. . . and more praise for Kristine Kathryn Rusch

"A masterful writer."　　　　　　　　—Orson Scott Card

"Whether [Rusch] writes high fantasy, horror, sf, or contemporary fantasy, I've always been fascinated by her ability to tell a story with that enviable gift of invisible prose. She's one of those very few writers whose style takes me right into the story; the words and pages disappear as the characters and their story swallows me whole."　　　　　　　　—Charles de Lint

"Accomplished . . . exceptional."　　　　　　　—Edward Bryant

"Rusch's greatest strength . . . is her ability to close down a story and leave the reader feeling that the author could not possibly have wrung any more satisfaction out of the piece."
—The Kansas City Star

"Kristine Kathryn Rusch never stray[s] from the path of good storytelling as she dissects her characters and their situations for the reader's benefit. She integrates the fantastic elements so rigorously into her story that it is often hard to remember she is not merely recording the here and now."
—Science Fiction Weekly

"[Rusch's] writing style is simple but elegant, and her characterizations excellent."　　　　　　　*—Beyond*

"Rusch's . . . stories are exceptional, both in plot and in style."
—Ed Gorman, *Mystery Scene*

"[Rusch] is already far better than should be allowed." *—Nexus*

Praise for the Retrieval Artist novels

Consequences

"Ms. Rusch has a knack for creating interesting characters and a future that moves and breathes. I look forward to her next puzzle." —*The Weekly Press* (Philadelphia)

"An engrossing, thought-provoking murder mystery." —*Locus*

"Part science fiction, part mystery, and pure enjoyment are the words to describe [*Consequences*] . . . a strong murder mystery." —*Midwest Book Review*

"Both Miles Flint and Noelle DeRicci are interesting and likable characters. Rusch ably weaves the various plot threads together. . . . Readers who enjoyed the previous books in the series will definitely want to read this one as well. . . . It works equally well as a stand-alone novel." —*SFRevu*

"Rusch has outdone herself. . . . There are so many stories layered together in this novel that the reader is hooked from page one and reeled in through every page afterwards, as [she] interweaves the most complex, charged plot in the series so far. . . . Rusch has been clever in revealing degree by tantalizing degree what life in her future universe is like; in this book she shows us a lot more of that universe, and sets up threads for a galaxy of fresh stories. Fans of the Retrieval Artist series will be thrilled and gratified, while newcomers will become instant fans." —Wigglefish.com

"A satisfying SF mystery. Flint's internal conflicts are deftly portrayed, and the gritty realism of the murder investigation meshes well with the alien setting." —*Romantic Times*

continued . . .

Extremes

"A deft blend of science fiction and mystery devices. . . . This very fine novel incorporates a nice puzzle and a well realized lunar setting, and the interplay between the protagonist and another detective is convincing and entertaining."
—*Science Fiction Chronicle*

"Rusch achieves a thrilling momentum, and her attention to procedure and process contributes greatly. This is a sci-fi mystery that thinks, and thinks hard, about questions of justice and survival in a universe full of conflicting imperatives."
—Wigglefish.com

"Good all around . . . an exemplary futuristic detective thriller."
—*Booklist*

The Disappeared

"A very readable, very thought-provoking novel that lives up to every expectation we have of Rusch and her considerable talent. Buy and enjoy." —*Analog*

"Rusch's handling of human-alien interactions puts a new and very sobering face on extraterrestrial contacts that few authors have thoroughly explored. . . . I am hopelessly hooked. . . . Rusch's characters . . . keep you reading long after everyone in the house has fallen asleep. . . . *The Disappeared*, like all the best science fiction, achieves a higher purpose: to make us look at the world around us with a new understanding and question the status quo." —Lisa Dumond, SF Site

"As well known for her fantasy and horror as she is for her science fiction, [Rusch] especially excels in tales of the collision between human and alien cultures. *The Disappeared* is a fine example of her skill." —Science Fiction Weekly

"An entertaining blend of mystery and SF, a solid police drama that asks hard questions about what justice between cultures, and even species, really is." —*Booklist*

"Feels like a popular TV series crossed with a Spielberg film—engaging." —*Locus*

BURIED DEEP

A RETRIEVAL ARTIST NOVEL

Kristine Kathryn Rusch

A ROC BOOK

ROC
Published by New American Library, a division of
Penguin Group (USA) Inc., 375 Hudson Street,
New York, New York 10014, USA
Penguin Group (Canada), 10 Alcorn Avenue, Toronto,
Ontario M4V 3B2, Canada (a division of Pearson Penguin Canada Inc.)
Penguin Books Ltd., 80 Strand, London WC2R 0RL, England
Penguin Ireland, 25 St. Stephen's Green, Dublin 2,
Ireland (a division of Penguin Books Ltd.)
Penguin Group (Australia), 250 Camberwell Road, Camberwell, Victoria 3124,
Australia (a division of Pearson Australia Group Pty. Ltd.)
Penguin Books India Pvt. Ltd., 11 Community Centre, Panchsheel Park,
New Delhi - 110 017, India
Penguin Group (NZ), cnr Airborne and Rosedale Roads, Albany,
Auckland 1310, New Zealand (a division of Pearson New Zealand Ltd.)
Penguin Books (South Africa) (Pty.) Ltd., 24 Sturdee Avenue,
Rosebank, Johannesburg 2196, South Africa

Penguin Books Ltd., Registered Offices:
80 Strand, London WC2R 0RL, England

First published by Roc, an imprint of New American Library,
a division of Penguin Group (USA) Inc.

First Printing, April 2005
10   9   8   7   6   5   4   3   2   1

Copyright © 2005 White Mist Mountain, Inc.
All rights reserved

The Edgar® name is a registered service mark of the Mystery Writers of America, Inc.

Cover art by Greg Bridges

  REGISTERED TRADEMARK—MARCA REGISTRADA

Printed in the United States of America

For my nephew, Tim Rusch, with love

ACKNOWLEDGMENTS

Thanks on this one go to my husband, Dean Wesley Smith, who kept me focused on the heart of this book, and to Loren Coleman for one important late-night brainstorming session. Much appreciated, you two.

1

By the time Sharyn Scott-Olson had reached the crime scene, she already knew something was seriously wrong. The three-block area surrounding the construction site was empty except for three police carts, five officers, and Petros Batson. Petros stood at the edge of the site, staring down the street, obviously waiting for her. His long coat brushed against the rust-colored Martian soil, and his boots were covered in dust, making them look pale orange instead of black.

There were no Disty. Not on the streets, not leaning against the doorways in the nearby buildings, not guarding the site, even though the excavation equipment was clearly Disty made.

The Disty had fled, and that made a shiver run through Scott-Olson. She knew that the Disty didn't like death. One of the many reasons vengeance killings worked in Disty culture was because the Disty believed that dead bodies contaminated the environment—not just for the moment those bodies touched the ground, but for all time.

But the Disty also valued their homes, their businesses, and their possessions. Scott-Olson had entered hundreds of locations in Sahara Dome, always to examine a dead body, and never before had she arrived at a scene without at least one Disty there. Usually the Disty was a member of the Death Squad.

Scott-Olson had never been to a scene so unclean that not even the Death Squad would stand guard.

The surrounding neighborhood looked no different than it had ten years before. The buildings appeared haphazardly built, although they weren't. Their doorways, tiny by human standards, were made for the adult Disty. There were no windows. The buildings seemed to grow off each other.

Only one open street went from block to block, and that was a nod toward the initial human requirements of Sahara Dome. Most of the streets, especially in this section, were little more than tunnels, with buildings on top that stretched all the way to the dome roof.

The tunnels were so low that no adult human could walk through them without crouching. The walls were narrow, as well. Humans who lived on Mars learned to stay thin if they wanted to travel inside the domes. Heavyset humans sometimes couldn't fit inside the tunnels at all.

Scott-Olson was too thin, but sometimes even her arms brushed against the walls of Disty tunnels. She was lucky she wasn't claustrophobic, since her job often took her into the Disty-only sections, where the tunnels seemed even narrower.

Perhaps what surprised her most about the crime scene was that it wasn't narrow or covered with buildings. It was the widest-open space she had ever seen in the Disty section. An entire human-sized city block—perfectly square, just like the blocks in the human section of the dome—had been torn down. Someone had removed the Disty brick and piled it against the back side of the square as if building a wall.

Scott-Olson looked up, saw the yellowish light on the underside of the dome, the shadow of the inexorable dust on the top of the dome, and the darkness beyond.

Martian winter.

Even though she had been here for nearly twenty Earth years, she still couldn't get used to the darkness. She used to imagine that she'd leave before the next winter set in.

She had no such illusions now.

"It's about time," Batson said as he walked toward her. He looked gigantic against the twisted Disty buildings and the tiny carts. His long coat swayed behind him, creating eddies of reddish dust.

She had forgotten how ubiquitous the dust could be inside the Dome. The Disty had developed an excellent filtration system to keep the dust outside, and almost all of the dome's interior was paved.

Except when buildings were torn down, and construction was underway.

Batson even had dust on his face. His dark skin seemed unusually ruddy, and his eyelashes, long and beautiful, accenting startling green eyes, looked like they'd been coated in red dye.

"I had to walk," Scott-Olson said. "I couldn't get a cart small enough for the all-Disty section."

He grunted, shook his head, and then took her kit from her.

"Where's the Death Squad?" she asked.

He looked at her sideways as he led her to the construction site. "We've got a major contaminant, as far as they're concerned," he said.

"Major contaminant?" In all her years as medical examiner for the Sahara Dome Human Government, she had never heard of anything categorized like that.

"They took one look, decided the body'd been here for years, and ran off. I managed to catch one, and he yelled something about tearing down the entire community—at our expense."

Scott-Olson frowned. "Our expense?"

"The body's human," he said.

She had figured that much. Otherwise, she wouldn't be on the scene. The Death Squad dealt with their own in this section of the dome. She got Disty who died in the human section, and had learned to perform Disty autopsies because the Disty were so squeamish about doing one themselves.

"I've handled human bodies in the Disty section before," Scott-Olson said.

"Not one like this." Batson stopped at the edge of the construction site. There were several large dips in the sand, caused by the weight of the buildings that had been on this site. She counted five separate rectangles, and stopped when she realized she couldn't take in the entire leveled area.

She scanned the site. Aside from the Disty excavation equipment—something that resembled a miniature backhoe, a claw-shaped digging something-or-other, and a tiny truck that carted the recyclable building materials to another location —she saw nothing except flattened sand.

"Where's the body?" she asked.

Batson set her kit on the side of the site, then jumped down the meter or so to the main part of the dig. He extended a hand to help her down, making her feel old.

She was old, or at least older than he was. She took his hand, let him ease her down, then grabbed the kit.

From here she could see Disty prints, with their distinctive three-toed mark barely deep enough to be called an impression. Disty bones were hollow, and the Disty themselves weighed next to nothing.

Batson walked in his original prints. He was a good detective, if a bit blunt and brash. She liked working on his cases because he actually cared. So many people on Sahara Dome's Human Police Force didn't.

He walked almost to the center of the large excavated area and then stopped. He crouched and pointed with one dust-coated finger.

She was probably dust-coated as well. Already she could taste the sand in the back of her mouth, grinding as she pressed her teeth together. Her eyes felt dry and gritty.

Amazing how little of the dunes had to appear before they coated the entire area, even with the fantastic filtration system.

She still didn't see anything. The area near Batson's finger was raised slightly, and nothing else.

She crouched beside him, removing a paintbrush from her pocket. She had learned during her first year that any case involving Martian sand required a delicate tool for brushing it away.

"What am I looking at?" she asked.

"I'm no expert, Doc," he said, "but I think that's a pelvis."

His finger outlined the air above the sand. She squinted and finally saw what he was pointing at. Ridges, whirls, edges.

Bone.

She blinked twice to clear her mind, and looked again.

Bone.

Bone the same color as the sand, a dusty reddish-orange. She leaned forward, clutching her brush, and tried to rub off the sand. It came off in delicate chunks, floating to the side.

But no matter how hard she dusted, she still couldn't get all of the sand out of that bone.

She pressed a button on her sleeve, starting a recording of the site. She probably should have started that when she arrived, but she hadn't seen anything, and now she didn't believe what she saw.

Scott-Olson rested her brush on her knee, reached into her pocket, and pulled out the thinnest pair of gloves she owned. She still wanted to be able to feel through the material, but she didn't want to contaminate the site any more than necessary.

The gloves felt like rubber against her skin, then that feeling faded, replaced by a slight pulling sensation, as if the gloves made her middle-aged skin taut again. Slowly, she eased her hand down and touched the innominate.

It was hard, the surface clean. She had gotten all the dust off, and still the bone was reddish-orange, exactly the color of the soil. If the bone had been placed here recently, it should have been yellowish-white.

She cleared dust away from the pelvis to find an intact sacrum, and a wide subpubic angle. From the look of this—and she was only going by gut at the moment—she was working on part of an adult female skeleton.

Slowly, she worked around it, removing more sand with her brush, coming away from the bottom of the pelvis and toward her. It took very little digging to find the vertebrae, and slightly more to find the attached rib cage.

She kept going upward, digging even deeper than she expected, until she found a skull near her feet. The eye sockets, empty except for sand, had sharp upper borders, confirming what she had already suspected.

She was looking at a dead human woman.

"I don't get why the Disty are so upset." Batson's deep voice startled her. She had forgotten he was there. "They've seen skeletal remains before."

"Not many of them," she said.

"Enough. I've even had a case or two. That woman who died in her bathtub, remember her? The—"

"I remember," Scott-Olson said, thinking mostly of that water, with the fat floating along the surface. The moisture and exceptionally warm temperature in the apartment had sped the decay. Strangely, no one had reported the smell, which had to have been fierce, and by the time the body had been discovered—by the landlord, who thought his renter had skipped—the woman was long past bloated, little more than a skeleton, with flesh hanging off the bones.

"There was a Disty at that scene. Death Squad, but still." Batson shook his head. "He didn't run screaming."

"Were they really screaming?" she asked, finally looking at him.

The dust on his face had grown worse, almost a reddish mask over his skin. Her face probably looked the same. This stuff clung.

"Close enough," he said. "They acted as if they'd been contaminated. I don't know what the hell would cause that."

"Disty found the body?" she asked.

He nodded.

"How?"

"Excavating," he said. "I didn't get the entire story because of the, you know, running, but I guess they were getting the last of the Disty bricks out of this section when their whatchamadingy over there hit something that wasn't Disty. They dug enough to find this, sent for the Death Squad, and then sent for us."

He brushed at his lower lip, making the dust layer worse.

"We got here same time as the squad and they went in first to secure the site."

Protocol, she knew. Apparently, there were things in the Disty section not even the human police were allowed to see.

"We haven't even waited five minutes before they hurry past us so fast that I nearly get knocked over. And those little guys usually can't budge me."

Scott-Olson frowned, trying to imagine it. She'd never seen anyone on the Death Squad panic.

"Then," Batson said, lowering his voice, "this is the creepy part. A bunch of Disty start pouring out of the buildings and onto the street like they all got a bulletin telling them to flee."

"Maybe they did," she said.

"But no one would tell us why," he said.

"Except major contamination," she said.

He nodded.

"You've worked these cases before," she said. "You've heard them talk about contamination, right? Death coats everything. If the body's allowed to remain too long, it takes forever to clear out the contamination."

"So major contamination would be what? That the body's been here so long they can't clear out the 'coating'?" He looked at the partially revealed skeleton. "How would they know? Before everyone skipped out, I talked to one of the Disty in charge of the construction. He said they'd just started their day's work. Anyone could've dumped the corpse here and poured sand on top of it."

"I suppose." Scott-Olson brushed a bit more sand away from the skull. It had been buried deeper than the rest of the skeleton, almost as if it had been thrown halfway into a hole, legs on the edge, head inside.

But the settling of two different buildings could have caused the same effect.

"You suppose," he said, "but you don't agree. You think this was under the building? You think they're telling the truth?"

"I don't know why they'd lie." She had stopped brushing again. Her knees ached. Her back ached too. Her own skeleton would probably show stress in those two areas, all because she had lived too long on Mars.

She stood, stretched, and looked up, reveling in the empty air above her head. Her back cracked.

"How long has this building been here?" she asked.

"I don't know," he said. "I don't study the history of the Disty section."

"Ten years? Twenty? A hundred?"

"I don't know," he repeated. He was sounding testy. "Why does it matter? That body couldn't've been here the whole time. It'd be a mummy."

He'd seen a number of those, just like she had, buried in the Martian soil, waiting for someone to find them.

"Yeah," she said. "That's the problem."

"What, exactly?"

"That she's not a mummy."

"She," he muttered. "So someone dumped the bones. It had its effect. It scared the Disty. Now we tell them that they can bring back the Death Squad and we'll help them find whoever contaminated their site."

"We can't," Scott-Olson said. "I think they're right. I think this is a major contamination by their definition."

He frowned at her. Dust gathered in the fine lines around his eyes, accenting them.

"C'mon, Sharyn," he said. "Even I know that bodies don't decay like that here. Not in the sand. These bones were placed here."

"Yes," she said. "They were. I agree with you on that."

"Someone transported the skeleton and tossed it on this construction site."

"First, they didn't toss it. The connecting tissue is still holding the bones together, even the small ones. They set it here."

Batson grimaced.

"And second," Scott-Olson said, "this happened at the previous construction site. I'd bet my apartment on it."

Batson let out a small sigh. She had an apartment with windows, high ceilings, and more floor space than half the apartments in Sahara Dome. It was a luxury place that she had bought back when prices were low and everyone thought the humans were going to leave Mars altogether.

"How can you tell?" he asked.

"The color," she said. "Human bone is porous. After several years of burial, it'll take on the color of the surrounding soil."

"Several years?" he asked. "You're sure?"

"No," she said. "I'm not. I'm making an educated guess. I'll have to do some testing to see if the color in the bones is from the sand or from something else. But if it's from the sand, then she's been here longer than that building they tore down."

"Contaminating for years or decades," he said.

"Major contaminating," she said.

"Oh, God," he said. "Either way, this is a disaster. I don't even know what the Disty'll do if this body's been here forever. And if it hasn't, then I have to find out who knows more about Disty death rituals than we do, enough to make them think the whole area's been ruined."

"Disty death rituals," Scott-Olson said, "*and* the vagaries of postdeath human anatomy."

"The brass isn't going to like this," he said.

"The brass, the Disty." Scott-Olson picked up her brush again. Her annoyance, the product of too many years of examining human death in a dome that didn't care, surfaced. "Already she's insignificant."

"The skeleton?" Batson's voice rose. "It's not insignificant. It's going to cause a major incident that I hope will only impact Sahara Dome. I hate to think about what's going to happen to the human-Disty relationship on the rest of Mars."

"See what I mean?" Scott-Olson said. She crouched again and started working at the sand, making sure she was still recording. "Already you've forgotten the center of the case."

He stared at her. "What are you talking about?"

"This woman," Scott-Olson said. "She was someone once. And she ended up here, probably murdered."

"You know that?" he asked.

She let out a sigh of impatience. Usually Batson wasn't slow. Usually he had some compassion for the victim.

"No," she said. "I don't know it for sure. But think about it, Petros. She's dead. If I'm right, she was hidden here. Someone either waited until she decomposed, which in this atmosphere had to take a while, or cut the flesh off her bones, or boiled the skin away."

He grimaced and turned away from the exposed skeleton. "Why would someone go to that kind of work?" he asked. "Why not just bury the dead body in the construction site and leave?"

"I don't know," Scott-Olson said. "But I can tell you we're going to have a hell of a time with this case."

Batson cursed. "This just keeps getting better and better."

He had no real idea. He'd never had a case that put him at odds with the Disty. She had.

She had barely survived it.

She wondered if she would survive this one, as well.

2

Aisha Costard already hated Mars. She hadn't been in Sahara Dome for more than two hours, but those two hours felt like two weeks.

Her seat companion on the passenger shuttle from Earth had warned her. He'd said that Mars induced claustrophobia in people who lived their entire lives on Earth. He'd said that to Earthlings, Mars was the most inhospitable planet in the Alliance.

He'd been talking about the buildings. He hadn't even mentioned the dome.

Costard had been in a domed environment only once before, the only time she'd been off Earth. She'd worked a summerlong dig sponsored by Glenn Station University on the Moon, looking for twentieth-century space travel artifacts, and finding very few.

The dome hadn't bothered her then. But Glenn Station's dome had a visible ceiling. It wasn't compressed by buildings that were little better than square nests that rose to the sky. Rabbit warrens. Ant tunnels.

She could think of a thousand comparisons to this place, none of them pretty, and none of them places she ever wanted to be.

And that didn't count the recycled air, which smelled faintly of rotting vanilla, or the strange dome lighting, which was thin and yellow. The light actually reminded her of some

historic Earth buildings that still ran early twentieth-century
electricity. This place had the same feeling of unreality, as if
she had stepped into an antique, badly lit photograph.

Her guide, a slender young man who had picked her up at
the space port, acted like he was afraid of her. He didn't want
to carry her bags, even though she needed his help—she had
brought a lot of equipment, uncertain what she would need
here. Her clothes were the lightest thing about her.

He had steered her into a small cart attached to the back
of his cart. He then drove through the rabbit warren/ant tunnels that Sahara Dome dwellers thought of as streets. By the
time the carts stopped in front of a normal-sized building,
Costard was lost.

The ceilings were very low inside the building. If Costard
reached up, she could touch them—something she couldn't
normally do on Earth. She had a medium build, and she
stayed in shape because she never knew where she was going
to end up. She kept her black hair short and her clothing practical, although she really wasn't sure what practical was here
on Mars.

She slung her clothes bag over her shoulder and carried
her equipment case. The guide carried two other kits, holding
them as far away from his body as he could. He walked past
several pasty humans in uniform and the large front desk,
with its glowing digitized warning to Sign In.

The corridor branched, one part leading toward the back
of the building, the other part leading to a flight of stairs. Her
guide went down, taking the stairs cautiously, as if they were
dangerous.

She followed, her shoes clanging on the metal. She hadn't
expected metal here. She hadn't expected anything here.

What she knew about Mars could be placed in a three-
page pamphlet, and two of those pages would have been
wrong.

Had she known, when she accepted this job, that she
would feel so out of place right from the start, she might have
referred it to someone else.

Then she smiled. She was lying to herself. The Sahara

Dome authorities had appealed to her professional vanity. They had contacted several forensic anthropologists, all of whom recommended her for this job. At the time, everyone thought that she could do the work in her lab at the University of Wisconsin.

It wasn't until she told the authorities that she needed the actual bones that things became complicated.

The guide reached the bottom of the stairs, pulled open a door, and held it for her. Cooler air hit her, mixed with the faint scent of human decay and disinfectants. Morgue smells were apparently the same on Mars as they were on Earth.

Oddly enough, the odors calmed her. She walked through the door, saw the familiar coolers stacked against the right wall, several examination tables made of the same silver metal as the ones in the morgues she'd worked in on Earth, and in the back wall, five odor hoods dominating the square stations where remains were often boiled clean of their flesh to prepare them for certain kinds of examination.

Near one of the empty tables stood a woman so thin that she looked like a strong wind would snap her in half. She wore a smock over a pair of dark pants and a matching blouse. Her hair, a mousy brown, rose in spikes along the top of her head, but had been buzzed away from the sides and ears. She would have looked like a teenager if it weren't for the frown lines that ran beside her generous mouth.

"Dr. Costard?" The woman came forward, holding out her hand. "I'm Sharyn Scott-Olson. I'm so glad you could come."

Costard shifted her bag on her shoulder before taking the other woman's hand. It was dry and rough, almost leathery. In comparison, Costard's own hand felt moist and much too soft, as if she hadn't had much of a life at all.

"I'm still a little stunned to find myself on Mars," she said.

"Aren't we all?" Scott-Olson took Costard's kit, then nodded at the guide. "You can leave her equipment here. Has he taken you to your hotel yet?"

That last was directed at Costard. "No. We came directly from the space port."

"You must be tired. And famished." Scott-Olson set the kit next to the door. The guide was putting the others down carefully, as if he were afraid they would break. "Get us a couple of sandwiches, Nigel. Whatever Dr. Costard wants—unless you want to go to the hotel."

Costard was tired enough that Scott-Olson's way of holding a conversation—half with her and half with the guide, Nigel—was beginning to confuse her.

"I'm not hungry," Costard said. She was too stressed to eat. "I'd like to see the skeleton first. I had time to sleep on the shuttle."

Although it was interrupted sleep. First because her seatmate snored, and then because the attendants insisted on waking everyone up for meals. Costard would have liked to slept through the entire ordeal, but apparently that wasn't allowed. People had to have a lot of water when they traveled in an artificial environment, and one way of encouraging the right amount of liquid was making sure everyone had plenty of food.

"Great," Scott-Olson said. "I was hoping you'd take a first look. We're getting all sorts of flack from the Disty Government. We've managed to hold them off until you got here, but they're getting impatient."

"I don't release findings until I've done a complete evaluation," Costard said.

"I just need a timeline question answered," Scott-Olson said. "We need to know how long the body was in the soil."

"I won't be able to tell you that until I do a soil analysis as well as examine the corpse." Costard's head was starting to ache. She knew there would be political issues—she'd been informed of that from the beginning—but she hadn't expected them to crop up so quickly.

"You don't need me then?" Nigel asked, his reedy voice sounding curiously tentative in the large space.

Scott-Olson grinned at him. "I always need you, Nigel,

but I can't pay you for the overtime. So I guess you're free to go."

He nodded at Scott-Olson, but couldn't meet Costard's gaze. He slipped out the door and ran up the stairs.

Scott-Olson shook her head as she watched him leave. "Poor kid. He signed on for an intersession internship at the SDHPD, and ended up here. Who knew a person could be that squeamish?"

"SDHPD?" Costard asked.

"Sahara Dome Human Police Department," Scott-Olson said. "We're acronym happy around here. You'll get used to it."

Costard hoped she wouldn't be here long enough to get used to anything. "Human Police Department. That's a curious designation. Does that mean the Disty have one?"

"Oh yeah," Scott-Olson said. "Normally, in a case like this, we'd work in tandem with them, but they won't come near this place, not right now."

"Why not?" Costard asked.

Scott-Olson waved a thin hand. "It's too complicated. Let's just look at our mystery woman, and then we can get you to the hotel."

"All right," Costard said. She set her bag down beside the kits, then stretched. Her muscles ached from the heavy equipment, the long time she'd spent in the shuttle, and the unusually cramped seating in that cart.

Scott-Olson walked around the tables to the left wall. She pulled open a drawer that had been painted the same color as the wall, so that it wasn't even noticeable until she touched it.

Costard followed her. As she got closer, she saw a rib cage floating above the drawer's edge. The rib cage was a burnt orange.

By the time she reached the drawer, she could see the whole skeleton. The entire thing was orange. There was no smell of decay, just a faint dusty odor, as if the skeleton had been stored in a box for a long period of time.

Costard examined the bones without touching them. The

skull itself was small, relatively polished, and even surfaced. The breastbone had become a single bone, so the victim was an adult, but the spinal column hadn't fused and showed no sign of the elasticity tampering that Costard often saw in elderly corpses. There were parturition scars on the pelvis.

"She's had children," Costard said.

Scott-Olson nodded. "I didn't try to determine age. I took a little bone marrow so that I could ID her, but aside from taking her from the site and bringing her here, that's all I've done."

"Do you know who she is?" Costard asked.

Scott-Olson shook her head. "I had to apply to the Alliance database. Most of our idents are done by chip or nuclear DNA. We almost never have to use mitochondrial DNA."

That caught Costard's attention. Nuclear DNA came from living cells or cells that hadn't had a lot of time to decay. "Don't get a lot of old corpses?"

"Most of the dead around here are locals. People don't come to Sahara Dome except on business, and if they've traveled, they have an identi-chip in their shoulder or hand, somewhere easy to find. I usually use that, and yes, because of the Disty, we don't get many old corpses."

"What do the Disty have to do with it?" Costard asked.

"They can't tolerate death," Scott-Olson said. "They'll ferret out a corpse faster than anything. The old ones we get are usually in the human section, where the Disty rarely travel."

Costard frowned. She'd been around a lot of strange death traditions, but almost all of them were human. She had some training in alien physiologies—she had to in order to rule out alien bones at an Earth death site—but she had almost no interactions with alien cultures.

"She's an amazing color," Costard said.

Scott-Olson nodded. "I'm guessing it came from the soil."

Costard touched the edge of one of the bones, rubbing her thumb and forefinger across the surface. Still surprisingly strong, although there was some flaking. But the color had embedded into the bone itself.

"It came from whatever she was stored in. But you told me she might have been moved," Costard said.

"She was moved," Scott-Olson said. "Corpses mummify here. Someone placed the skeleton there."

"And you have soil samples from the site?" Costard asked. She moved her fingers away from the skeleton. Poor thing. The woman hadn't been much taller than Costard in life. And she had children, which meant that once upon a time, she'd had a family, someone who cared about her.

Someone who missed her when she disappeared.

"I have soil samples, video of the site, stills, and air composition as well as odor tracking as we slowly brought her out. The crime scene unit has the blade of what we would call a backhoe—the Disty have their own name for the damn thing, and it is slightly different—as well as some of their equipment. We could have had all of it. I doubt they'll ever touch it again."

Costard looked at her. Scott-Olson was staring at the skeleton, too. "You're going to have to explain the Disty death thing to me."

"Believe me," Scott-Olson said. "I will."

"First things first," Costard said. "We're going to have to test the soil and see if it colored her bones. We'll have to figure out her age and her identification. And we'll have to figure cause of death, unless I'm missing something obvious."

"She has a lot of scratches and cuts in the bones," Scott-Olson said. "But I'm not sure if they're postmortem. I'm not sure how she became a skeleton, whether the flesh was cut off her or not. I assume so, since the killer left enough connective tissue so that the bones are still attached to each other. I could have figured some of this out, but since you were coming, I thought I'd leave it to the expert."

Costard appreciated that. Bone work was her specialty. Medical examiners didn't specialize in anything except the various forms of human death.

"How much time do I have to complete the work?" Costard asked.

"The faster you get it done, the better," Scott-Olson said. "The Disty won't go near the death site. More than a thousand are temporarily homeless, and they're getting angrier as each day goes by."

"A thousand homeless?"

"They cram into these buildings like you wouldn't believe. I'm probably underestimating. And that really doesn't matter. What matters is that the Disty are going to assign blame for her death if we don't."

"Figuring out who killed her isn't my job," Costard said. "I can tell you how she died and how long she's been dead— roughly anyway—and help you identify her, but that's all I can do."

"I know," Scott-Olson said. "But we need those things before we find her killer."

Costard had never heard an M.E. sound so unrealistic before. "You might never find her killer. You do know that, right?"

"We have to find her killer," Scott-Olson said. "Or the Disty will do it for us."

"I thought you said they don't like death. They investigate it?"

"Not like we do. And their ideas of justice aren't the same as ours either."

Costard felt cold. "Are you saying they'll just pick someone at random?"

"No, although that might be better."

"What will they do, then?" Costard asked.

"They'll blame us."

"Humans?" Costard asked.

Scott-Olson shook her head. "You, me, anyone involved in the investigation."

"Legally, they can't do that," Costard said.

"Legally, they can do what they want," Scott-Olson said. "Mars is Disty territory. I thought you knew that."

"But you have your own law enforcement," Costard said, not sure she understood this correctly.

"It's a courtesy," Scott-Olson said.

"They'll kill you?" Costard asked.

"It's a risk," Scott-Olson said. "We've touched the body. We've been contaminated by it. We're useless to them."

Costard felt a surge of anger. Someone should have told her. "I think I'll just take the next shuttle to Earth. I am not volunteering for this."

"It's too late," Scott-Olson said. "You already have."

3

Miles Flint stood in the back of the press conference room in Armstrong's Police Headquarters. He made sure he was close to the door, so that he could duck out quickly if he had to. A year after he quit the force, he had no longer felt a part of it. Now he felt like a complete outsider.

He had his arms crossed and his back pressed against the wall. Several other people stood next to him, many of them focused on their multimedia equipment. A few spoke softly, narrating the events for viewers who couldn't attend.

Ahead of him, a sea of blue Armstrong Police uniforms filled the room. They were present because this wasn't just a press conference, it was also a ceremony—a ceremony that had surprised Flint as much as it surprised its intended victim, Noelle DeRicci.

DeRicci sat at the edge of the stage, her legs crossed, her hands resting comfortably in her lap. She wore a skirt-and-blazer combination with chiffon accents, making her seem very stylish. Her dark hair, which once had touches of gray, now had streaks of black in its professional cut. She even wore some makeup, something the old DeRicci—the woman who had once been Flint's partner back when he was a detective —would have scorned.

Still, she was the same woman, brash, brilliant, and insecure. When she had mounted the stage, she had scanned for him, then smiled when she saw him.

He had smiled too. He liked her and he had come to support her in this, one of the more important press conferences of her career.

It hadn't been fair of him to think of her as a victim. DeRicci was no one's victim except her own. She was about to become the recipient of Armstrong's highest honor, the Silver Moon, given to public servants who acted with bravery above and beyond the call of duty.

DeRicci had deserved this for her work a few years ago, stopping a highly infectious virus that would have contaminated the dome and killed most of its inhabitants. She hadn't received the award then, partly because she had no political clout at the time, and partly because of Flint's involvement in that case—something the city had wanted to keep hidden.

But Flint had no involvement in this latest triumph of DeRicci's. She had investigated, along with the help of an impressive team, last year's bombing of Armstrong's dome. In the course of her work, she had found structural cracks in the dome that would have caused it to disintegrate suddenly and without warning.

Once again, DeRicci had saved the Moon's largest city. And this time, she was getting recognized for it.

Arek Soseki, Armstrong's mayor, had been droning for nearly ten minutes now about the bombing, the costly aftermath, and DeRicci's actions. The group on the stage, most of whom knew all of this, tried to pay attention.

That group included a whole host of political dignitaries, including the Moon's governor-general. The only police officers included, besides DeRicci, were her immediate boss, Andrea Gumiela, and the chief of police.

"He can talk, can't he?" Ki Bowles leaned against the wall next to Flint. Bowles worked for InterDome Media. She had made her reputation as an investigative reporter, but in the past few months, she had spent most of her time behind a desk, framing other reporters' stories for the nets' constant live broadcasts. Flint had no idea if that was a demotion or not.

"Isn't talking his job?" Flint asked.

She smiled at him, her almond-shaped eyes twinkling. Her hair, which had been curly and multicolored when he met her more than a year ago, was now a strawberry blond, which made her dusky skin seem even darker than usual. Her lemon-scented perfume was light enough to seem tasteful, but strong enough to announce her presence.

"Talking is *my* job," she said. "Governing is his."

"And I believe that as much as I believe you've gone back to your natural hair color."

"So says one of the few remaining natural blonds in the universe."

Flint felt color rise in his cheeks. He had always been self-conscious about his looks. His hair was blond and naturally curly, his eyes blue, and his skin so fair that his blood vessels were visible on the underside of his arms. His looks underscored the narrowness of his gene pool and displayed his family history for all to see.

"I didn't expect to see you here," he said. "I thought press conferences got assigned to cub reporters, not to big-time investigators."

She tugged on the silk scarf around her neck. Her hair had tamed, but her clothing hadn't. She wore vivid reds and golds, colors that accented her skin and hair. "Have you read the report?"

"No," Flint said.

"It's amazing how much information is missing."

Flint nodded toward the podium. "All of the speakers so far have called it comprehensive."

"It is," Bowles said, "except for one teeny-tiny detail."

Flint waited. Bowles wanted him to ask what that detail was, and he wasn't about to. Instead, he listened to the murmur of voices mixing with the scripted eloquence of Mayor Soseki.

"That detail is," Bowles said, letting a bit of annoyance color her voice, "the thing we all want to know. Who placed that bomb? The report says that detail is unknowable. If the bomber was a suicide, then the remains were lost in the blast."

"I thought the bomb was remote detonated," Flint said.

"They don't know. They don't know anything, and they're hiding it under words, vids, analysis, and thousands of footnoted details. This report is truly a multimedia event, burying the most important information beneath stuff that seems relevant."

"Like that's never been done before," Flint said.

"No one has successfully blown a hole in Armstrong's dome before," Bowles said. "Don't you think it's a little disingenuous to give a medal to the person who couldn't solve the crime?"

"That person is an old friend of mine," Flint said. "I'm here at her request."

Bowles shrugged a single shoulder, but the brightness in her eyes told Flint that she already knew Flint and DeRicci had once been partners. Bowles had probably stopped beside Flint for that very reason.

"I wondered why a Retrieval Artist would voluntarily come into Police Central," Bowles said.

"And now you know." Flint smiled at her. "Retrieval Artists have lives too."

Although that technically wasn't true. The most effective Retrieval Artists had no solid ties. That prevented blackmail, or worse—the kidnapping or loss of a loved one in the middle of a particularly sensitive case.

Flint had no family, unless an ex-wife he hadn't seen in years counted. He was an only child. His parents and grandparents were long dead, and his marriage ended after his daughter Emmeline died at the day care center where Flint had left her every afternoon.

"Lives and secrets and friendships," Bowles said, as if she wanted to discover every single aspect of his. "Tell me, what kind of partner was Noelle DeRicci?"

She had the audacity to interview him. She knew better. He had told her over and over he had no interest in talking to the media.

Flint turned so that he looked at Bowles directly. "Ki," he said softly, "if I find you were recording this conversation, I will sue you and InterDome."

"I'm just asking about an old friend," Bowles said.

He moved away from her, crossing behind several of the standing visitors, and moving to the other side of the door.

Soseki had finished his speech and was turning toward the governor-general. Apparently, she was the one who would give out the award.

DeRicci's back was straight, and although she hadn't really moved since she spoke at the podium half an hour before, she looked tense. She hated public attention.

The governor-general walked to the podium. She was a tiny woman with a deceptive delicacy. As she hit the button that adjusted the podium's size so that it was appropriate to her build, she smiled at the audience.

Flint suppressed a sigh. He hadn't meant to spend the entire afternoon here. DeRicci had asked him to come, promised him dinner and time to catch up, which they hadn't had much of these last few months. He was beginning to think they wouldn't have any of that time tonight either.

Bowles hadn't moved from her place on the other side of the door. When she noticed that he was looking at her, she smiled and shrugged.

Flint turned away. He certainly hoped she hadn't recorded him. Now he would have to have one computer monitor InterDome, and make certain he didn't appear on any of the media conglomerates' holdings.

The governor-general finished her little speech, then waved a hand at DeRicci, commanding her to rise.

DeRicci did, tugging at her skirt, showing her nerves. She was taller than the governor-general, which surprised even Flint. He used to tease DeRicci about her height—or lack of it.

The governor-general took a jeweled case from an assistant, opened the case, and showed everyone the medal inside. From his place in the back of the room, Flint could only see a flash of silver. Then she turned to DeRicci, took the medal out of the case, and handed the case back to the assistant.

DeRicci looked as if she were queasy. Flint wished he

were closer, so that he could wink at her, or mouth words of encouragement.

But he couldn't. He had to wait, and watch.

The governor-general pinned the medal on DeRicci's lapel. The material bowed forward, and both women laughed at the awkwardness. DeRicci helped as the governor-general pinned the medal again.

Then the governor-general turned DeRicci toward the audience, and the entire room erupted into applause. DeRicci's face was flushed and her eyes seemed too bright.

And then, with surprising suddenness, the event was over. Soseki waved his hands and thanked the crowd for coming, then turned toward DeRicci. People stood in unison. Most of the crowd filed out of the room. The press stayed, of course, and so did Flint.

DeRicci started down the stairs to the side of the stage, but the governor-general caught her arm. Soseki approached them, followed by several other politicians. Andrea Gumiela and the police chief stood off to the side, looking confused.

Flint felt his shoulders tighten. This whole ceremony was part of a larger event, something the police hadn't been told about. He couldn't see DeRicci through the crowd of people surrounding her.

He wondered if he should just leave.

Instead, he worked his way toward the front, in case DeRicci needed an excuse to escape.

4

Ki Bowles touched the information chips on the back of her hand. She filtered her sound meters for room noise, trying to get rid of the surrounding chatter. Chairs clanged, voices rose, and people laughed, preventing her from hearing anything that happened near the stage.

She already felt out of touch. She had shut off her infotainment feeds when she had come into the room, hoping her focused concentration would help her find other leads. Instead, she'd actually had to listen to this press conference rather than multitasking.

She had been about to turn the infotainment links back on when she saw Miles Flint. He had provided enough of a distraction that she had made it to the end of the goofy medal-pinning part of the conference.

Now all she had to do was double-check her recording links, make sure she got everything going on in the room, and hope that she happened on something important.

She had worried about this. She hoped that the sound chip she had placed against the stage's edge when she arrived would get the information she needed.

Bowles continued recording, using wide-angle on her wrist chip, a double-link to the provided overhead camera on another chip, and an eye-level zoom that she had just recently installed. She would get and keep her own personal perspective, just in case this story went big.

Flint hadn't left yet. His lanky frame dominated the left side of the room. He was a distinctive man, and too smart for his own good. When she had first spoken to him, she had been struck by his pre-Raphaelite looks. Those looks—so rare these days—had helped her remember Flint from a previous story.

She had watched him years ago, her gaze caught by his striking resemblance to the European art she had studied when she had been an art history major, before she had come to her senses and had started pursuing a career.

Since she had never seen anyone who looked like him before or since that moment, she was able to make an instant connection between the Retrieval Artist she knew and the grieving father she had first seen when she was a cub reporter.

In those days, he had been conducting a war against the day care center where his daughter had died. Bowles had never seen a man as angry as Flint had been when he discovered that yet another child died from the same trauma as his daughter. Shaken to death by a worker. A preventable death.

Another death had preceded his daughter's. If that death had been properly investigated, Flint's daughter and the other child would have lived, and he would never have quit his job as one of the best computer specialists in the city. He would never have applied to the police academy, worked the space ports, and then got promoted to detective.

He would never have met Noelle DeRicci, and he would never have become a Retrieval Artist.

From the second time Bowles had seen Flint's unique face, she had known that a major story lurked there. She just wasn't sure what the story was or how to tell it.

Or how, even, to discover it.

Bowles moved closer to the stage, careful to stay as far from Flint as possible. She had worked her way to a comfortable living. She was well-known in Armstrong as one of InterDome's main reporters. She had taken a job anchoring live feeds so that her face would become even more recognizable.

All of her work was good. But the great reporters, the ones who became famous throughout the Alliance and the Outlying Colonies, all had one great story—a career-making story—that sent them on their way. And the really great ones continued to get the best of the best, parlaying an excellent career into a memorable one.

Bowles wanted that, and she knew the only way to get it was through incredibly hard work and a lead that no one else had, a perspective that was uniquely hers. That was what succeeded in the Alliance. Vision, voice, and a spectacular hook, something none of the thousands of other reporters on all the Allied worlds had.

She edged closer to the stage. She still couldn't see Assistant Chief DeRicci, but Soseki bent forward, as if he was talking to someone shorter than he was. Two other mayors from nearby domes hung back, more as protection for the discussion, it seemed, than part of it.

Bowles counted five members of the United Domes of the Moon's Governing Council, three of them representatives of Armstrong and its environs. They were all participating in the discussion. Something was happening here. Something important. And with luck, Bowles had it all.

She tapped another chip on her wrist, opening a link with the sound chip she'd pressed against the lip of the stage. Still too much chatter. Voices of cops greeting each other, a few saying hello to Flint, someone making a date, and earnest conversation beyond. She couldn't get anything, but maybe she could filter it when she got back to the office, see if she could isolate some of the famous voices.

A hand covered hers. She looked up to find Andrea Gumiela peering at her. Gumiela was being groomed for the next chief's position. She was ambitious, not that smart, but incredibly political.

Rumors around the city now floated the idea that DeRicci would get Gumiela's position. Or maybe even become Assistant Chief of Police, instead of Assistant Chief of Detectives, leapfrogging over Gumiela herself.

"Press conference is over, Ms. Bowles," Gumiela said.

"I know." Bowles made sure there was no animosity in her tone. "I'm getting ambient noise and some extra vids for background."

"That's all it better be," Gumiela said. "If I found out you've been recording private conversation—"

"I wouldn't do that," Bowles said. "But for the record, it seems to me that any conversation held in a press room before members of the press couldn't be considered private."

Gumiela's grip tightened on Bowles' hand, crushing the embedded chips. One chip clinked as it went off-line. Bowles pretended like nothing had happened.

"That sounds like an issue for the courts," Gumiela said. "And you know they hate deciding freedom of the press issues after the offending story has already made its way into the media."

Bowles shrugged. "I'm not doing anything wrong, Chief. I'm just getting background, like I said."

"I hope that's all." Gumiela let go of Bowles' hand. "It's probably time we clear the room anyway."

Bowles gave Gumiela her best smile. "Do you have a few minutes for an interview? I need some background on Assistant Chief DeRicci for my extended piece on the medal ceremony. I'd also like to find out about the future for Andrea Gumiela."

As Bowles expected, Gumiela's entire expression softened. That woman loved media attention. "How about we go to the hallway, so that we aren't interrupted?"

"That or your office," Bowles said. "Whatever is more convenient for you."

Her chip would have to do its job on its own. Bowles needed to keep this interview short, so that no one had time to sweep the room before she had a chance to return and retrieve the chip.

As she followed Gumiela out of the room, she dropped

her scarf beside the door. She needed a reason to return. That was as good as any.

By then, she hoped, she would know what the big conference was with DeRicci and the politicians.

That might not be Bowles's great story, but it would do.

5

Noelle DeRicci sank into the overstuffed couch on the far side of the mahogany table. Her stomach growled. The restaurant smelled tantalizingly of roast garlic and baking bread.

Flint stood at the edge of the table. A large light with a moonscape painted on the shade hung over the table's center, half obscuring his face.

She motioned for him to sit down. To her surprise, he sat beside her on the couch.

"It'll be easier to talk," he said.

They were in a private room in the Hunting Club, one of Armstrong's most exclusive restaurants. The Hunting Club kept its private rooms free of listening devices. This particular room automatically shut off people's links, all except emergency links.

It surprised DeRicci that Flint felt they would need even more privacy.

But caution was part of his job—and his nature. He had kept secrets from her even when they were partners. Over the years, she had come to realize she would never get to know Flint well. It wasn't until he nearly died on his last case that she realized how much she valued his friendship, whether she knew all his secrets or not.

A waiter came over to the table. The Hunting Club vetted its employees, paying them a tremendous amount so that they'd be incorruptible (theoretically) and requiring that they have no links whatsoever. DeRicci hated her links—she had gotten in trouble more than once for keeping her emergency links off, something she was now forbidden to do—but she couldn't imagine life without them.

The waiter went through a list of specials, offered drinks, and took their order by writing everything on a piece of paper—one of the most inefficient and expensive methods DeRicci had ever seen. This dinner was Flint's treat—even DeRicci, with her high salary and three outrageous bonuses, couldn't afford an average meal at this place.

When the waiter left, DeRicci sighed. "Do you know what they offered me today?"

"Who?" Flint asked.

"The governor-general, basically, speaking for the entire United Domes of the Moon." DeRicci's head was still spinning. She couldn't believe that such illustrious people wanted to talk to her, let alone offer to work with her.

"What did they offer?" Flint asked.

"They want me to be the first appointee to a new office," she said. "I'm supposed to be the Chief of Moon Security. I'd make policy on how to defend the domes, coordinate with the head of security for each dome, and—"

"The domes have heads of security now?" Flint sounded surprised.

DeRicci shook her head. "This would be new, and organized by the UDM, not by the Domes themselves. After the two attacks on Armstrong, the UDM Council figured it was only a matter of time before the other domes had major security problems, and it was time to coordinate them."

The waiter returned, carrying their drinks on a tray. Flint had ordered real coffee, made from beans imported from Earth. Leave it to him to indulge in a stimulant instead of something that would relax him. DeRicci had thought of ordering wine, but instead she had settled for water.

As much as she wanted to escape the conflicting emotions of the day, she needed to be clearheaded. Flint was one of the few people—maybe the only person—she could confide in, and she needed to pay attention to whatever he had to say.

"So that's what the whole press conference was about?" Flint asked. "It was an excuse to get some of the mayors, the councilors, and the governor-general together to talk with you?"

DeRicci shrugged. "I'm as taken aback as you are. Maybe more so."

Probably more so. No one had told her about the medal ceremony. When she had left Police Central, she had removed the Silver Moon from her lapel and replaced the medal in its little box. She strongly objected to being rewarded for doing her job, especially when that job had been predicated on the loss of countless lives.

She hadn't succeeded during the Moon Marathon, no matter what Soseki had said. A lot of people had died that day. And she had done nothing positive in the bombing case. There was still no suspect, and no real understanding of why someone (or many someones) had tried to destroy the dome.

"The United Domes are a loose confederation," Flint said. "The mayors have more power than the governor-general. A moon-based post seems to me to be a political move on the council's part, a power grab so that the UDM would eventually dictate policy to the domes."

"I said that." DeRicci sipped her water. It was cold and fresh and tasted better than any water she had ever had before. She resisted the urge to check the paper menu, cleverly disguised to look like an ancient book, to see where the water had come from—or how much it cost.

"And?" Flint asked.

"They denied it, of course," she said. "All the while promising me enough power to make sure each dome followed my security recommendations. My head aches from all the doublespeak."

"Doesn't it strike you as odd that they'd do this at a press conference?" Flint asked.

DeRicci shook her head. "They want this to leak. People are scared right now. They want someone to do something to protect them. There's been talk in the Armstrong City Council of confining aliens to particular parts of the city—"

"But there's no proof that aliens bombed the dome," Flint said. "And the attack at the Moon Marathon came from a human."

"I said that too." DeRicci rubbed her fingers against the cold side of her water glass. "You know, in the past, I would've gotten yelled at for that kind of outspokenness. Now everyone listens as if what I have to say is important, and then they find ways to contradict me. I think I like the yelling better."

The political realm was completely new territory for her, and she couldn't escape the feeling that she was being used.

"I don't see how leaking this whole idea to the press will make people feel safer," Flint said.

"Here's the psychology," DeRicci said, annoyed that she understood this much of the game. "People don't believe official statements. They do, however, believe leaks, thinking that information ferreted out is somehow closer to the truth."

"But overall security," Flint said, "that's like a UDM police force. We've avoided that since the Moon was colonized."

Double doors in the paneled wall opened wide, revealing the steel walls inside the kitchen. The waiter entered the private room, carrying a tray on one hand as if he were some kind of entertainer.

DeRicci sighed. Maybe Flint had been right about privacy. Every time the conversation got going, it felt like the waiter had to interrupt.

He bowed before them as he took a large bowl off the tray. He set the bowl in the center of the table, then grabbed two plates and placed them before Flint and DeRicci. The bowl was filled with greens and multicolored vegetable bits, all cut so fine as to be unrecognizable. The waiter took some bottles of various oils from a nearby wait station. He dashed each oil onto the greens, then used two large wooden spoons to mix up the entire mess.

The air smelled of olive oil and basil, with a hint of vinegar. DeRicci's stomach rumbled again.

The waiter left. After the double doors had closed, Flint asked, "Are you going to take the job?"

"What do I know about dome security?"

"Seems to me that you're well-known as a public speaker on that topic."

She looked at him sideways. He had gripped both spoons and was trying to dish some greens out of the bowl. He was failing miserably.

She moved the bowl closer to his. "That was more than a year ago, and those talks were about the threats to the domes, not about how to secure the domes."

"Seems to me you have to understand the threats before you can prevent them." Flint managed to drip some greens onto his plate. The greens looked soggier outside of that bowl. The smell of vinegar grew.

"Sounds like you want me to take this job," DeRicci said.

"Better you than most of the so-called security experts I've met," Flint said. "At least you understand the unfairness of most Alliance laws, how complex it is dealing with more than fifty legal alien species, and how humans are just as dangerous as the rest. If we get some xenophobic person establishing policy, then the Moon becomes an unpleasant place to live."

DeRicci grabbed the bowl, tilted it slightly, and pushed greens onto her plate. Then she set the bowl back in the center of the table.

"I was thinking of not taking the job."

That caught Flint's attention. He set his forkful of greens on the side of his plate, and looked at her, a slight frown creasing his forehead. "Why?"

"That's not me," DeRicci said. "I'm not political. I'll make everybody mad."

"Is that what you're worried about?" he asked.

She shook her head. "I'm an investigator. I've already been promoted past my skill level. This'll be a nightmare."

"Then say no."

He made it sound so easy. But he was right. Someone else would get the job. Someone else would be the person who used the threat of bombings and biological attacks to create a strong interdome government.

The greens tasted bitter. The vinegar accented the bitterness. DeRicci pushed her plate away.

"I don't want them to create an overall security post. I went to various domes last year and talked to the governments so that they'd make their own policy. What the City of Armstrong needs is very different from the needs of Glenn Station. We have the largest port on the Moon. They have a small private port that's rarely used, and bullet trains. They're not facing external threats."

"I thought you said we weren't either," Flint said.

"Of course we are," DeRicci said. "But we can't shut down the port. We can't move all the Peyti to one side of the dome and the Rev to another. I'm envisioning checkpoints and more identification than we've ever had, and files and files of information just to get from one section of Armstrong to another. Who'd want to live like that?"

"Why don't you mention it to the council?" Flint asked. "Or are you supposed to deal directly with the governor-general?"

"I don't know," DeRicci said. "There's going to be a meeting tomorrow."

"So tell them." Flint finished his greens and set the plate aside.

"I'm afraid to," DeRicci said. "I'm afraid any objection I make will become an idea, and if I turn the job down, someone will remember the objection as a suggestion, and suddenly it'll all become policy, whether I like it or not."

"It sounds like you have no choice," Flint said. "You have to take this position."

"If only I could show them that this bombing was an isolated incident. Maybe they'll abandon the entire idea."

"The bombing may have been isolated and the marathon attack was isolated, but they came back-to-back," Flint said. "You were involved with both. They feel related."

She knew that. She felt trapped, leaning against the velvet couch, the beautiful table in front of her.

"I used to want the respect," she said. "Now I have it, and I hate it. It's forcing me into positions that I don't want to hold, places I don't want to go."

Flint templed his fingers, his eyebrows raised. He studied the double doors as if willing them to remain closed.

"But I'm really torn," DeRicci said. "They're going to create the position, but they've given me the chance to create the rules. I'd be a fool to balk at that."

Flint took a sip of his coffee, then ran his finger along the cup's rim. "No one would ever call you a fool, Noelle."

"People used to," she said.

He smiled at her. "And they were wrong."

6

Aisha Costard was shaking. If someone had told her two weeks ago that she would visit the Moon before she returned to Earth, she would have laughed. At that time, she had thought her Mars case something simple—an adventure really, instead of a disaster that had already changed her life.

She stood on the curb, waiting for Port Rentals to bring her an aircar. To other people, she probably looked like a typical traveler, clothes wrinkled from days on a shuttle, a bag over her shoulder. The clerk inside the rental office hadn't given her a second glance, merely took Costard's hand, pressed it against the identification box, and then touched a separate screen, confirming that Costard was who she said she was.

No mention made of the limited warrant, no comment on the fact that her travel visa came from Mars instead of her home planet of Earth, no discussion of the alert that had tinted Costard's file orange.

Apparently, Armstrong's customs had cleared all that. Or maybe they had simply modified it, giving whomever looked up Costard's identity specific instructions.

Costard had been too afraid to ask, especially after the last few days.

The Disty had given Costard clearance so that she could settle the major contamination case. But they had warned her that they would come for her if she tried to run. They would hunt her down, even if she disappeared.

She was working for them at the moment, even though they wouldn't come into the same room with her, even though they considered her as contaminated as the bones she'd been studying.

But the Disty did concede that she was making progress. Her work on the skeleton had brought the contamination area down from three square blocks to two, because she could prove that the skeleton had been at that site only as long as the building, which was about thirty years.

The area still reeked of death as far as the Disty were concerned, but it wasn't as bad as it had been. And if Costard could find the dead woman's family, then maybe the contamination would disappear for good.

A man stopped beside her. He wore a long brown coat and thigh-high boots. His hair fell against his shoulders. On one arm he wore a corporate patch. He didn't give her a second glance.

She resisted the urge to move away from him. She didn't want him to look at her. Ever since she had gone to Sahara Dome, she had felt like the ground could shift under her at any moment.

She made herself take a deep breath of the recycled air. Dome air always had a metallic taste to it, no matter how fresh the engineers tried to make it. At least here the dome's ceiling was visible, and the buildings towered above her. Real streets, with no rabbit warrens, no need for her to crouch every time she went from one location to another.

Armstrong Dome was big enough, and the roof of the dome high enough, that aircars were practical here. That, at least, was enough like Earth to reassure her.

"How long you been waiting?" the man next to her asked.

Costard started. She glanced at him sideways, then realized the movement probably looked furtive. She made herself smile at him. "A while."

"They're always backed up here," he said. "I don't know why I schedule everything so tight."

"You're not local?" she asked, then realized it was a dumb

question. Why would a man from the city need to rent a car at the port?

"I'm from the Outlying Colonies," he said, "but I do way too much business in this solar system. Seems like I'm in Armstrong half of my year."

She swallowed, trying to imagine that kind of travel and failing. "The literature says Armstrong is human controlled, right?"

He gave her a surprised look. "That's a strange question."

She shrugged. "I—had some trouble on Mars. I didn't realize the Disty had so much power."

"People rarely do." He rocked back on his heels, checked over his shoulder as if he were looking for his car, and then looked forward again. "You here on business?"

"Yes."

"I can show you around, if you like."

Months ago, she would have taken him up on the offer. She might have still if this had been Tokyo or London. But she was in another damn Dome, and she wasn't sure how to behave.

"I'm not going to be here long enough for that," she said. "But thanks."

He nodded, as if he had expected the answer. "You're from Earth, right?"

She almost blurted, *How do you know?* but caught herself just in time. "Why?"

"People from Earth rarely research their destinations. You live outside of the home world, you learn pretty fast that you have to know exactly what you're walking into."

She felt her face heat. "You never answered my question."

"About Armstrong? It's about as human as a domed colony can get. Maybe it'll get more human real soon now. I don't know."

"What do you mean?" she asked.

"New security laws coming in," he said. "Armstrong's been attacked twice in the last two years. The city's become paranoid."

An aircar rounded the corner of a nearby building and

slowed down. It hovered above the waiting area, then eased its way to the pavement in front of Costard.

"Looks like yours," the man said.

She nodded.

"The navigational equipment in the vehicles here are old by Earth standards, but still real functional. The only thing you have to worry about with these babies is that they're pretty easy to break into. Don't leave anything important in them."

He was being friendly. He was being helpful. She wanted to trust him more, but she didn't dare.

"Thanks," she said, as she went around to the driver's side.

A Port Rental employee, wearing a dark green uniform, got out. He took her hand, just like the woman inside had, and pressed her palm against a screen.

"How come you don't use 'bots or straight computerization?" she asked, getting irritated at the way these people just grabbed her and pulled her hand toward the screens.

"Living flesh," he said without looking at her. "We have to make sure the part is attached."

The answer made her stomach turn. She wasn't sure she wanted to know how the whole living-flesh identification system could be compromised by a cutoff limb. The blood had to be flowing through the palm, and the skin had to be warm. How did someone fake that?

The screen beeped its verification and the car chirruped a greeting at her. She hadn't heard that particular aircar electronic voice since she was a child. The man who had helped her hadn't been kidding when he said the equipment was old here.

He grinned at her and nodded as she got into the car. She put her bag on the passenger's seat, strapped herself in, familiarized herself with the controls, and hesitated.

If this had been Earth, she would have gone straight to her hotel, checked in, and cleaned up. She would have let the hotel information screen tell her about Armstrong, its history and its sites, while she prepared for her meeting.

But she was behind schedule, and even though she'd notified everyone in Sahara Dome who needed to know about her delay, she didn't trust them to act rationally about it. She had only gotten four days away from the project, and she had spent half of one in travel, the rest of it and all of another day in customs, and now half of this day trying to get out of the port.

She didn't have time to follow her usual leisurely plan. She would have to see if she could meet with the Retrieval Artist first.

Then she would settle in. Then she would spend at least one evening pretending she was still free.

7

Miles Flint sat at his desk, watching the report on InterDome Media for the third time. He had downloaded it nearly an hour ago, and ever since, he'd been watching like a man who couldn't take his eyes off a particularly devastating accident.

His office was cooler than normal. He had turned the temperature down when he had come in, mostly to stay awake. He'd been napping in his office too much lately.

Of course, that had been before he had seen Ki Bowles's news report. He had punched a button beside his desk, calling up one of the screens that he had hidden in the antique permaplastic walls. He usually let one of the news programs run all day, covering stories from all over the Alliance, never repeating them, always "Fresh! Up-to-Date! Surprising!"

Usually the packaged reports for the various media companies were high on sensationalism and low on details. But they provided a background-noise overview of the "important" events in Alliance space. Flint could always download reports from various sources, including the noncorporate sites, to get greater detail.

Often he spent his days that way, chasing news stories, keeping himself informed so that he would know which country had internal strife, which part of which planet was torn apart by civil war, which corporation had screwed its employees yet again.

All of that might be unimportant, and yet all of it might matter later if he took a case that involved it.

He had been reading a long report on the mines of Igesty when he had heard DeRicci's name. He looked up from his e-reader, but couldn't see past one of his raised desk screens to the newscast. He did recognize the voice narrating the piece, however. It belonged to Ki Bowles.

He set his e-reader on the desktop, stood, and faced the left wall. The front part of the office was small, with very little furniture—only his desk and his chair—which made it seem even smaller. Or maybe the large image on the wall did that. Ki Bowles had been to this office, and she had never taken up as much space as her recorded face now did.

". . . Filed reports branded her a screwup," Bowles was saying. "Someone who couldn't take or understand orders. Guaranteed, one supervisor said, to ruin any assignment she was given."

Flint pressed a corner of the screen and got the piece's title, along with its running time. He'd already missed five minutes of the report, and there was only a minute to go.

He had left the screen running, returned to his desk, and pushed a button on the underside of his desk, raising yet another screen. This one was part of his main system, unlike the wall screen. He went to InterDome's site, looked for Ki Bowles's most recent reports, and found the one he was listening to: NOELLE DERICCI: ACCIDENTAL HERO?

He downloaded it, then logged off, not caring that Inter-Dome had a record of his download. If Bowles somehow learned of his download and asked him about it later, he would simply say he was making certain she hadn't used any of her discussions with him.

And now, after he had watched the report three times, the content had broken his heart. DeRicci had a bad history, one that he thought she was past with her various promotions, and now with the new position as Chief of Moon Security.

Apparently, however, Bowles saw DeRicci as a story, maybe even a career-making one. And it didn't hurt that

Bowles had DeRicci's former boss, Andrea Gumiela, on record saying what a screwup DeRicci had been.

"We were all surprised when she came into her own at the Moon Marathon," Gumiela said.

She wore a little too much makeup and had a few enhancements to make her look younger. She had never looked that pretty when Flint worked for her.

"If you thought she was such a bad detective," Bowles asked in voice-over, "why did you keep her on the force?"

Gumiela seemed unfazed by the question. Instead, she had smiled as if she had expected it. "Noelle is brilliant, strong, and very driven. We look for those qualities in our officers. She had never been engaged before. Apparently, her heart wasn't in solving crime. It was in preventing crime."

When she gave that interview, Gumiela probably thought she was doing DeRicci a favor. Flint suspected there were a lot more statements like the last, statements that, in context, praised DeRicci. But Bowles only took snippets of what had obviously been a long interview, interspersed them with video reports and confidential memos about DeRicci's job performance, all of which must have been leaked by someone, maybe even Gumiela herself.

The whole thing made DeRicci sound like the biggest failure to ever join the Armstrong Police Department. It also sounded like the governor-general's assignment of her to the new United Domes of the Moon Security Department was a great mistake.

DeRicci only took the oath for her office the day before. She hadn't had a chance to do anything except give a gracious acceptance speech when Bowles's attack came out.

Flint was relieved Bowles hadn't used anything he said, even inadvertently, the day he had seen her at the press conference. She had mentioned his name, however: "Miles Flint, a local Retrieval Artist, had been one of Detective DeRicci's partners. He got rich shortly after he resigned from the force, some say off a case that he had worked with DeRicci herself."

The first implication, of course, was that Flint had gotten

rich through illegal means, which, he supposed, he had—saving hundreds, maybe thousands of lives in the process, something he would never discuss. The other implication was that DeRicci had helped him, and was somehow hiding millions of credits from her nefarious activities in the police department.

The irony was that she could have gotten rich if she had only quit when he did. He would have worked with her. He even offered to.

But she had turned him down, preferring to stay on the known path, even though it branched into places that made her morally uncomfortable. She had stayed with the police because she believed in the law, because it was the only thing she completely understood.

And now she was getting pilloried for it.

A screen opened on his desktop. The screen only opened when his perimeter alarm went off. The perimeter alarms were set in a half-mile radius around his office, so at least one of them went off once a day.

Some days, the alarm went off several times, providing a much-needed distraction. Usually, he would look at the screen that displayed the section where the alarm had been triggered, and see a neighbor coming home, or the seedy lawyer who had rented the office next door coming to work.

This time, however, Flint saw a rented aircar park in a little used lot. He pulled out the keyboard shelf. His mentor, Paloma, from whom he had bought the business, had taught him a healthy aversion to touch screens and voice commands. They were too easy to replicate or overhear. So he did most of his work on an old-fashioned Earth English-language keyboard, augmented with special keys for special commands.

He pressed a command key, and the image on the screen zoomed closer to the aircar. He had the system check the license. The car belonged to Port Rentals, the largest aircar rental firm on the Moon.

He transferred the still image of the car and license to his private system, however, the one that he never linked to a network. If he had to, he would make yet another copy, and use that image to hack into Port Rental's system, to find out who had rented the car.

He always liked to be prepared.

The car landed with a caution that only Earth drivers used. Most Moon-based drivers and drivers who were used to domes landed at the same speed they drove, knowing there would be little interference from wind or the ground. People who grew up in Earth's constantly changing environments never knew what to expect, so they acted with extreme caution.

He was intrigued now, even though he knew the chances of the aircar's driver coming to see him were slight. His office was in Old Armstrong, where the Moon's first settlement had been. Most of the buildings here, including his, were made of the original colonists' permaplastic, and were on a number of registers of historic places. A lot of tourists came down here to walk to the streets and touch the past.

The car's driver's door opened and a woman got out. She had an athletic build that came from exercise, not thinness enhancers. Her black hair was cropped short and curled under her ears. She wore a loose blouse that looked too wrinkled to be Moon-made, and tight pants that showed off her muscular legs.

Flint didn't recognize her. He transferred her image to his private system and ran it through known Earth records. If he didn't get a hit there, he would go to Moon records and maybe beyond.

She looked around as if she were expecting to be attacked at any moment. Then she looked up, a sure sign of a non-dome dweller. The dome was in Dome Day, radiating pure sunlight on the city below, but the sunlight was artificial. This side of the Moon was in complete darkness, and had been for the last two days now. It would remain in darkness for another ten.

The woman bent slightly, grabbed a bag from the car, and slung the bag over her shoulder. The bag was too large to be a shuttle gift, something the passenger shuttles handed to tourists who carried too many personal belongings. It looked more like a suitcase of some sort.

Apparently, someone had warned the woman about the neighborhood. Flint wasn't sure if wearing the bag was any better than leaving it in her locked aircar.

Her shoulders went up and down in a visible sigh, then she left the lot, crossed the sidewalk, and entered the street, looking around as she did so. Such a naïve thing. He wondered how she had made it so far on her own. Anyone watching her could tell she was a newcomer to Armstrong, probably with all of her belongings on her.

A victim ripe for the taking.

He zoomed in even closer, so that he got a better view of her face. She touched the edge of one eye, then blinked, and he realized she was following an overlay map that she had downloaded through her links.

She had a specific destination.

His private screen rose to full height. It was clear, so that he could see the office in the background. The screen displayed the still image of the woman, and beside it, a lot of tiny print.

Obviously, his system had found her.

He glanced at the information, blocking the photo, and making the print readable.

Aisha Costard
Forensic Anthropologist
Permanent address: Madison, Wisconsin, Old USA, Earth
Last requested visa [information two days old: system has not updated]: Sahara Dome, Mars
Visa approved by Sahara Dome Human Police Department. Reason given for issuance: forensic assistance on an unidentified corpse . . .

Flint stopped reading and frowned. A forensic anthropologist. He had heard of the job title when he was at the police academy, but had never had cause to bring one in on a case.

Apparently, she was good enough at her profession to be summoned to Mars.

None of which explained why she had come to Armstrong.

He scrolled through the information, scanning, until he reached:

> Warning given: subject must report position daily to Sahara Dome Disty Police Department. Failure to do so will result in drastic action.

That surprised Flint. He'd seen enough of these when he'd been space patrol to know that *drastic action* meant she was subject to Disty law. The only way she would be subject to Disty law outside of Disty territory was if she had committed a crime that the Disty considered particularly heinous.

Another screen went up and a silent alarm buzzed against his hip. She had come close to his building. Now he watched her on two screens, moving closer to his door.

When she reached it, she paused, blinked, and rubbed one eye. She had probably switched off the overlay map.

He shut down the hip alarm but kept the screens up. Her face looked unnaturally large in the building screen. She looked for something that identified the building.

She paused, as most people did, over the plaque that declared the building's historic value to the city of Armstrong. Then she saw, just below, the tiny sign that declared a Retrieval Artist worked in this office.

For a moment, she closed her eyes, as if she were terribly exhausted or extremely disappointed to find him. Then she took a deep breath, opened her eyes, and knocked.

He saved the information on her and shut down his alarm screens. He kept the wall screen on but muted it, and put his e-reader on the desktop as if he had been working with that. He shoved the keyboard into its place under the desk.

She knocked again.

"It's open," he called, even though it hadn't been a moment before.

The knob turned and she stepped inside, stopping suddenly as her links shut down. Most people had some kind of information being fed to them constantly, so much that they had gotten used to the constant crawl along the bottom of their vision or the soft voice droning inside their heads.

A handful of Flint's potential clients had fled the moment the links quit.

"You didn't have to do that." Her voice was soft, almost musical. Its depth surprised Flint. "I'm a client."

"I do that to everyone. The only systems that run in my office are mine." He hadn't stood. He hadn't done anything by way of greeting. It was his job to make potential clients uncomfortable so that they wouldn't hire him.

Hiring a Retrieval Artist usually put the Disappeared in jeopardy. He usually worked cases in which he felt the Disappeared was already about to be found, had been reprieved, or was in new trouble anyway. He rarely took on cases in which he was the first to search for the Disappeared.

She still held the door open, almost as if her muscles had stopped working with her links.

"If you don't like the silence, you can leave," Flint said. "Otherwise, close the door. I have a lot of sensitive information here that I don't want hacked. The longer the door is open, the more danger you cause countless people you don't even know."

She started, as if she were embarrassed, and pushed the door closed. Then she wiped her hands on those tight trousers.

"You're Miles Flint?" she asked.

"That's what the sign says."

She took a step closer to him. "You're the eighth Retrieval Artist I've seen, and the only one who has been this rude."

"I'm sorry to hear it," he said. "All of them should have been more cautious."

He was curious why she had seen eight previous Retrieval Artists, but he wasn't going to engage. He had learned, in the past few years of doing this job, that his curiosity often drew him to cases he shouldn't take.

"You're being rude on purpose?" she asked.

"I'd hate to think that I'm so socially inept that I'd be rude by accident." He crossed his arms and leaned back in his chair.

Her face was very pleasant. Her eyes were dark, her skin a light chocolate. She had round cheeks and a button nose that seemed at odds with her generous mouth. Yet all of the features worked together into something more, something quite appealing.

"I don't understand," she said. "You're in *business*."

He shrugged. "I don't need the money. Any Retrieval Artist who does is more of a Tracker, and probably doesn't care if he inadvertently exposes a Disappeared."

"I thought Trackers and Retrieval Artists were the same thing," she said.

He felt a flare of anger. He hated that comparison. "If you believe that, then why are you visiting Retrieval Artists? We're much more expensive."

"I thought—you know—Trackers worked in the public sector and Retrieval Artists were private."

"You thought wrong." He touched a key on the board under his desk. The door swung open. "Thanks for this little enlightening conversation. Your ignorance has been the highlight of my day. I hope I don't see you in my office again."

"You're kicking me out?" she asked. "You haven't even heard why I need your services."

"You probably need a Tracker." He stood, letting his height give his words added strength. "I will throw you out if you don't leave."

She looked panicked, as if he had already touched her, leaving bruises. Then she fled out the door. It closed behind her.

Flint sat back down and sighed. The case, whatever it had been, sounded like it might have been interesting, but he couldn't trust someone who didn't know the difference between Trackers and Retrieval Artists.

He hadn't lied to her when he said her very ignorance might put someone in jeopardy.

He pulled out the keyboard as he tried to dismiss Aisha Costard from his thoughts.

8

He had run her out. That arrogant man had tossed her into the dusty street as if she had been nothing more than a child.

Aisha Costard stopped on the tilted sidewalk outside the Retrieval Artist's office and coughed as the Moon dust swirled around her. Nowhere in Sahara Dome had she seen so much dust, not even at the open gravesite. Here it seemed like the dust filtered in from outside, as if the Dome weren't properly sealed.

Her stomach lurched, and the fear she'd been trying to suppress rose again.

She had a list of two dozen Retrieval Artists. She had already seen the eight "trustworthy" ones on Mars. This Miles Flint was the only Retrieval Artist that SDHPD felt worthy on the Moon.

If she had to hire someone else, she'd have to go to Earth, and in order to do that, she'd need special permission from the Disty themselves.

Two more trips through customs and security. Two more trips that were probably going to be worse than the one she had just endured. Earth's security was tighter than anywhere else in the solar system. Earth made most suspicious outsiders go to the Moon, rather than risk the center of the Alliance.

She'd probably be in custody for weeks rather than days.

She couldn't face it.

That arrogant man was going to listen to her, no matter what it took.

She turned around, walked back to the dirty plastic alcove that served as a front doorstep for this rundown place, and knocked again. She waited.

No answer.

She knocked again.

Of course, he probably had some kind of surveillance. He knew it was her and he wasn't going to let her back in.

"You should really listen to people before you make judgements," she said as loudly as she could. "I'm not your typical client."

Her words rang against the plastic. She had no idea if this Flint was listening to her. She had a hunch anyone else on the street could hear her.

"I'm here on official business," she said. "This is really important."

Silence.

She had never, in all her years traveling to all sorts of different places all over Earth, encountered anyone as rude as this man. She had run into people she didn't like, people who didn't like her, and people who didn't want her on a case. She'd even faced the Disty who had already decided that she was an enemy, and she had made them listen to her, with partial success. She wasn't going to let some low-rent "artist" get the better of her.

She tried the doorknob, but it wouldn't turn. She shoved, but the door didn't open.

Bastard.

He probably didn't appreciate her discussing this on the street. She didn't appreciate it either.

What had he said? That leaving the door open would jeopardize information in his files. Was he pretending to care about the clients he had been rude to? Or was it the actual Disappeareds who were important to him?

Maybe this was just a negotiating ploy so that she would pay any fee to get him to help her.

She backed away. She wouldn't do that. This trick

wouldn't get her to pay any price, not that it was her money. It wasn't. The money came from Sahara Dome—the human branch. It didn't matter if she saved them money, at least not to her, but it was the principle of the thing.

Principle.

He seemed to want her to believe that he was principled. Well, fine. She could play that game, even if she didn't believe him.

"No one's going to get hurt," she said. "The Disappeared is already dead."

Silence again. She was about to turn away when she heard a slight click. The door eased open.

He was sitting behind that crummy little desk, looking like a pale ghost in the cold room. "Shouting on the street is a sure way to get someone hurt."

She stepped inside, braced for the double clunks she had heard the last time when her links closed down. She wasn't one of those people who had information running all the time, but apparently, the links came with some white noise that she hadn't recognized until now.

She actually missed it.

The door closed behind her. She shivered involuntarily. He kept this room unbearably frigid.

Her bag shifted slightly, then slipped off her shoulder. She let the heavy thing fall onto the floor.

"Are you going to listen to me?" she asked.

"If it's the only way to get rid of you," he said.

She hesitated, the rudeness catching her again, making her anger work.

His expression softened. He leaned forward, looking engaged for the first time.

"Go ahead," he said. "Tell me what's going on."

So she did.

9

Flint paid little attention to her saga of woe: How she felt she had been tricked when she went to Mars; how she was unfamiliar with Disty customs; how she had stayed four times longer than she had expected. She spoke with an intensity he hadn't seen before, as if each thing that happened to her had been a personal affront.

Obviously, she had taken his attitude as an affront as well. She seemed like a timid thing; maybe anger was the only emotion that got her to stand up for herself. It certainly put some color in those round cheeks of hers, and added an even richer timbre to her already deep voice.

He was determined not to ask questions, to listen to her and then get her out of his office. If she had already seen eight Retrieval Artists, then she had failed to engage them as well.

Although this time, he wouldn't use the ignorance as his reason to turn down her case. He'd find something in this litany of woe that would sound plausible. Rudeness seemed to get her back up; maybe she would respond better to kindness.

After a few minutes, he held up a hand. "Enough. I want to know about the case. The background can come later."

"The background is very important." She shifted from foot to foot, but unlike most of his visitors, did not ask for a chair. It was as if she hadn't even noticed the chair's absence because she had been so focused on convincing him to pay attention to her.

"I can't understand the relevance of the background unless I know why I'm hearing it," Flint said.

She nodded and said, "I was called to Mars to view a skeleton, Mr. Flint. Bodies that decay in the Martian soil should mummify, just like they do in the real Sahara."

"This still feels like background, Ms. Costard."

Her face flushed. "It's not."

"I deal with Disappeareds, Ms. Costard, not skeletons. You mentioned a Disappeared. You also said she was dead. If you know that, and know who she is, then you don't need a Retrieval Artist. A detective maybe, or even a lawyer if the problem is with the estate, but—"

"My skeleton is the Disappeared," Costard snapped. "She was planted in Martian soil like a clue to a crime I don't even understand. She was killed somewhere else, probably stabbed, judging by the slash in one of her ribs, and then whoever killed her cut the skin off of her. This was deliberate."

Flint winced at the description. He had seen a lot of violent death during his years with the police force, and the sheer creativeness of it never failed to disgust him.

"Her real name is Lagrima Jørgen. She's been missing for the last thirty years, and I think she's been dead at least that long."

Flint shrugged. "I'm sorry to hear of it, but there's nothing I can do. You have her body, her name, and probably a lot of her history. I find people, Ms. Costard."

"I know," she said. "I may have made a mistake about Trackers, but I know what Retrieval Artists do, Mr. Flint. I really do. Lagrima Jørgen angered a group of M'Kri Tribesmen by selling the mineral rights to their homeland. She tricked them out of those rights, and when BiMela Corp's engineers arrived to stake their claims, the Tribesmen killed them. The case went before the Fifth Multicultural Tribunal, who ruled for the corporation—which was no surprise, because the documents were in order. But the Tribunal noted that the Tribesmen actually had a case against Jørgen under tribal law for using a type of language that they had forbidden in negotiation. They had lost the rights because they had failed to engage an Alliance lawyer to protect them—which is simply incompetence, not illegality—but they still had redress under their law for the actual trickery itself."

Flint frowned. "The M'Kri aren't known for their inhumane treatment of people who break their laws."

"The Tribesmen are a subculture. They follow different laws—which is, apparently, another reason they lost their case. They weren't the dominant culture of their region." She sounded a lot more confident and authoritarian than she had before.

"As a subculture, they allowed killing to redress crimes?" Flint didn't understand. Usually—although not always—subcultures were subject to the dominant cultures laws.

"The Tribesmen don't kill, Mr. Flint. They enslave. And that is legal. They call it servitude, and the punishment lasts as long as the effects of the crime itself. A week for a damaged pot, until that pot can be remade, all the way to life and beyond if the crime has changed the very way the Tribesmen or the ones affected live."

"The loss of the mineral rights was permanent?" he asked.

Costard nodded. "So Jørgen's children and her children's children would be in service to the Tribesmen, unless the mineral rights could be released to them. Even then, her family might not have gone free. If the minerals were taken, then the effects of the crime continued."

Flint sighed. He understood why Lagrima Jørgen had disappeared. But he still didn't understand what Costard thought he could do about this case. "Tell me, in one sentence, why you believe you need a Retrieval Artist."

"I'll give you two," she said. "I don't think Lagrima succeeded in disappearing."

Flint wouldn't necessarily agree, but he didn't say that.

"But no one has seen her two children in thirty years either." The color had risen even further in Costard's face, making her eyes seem incredibly bright.

"You think she got her children to disappear?" Flint asked.

"They're not with the Tribesmen," Costard said. "The

SDHPD already checked that. And the warrant is still outstanding."

"They were probably murdered then," Flint said.

"There's that chance," Costard said. "But their bodies haven't turned up anywhere."

"You've checked the site where you found hers?" Flint asked.

Costard nodded. "The SDHPD is still looking, but they doubt the children are there. The team has already gone through too many layers of soil. They're convinced that no more bodies were buried at the same time as Jørgen's."

"But you say she wasn't killed there," Flint said.

"And therein lies my problem, Mr. Flint. I can't prove anything. I know she tried to disappear. I know she took her children with her and no one saw them again. I know she ended up dead, probably murdered. Clearly, her corpse has been violated, and done so with a probable intent to upset the Disty. And that's all I know."

Flint frowned, feeling a mixture of irritation and excitement. She had certainly aroused his curiosity. He was interested, partly because the case was so different from anything that anyone had brought him.

But several things still nagged. "Do you know how expensive my services are?" he asked.

"Not exactly," she said. "But I hear that a Retrieval Artist can cost a small fortune."

"I take a retainer of two million credits," he said. "I always investigate the information you gave me myself. If I decide, after my investigation, not to take the case, the two million is all this will cost you. If I decide to take the case, I bill weekly for expenses, which can run into a great deal of money. I also collect a weekly fee. I may terminate our arrangement at any time. If I take your case, you cannot terminate. If it takes me five years to solve this case, you will pay the weekly fee and expenses for those five years—"

"Five years?" She took a step backward. "It could take that long?"

"It could take longer." He folded his hands together. "Why

should that matter you, Ms. Costard? This is an intellectual puzzle to you, right? Nothing more."

Except maybe the money. But if it was just the money, she would probably have left when he mentioned the two million credits. He had no idea how much forensic anthropologists got paid, but he doubted it was enough to indulge an intellectual whim.

She blinked hard several times. "Five years, Mr. Flint. I don't have five years."

"To solve the case?"

She shook her head, swallowing visibly. "To live, if we don't find those children."

"What do the children have to do with it?"

"They're the only ones who can clear the contamination," Costard said. "I have to give them to the Disty in order to go free."

10

Sharyn Scott-Olson couldn't shake the feeling of déjà vu as she walked in the freshly dug Martian soil. The hole was deeper now, still square, and still a wide-open space inside the Disty area.

The main difference was that the buildings looked abandoned, not empty. Amazing what a few weeks could do.

Petros Batson leaned against one of the backhoes. The human-made machines were bigger than the Disty ones. Scott-Olson wondered how they had been brought into the Disty section. Probably in pieces—that was how large things made their way in here—and probably at considerable effort on the part of the human workers.

"I don't believe that you found another body," she said as she got close.

Batson gave her a baleful stare. His face was covered with dust, just like it had been the first time, only this time, the dust had gathered in even more creases in his skin. Batson had aged in the last few weeks, just like she had.

The fear ate at all of them. It hadn't helped that Costard, the Earth advisor, had gotten so angry about her own involvement. They should have told her, she said. They should have warned her. They should have realized she had very little interaction with alien cultures.

Maybe Scott-Olson should have. But Costard taught at a university, and Scott-Olson remembered from her own student days on Earth how diverse the campus population was. Various alien races on exchange programs; some who lived locally, others who had come in spending their own credits just to get whatever specialty the university offered.

Besides, everyone knew that Mars was controlled by the Disty. The fact that Costard had been ignorant of Disty law wasn't Scott-Olson's problem.

Batson hadn't answered her comment. In fact, he hadn't moved from his position beside the backhoe. His long coat was stained brownish-red, and his hair was mussed.

"Don't tell me it's another skeleton," Scott-Olson said.

"It's not." His voice was flat.

She turned around. They were in the very center of the square hole. It was twice as deep as it had been when they discovered the skeleton. The Human-Disty Relations Department of the Human Government had continued the dig at the Disty's insistence, in an effort to show that the contamination was a onetime thing. The Disty required that the hole be doubled in depth—some kind of weird tradition. The backhoes hadn't quite reached that level, but they were close.

Batson still hadn't moved.

"You gonna show me or not?" Scott-Olson said.

"We're going to have to keep this quiet," he said. "I have the backhoe operator and his assistants in custody. Fortunately, they called me. If they'd called a street officer, then we'd really be screwed."

His flat tone chilled her even more than his words. She'd never heard of humans taking each other into custody over a discovery.

"They hurt someone?" she asked.

He shook his head. "Come on."

He led her across the sand. It was darker at this level than it had been at the upper levels. The lines on the side of the hole showed definite strata—the color varied from a bright orange to a rust to a near brown, with just a touch of white weaving through. The white, she knew, came from chemicals leaching from the Disty buildings. She had seen that before.

Only one set of footprints crossed the backhoe's path. Batson was careful to step in them. Apparently, they had been his own.

He stopped at the edge of a deeper section of the hole. Then he turned his back to it, tipped his head backward, and walked away.

In all the years she had worked with him, he had never done that before. He left her alone without explanation, without guidance.

She was shaking when she peered into the section.

At first, she saw nothing. Just an uneven sand surface, caused by the blade. Then she hopped down inside and nearly stumbled.

Her boots had caught on a hard surface, like brick or rock. But there weren't rocks here. That was one of the charms of the dunes, the fact that there was only sand to contend with instead of giant rock.

She crouched, her breath catching in her throat. Everything had combined to make her nervous: Batson's strange behavior, the abandoned look to the buildings, the pressure she already felt from the Jørgen case.

Her feet hadn't caught on a rock. They had caught on an arm. It poked out of the dark red sand like an arm poking out of a blanket. She followed it, found the shoulder, and a little farther up, a bit of an ear.

A mummy. That, at least, was normal. And judging by the depth at which it had been uncovered, it had been here for a very long time.

She put on her gloves. They tightened automatically against her skin. She brushed a bit at the sand, then stopped and studied the entire uneven surface.

Bile rose in her throat. She swallowed hard, forcing the bitter-tasting fluid back down. She hadn't thrown up at a crime scene in her entire life. She wasn't about to start now.

But clinging to her professionalism meant she had to deal with the scene before her, and she wasn't sure she wanted to do that, either.

Because the scene before her defied any other scene she'd ever witnessed. What she had initially taken for an uneven sand surface caused by the backhoe was a sea of body parts, rising from the depths like corpses leaving their graves.

Arms, legs, hands, heads. All mummified, all apparently still attached to the bodies, strewn before her like rocks on a beach. The parts continued to the walls of the section, disappearing under the sand in ways that told her this mass grave continued beneath the yet unturned dirt.

Her mouth was open, already dry from the air and the sand floating in it.

Sand and whatever else, particles, perhaps, of the unfortunates in front of her.

The bile rose again, and this time she covered her mouth with her gloved hand. She scrambled out of the hole and lay at the edge, swallowing against the dryness in her throat.

Swallowing, swallowing, completely unsure what to do.

She wanted to go to Batson, tell him to order the workers back, have them cover this space, cover everything, and lie to the Disty, telling them everything was fine.

But they wouldn't believe it. The Disty knew better. Most of them never even bothered to learn English, but even those had one phrase that they used like a mantra:

Humans lie.

Yes, they did. It was innate, a survival mechanism. Sometimes it was the only option that humans had.

Scott-Olson wished she could lie, pretend this never happened, pretend she had never seen it.

Because if the Disty considered a single skeleton that had been in the ground for thirty years to be major contamination, what would they consider this? Did they even have a word for it? And if so, what was it? Could it express the horror she felt even now?

Because if the Disty thought her contaminated by that skeleton, what would they think of this?

11

"I'm not going to help you find two people just so that the Disty can treat them to a vengeance killing." Flint was appalled that this slight woman had suggested such a thing. She had seemed so mild a few moments ago; he had even been slightly amused by her anger, as if it could have no real impact on the people around her.

It turned out that she had a lot of impact. She was willing to sacrifice two lives to save her own.

No wonder the other Retrieval Artists had turned her down.

"No," she said, her hands up as if she were warding off a blow. "It's not about killing."

"What's it about then?"

"It's a Disty ritual. I don't entirely understand it, but here's how it was explained to me."

She took a step closer to the desk, as if she wanted to confide in him. Her voice lowered as well.

"If the Disty avoided every place where someone died, then they'd have no place to live in the entire universe."

"In theory, I suppose," Flint said.

She glared at him, then took a deep breath. "I'm giving you my superficial understanding of all of this. I'm new to the Disty, unfortunately. If I weren't, I wouldn't be in this mess. All I can tell you is what I learned from some Sahara Dome official who spoke to the Disty and then talked to me.

Right now, I'm so contaminated that I can't talk to any Disty."

Flint frowned. She had said something about contamination, but that had been when he wasn't paying a lot of attention.

"Anyway, the Disty have a way of cleansing areas where corpses are found. Family members of the deceased do some kind of thing with fire and sixteen days of silence, and sprinkling a special kind of liquid on the spot. Then no one goes near the site for a month or more, depending on the length of time the corpse spent there. Finally, some other Disty is sent in to make sure the decontamination happened. If he clears it, then the area's safe again."

"And the people who are contaminated?" Flint asked.

"They have to go through some other kind of ritual, also with the family of the deceased. No one would explain that to me, except to say it's harmless."

Flint had heard of stranger rituals, so he didn't doubt that this one could exist. But he would look up the Disty death contamination rites when Costard left, whether he took the case or not. His curiosity again. It always got the best of him.

"What happens if the family members can't be found?" Flint asked.

She blinked rapidly, as if her eyes were filling with tears. She bent her head, wiped at the corner of one eye, and then took a deep breath.

"Ms. Costard?" Flint made certain his voice was harsh. He couldn't give her sympathy at this moment. He had a hunch she would respond to it badly.

She nodded once, acknowledging him but not looking up. Then she held up a hand, took another deep breath, and raised her head.

Her eyes were red and so was the tip of her nose. She looked helpless and frightened. He had a hunch he was finally seeing her core personality. She was overwhelmed and out of her league, and from what he had listened to in her story, no one had tried to make things easier for her.

He wouldn't either, just by the nature of his job. Yet for

the first time since she had come in the door, he felt compassion for her.

"What do they do?" he asked again.

She swallowed hard, squared her shoulders, and straightened her spine. She raised her chin slightly. "They use the people involved with the body—and I use 'people' loosely. It could mean Disty, it could mean humans, it could mean Revs—anyone who was near the body when it was found— and these people have to do the decontamination work."

Her voice hitched and she stopped. When it became clear that she wasn't going to say anything else, he spoke.

"Is this decontamination work a ritual as well?"

She nodded. "I wasn't told the details, so I looked them up. Torture—that's what we'd call it. The use of bodily fluids— not necessarily blood, although that's the preferred fluid from humans—combined with an exchange of body parts, detached, and some other really grotesque things that I don't want to describe. I don't even want to think about them."

Her voice sped up as she recounted this. She had threaded her fingers together and she was twisting them, twisting, twisting, twisting, as if the very act could make her words disappear.

"I'm told that not many humans survive this decontamination process."

"What about Disty?" he asked. "Do they survive?"

She shrugged. "I didn't ask."

He leaned back in his chair and templed his fingers, tapping them against his chin. He had seen the results of Disty vengeance killings—corpses splayed, their intestines removed and used to decorate a room. The blood spatter around the human victims of vengeance killings always indicated the victims were alive while they were being disemboweled.

If the Disty could do that, they could come up with equally vicious things for a "decontamination ritual."

"How long do you have before the Disty conclude that the children no longer exist?" he asked.

"Initially, only a month," she said. "But I was able to show the Disty that Jørgen's body had been under a building for thirty years and that she hadn't been killed on site."

"Show them?" Flint asked. "I thought you couldn't interact with them because of your contamination."

"Apparently, contamination doesn't spread to equipment," she said. "Or at least to vids. I made a recording of my evidence, explaining everything clearly, and the SDHPD showed that recording to a Disty Death Squad. The Death Squad determined that the contamination wasn't quite as bad if the body had been killed off-site, so they gave us an extension."

"An extension?" he asked. "As if you hadn't paid your rent on time?"

She gave him a distracted smile. "Not quite like that. Their laws determine the level of contamination and the time it takes to recover. The longer the corpse remains at its place of death, the more the contamination grows, but apparently, the corpse takes less contamination with it when it moves to a new location. The thirty-year time span was shorter than the Disty had expected, and the fact that Jørgen was killed off-site took some pressure down too. So we have six months to find family members."

"Six months," Flint repeated, thinking about the magnitude of the case. He hadn't had a case this involved, but during his training, Paloma had told him of cases she had worked on that had taken years to resolve. She had given him a rule of thumb: The more alien groups involved, the more off-Moon locations involved, the longer the investigation would take.

"It's not really six months anymore," Costard said. "I used up a week making my determinations, and the Disty used another week before they decided to believe me. Then I've spent another week searching for a Retrieval Artist to take my case."

"There aren't any Trackers on staff at the Sahara Dome Human Police Department?" Flint asked. A lot of departments all over the galaxy had Trackers, many of whom were cops as well.

She shook her head. "The SDHPD is a for-show police force. They keep the humans in line for the Disty and take care of human-on-human crime, which the Disty don't want to deal with. But anything that happens outside the Dome isn't the Disty's concern—unless it had some kind of impact on them, and then they handle it, in ways that I don't entirely understand."

Flint flashed on the last vengeance killing he had seen. Three humans, murdered in a space yacht, their bodies splayed in typical Disty style. The mess had been awful. The stench had been worse.

"You could hire a private detective," Flint said. "It would be cheaper."

"Jørgen disappeared," Costard said.

"Jørgen *tried* to disappear," Flint said. "From what you tell me, she failed. Chances are the children failed as well. For all you know, they could be buried under nearby buildings."

Costard shuddered. "I like to think they disappeared."

Flint stood. The walls of the office felt closer than they had, probably because of all the talk of the Disty and their nasty ways.

"I used to be a police officer, Ms. Costard," he said. "You learn pretty quickly that the most obvious solution is usually what happened. The obvious thing here is that Jørgen and her children were caught before they could finalize their disappearance, they got killed, and their bodies were scattered on building sites. A good private detective can find this out for you, and charge you so much less than I can."

"But what happens if you're wrong, Mr. Flint?" she asked. "What happens if the children did disappear? Aren't I better off hiring you, a man who is trained as a detective and who knows how to find the Disappeared, than hiring someone who could screw up a disappearance investigation?"

He said nothing. She had finally caught his attention. All of it.

"To me," she said, "the worst-case scenario is that Jørgen managed to get her children away from the M'Kri Tribesmen but wasn't able to save herself from . . . whatever killed her. The children are safe. They grow up, they're functional adult humans, and then my hired detective blunders his investigation. The M'Kri Tribesmen find the children, take them away, and will not let them come to Sahara Dome to help us decontaminate their mother's final resting site. Whereas if I hire you, the children would be safe and they could come to Sahara Dome and—"

"There's no guarantee that they'd be safe just because you hired me," Flint said. "I'd be more cautious than your fictitious detective, that's for sure, but I could still trigger an investigation that would end up in their getting captured by the M'Kri. That's one of the risks you take any time you hire a Retrieval Artist."

"But theoretically, you do your best to minimize that risk," she said. "That's why I would hire you. To protect all sides—the children, me, the others from the SDHPD—and to give us a chance. Please, Mr. Flint. We don't have a lot of time."

He wasn't going to let that pressure make him decide to take a case. "Why did the other Retrieval Artists turn you down?"

She flashed him that glare again. "Let's see. The first three—all of whom worked in Sahara Dome—didn't want to cross the Disty. You see, if you get near this corpse, you could be contaminated."

"I wouldn't get near it," Flint said.

"That was my argument," she said, "but those three wouldn't hear of it. So I talked to a Retrieval Artist in White Rock. He only worked with Disappeareds who might be on Mars, and he figured if Jørgen managed to get her children away, they wouldn't be on Mars, particularly if she died there."

"That's false reasoning," Flint said.

"No kidding." Costard was using the voice she had originally used when she came into the office, the voice that spared no one and covered a litany of problems, all as if they had personally offended her—which, Flint supposed, they had.

"And the other four Retrieval Artists?" Flint asked.

"Two were in Pathfinder City. One refused to deal with a nonrelative, and one only worked with insurance companies and lawyers. The last two were in Aram Chaos, and like the others, they only spoke through my links. One of those Retrieval Artists promised to get back to me but never did, and the other told me that taking my case was a death wish, not just because of the Disty, but because of M'Kri Tribesmen."

"I thought you told me they don't kill," Flint said.

"They don't. I told him that, and he said I was misinformed. So I went back later and checked my research. They don't kill, but I couldn't convince him of that, and since I couldn't convince him, I couldn't hire him either. I traveled all over that damn planet, and no one would help me. So I came here." She put her hands on her hips. "And now I'm beginning to believe I have to apply to the Disty for a special permit to return to Earth, because you're not going to help me either, are you, Mr. Flint?"

"There are other Retrieval Artists on the Moon," he said.

"I've researched them. Most seem pretty unreliable."

"You found a lot on me?" he asked, stunned. He had been careful to keep the information about himself to a minimum.

"Not as a Retrieval Artist," she said. "But I like your police background, and you have some computer experience as well. And . . ."

Her voice trailed off. His heart had started beating hard. He had a hunch that he knew what she was going to say, but he didn't want to assume. He wanted her to tell him.

"And?" he asked.

"I saw you plead with the authorities to shut down that day care center. That old vid is really affecting. And I figured someone who cared that much once might do so again."

Flint's stomach churned. He wanted to snap at her, *Anyone would care about that. My daughter died there.* But one of the main rules of Retrieving was to keep his emotions to himself. Keep the personal private at all times.

He wished he could get that vid out of all the various archives, so that it never came up when someone searched his background. But he couldn't. It had been duplicated so many times, he would never find all of the copies.

It was there for his future and former clients, as well as his enemies, to find.

"You would base your future on an ancient news story?" he asked, careful to keep his voice level.

She shrugged. "You Retrieval Artists like to be mysterious. I'll do what I can to find the best person for the job. But you don't want it, either, do you?"

He wasn't afraid of the Disty—at least, not in the ways that Martian Retrieval Artists were. And he was intrigued. But he had a lot of hesitations.

"I don't make decisions on the spur of the moment," he said.

Her shoulders fell. She looked almost as if she had collapsed in on herself.

"But," he said, "I'll take a retainer, and research all that you've told me. If it checks out, I'll take the case."

For a moment, she didn't move. Then she raised her head, her lips parted slightly. "What?" she whispered.

"I'm going to investigate you," he said. "You and the Disty and the Tribesmen and Ms. Jørgen. If I'm satisfied with what I find, I'll take the case. If not, I'll keep the retainer for my time, and send you to someone else."

"You will?" Her voice rose. "Really?"

He wasn't sure she had heard him. Or if she had, that she understood him. "I'm not saying I'll take the case yet."

"But you'll at least listen. You'll see that I'm not lying to you. Oh, Mr. Flint, I can't thank you enough."

"I don't care about thanks," he said. "I care about credits in my account."

"Right," she said, as if she were in a daze. "Right. Credits."

She grabbed his hand. The warmth of her skin startled

him. He couldn't remember the last time someone had voluntarily touched him.

"Thank you," she whispered. "Thank you for giving me a chance to save my life."

12

RADIANTE   81

with the sudden. Happened at home. Attempt. My wife—
silently changed him.

Forgive me, she whispered. Thank you, he began and
said he by side up, his a.

12

Noelle DeRicci stood before the floor-to-ceiling windows in her new office. It smelled of fresh paint and varnish. She'd had the environmental controls on for two days now, but it hadn't made any difference. The smell still lingered.

The windows made her nervous. Ever since the explosion more than a year ago that knocked a hole in the dome, she'd been leery of windows. They seemed artificial, unnecessary, a danger. She worried about them shattering, about crooks or terrorists breaking in through them, about air seeping out of them.

She worried about everything.

She sighed. From here she could see the section of the dome where the explosion had occurred. In the arching curve of the dome that controlled Armstrong's light and environment, she could still see cracks that ran along the interior of the frame.

No need to worry, the engineers told her. There were four levels of redundancy in the dome itself. The cracks were only in the lower layer, the one that didn't expose the dome to the Moon's harsh environment.

No need to worry.

But she did anyway. That was her job.

She sighed and looked at the scorch marks still visible during Dome Daylight. The fire in that section of the dome had leveled everything. The scorch marks were less important than the cracks. Since no one had fixed the cracks yet, no one had even thought of the scorch marks, black against the artificial light that hid the Moon's sky.

DeRicci clasped her hands tightly behind her back. She had taken this office precisely for its view. She wanted the reminder of the horrors the Dome could experience.

She wanted to remind herself every day what could happen if she screwed up.

DeRicci turned away from the windows and headed toward her desk. The office had been designed by some fancy architect who was trying to make his name outside the Moon. Of course, the United Domes had sponsored him, giving him this commission as if they were bestowing a gift, and he did all sorts of fancy things that would impress all the outsiders who visited Armstrong on business.

DeRicci hadn't known anything about the project, of course. When the powers that be had decided on a Moon-wide security office, she had been a lowly detective, working murder cases.

After she had taken this job, she had learned that the security position had been in the works for years—since before the Moon Marathon. Somehow she had thought that the twin disasters of the marathon and the explosion had frightened the politicians into creating this office.

Instead, those disasters had simply given the politicians an excuse.

Learning that had convinced her that she had made the right decision. The job needed someone like her, someone who had been in the trenches and yet knew how regulation could tie people's hands as well as protect them. She knew all the dangers and she was determined to avoid them.

DeRicci couldn't bring herself to sit down at her new desk. Some interior designer had thought that transparent furniture would go with the window-covered walls and the clear ceiling. The chairs had lines around the frames—faint white lines, so a person didn't sit on a chair that wasn't there—and so did the desk. The tables had no such outlines, and were only visible because of the items placed on top of them.

The architect—or maybe it was the interior designer—had ordered that greenery be the other feature of this place, and not just fake greenery like there had been in her detective's office, but real plants that required some real plant person to come in every day, mist them, water them, and feed them as if they were children.

As soon as DeRicci felt like she had freedom of movement, she would order those plants out of here. She wasn't sure that freedom of movement would ever come. Right now, each breath she took was scrutinized, each tremble of a finger looked at as if she were signaling an order to one of her minions.

She didn't really have minions yet. She hadn't hired them. The only people on her staff were the security team assigned to guard her, and the skeleton staff that any government office had. Right now, they were all being paid by the City of Armstrong. No one had worked out the logistics of having the United Domes pay for any of this.

That, the governor-general had assured DeRicci, would happen in the next biennium—whatever the hell that was.

A big office, no real staff, and only a vague mission. At the moment, DeRicci wasn't even sure how to begin doing her job, let alone what kind of job she was supposed to do. She'd asked, of course, and everyone had given her the same answer: *It's your job to make the Moon more secure.*

But she didn't have a budget or any way to enforce the changes she made. She didn't even have a plan.

And everyone outside of the government treated her like she had just become the Moon's military dictator. All that popularity she had worked up after the marathon and her work on the commission had vanished like it had never been.

Of course, Ki Bowles wasn't helping. Those horrible news pieces, talking about all of DeRicci's past screwups without discussing anything positive she'd done, made it sound like she had bungled her way into this job.

Maybe she had. She certainly couldn't remember anything she had done right. Only the demotions and the reprimands and the anger she had carried in her very bones when she worked for the police department.

Then she used to think if only she could run the department for one day, she would make such a difference. *She* would understand all the problems the street officers and detectives had. She would know how to treat everyone well.

Now she just shook her head at her own naïveté. Here she was in charge of a fake kingdom, almost afraid to make a move for fear that someone somewhere would make a valid objection.

Right now, her new department had bad press, no real design, and no power.

And she was so politically inexperienced, she had no idea how to put any of this right.

<u>13</u>

Flint wasn't trying to save her life. He was just trying to find out if she was telling the truth.

He made Costard pay the retainer directly into one of his accounts, explained the rules and procedures to her, and sent her on her way. She left him the name of the hotel she was staying at, and he promised to contact her in no less than forty-eight hours.

He had a lot of research to do during that time.

Some of the research was easy. He started with Costard herself, going deeper than the cursory information he had received when he had gotten her facial recognition through his network. Everything she had done was in some database or another. Her parents were well-known archeology professors who had traveled the Earth, looking at artifacts. They had died on a dig in a region known as the Middle East, after some sort of accident had caused the remains of an ancient stone building to collapse around them.

Costard was their only child. She had accompanied them on their travels when she was young, but as she got older, they had left her behind in various schools. She had worked her way to the top of all of her classes, and had shown great promise in several fields.

When her parents died, she had been working on a master's in history. She had dropped that and had started all over again, focusing on physical anthropology, a field related to her parents' expertise, but not in that area. Over time, she had specialized in forensic anthropology, essentially working with bones recently found to figure out how the person who had once worn those bones had died.

Flint wondered if she ever thought about the irony of her work: that she dealt with people who had often been long buried—hidden by dirt or debris or ancient stone buildings. People like her parents, who, because of some misfortune, had ended life early and painfully, their bodies hidden by the ground itself.

If she had thought of it, he found no record of it in her writings or the interviews she had done. Costard was passionate about her work and had become well-known, one of the true experts in her field.

Only her field was Earth-centric. There was little call for forensic anthropologists outside of the nurturing, oxygen-rich, humid environment of the mother planet. The more artificial the environment, the easier it was for medical examiners, doctors, and coroners to find the secrets of the dead.

Flint learned, in his study of Costard, that the dead who kept their flesh had fewer secrets than the dead who had lost theirs. He had found it a ghoulish job, one that seemed almost irrelevant. He hadn't talked with her about it; he wasn't sure he really wanted to know what it was about the work that truly inspired her.

Like most forensic anthropologists, she spent a few years at the Smithsonian Institute, doing work in their labs, and that was where she discovered an aptitude for solving murders. *Current death,* she called it in one of the many profiles he saw. Current death instead of carbon dating bones thousands of years old.

This way, she had said in an interview, *I can make an actual difference. I can let families know what happened to their loved ones. If the case is truly current, I can help put criminals in jail.*

And she did. She became well-known throughout Earthly

police circles for her unerring expertise and her willingness to throw herself into a job.

Perhaps that was what led her to Mars in the first place, that willingness to get overinvolved. She hadn't done her research, just like she had said. Her problems on Mars weren't human problems; they were Disty problems, problems she rarely encountered in her work on Earth.

Flint could have spent days developing a profile of Costard, but the deeper he dug, the more consistent she seemed. After the death of her parents, everything she had done seemed to follow a straight-line pattern. Each decision was logical, moving from one point to another.

Even her decision to remain alone and uninvolved outside of her work made sense to him.

But of course it would. He had made the same decision after Emmeline died.

When he came to that realization—that he and Costard had their reaction to familial death in common—he had stood up from his desk and paced the office, trying to evaluate his own stance on this case. If he felt a thread, a common tie to Costard, could he keep his objectivity?

And did it really matter?

After all, her involvement in this case wasn't personal. She hadn't killed Lagrima Jørgen. Costard hadn't been old enough to be a part of this case, even if she had some ties to the Jørgen family.

Finally, Flint calmed himself enough to return to his desk. There he set aside the work he had done on Costard—he had done enough to get a sense of her—and turned to the most troublesome part of the preliminaries: Disty death rituals.

When he looked them up in the alien database he'd kept from his police academy days, he nearly stopped work at that moment. The Disty had ten thousand known death customs, and several thousand more variations.

Death frightened them and appalled them, although unlike some other alien groups, the Disty did kill when they had to.

But their society had strong structures and taboos about death, so strong that the Alliance found no way to negotiate with the Disty over these issues. Eventually, the Alliance had decided to accept the Disty into the fold with warnings to anyone who did business with them: Avoid the Disty death traditions. That seemed to be the most sensitive side of their society.

Flint leaned back in his chair and threaded his hands behind his head. The cursory glance told him that Costard had not been making up the Disty paranoia. She had walked into the middle of the most troublesome part of Disty culture without a clue about its impact on her.

He had done the same as a police officer. He had never realized that his work with corpses who died by Disty vengeance killings had made him unclean to other Disty. Of course, they hadn't known that he had gone near victims of vengeance killings. If they had known, they would have insisted on other investigators, or worse, that he be punished for violating Disty law as agreed to under a variety of Alliance contracts.

Costard hadn't lied about the Disty death rituals. In fact, the deeper Flint dug into them, the more he realized how cursory her understandings were. The purification ritual without family members was gruesome no matter which variation the Disty performed; Costard definitely would not survive it, but she would live long enough to regret ever seeing Jørgen's remains.

Flint felt a flash of empathy: Living in this modern universe was like living in a war zone without knowing the combatants or the rules. The laws that governed the Alliance and its many peripheral allies were so complex that any venture off familiar turf brought with it dangers that initially seemed innocuous.

It wasn't hard to see how Costard had gotten into this situation.

Flint had to make sure he didn't make similar mistakes.

14

Scott-Olson sat down in the reddish-brown sand. She wrapped her arms around her legs and rested her cheek on her knees.

She was exhausted. She had worked for five hours straight, uncovering three mummies, all in the area where Batson had first led her. Limbs still peeked through the surface in all directions. If she had to guess, she figured there were a least a hundred corpses here, all buried at the same time.

Batson had brought her water but no food. Like most normal people—the kind who didn't spend their days around corpses—Batson figured she would be too nauseated to eat while she worked.

But what she really needed now was a good meal and a hot shower, and a couple dozen assistants to carefully separate the corpses from the ground.

Scott-Olson closed her eyes. She couldn't get the assistants. She wasn't even sure she could bring in her own medical examination team. Were they already tainted by the Jørgen corpse? That was one of the finer points of Disty law that she didn't entirely understand. If they were, she had no problem bringing them in.

If they weren't, she didn't want to bring them anywhere near this gravesite.

She sat up and straightened her spine. Something cracked,

sending a shiver of pain through her neck. She was getting too old for this kind of concentrated work.

What she really wanted to do was go back to her lab, analyze the soil samples, look at the detritus she had bagged from the sand around the corpses, and then analyze the three corpses themselves. She had a hunch—more of an educated guess—that these corpses had been here long before someone placed Jørgen on top of them, but she wouldn't know that for certain until she did her job, and did it meticulously.

Something crunched behind her, and she turned, startled. Batson was approaching, his boots making soft sounds in the sand.

"What have we got?" he asked, handing her a bottle of water.

She took it and opened the cap and drank. The water was warm but filling. It revived her. She drank until the water was gone, then handed Batson the bottle back.

"We have a disaster," she said.

"That I know," he said.

She shook her head. "Not just in the Disty way, or even in the major-major-contamination way. These are human corpses, Petros, and they deserve a real investigation."

"Maybe this is one of those—what do they call them on Earth? Cemeteries. Maybe an early settlement did this." He had his hands clasped behind his back as he looked down at the field of bodies.

"I wish it were," Scott-Olson said. "But we've never buried bodies here. It's been against human custom from the very earliest colony. The Domed land was too precious, and no one wanted to put the bodies outside a Dome. Besides that, if it were a cemetery, the bodies would be in individual boxes, buried with care, and probably marked with some kind of stone or metal plate. You found no evidence of markers, right?"

Batson shrugged. "I'll ask."

"I doubt you'll find anything. The lack of boxes tells me that something bad happened here—or was covered up here."

Batson sighed. "Is this connected to Jørgen?"

"I don't know." Scott-Olson peeled off one of her gloves and rubbed her face. Her skin felt gritty. She was probably rubbing the sand into her pores. "I may not be able to find that out for you. Whoever killed Jørgen might have known this was here. Or not. I'm not even sure how long these bodies have been here."

"Do you have a guess?"

"Not an accurate one."

"Then give me an inaccurate one."

She stared at the uncovered bodies. Two men and a woman, their faces wrinkled, mouths open, teeth as orange as Jørgen's bones.

"Older than her, I think," Scott-Olson said, "just judging by the depth at which they were buried."

"You can't tell from looking at the corpses?"

She glanced up at him sideways. He was still staring at the field. "This isn't like a fresh corpse, Petros. I can't give you a guess that's accurate within a few hours. I might not even be accurate within a decade."

"So these could have been here since the colony was founded?" he asked.

"It's possible. Or they could have been here fifty years or a hundred. I don't really know." She peeled off the other glove and reached into the pocket of her shirt, removing a cleansing tissue. She pressed the moisture chip on the side, felt the cleansing fluid fill the fibers of the tissue, then wiped her face. The tissue was cool and smelled faintly of soap, but she could tell from Batson's look that all she managed to do was cover herself in orange muck.

He reached into his pocket kit and removed more tissues. "Let me," he said, and crouched.

He cleaned her face as if she were a child, and she thought, as he pressed and pushed and scrubbed, that she finally understood why babies moaned and complained when their parents did this. It looked nurturing, but it hurt.

"There," he said after a moment, taking the tissues and putting them in the recycler that came with his kit.

Her skin burnt where he had pressed on it. She wanted to

close her eyes and indulge in a good long cry—not because she was mourning the people in front of her, but because she was so tired and she saw no way out of this situation.

"You okay?" Batson asked.

She shook her head without opening her eyes. "I can't do this, Petros."

"What exactly?" he asked.

She opened her eyes and looked again. Her imagination hadn't added to the bodies; if anything, she had underestimated the task in front of her.

"If I'm the only person uncovering the corpses, using proper procedures and working the way that I'm supposed to—let's not even discuss the lab, and how I'm supposed to hide so many dead people. Let's not even think about that." Even though, now that she had mentioned it, she felt as if an even heavier burden had fallen on her. "Let's just talk about the physical labor in front of me. It'll take me months to get everything dug up, separated, and catalogued. If there are more bodies underneath, you might want to make that a year. And we can't keep this secret that long. I'm not even sure we can keep it secret for a day."

He sank down beside her, sitting in the sand. She didn't want to tell him that he might be sitting on top of even more bodies. The only difference here was that the backhoe had dug away from their perch instead of into it.

"You're not exaggerating?" he asked.

"If anything," she said, "I'm underestimating."

He crossed his legs and rested his hands on his knees, almost as if he were meditating. "You'd think we'd know about this. Fifty people, maybe more, all dead and buried here. Fifty missing people would get noticed. Wouldn't they?"

She shrugged. "I don't know enough about the history of the Dome. Was this ever outside? If fifty people were buried here before the dome was put in place, then I'd wager no, they wouldn't be noticed."

"That's a long time ago," he said, "and besides, who would do that? The winds are fierce here. If I were going to bury anyone on the Martian surface, this is the last place I'd come—at least outside of a dome. I'd find a small crater or someplace protected that clearly didn't get a lot of wind."

She hadn't even thought of that. The sandstorms here were legendary. They still caused consternation. The severe ones sandblasted the dome, and repairs had to be done constantly. The Disty had worked out a system of repairing the dome from the inside out, so there was always a thick inner layer. As the sand destroyed the top layer, there were always more to replace it.

There was no predicting how the sand would cover things. Sometimes the dome roof was covered with sand, and sometimes the sand was gone. It depended on the direction of the wind, on the power of the sandstorm, and on whether or not there were dust devils—such small words for what was essentially a tornado filled with sand.

"A lot of people buried without care or love or thought," she said. "They look like they were buried where they fell."

"As if in battle?" he asked.

"I don't remember studying any wars fought here," she said.

"The early years with the Disty were rough," he said. "I've heard that there's a lot that happened that never made it into the official histories."

She shook her head. "These can't be victims of the Disty. These corpses are intact."

"At least the first three," he said.

"It doesn't matter," she said. "They don't kill like this."

"Even in battle?" he asked.

"Especially in battle. The Disty have always preferred distance weapons, things that incinerated, so that the area would be purified and no part of the corpse would remain. The Disty could build here then. Otherwise they wouldn't have been able to."

"Not even if the information was lost?" Batson asked.

"I don't think the Disty would lose this kind of information," she said. "But this is all speculation. I have no idea what killed these three or how long they've been here, or even if they all died of the same thing. I need to work in my lab. I need good people to disinter the corpses, and I need to work with the evidence."

"How about training us?" Batson asked. He was sincere, but she could hear the reluctance in his voice. He wanted her to say no, even though he would do the work if she agreed.

"Maybe," she said. "But I can't supervise you, and frankly, I'd worry that you'd be doing things wrong. Besides, how're you going to keep this secret—eight people coming to work at this site every day, digging up the dead? Eventually, someone will investigate."

"What do you suggest?" he asked. "We can't let the Disty learn of this."

"Why not?" she asked. "What'll they do? They emptied out three square blocks for one human skeleton. What would they do for this many corpses that have been here this long? Evacuate the Dome?"

"Maybe," he said.

"And that would harm us how?" she asked.

He looked at her. She could see the thought penetrate, then he blinked, frowned, and shook his head.

They'd been afraid of the Disty for so long that they couldn't imagine life without them. What would happen if the Disty left the Dome? Humans could reclaim it.

"Mars is theirs," he said. "I doubt they'd abandon any of it."

"They abandoned these blocks fast enough."

"And demanded that we fix this," he said. "It's the fixing that scares me, Sharyn. They could incinerate the whole Dome, purify the place somehow, do something to the ground, and kill us all. Who'll argue with that? It fits into their laws."

"Does it?" Her voice remained calm, but she shuddered just the same. She didn't know how their laws worked on something this extreme. All she knew was that she was trapped here now, facing an even more uncertain future.

"What do you suggest?" he asked. "I'm out of ideas."

She slipped on her gloves, then picked up a handful of sand. Who knew that it hid so much?

"I don't think we should make the decision," she said after a moment. "I think we take it to the chief."

Batson was shaking his head even before she finished her sentence. "There's too much corruption in the SDHPD. They'll tell the Disty."

"Maybe they should tell the Disty. Maybe they should insist that the Death Squad get involved."

"But the Death Squad wouldn't touch Jørgen. They're not going to get near this."

"We don't know." Scott-Olson was pouring sand from one hand to another. The repetitive motion was almost hypnotic. "If they already knew about this, they might."

Batson continued to shake his head. "I'm not going to the boss."

"Everyone'll find out. No matter what we do, Petros. Better to control the outflow of information."

He was silent for a long moment. Then he said, "What about the mayor of the human section of Sahara Dome? What about the Dual Government?"

"The Disty laws take precedence with them."

"They'll take precedence with the Alliance too. The Alliance always goes with local laws." Scott-Olson balled her hands and pressed them against her knees.

"No," Batson said. "The Alliance goes with the laws prevailing at the time of the act. If you can show that this occurred before Disty took over Mars, then we might have a shot."

"I don't know if this occurred then."

"Lie," he said.

She looked up at him. She had never lied about her work. Not once. Her stomach muscles tightened. The hunger turned to nausea. "What if I get caught?"

He turned toward her, his eyes bright. "It won't matter. We'll be news by then. The entire solar system will want to know what happened to these humans. If the Disty mistreat the investigators, we might get protection. Or a place to go. We won't be at their mercy."

"Unless we're needed to clear the contamination."

He froze. He knew about those strange rules as well. And unlike Aisha Costard, he hadn't flinched when he heard what would happen to them if the relatives weren't found.

Scott-Olson stood. "I'll work. You go upstairs. You tell them that this happened before the Disty took over. If you're wrong, no one'll care."

"And you can deny that you told me."

"Yes," she said. "Don't let them come to me until they decide to help."

He looked at her. She saw hope in his eyes for the first time in weeks. She wished her eyes reflected the same thing. But she didn't feel hopeful. She felt overwhelmed and strangely sad, as if all these corpses, all these former living and breathing humans, had infected her with their great tragedy.

She had been right: In the end, the work mattered most. She wanted to know what happened here. She wanted to know how many were dead and who caused it, and why it happened.

Batson stood. His hand brushed her shoulder. "We're going to get out of this."

He sounded like he believed it.

She was glad he did. One of them had to.

15

It took Flint nearly two days to finish his work on the Disty. He didn't like what he found. The Disty death rituals were complex and violent. They also seemed to benefit only the Disty, and in ways that Flint didn't entirely understand.

Costard had been right; family members were her best chance out of this crisis.

Now that he was certain that Costard was who she said she was and that her problem was as bad as she had claimed, he was ready to research Lagrima Jørgen. Only he wouldn't do most of the work from his own network. Instead, he would go to a public system that required no identification, and work from there.

One of the first things Paloma had warned him about was that Retrieval Artists left tracks in the system. Trackers often traced the work of Retrieval Artists, then went after the Disappeared before the Retrieval Artist could do so, collecting the bounty on the Disappeared and moving on to the next case.

Trackers didn't care whom they gave the Disappeared to. Flint and most of the other Retrieval Artists would do everything they could to make certain no Disappeared was found by someone who meant them harm.

The public information on important Disappeareds was often monitored by the very governments that wanted them. A Retrieval Artist's tracks sometimes let those governments know the Disappeared was still alive or might come home or might actually be on the move again.

Flint was always careful, not just because of the Trackers and the alien governments, but because he knew that bringing up old material sometimes brought back old animosities. Even if the Disappeared was never found, the arguments that sent the person away might be revived, and others—the families, friends, even business associates—could be hurt in the resulting crossfire.

Touching the records was probably all right in this case since Jørgen was already dead, but there were others involved—missing children, perhaps even more family living safely off Mars somewhere. Flint hoped that they remained unharmed and unnoticed, despite any preliminary work that Costard had done.

For his first foray into researching Jørgen, he went to the main library at Dome University's Armstrong campus. The library had screens in all of the carrels, and the screens used university identification to access information.

Flint had gotten several student identification numbers over the years, and routinely varied his use of them. He also updated from time to time, so that even those IDs wouldn't lead anyone to him.

The library was in the very center of campus. The building was rectangular and was one of the few buildings in the entire city that had no windows at all. Initially, the building had been built to house rare books only—actual volumes, many of which had been brought to the Moon after the original settlers had colonized Armstrong. The books were gifts, a sign that the city would remain stable and would be able to handle such esoteric and expensive things as paper books.

But over time, the university realized that it would never get enough paper volumes to fill the large building. The students needed a place for group study, and the coffee shops and cafés, which were not under the control of the university, didn't provide the quiet that the students needed.

Most public places also charged for access. Students who didn't have enough money for good personal networks, which allowed them to feed off the public ports wherever they went, also didn't have enough money to pay the exorbitant access fees charged by these places.

So the university covered the fees at the library for anyone with a student identification. Money wasn't the issue for Flint. Identification was. So he made certain he donated a large sum of money every year to the university's library system. In return, he cadged student identifications and used them as his very own.

He had a favorite carrel on the second floor, the main study floor of the library. Here students worked in silence, touching screens, marking their own pads, tapping silently at keyboards as they learned how to put their thoughts into writing.

The second floor also had a few books locked up in clear plastic cases. The cases ran from floor to ceiling and had special shading that protected them from glare.

Flint's carrel was between two of the cases. The carrel faced outward so that he could see around it into the floor itself. People could see that the carrel was full only by seeing his feet and an arm, but they couldn't see his face. He could see theirs, though, and he would know if any trouble approached.

He slipped inside the carrel, entered one of the newer student IDs into the special keyboard at the base of the desktop, and waited while the system booted up. That was a university fail-safe, something someone told them would prevent identity theft. It prevented the amateurs, but made things easier for practical people like Flint. All he had to do was stand behind a student as the student typed in the code. Oddly enough, because of touch screens, very few people worried about something that simple anymore.

The system blinked on, the touch screen directly in front of him glowing blue for a moment before linking to the university network. A canned welcome message said hello to the student he was pretending to be and asked for the identification number again.

This time, Flint pressed numbers on the touch screen.

The system winked out one more time. He glanced around while he waited. Only half of the carrels were full. Most of the students were in class or goofing off. This was midsemester, and a lot of the students didn't begin serious work until a week or two before the semester's end.

The screen winked back on, a specialized menu providing a full range of options. Because the second floor was quiet space, the vocal processors on the machines had been shut off, which was another reason Flint liked to research here.

He had very little information to start with. Jørgen's name, her connection to BiMela Corporation, the writs against her from the M'Kri Tribesmen, and the judgements of the Fifth Multicultural Tribunal. He quickly realized that Jørgen hadn't worked for BiMela. They had bought the mineral rights from her. She had negotiated those rights for Arrber Corporation, which Flint couldn't locate at all.

A legal representative of Arrber Corporation showed up at all of the proceedings of the Multicultural Tribunal to represent both Jørgen's interests and Arrber Corporation's, but Flint couldn't even find the name of the representative in the records. The representative was listed only as *Legal Council for Arrber Corporation.*

He had other problems. Not only could he find no other listing of Arrber Corporation, he could find no listing of Lagrima Jørgen's children outside the M'Kri Tribesmen's writs.

In those writs, Lagrima Jørgen supposedly had a large family, consisting of two parents, two stepparents, several aunts and uncles (not counting the relatives of the stepparents), many cousins, and two children from her first marriage.

The mention of the first marriage led him to believe there were other marriages. He wondered if the spouses from those marriages counted as family under the Disty definition. Perhaps saving Costard would be as simple as finding an ex-husband of Jørgen.

If, indeed, that was her name. None of these family members were listed by name, nor was their location mentioned. Flint couldn't access the M'Kri Tribesmen records— apparently, that required some sort of legal proceeding, since the Tribesmen did not consider themselves part of the Alliance (even though they were, by M'Kri law).

The more he dug, the more confused Flint got. As far as he could tell, Lagrima Jørgen came into existence shortly before the negotiations with the Tribesmen started, and stayed in existence as long as she was needed for the various court cases. When the writs came down, Jørgen did disappear off the public records—only to reappear a few weeks ago as an orange skeleton in Sahara Dome.

It unnerved Flint that Jørgen's reappearance had made the news in several smaller markets. Some of the larger markets covered it as a two-second item, something that might interest scholars and news junkies who remembered the M'Kri Tribesmen cases from the Fifth Multicultural Tribunal.

Apparently, a number of people followed the rules of all the various Multicultural Tribunals, believing the rulings to be skewed in favor of the corporations, rather than following the agreed-upon rules for interstellar law.

Flint sighed. He had more than enough information at the moment. He had to let it soak in. If he was going to get deep into this case, he would have to learn a lot more about the law and the tribunals, as well as the Tribesmen and the Disty.

Obviously, Costard had done a small search and had answered questions to do so. That was how Jørgen's name hit the various media.

But that small search had probably caused more problems than it solved. It had flagged the Jørgen case for anyone who was watching, it had reminded people of the interstellar implications, and worst of all, it had given Costard hope.

Flint no longer believed that hope was justified in this case. He would wager there were no children, and if there was family, it would take years to find.

He logged off, and the screen went down. Then he stood, stretched, and stared at the old books.

Once, people could record all of their laws between bindings, keep track of each minute detail, and know to whom they would answer if they did something wrong.

Life was no longer that simple.

And he would have to remind Costard of that this very afternoon.

16

Ki Bowles hadn't expected him, this shy, dumpy little man with his wide brown eyes and his hesitant smile. He hovered over the chair, his hand on the heart-shaped faux ironwork along the back.

"Join me," Bowles said with a warmth she didn't feel.

She was at an outdoor café near the far edge of the Dome University. *Outdoor* was a misnomer—she was still inside the Dome. But the café's designers had gotten special permission to push up against the dome's edges and to use the dome's wall as their own. Real flowers tumbled out of planters built into the waist-high stone fence that separated this café from the sidewalk. The air smelled of perfume and baking bread, a combination that Bowles couldn't resist.

Ezra Farkus sank into the chair. She'd never seen anyone collapse into a seat like that, almost as if he had no spine. He rested his elbows on the clear tabletop and leaned forward so hard that two of the table legs rose off the ground.

Bowles had to catch the edge of the table to keep it from tipping over.

"Thank you for coming, Mr. Farkus," she said.

He nodded. Maybe he was too tongue-tied to talk with her. That would be a disaster.

"I'd like to make a recording of the conversation," she said. "Do I have your permission?"

He nodded again.

She touched the main camera chip on the back of her hand. That chip started the sound on four other cameras—one attached to the edge of her eye, like a diamond teardrop; another she had planted on a nearby post; one behind Farkus so that she could get good views of her face; and one on her lapel that sent material directly to InterDome.

They had strict instructions not to use any of her DeRicci material until Bowles told them they could.

"Mr. Farkus, I need you to state your permission for the record."

He nodded a third time, and she actually thought he wasn't going to say anything. Then he opened his mouth and said slowly, "I, Ezra Farkus, hereby grant Ki Bowles and Inter-Dome Media the right to use this conversation as news. . . ."

She tuned out the rest. It still astonished her how many people knew the permissions statement by heart. These people had to be constantly linked, always getting news or entertainment through the various networks.

". . . in all forms, irrevocably." He took a breath. "There. Is that okay?"

She hoped so, since she missed the middle. But she smiled at him. "Yes."

A Waiting Tray floated by with waters on it. Bowles took one. Farkus looked at it hesitantly.

"I'm afraid this place is serve yourself," she said.

He grabbed one of the waters quickly, before the tray floated away.

"You do know why you're here?" she asked.

"I'm a little stunned by it," he said. "In all the years we've been apart, you're the first person to ever contact me."

It took Bowles a moment to parse his sentence. She hoped he wouldn't be that inarticulate throughout the interview.

"No one contacted you after the Moon Marathon?"

He shook his head. His hair flopped against his ears, obviously a bad regrowth, probably very cheap.

"I'm amazed," Bowles said, and she was. Ezra Farkus was Noelle DeRicci's ex-husband. Her only ex, in a relatively long life. Granted, DeRicci had married Farkus decades ago and divorced him shortly thereafter, but former intimate partners usually made good—and dishy—interviews. DeRicci had been in the news for more than two years now. Someone else should have found him.

"I'm not," Farkus was saying. "Noelle and I weren't together that long."

"But you married," Bowles said. "That's public record. Surely someone would have traced it."

"Long before she became a cop," he said. "I thought she was going to be a teacher."

Bowles couldn't imagine the tough-spoken DeRicci around children. "Was that her major in college?"

"She didn't have one. Too many interests." He sighed. "Guess that should have been a sign."

"Of?"

"The fact she couldn't settle down." He looked up at Bowles. "Noelle did things her own way."

"Even marriage?" Bowles asked.

"Especially marriage," he said.

Bowles discreetly touched the back of her thumb, sending a marker to that section of the interview, so she could find it again. A pithy quote that, she hoped, would capture the essence of the interview itself.

"You'd better go back to the beginning," she said. "You met Security Chief DeRicci how?"

"Security Chief." He shook his head. "That's terrifying."

He meant for Bowles to pick up on that comment. If she jumped on that now, he would think he could control the entire interview. So she ignored it, although she would pick up on it later if she felt it was worth her time.

"How did you meet her?" Bowles asked again.

He blinked, frowned slightly, and then propped himself up on one elbow. He stared behind her so fiercely that Bowles almost looked behind herself.

Another tray floated by, this one with fruit salads, dessert compotes, and pies. She took one of the salads while she waited for his answer.

If he didn't respond in another minute, she'd end the

interview—always wondering, of course, how DeRicci managed to live with this jerk, even for a few months.

"Noelle and I met when we were four." His voice startled Bowles. She was so convinced he wasn't going to say anything that she had already started to ignore him. "My parents moved next door to hers."

He still didn't look at her, but he did take a piece of pie from a nearby tray. Bowles walked him through the early years: their childhoods in one of Armstrong's poorer neighborhoods, the death of DeRicci's parents, the way his parents took her in despite their poverty, and how his parents had managed to send them both to college, despite their difficult teenage years.

It sounded almost like DeRicci had married Farkus because she felt she had no choice, or because she had felt gratitude toward his parents. Or maybe she hadn't wanted to leave the warmth of that family, the only real family she had known.

The marriage collapsed in Moscow Dome. They had gone to Moscow Moon University, about as far from Armstrong as they could get. Apparently, life alone, just the two of them, with no parents, no old neighborhood, took the marriage apart in less time than either could imagine.

"You were both very young," Bowles said with as much sympathy as she could muster.

Finally, his gaze focused on hers. His eyes were naturally watery, his skin etched with the kind of lines that told her he still didn't have a lot of money.

"I loved her." He said it defiantly, as if it were a badge. "I still do."

"Have you seen her recently?"

He shook his head. "We agreed to have no contact."

"Was that part of the divorce decree?" Bowles asked.

He flinched. "So what if it was? We still agreed."

"It's unusual to have that as part of the decree," Bowles lied.

He shrugged. "We didn't have children, and we fought all the time. So the judge asked that we didn't see each other again, and we agreed."

There was more to the story, Bowles was sure of it. She would read the decree herself—divorces were public record—and then she would come back to Farkus if she had more questions.

"You still love her," Bowles said, "but you haven't seen her in a long time."

"I see her on the news." He sat up a little straighter. He hadn't touched his pie.

Bowles hadn't touched the salad either. The ingredients weren't real fruit. She recognized the sheen of the synthesized stuff along the edge of the watermelon cubes.

"And that's enough?" Bowles asked. "Enough to know that you still love her?"

He raised his chin. "Is that strange?"

Yes, Bowles wanted to say, but didn't. This man was strange. Now that she knew how DeRicci had married him, Bowles wasn't quite as interested, although she still wanted to see that divorce decree.

"When I contacted you," Bowles said, ignoring his last comment, "you said that it was about time someone asked you about Noelle. Why is that?"

"She's flighty," he said.

Bowles had never heard anyone describe DeRicci as flighty. From her observation, DeRicci was anything but flighty. She was solid and unimaginative and a little too serious. Certainly not flighty.

"Flighty?" Bowles prompted.

"Yeah," he said. "She goes from one thing to another, never thinking about what's behind her, always moving forward. There's no thought, no analysis, no real caring. None."

He was revealing himself in those statements. It was in his tone, half angry, half sad. Bowles decided to guess.

"One thing to another," she repeated. "You mean one person to another."

His skin flushed instantly, revealing white acne scarring along his chin. Bowles hadn't seen that outside the slums in Gargarin Dome.

"Look at her history," he said. "She even did it with her partners on the police force."

DeRicci had had a series of partners. Bowles hadn't really investigated that yet.

"But she did it to you too," Bowles said, keeping her tone compassionate. "That must have hurt."

His eyes narrowed. "She said it hurt her worse than it hurt me. She was such a *liar*!"

He slapped the table and shouted the last word, startling Bowles. Until that word, he had been soft-spoken, almost reserved.

"Why would an affair hurt her?" Bowles said.

"I never did understand it," Farkus said. "You ask her."

Bowles took a deep breath. "Guess."

He shook his head and pushed away from the table. For the first time, Bowles noticed the muscles in his arm. For an unenhanced male, he looked pretty strong.

"Look," he said, lowering his voice again. "She couldn't protect our home, our family, or our lives together. She certainly can't protect the Moon. Obviously, the idiots that hired her haven't checked into her background. Obviously, they think this is just political and she'll be just fine as a figurehead. But Noelle doesn't do pomp and ceremony and ritual. She's no good at being assigned anything."

"Not even the role of wife?" Bowles asked.

"It's not a role," he said, now nearly whispering. "It's a promise. And she couldn't live up to that either."

He took his glass of water and drained it.

"I still love her," he said, "but she's the biggest screwup I've ever known. I have no idea why they're giving her so much power. Unless it's all a sham and they're using her to cover up for something."

That took Bowles by surprise. She wasn't even sure she could follow the logic. "What do you mean?"

"Don't you pay attention?" he asked. "Governments hire people like Noelle all the time. Rehabilitated screwups in a precarious position, so that if something goes wrong, there's someone to blame. 'We didn't realize she had so many problems in her background,' they'll say, and most people will believe them."

"But you won't," Bowles said.

"I know they know about Noelle," he said. "I've told them. I've sent vids and messages and warnings, and no one has ever responded. They know and they don't care."

Bowles patted the tabletop. "Maybe you should sit back down and tell me what you do know."

He almost sat down. Then he stopped, midmovement, and shook his head. "You're humoring me, just like they did. You'll listen to everything I have to say, then you'll use one quote, like the one about me loving her, and ignore all the bad stuff. You're part of the problem, lady. I've given you enough."

He whirled, then left, hurrying out of the enclosed area. Bowles watched him leave.

He was right; she would only use a quote or two. But he had given her several good ones, ones that would help her make her case against the Moon's new security czar.

17

Aisha Costard's hotel was not too far from the bombed-out crater that still scarred Armstrong. Flint wondered what Costard had thought of that when she had seen it. She had already come here, terrified from her ordeal with the Disty, and then she had managed to find a hotel that seemed like one of the most unsafe buildings in the city.

Or maybe he just thought that because he knew a lot of nicer hotels in the same price range, and a lot of better neighborhoods. This had been a lovely neighborhood before the bomb had blown up in its backyard. People had moved out after that, many going to other cities, some even leaving the Moon.

However, the hotel known as the Domeview had done a banner business in the last year. A lot of the hotels in this area had. Ghoulish tourists had arrived to see the damage; many of them wanted to stay as close to the disaster site as possible.

Flint didn't understand it. Although he did know that Costard hadn't come here for the disaster. Neither had he. He rarely came to this part of town now.

It made him uncomfortable. Part of that was the smell. The area still had the faint odor of burning plastic. The city acknowledged the smell was a problem. It had gotten into the filters, and no matter how many times the engineers changed them, the smell lingered.

The hotel was tall and not very wide, built nearly a century ago as one of the luxury hotels in Armstrong. The building's height had once given it an excellent 180-degree view of the Dome, but as Armstrong grew around it, that view went away.

Flint pulled open the double doors, resenting their weight. Once, doing physical labor like that was considered luxurious. Luxury hotels from this period seemed to believe that making guests do things like pull open heavy doors and carry their own luggage was worth the extra price. That fad faded almost as quickly as it started, leaving the Domeview's doors and a few other places as quirky reminders of that strange moment in the past.

The air smelled fresher inside. It was certainly cooler. The tile floors shone. A long desk ran along one wall. Automatic check-ins ran along another. A single woman stood behind the main desk. She didn't look up as Flint entered.

He went to the automatic screens and punched in Costard's name. The hotel wouldn't tell him what room she was in, wouldn't even really tell him if she was a guest.

All it invited him to do was leave a message. If she answered, then the screen would tell him how to proceed.

"Tell her Miles Flint is here," he said in his normal tone.

The system asked him to wait. It tried to entertain him with a listing of the hotel's amenities and the amenities of the other hotels owned by the same corporation. The screen had cycled through the Moon and Earth and had just started on Mars when Costard answered.

Her face filled the screen.

"Mr. Flint." Her voice was cool. "I didn't expect to see you here."

"I know," he said. "I've done some of the preliminary work, and I need to speak with you."

"Come on up," she said.

He shook his head. "Meet me down here. We'll walk back to my office."

"Mr. Flint—"

"Don't argue, Ms. Costard. The hotel is required by law to monitor the actions of its guests. If you want a private conversation, you have to leave the premises."

She sighed, and the screen went dark. For a moment, he wondered if she wasn't willing to talk with him. Then the system floated a message, telling him that Ms. Costard would join him shortly.

Flint walked into the middle of the foyer. Five chairs surrounded a round coffee table. The tableau was uninviting: The chairs looked hard and uncomfortable, and it seemed impossible to have a conversation in that space.

The woman behind the desk looked up at him, as if she was seeing him for the first time. Her gaze met his and held it, her expression cool. He felt unwelcome suddenly, and wondered if the system had tracked his identity and informed her. Retrieval Artists weren't always well liked, especially in places like this, where keeping the guests comfortable was a top priority.

The elevator doors shushed open. Costard came out, her hair slightly tangled, deep shadows under her eyes. She wore a long sweater over a pair of dark pants. The outfit looked as haphazardly assembled as she did.

She approached him, and when she arrived, he put a hand under her arm. Her skin was slightly clammy.

"Let's walk," he said.

She nodded. The woman from the desk watched them both. Flint was happy to get away from her.

When they stepped outside, Costard stopped. She wiped a hand over her face. "I have an aircar. We can go to your office."

"I prefer not to," Flint said.

Her hand dropped. She looked at him as if she didn't understand him.

"I don't want to have this conversation on my records."

She touched the chips on the back of her hand. "Surely you're linked."

He nodded. "But I'm going to shut down my networks. I suggest you do too."

"What's going on?" she asked.

He put his hand on her arm again, and led her away from the building. There were several outdoor cafés a few blocks from here. He would lead her there, and maybe they would sit down when they arrived.

By then, she might not want to either.

"I did a lot of preliminary research on your case," he said, "and I am not going to take it."

She wrenched her arm from him. "You brought me out here to tell me that? You wasted three days of my time."

"I brought you out here to tell you more than that. Keep walking with me." He looked in all three directions, including up, before crossing the street.

She hesitated on the curb. He didn't look back, but he had kept a few of his links on. He was using a camera chip to monitor several directions, making certain no one followed them. One of his other chips pinged for theft networks, the kind that searched for active links and stole information from them.

After a moment, Costard's shoulders sank. She hurried to catch up to him. Flint slowed down so that she could.

They were heading away from the bombed-out area, toward a group of shops and restaurants that catered to the university crowd. The shops claimed to have the latest Earth fashions, while the restaurants advertised cheap food. A few downscale hotels crowded each other in the next block.

"All you had to do was tell me you don't want the case," Costard snapped as she reached his side.

"No, that's not all," he said. "I learned a lot of things the last few days. One of them is that the Disty death rituals are a lot more complicated than you mentioned. There are dozens, maybe hundreds, of variations of each law."

"Are you telling me that we can pick which one applies?"

"I'm telling you that finding the children might not be enough. There might be other steps involved."

She shoved her hands in the pockets of her sweater and stared straight ahead, almost as if she hadn't heard him.

Students poured out of a nearby building, laughing and holding some sort of fabric he didn't recognize. He waited until they passed before continuing.

"I looked up your Disappeared," he said. "She's not Lagrima Jørgen."

That caught Costard's attention. She glanced at him, eyes wide. "Who is she, then?"

"I don't know," he said, "and we may never know. There are layers of identity, and so far as I can tell, they were designed for one shady deal after another."

"Shady," she said. "You mean illegal?"

He shook his head. "She seemed to be working with a team that knew how to use laws to their own advantage, skirting the edge of the law's intent in such a way that the action would hold up in court if, indeed, the case was ever taken to court."

"Like the M'Kri Tribesmen," Costard said.

"Exactly." Flint crossed another street, this time heading to the paths that wound through the university's main campus. "And this is the problem. I think, in order to take the attention off of her, she invented that family listed in the court records."

"Invented." Costard breathed the word. She stopped near some oak trees. They were real and very tall, nurtured by the Environmental Department. "She couldn't have invented them. Her pelvis had parturition scars."

Flint stopped too. "What?"

"A woman's pelvis actually shows how many times she's given birth. Jørgen's pelvis confirms the record. She had two children."

He glanced around. No one stood near them. Flint had brought Costard here for a reason: The campus had pockets that had no links at all.

"Well," he said, "the family only shows up in the court documents. The other information I found about Lagrima Jørgen doesn't mention family at all—and it should have."

"That's impossible. She had children."

"But we don't know if she raised them. We don't even know if they survived childhood," Flint said.

A young woman carrying a pile of old documents came out of a nearby building and started down the path.

"We need to move," Flint said.

Costard looked at him as if he had told her she had to run in the Moon Marathon. "I'm done with the conversation."

"No," he said. "I need to tell you a few more things."

"You've already said you're not taking the case. You've already said that things are much worse than I thought they were—and I thought they were awful. What else can you tell me?"

"Let's walk." He beckoned her forward, into an enclosed area between the naturally growing trees. This was a modified greenhouse with open ends. The greenhouse wasn't designed to grow food, like the greenhouses outside the Dome. This one had only green, leafy plants that seemed very overgrown.

The university had dozens of these open-ended greenhouses all over campus. For the last several years, they had been running experiments on the production of pure oxygen.

This was the natural section, near the trees that had been planted decades ago by some environmental sciences students who believed that the Dome would be better off if greenery dominated the interior. Flint knew, because he had studied it, that the natural greenhouses worked on old-fashioned systems—no automation at all. The plants were watered by hand, nurtured by hand, and fertilized by hand.

No electronic devices were allowed near these greenhouses, and even the cameras, which kept track of the moment-by-moment growth, had to film from a distance of at least twenty feet. Because previous studies had shown how sensitive the plants were to what humans called white noise, no sound equipment was allowed nearby either.

Hand-painted signs tucked into the grass warned that anyone who entered this area had to shut down their links or be subject to huge fines. Costard started to turn away from the area, but Flint put a hand behind her back.

"Shut down your links," he said, "including emergency links."

Her breath caught. It was a matter of trust. If she believed in him, she'd go into a secluded place with no outside access at all.

She touched the back of her hand. He waited until his system confirmed that hers was off before shutting down his own.

They stepped into the greenhouse proper. The air did seem cleaner here. It had a tang to it that Flint found nowhere else on Armstrong, not even in the artificially designed greenhouses. He sometimes came here to sit and think, especially after his injuries last year. He had found this a good place to heal.

"Why the secrecy?" she asked.

"Because," he said, "what I'm about to tell you can't go on any record."

Her face hardened, almost as if she were bracing herself for his words.

"When you queried about Lagrima Jørgen, you aroused interest all over the known universe," he said. "There were news reports, most of which recycled the M'Kri Tribesmen case, but a few were about the skeleton itself."

"Why is this bad?"

"We don't know who she was or who she worked for," Flint said. "Someone did kill her and plant her body on that site."

Costard nodded. "I've thought of that."

"That someone may still be alive."

"I thought of that too."

"And may not be human," Flint said.

Costard sighed. She obviously hadn't thought of that. "Meaning they might have weird laws about people who discover the bodies of the dead."

"Or something about passing guilt through touch, or any kind of strange thing you and I can't imagine. The news stories weren't very specific. For all these people know, you could have found some incriminating evidence with that body, or something else that might frighten them."

Costard reached for one of the long, thin leaves, nearly touched it, then brought her hand back as if she wasn't sure she could. She looked very small among the overgrown plants; the hardened expression had morphed into something resigned and sad.

"This frightens you, so you won't take the case," she said.

Flint shook his head. "I see no reason to take the case."

She frowned at him.

"It might take years to uncover this woman's identity. I don't believe she had a family—or at least one that we can find in your time frame. And now, besides the Disty, there might be other aliens involved."

"Do you think anyone will take the case?" Costard asked.

"I don't think you should go to anyone else," Flint said.

"What? Are you saying I should just accept this? I should go back to Mars like a good little soldier and let them dish out this stupid fate without even trying to stop them?"

"No," Flint said. "I think you should disappear."

She stumbled and gripped a nearby table. One of the plants started to fall, and Flint caught it.

He set it back on the table. Costard stood next to him, both hands on the table.

"You're a Retrieval Artist. You're not supposed to tell me to disappear," she said. "Can't you lose your license for this?"

"We're not licensed," he said. "I can do whatever I want."

"Why would you tell me to disappear? You, of all people?"

"Because I, of all people, know what you're fighting. The Disappearance Services were set up for precisely this kind of situation. Under our laws, what you did was normal behavior, helping another agency, doing your work. To the Disty, you have made yourself a part of that death scene, and only a few things might get you out of it, if that."

"So you're advising me to break the law?" she asked.

"I'm advising you to take advantage of a loophole. You haven't been charged with anything on the Moon. You were sent here to solve a problem, with the Disty government's permission. If you go back to Mars, you'll be subject to their laws. If you go back to Earth, you will as well. And once that time limit is up, the government of Armstrong will have to give you back to Sahara Dome. There's no place in the Alliance that Aisha Costard can go and be safe. But if you take a new identity, you will have a lot of places you can go. You will be safe."

"Except from people like you," she said.

He suppressed a sigh. She was horribly uninformed. He supposed most people were. They had simple jobs and even simpler lives, and probably didn't even think about the intricacies of interstellar justice from day to day.

"Thousands of people, maybe hundreds of thousands throughout the Alliance, use Disappearance Services every year," he said. "Most of those people are never thought of again. Most of them escape. Most of them go on to live productive lives somewhere else."

"Productive," she muttered.

"Only a few are important enough to have the alien governments or some lawyer or some law enforcement agency spend the money on a Tracker. Fewer have family with enough money, or businesses with enough incentives, to hire a Retrieval Artist to track them down. Even then, our mission isn't always to bring them back. We also find them to give them inheritances or to notify them that their parents died or to tell them it's safe to return to their old life. Trackers bring them back to face the legal charges they'd fled. Retrieval Artists often leave Disappeareds in their new identities, living their new lives. Most disappearances work, and work well."

"I can't live somewhere else," she said. "My work is on Earth. All I know is human bones."

"You'll learn something new," Flint said.

"I don't want to learn something new," Costard said. "I want to go home, to my university and my friends and my house. I don't ever want to see Mars again, and I certainly don't ever want to hear of the Disty."

"If you stay in your current life, that won't happen," Flint said. "You probably won't go home, and you'll probably have to deal with the Disty until the end of what's going to be a very short life."

She closed her eyes, her frown deepening. "You can't see any other way out of this?"

"There's no easily locatable family for Lagrima Jørgen," he said. "That I do know. And I don't know the Disty law well enough to know if they'll accept the family of the woman who posed as Lagrima Jørgen, whatever her identity might be. As I mentioned, the variations are extreme. Check it out. Disty laws are in all of the databases. You can probably access them from the hotel."

She opened her eyes. They were lined with tears. "I'm not doing this just for me. I'm doing this for the entire team back in Sahara Dome. Everyone, from the detective to the medical examiner, who got near Lagrima's body are considered contaminated by the Disty. What about them?"

"They'll have to solve it their own way," Flint said. "I can't give them this advice, and neither can you. If you do, the Disty'll monitor the Disappearance Services and none of you will survive."

"So it's better for me to get out and leave them behind."

"Yes," he said. "At least you'll go on living."

She let go of the table. "You're so cold."

He nodded. "You asked me to work for you. The best way I can work for you is to tell you this."

She stepped toward him, and he saw that switch again, the one she had done when she came to his office. The anger came just as suddenly and just as powerfully.

"I hired you for all of us. Finding the children wasn't just going to benefit me. It was going to help Sharyn and Petros and everyone else in the SDHPD who worked on this case. I'm using their money to pay your salary, and you tell me to run away from them? How dare you."

That last she said very softly, as if he were the one who created this entire mess.

"I'm telling you to save your life," he said. "We can't save theirs."

"You don't know," she said. "All you have is guesses. You *guess* that there's no family. You *suppose* that the Disty won't accept family from the same woman if she has a different name. You *think* the Disty ritual is more complicated. That's not proof."

She had a point. But it was more minor than she thought. Her naïveté had been the problem from the beginning. It continued to be the problem now.

"Actual hard facts are rare in my business," he said, "and they come at great cost. I might be able to find out who Lagrima Jørgen really was, what happened to the children she gave birth to, and who she worked for, but I might not. I might find her family, and I might not. At that point, this will have cost a lot of money—"

"I don't care about money," Costard snapped.

He ignored her. "And by the time I find out, you and everyone you seem to be protecting will be long dead."

"You can't be sure."

"No," he said. "I can't."

"So try," she said.

"At the risk of your life?" he asked.

"It's already at risk," she said.

He wanted to take her and force her to face the difficult position she was in. But he doubted she'd listen.

He tried one last argument.

"Look," he said. "I'll stay on the case if you promise me you'll disappear."

"Don't make conditions." She was shaking with anger. She hadn't moved away from him, and he could actually feel the force of her emotion.

"If you'll do that," he said, "I promise you that I'll find you the moment your name is cleared."

She had her mouth open, obviously to continue arguing with him, and then she paused. "You can promise that?"

"Yes," he said. "Finding Disappeareds is my job."

"So I might be gone six months," she said.

"Or six years," he said.

"But I'd have the chance to come back, and you'll help the others."

"To the best of my ability, yes." He hadn't planned this, but he was curious. Lagrima Jørgen, through her death, might cause a dozen others. It would be nice to know who this woman was, what she had done, and if there was any way to protect all the people who had been "contaminated" by her.

Costard frowned. "I don't know anything about disappearing."

"Most people don't," Flint said. "That's why there are Disappearance Services."

"And you won't tell me which one to go to, will you?" she asked.

He shook his head. "That's not part of my job."

"With me gone, how will you get paid?"

"You and I will go to my office and set up a system for billing and payment through the SDHPD. It is their money, right?"

She nodded.

"Then I'll work with them."

"All right," she said, and let out a vast sigh.

Flint started to leave the greenhouse, but she didn't follow. Her gaze met his, her eyes wide and vulnerable.

"I'm terrified," she whispered.

"I know," he said, and offered her no more comfort. She was about to change everything in her life.

There was no comfort left to give.

18

Sharyn Scott-Olson had never met with the Human Advisory Council before. Until a few hours ago, she hadn't even been certain she knew their names.

The meeting was held in a clean room in the Stanshut Government Office Building. The building had been named for the first governor of Sahara Dome, a man who ruled over a completely human colony. At that point, no one had heard of the Disty.

Scott-Olson wished that were still the case.

She sat in a wooden chair, built with recycled wood from some of the human buildings that the Disty had torn down. Most everything in this room was made of ancient or recycled wood. The conference table was one solid piece of wood, and the walls and ceiling had been paneled with it.

Every hour, someone came through the room and checked for loose chips, planted cameras or microphones, or illegal links. She had watched them check after she had come into the room, and the sight reassured her. She had never seen equipment that sophisticated.

Before they let her into the room, they had shut off her embedded links and confiscated her embellishments. She had come into the clean room feeling naked and alone.

She wasn't even allowed to have Batson beside her. Batson, who had started this entire procedure. He had gone to the head of the Human-Disty Relations Department, who had apparently stopped Batson before he could say much at all.

"The advisory board needs to hear this," the man had said. "They're our buffer."

It was Batson who explained the concept of buffer to her. If the Human-Disty Relations Department heard each conflict, they might become tainted in some way, according to Disty law. So the department was set up in a particularly Disty fashion: There were layers of underlings who heard items first, made decisions, or filtered information upward, through a series of meetings in clean rooms or with a handful of completely unlinked people.

The Disty looked the other way, just like they did in their own society, acting like the layers protected both original parties from any taint or tampering.

Scott-Olson still wasn't sure how that prevention worked, but she didn't question it. At least there was some sort of system in place.

Supposedly, she was meeting with the lowest of the low on the Advisory Council. At least three of the people at this level had never been networked. They were alone in their own heads. They had to use public boards just to get news, and those boards had to work on screens. No instant messages flashing across the bottom edges of their vision, and worse, in Scott-Olson's point of view, no emergency links.

If these people ever got into trouble, they'd be completely and utterly alone. They would have no way of getting help with just a single thought. They would have to hope someone saw the problem or was close enough to hear them scream.

Such a primitive system unnerved Scott-Olson. She could never have agreed to a job on this council if that were the main requirement, no matter how much she believed in the system.

She had been waiting nearly fifteen minutes when the councilors filed in. At this level, all five councilors were old, with a lot of experience in various aspects of Martian government. That was the other strange thing about this system: The more experience you had, the less overt power you had. People with the expertise to make the decisions about what information was valuable and what wasn't had to be several levels below Disty observation so that they wouldn't be subject to the arbitrary nature of Disty laws.

The councilors entered through a side door that had, until that moment, been hidden in the paneling. They were laughing as if one of them had made a joke a moment before coming into the room.

The laughter made Scott-Olson uncomfortable.

So did the councilors. All five of them—three men and two women—were unenhanced elderly. They had the wrinkled skin and rheumy eyes; they moved with that hesitation common to people who knew their bones were fragile.

To see the unenhanced look so vibrant seemed unnatural to her.

Still she sat stiffly, her hands clasped in her lap, her ankles crossed and to one side. She was the thinnest one in the room, and hence the coldest. The temperature felt ten degrees below government-accepted normal.

The councilors sat around the conference table. One of the women, whose white hair was so thin her age-spotted skull shown through it, beckoned Scott-Olson to come forward.

"Join us at the table, dear," the woman said, her voice husky with age. "We don't bite."

"Although we might nibble," one of the men said.

The group laughed.

Scott-Olson stood, trying to match faces with names without the aid of her links. The woman who spoke to her was Tilly Kazickas, whom Scott-Olson finally recognized by the hair. The other woman, Dagmar Yupanqui, had thick hair that looked like it had yellowed with age.

"We haven't got all afternoon, young lady," said a second man. He had a thin face, almost as if someone had cut the bones on either side with a very sharp knife and overlaid the work with wrinkled fabric.

He had to be Linus Squyres, who was well-known within the human government for his patronizing attitudes. Scott-Olson had certainly not been called "young lady" since she entered puberty.

Scott-Olson slipped into the chair in the exact center of her side of the table. Two chairs were open on either side of her. Squyres sat directly across from her, and the two women sat on either side of him.

At the end and the foot of the table were the remaining men, Ulric Middaugh and Kurtis Wheat. Middaugh was raw boned, with florid skin that suggested broken capillaries due to either some kind of space accident or too much drink. Wheat had perfectly smooth skin on his cheeks, but his black eyes were lost in a cascade of wrinkles. He looked like he was perpetually squinting.

"We've already heard about the disaster from your Detective Batson," Squyres was saying.

Scott-Olson wanted to correct him. Batson wasn't hers. If anything, he was more theirs.

"He assures us that this is not some kind of cemetery. He suspects these are from the same period as the Jørgen grave, and that makes me wonder if he knows a thing about his job."

So much for the timeline lie.

"So," Squyres continued, "you're here, young lady, to tell us what you know."

"What I know for a fact is that there are a lot of bodies in that plot of land," Scott-Olson said.

"Well, that's fairly obvious, isn't it?" Wheat asked. "We've seen the images that Batson brought us."

"He also told us the potential problem with the Disty," Yupanqui said.

"Although we are bright enough to figure that out for ourselves," muttered Middaugh.

"Can you tell us how many bodies there are?" Wheat asked.

Scott-Olson shook her head. "We've been working at the site for more than a day now, and I can see no end to them. I've removed six bodies from the same small patch, and found three more beneath them."

"What do you believe this is?" Kazickas asked.

"I'm hesitant to speculate," Scott-Olson said. "I don't know how old the corpses are. I haven't had a chance to autopsy any of them or do the standard tests. I don't know how long they've been there or whether they died on-site."

"Surely you have suspicions," Squyres said.

"Nothing scientific," Scott-Olson said.

"Does this predate the Disty?" Kazickas asked.

"It certainly predates some of the Disty architecture," Scott-Olson said, "considering the fact that the Disty wouldn't have built anywhere near this site if they had known what lay beneath it."

"True enough," Middaugh muttered.

"To do this right," Scott-Olson said, "we need a massive dig with lots of experts and a great deal of time. We might have to move more Disty buildings. I don't know how far this corpse field extends."

Wheat sighed and bowed his head. At his crown, he had a perfectly round bald patch. It made him seem endearingly vulnerable.

"I'm sure Detective Batson told you how worried we are that the Disty will find out about this," Scott-Olson said. "We don't know how to proceed, and felt it wasn't our decision."

"He said those last two things, but not the first." Squyres leaned forward on his elbows, folding his long fingers together. "In fact, he lied to us about the first. He said that if we told the Disty that it was from the same time period, everything would be fine."

Apparently, Petros wasn't the diplomat he thought he was.

"Would it be?" Scott-Olson asked.

"Are you prepared to lie for the human side of the colony, Dr. Scott-Olson?" Kazickas asked.

Scott-Olson wasn't sure how to answer that. She was becoming more and more willing to lie the more time that had passed.

"I'm scared for us," she said, giving them a nonanswer. "I don't know what's going to happen when the Disty find out, and I don't know what to do about it."

"Finally," Squyres said, "an honest answer."

He leaned back in his chair, a small smile on his face.

Scott-Olson realized that the others used his outspokenness to put visitors off guard.

"We'll worry about the Disty," Yupanqui said.

Scott-Olson shook her head. "I have to worry about them. I have to know how to proceed."

"What's to stop us from simply covering these bodies back over?" Middaugh asked.

"Besides simple decency?" Wheat asked.

"Too many people know," Kazickas said. "The Disty will eventually find out."

"And they'll blame us for deceiving them," Yupanqui said.

"They'd be right," Squyres said.

"That would make things much worse," Wheat said.

"I'm not sure how it can be worse," Middaugh muttered.

Scott-Olson watched each one speak, wondering how they could even have thought of that. The dead had rights, just like the living. She personally believed that dig was the site of a tragedy, one that may have more importance than anyone knew.

"I guess you're forgetting," she said slowly, not sure if she should break in, "that the Disty have already ordered us to dig up the site to prove no other bodies were there."

"They're going to check up on that, aren't they?" Wheat asked.

"They'll want to know about our progress," Scott-Olson said. "Even if we tried to keep this quiet, too many people know about it. The Disty will find out."

The councilors sighed. Middaugh crossed his arms and leaned back in his chair. Kazickas studied Scott-Olson.

"Have you suggestions?" Kazickas asked.

Scott-Olson threaded her fingers together, then twisted them until she could feel the ligaments stretch. "According to Disty law, I'm tainted because of the Jørgen case. So are Detective Batson and anyone else who has been in contact with the Jørgen corpse. The contamination is so great that the Death Squad wouldn't even get near the site to supervise us. They want nothing to do with this."

Squyres sighed heavily. Middaugh frowned and rested his chin on his hand.

Kazickas smiled, her gaze gentle. "We know this, dear."

"We're also bright enough to realize that this new case is even worse," Squyres snapped. "Move on, Doctor."

Scott-Olson met his gaze. His eyes were faded, their edges lined with liquid like those of a two-day-dead corpse.

"Dozens, maybe hundreds, of bodies on this site make the contamination extreme. I can work on that site—I'm already doomed. So are Detective Batson and a few of his men, and so is most of my staff."

"'Doomed' is a harsh word," Yupanqui said. "I'm sure we can settle that issue."

Scott-Olson decided to ignore the tangent—even though it was very important to her.

"I can put all of these already tainted people to work—my team in the lab, and the detective's grouping at the site. But the work would get done incorrectly. No one on the police force has the proper training and it would take months, maybe even a year, just to excavate the site properly and find out how extreme this entire thing is."

"Which is why you're afraid the Disty will find out," Squyres said. "We understand that too."

"No," Scott-Olson snapped. She was beginning to hate the way he spoke to her as if this were a debate instead of a fact-finding discussion.

"No?" Middaugh asked. He seemed to be the secondary antagonistic voice, useful when Squyres needed to take a breath.

"I told you up front that we need dozens of experts— *experts*—to excavate this site. We need people there all the time, working, digging, examining, taking soil samples. We need a large team, much larger than my small group and Batson's. We'd be putting experts from all over Mars at risk of contamination."

"Or people from other regions, like Earth," Wheat said.

"What of the Earth expert?" Squyres asked. "Can't she help?"

"She's on the Moon, trying to find a Retrieval Artist who will take the Jørgen case."

"That seems like an odd choice, to send her," Middaugh said.

"We needed our team. Once she finished examining the bones, her work was done, but she couldn't go home. The Disty wouldn't allow that." Scott-Olson heard some stridency in her own tones. She was more panicked about this than she allowed herself to believe.

"But they allowed her off-world," Kazickas said.

"With a long leash," Wheat said. "Dagmar and I were consulted on this."

"Without the entire group?" Squyres turned his sharp face toward Wheat. Wheat didn't even flinch.

"The decision had to be made quickly. You and Ulric were out of the Dome, and Tilly was at some conference."

"What kind of leash?" Kazickas asked.

"The charges are appended to her identification. She's on a strict time limit, and she's to report in daily with her findings. She has the backing of the entire Sahara Dome Human Government."

"And credits she can spend on a Retrieval Artist, should one be courageous enough to take the case," Yupanqui said. "I rather doubt one will."

"What's to stop her from disappearing?" Middaugh asked.

Scott-Olson's back stiffened. It felt as if she had left the room. The meeting was suddenly not about her or the potential mass grave. Suddenly, it was about Aisha Costard.

"Common sense," Wheat said.

"She doesn't have a lot of that where nonhumans are concerned," Scott-Olson said. "Did anyone tell her not to disappear?"

"She was told to get back quickly, that she could be subjected to Disty punishment if she didn't abide by the rules," Yupanqui said. "She will be all right."

"She should be back shortly," Wheat said. "You can use her."

"Good." This time, Scott-Olson deliberately let the sarcasm into her voice. "I get one expert when I need dozens. That doesn't quite work for me."

Kazickas pressed her fingertips together and tapped them against her lower lip. Yupanqui smoothed the back of one hand with the other. Squyres wasn't even looking at Scott-Olson anymore.

Only Middaugh and Wheat watched her. Middaugh as if he were waiting for her to slip up, and Wheat with a touch of compassion.

"You realize," Middaugh said, "if we go up the line and eventually our people talk with the Disty's representatives, that this could be the end of Sahara Dome."

Once again, the group was focusing on each other instead of Scott-Olson. She was amazed at the quickness with which they could make her feel invisible.

"I agree that they might abandon the Dome," Kazickas said.

"The Human Governments of Mars all signed documents swearing that there were no known Earth-style graves," Middaugh said. "If Disty believe those documents were signed falsely . . ."

"Then this becomes an issue for the Multicultural Tribunals," Kazickas said slowly.

"The costs would be astronomical," Wheat said.

"They'd have to broker something," Wheat said. "No one would let that happen."

His words hung in the air. The councilors stared at each other for a long moment. Scott-Olson hardly dared breathe. She wasn't sure if she should call attention to herself or not. They seemed to have forgotten all about her and the problem that brought her here. They had moved so far beyond it as to be in an imaginary world.

"Could it be some kind of grave site?" Kazickas asked.

"No," Scott-Olson said.

They all looked at her as if they had forgotten her.

"Graves don't function that way. It's one of the things we have to study before becoming M.E.s."

Squyres nodded. The edge that had made him seem so

angry was suddenly gone. "But someone could have taken all the dead bodies from a certain period of time and placed them there, maybe to thwart the Disty, right?"

"The Disty would have to know about it," Yupanqui said.

"And somehow these hypothetical people would have had to do this without being seen," Scott-Olson said. "Do you know how much work that would be?"

"You don't think it possible?" Kazickas asked.

"Anything's possible," Scott-Olson said. "But I don't think it likely. I suspect these people were killed around the same time, and then buried there to cover up the mass murder."

"Mass murder," Wheat whispered, as if he couldn't believe the term.

"Do you know how they died?" Middaugh asked.

"Not yet," Scott-Olson said. "Nothing obvious. But remember, I've only seen nine of the corpses."

"Only nine," Squyres said, and shook his head.

Yupanqui sighed and placed her hands heavily on the table. The others looked at her, startled. Scott-Olson was still breathing shallowly, not quite sure what had happened at this meeting.

"Doctor," Yupanqui said. "We thank you for taking the time to answer our questions. We'll try to figure out how to get you your team without compromising anyone else's health and safety. If we can figure out how to go about this without causing a panic, we'll get the Disty involved."

Scott-Olson swallowed heavily. The thought of the Disty knowing about this still terrified her.

"In the meantime, do what you can with the people you can. We would appreciate it if you can figure out, within a margin of error of a decade or so, when this mass grave was created. Then we'll assign someone to research the Sahara Dome histories—and not just the official ones—to see if we know when this occurred. Maybe that will give us some answers, as well."

"Thank you," Scott-Olson said.

They all stared at her. It took her a moment to realize she was dismissed.

She stood, her legs shaking. She had been even more uncomfortable here than she had realized.

The councilors looked away from her. Scott-Olson stood for a moment longer, but they acted as if she wasn't there. Finally, she turned around and headed for the door.

She couldn't shake the fear that had come to her while sitting in this room. The councilors weren't going to help.

They were going to make things worse.

Only she wasn't sure exactly how.

<u>19</u>

Aisha Costard felt exposed. She sat inside a windowless office not far from her hotel. She had had to cross the bombed-out section of Armstrong to get here, and a strange metallic smell now clung to her clothing.

The office was as sparsely furnished as Flint's. Nothing hung on the walls, and the main room had only three chairs. She sat in the center one. Its seat was uncomfortably hard, and the back felt like it wasn't made for human beings.

She had been told to come here. She had contacted one of the Disappearance Services listed in the public directories. She had no way of checking up on the service's qualifications. However, she had been smart enough to use a public system to make her inquiries, a system far away from the hotel. She hadn't even used her own personal identification to do so, instead paying for usage time on three separate screens, and accessing different information under different names on all three.

She felt like a criminal. Apparently, she was, under Disty law.

Her stomach ached at the thought of what she was doing—how she was abandoning the others and thinking only of herself. And then there was this place. It was so mean and small, in what was obviously a cheap section of Armstrong.

She had always heard that Disappearance Services made a fortune. If they did, how come they didn't have nicer buildings and some kind of receptionist? Whether that receptionist was a living, breathing being or a robot or a talking face on a screen, it wouldn't matter, just as long as someone, anyone, put her at ease.

Although she wasn't sure anyone could. She gripped the sides of her chair. At her feet was the bag of boxed synthetic food the contact had told her to bring here. If someone asked her where she was going, the contact told her, she was supposed to tell them she was going to a charity to drop off some goods.

A charity. Goods. Couldn't people see through that? Wouldn't they wonder why a woman like Costard, who didn't belong here, had never been here before, would involve herself in the problems of the local poor?

She was beginning to think she had contacted the wrong place, that this was some sort of scam. From what she could tell, there was only this little room in this strange building, near the destroyed section of Armstrong. What better way to make her an easy target than to have her come to an isolated place like this?

Damn Flint for not helping her find a good service. Damn him for telling her to do this, for making it a condition of his work. Damn him for having logical arguments, arguments that had taken her this far.

And damn her for considering them.

She stood.

At that moment, a panel opened behind her. A heavyset woman with long black hair smiled at her.

"Ms. Cunningham?" she said, using Aisha's fake name. "Please come with me."

Costard's heart was pounding harder than it ever had. The woman had startled her, yes, but the idea of going down that dark corridor frightened her even more.

If she went down it, she would have to commit to this silly path, and she wasn't sure she wanted to. She wasn't sure it was right.

What would her life be away from bones, away from the

university, away from Earth? Would her life be worth living? Would she be happy just to have survived?

"Ms. Cunningham?" the woman said again. "Would you like to join me?"

Costard glanced down the corridor, seeing nothing but darkness. Then she looked at the main door.

She didn't run from things. It wasn't her way. She had gotten into this mess on her own. She wasn't willing to trust her life to people who operated out of such a horrible office.

But mostly she was afraid to take that step, afraid to give up her very self just so that she could keep breathing.

"I'm sorry I bothered you," she said, picking up the bag of foodstuffs. She felt superstitious about leaving it, as if the bag itself were a commitment she didn't want to make.

The woman watched her, not speaking at all.

Costard hugged the bag to her chest and went to the main door, standing before it until it shushed open.

Then she stepped into the pallid light of the Dome's day, her breath coming in small gasps.

Running away wasn't the answer. Going back wasn't the answer either.

She would just have to figure out how to push Flint to work faster, to find a solution that would satisfy the Disty.

A solution that would somehow keep everyone alive.

20

Flint sat at his favorite table in the Brownie Bar, eating a bowl of cream of asparagus soup, made with real asparagus and real cream. He loved the Brownie Bar. It could afford to serve food with real ingredients at low prices.

The bar specialized in marijuana baked into brownies. The bar had been in Armstrong for generations, a holdover from the earliest settlement. Many of the early colonists had come to run away from government regulation, particularly regulation of their pleasures, and bars like this one—catering to specific drugs—had come into being.

The Brownie Bar was one of the few left, partly because marijuana's side effects were minimal compared with some of the heavier drugs, and partly because the place was so very profitable.

The bar was divided into several sections. Patrons called the very back the quiet section because it catered to the people who wanted a little relaxation on their lunch hour. A small brownie, an hour or so at the booth while they ate and did some work, and then they'd leave. The other sections focused on groups—parties of two or three had one room, and a newer room had just opened for groups that wanted to add alcohol to the brownie mix.

Flint didn't eat the brownies when he came here, preferring to sit by himself in the back, enjoy the spectacular food, and use the public access screen built into the table. At the

Brownie Bar, no log-in identity was needed, so Flint could work here on some of the more sensitive stuff.

At the moment, he was trying to understand the M'Kri Tribesmen. Their arguments in the Multicultural Tribunal had seemed filtered to him, and as a result, almost impossible to follow. What he had learned, however, was that the richness of their land had been a closely guarded secret.

He wasn't even certain the Tribesmen had understood the mineral wealth of the soil they had inherited. The various M'Kri cultures had never surveyed the land, and according to at least one witness in front of the Tribunal, no outsiders (read: no aliens) were allowed with a hundred kilometers of the Tribesmen's land.

If that were the case, how did Jørgen's company even learn of the minerals? How did the negotiations with the Tribesmen happen? And where did they happen?

None of those questions appeared to have been asked at the hearings, and none of those questions were answered in any of the documentation.

The more he dug into this case, the stranger it got.

He also spent some time researching Jørgen. He looked up Lagrima as a name, and came up with a very short list. Hardly anyone in any database named a child Lagrima—at least in modern times. It had been a somewhat more common name on Earth two centuries earlier—a lot of space travelers and adventurers were named Lagrima.

He would have to research them, but not here. Too much research on a single topic called attention to the place and material researched. The history of the owners of the name Lagrima would have to wait until he went back to the university. There, no one would take much notice.

The screen blanked, and he finished his soup. He wasn't quite full. He would order some of the Brownie Bar's fresh bread—the bar's baked goods (even without the herbal additive) were excellent.

With a touch of his finger to the edge of the screen, he summoned the waitress. Because the Brownie Bar specialized in drugs, it preferred human waitresses to keep an eye on the patrons. Flint liked the personal touch, even if it meant the waitress would occasionally ask about his work.

He kept the screen blank while he waited for her. When she did arrive, she was in a hurry, and didn't even look at the table as she took his order. She got his coffee first, telling him that the bread would be a few minutes, since some fresh loaves were just coming out of the oven.

Flint wrapped his hand around the coffee mug and leaned back in his chair, mentally reviewing the rest of the research that he had planned to do this day. Looking up the name Jørgen, after looking up Lagrima, might be a flag. He was better off doing more work on the M'Kri, and seeing if someone somewhere had done surveys that hadn't made it into the official records.

The waitress hurried back with a plate covered with bread and specialty cheeses. He hadn't ordered the cheeses, but he sometimes knew the bar tried new foods, just to see if patrons would enjoy them. He'd been the beneficiary of the bar's generosity a number of times.

He let the bread steam to one side as he pressed the screen. He was about to log in and state his question, when someone put a hand on his shoulder.

He looked up to see Ki Bowles smiling at him.

"I thought that was you," she said.

He did not smile back.

"I decided to say hello. We're heading to one of the private rooms, and I didn't think you'd see me."

It wouldn't have been a great loss. Flint darkened the screen with the touch of a finger. "We?"

She swept a hand toward the door to the quiet room. An amazingly short, slim man hovered near the opening. It took Flint a moment to recognize him.

That was DeRicci's old partner, Leif van der Ketting. Van der Ketting had been Flint's successor. Van der Ketting remained a detective after DeRicci's promotion. Whenever anyone discussed the Moon Marathon and the near disaster at the dome, they talked about DeRicci. No one mentioned her partner and his heroics that day.

"Still trying to see how dirty your hands can get?" Flint asked.

Bowles shrugged a single shoulder. "Your old partner is a fascinating woman."

"So are you," Flint said. "You might want to be careful. It looks like fascinating women are targets for on-the-make reporters."

She flushed. "That was uncalled for."

"No, it wasn't," Flint said. "I saw your latest piece on Noelle. It was filled with innuendo and suggestion, no real research at all. I thought you were an investigative reporter, Ki."

"I am. I'm investigating."

"Then you lack ethics," Flint said. "A real reporter would wait until she had the entire story before going public with any of it."

"A Retrieval Artist has no right to lecture me about ethics," Bowles snapped. "Maybe I should investigate how you got so rich the day you left the force."

"Go ahead," Flint said, knowing that his tracks were covered.

The color had faded from Bowles' face. She had, apparently, recovered. "I didn't come over here to fight with you. I came to say hello, tell you I'm still working on the story, and ask you to talk with me."

"I've already said no. I'll continue to say no for the rest of my life," Flint said.

Her lips twisted in an imitation smile. "You're not the kind of man who changes his mind."

"Obviously," Flint said, even though it was a lie. If he were consistent, he'd still be a computer programmer, inventing new software, new systems, working as deep into the networks and machinery of Armstrong as a man could get.

"You'll be the only one of DeRicci's partners I will not have talked to." Bowles said that as if it would convince him.

"Apparently, I'm the only one with a backbone." Flint glanced past her at van der Ketting, who still hovered near the door.

The man looked even smaller than he had after the

marathon. Flint wondered what kind of luck, what kind of career van der Ketting had had in the past two years.

"Why do you hate Noelle so much?" Flint asked.

"Why do you like her?" Bowles countered.

"Let me remind you that you cannot make a recording of any of our conversations. I will own InterDome Media if you do."

"As a private citizen, I can record anything," Bowles said. "You know that."

That was the first time she had come back with that response. It worried Flint.

"This conversation is over," he said.

Bowles frowned at him. "I'm not going to use anything without your permission."

"You even use my likeness and I'll sue InterDome. Do you understand me, Ki?"

"No," Bowles said, "I don't understand you. You're completely unfathomable to me. But I do understand what you're telling me, and I won't use your likeness—unless you do something on the public record that happens to be newsworthy."

He inhaled slowly and silently so that she couldn't see him holding back the angry response that had just tried to escape.

"The fact that I have come here for lunch is not newsworthy," he said. "Although I find it interesting you come to a drug bar for a professional meeting. Does van der Ketting have a problem? Or are you simply trying to loosen his tongue a little?"

"You're a very suspicious man," Bowles said. "There is kindness in the human soul, you know."

"In some." Flint pointedly looked around her. Van der Ketting had stepped just inside the room, but still looked nervous. "You're being rude to your subject."

"I'm sure he wouldn't mind if you joined us," Bowles said.

Flint studied her. Her hair had silver tips today, showing the usual care in her appearance, but there were lines under her eyes that came from lack of sleep.

"I'm sure you wouldn't mind," Flint said. "But as for van

der Ketting, I doubt he'd be happy about it. I doubt he's happy about the way you're wasting his time. Is that what you're trying to do? Make him angry so that you'll get some good quotes?"

Bowles eyes twinkled. "Why do you hate me so much?" she asked, mimicking his tone from before.

He decided not to respond to the flirtatious question in the same manner. Instead, he told her the truth.

"I don't hate you, Ki. However, I do think you're one of the most insensitive people I've ever met, and I don't think that makes for a good investigator, whether she is a cop, Retrieval Artist, or a reporter. Now, let me finish my lunch."

She took a slice of bread, the smile still pasted on her face. But the spirit had disappeared from it.

"One day, you'll realize I'm not so bad," she said, and walked back to van der Ketting. Flint watched out of the corner of his eye as the two of them disappeared down the corridor.

He didn't like what she was doing, but he didn't know how to stop her.

He wasn't sure anyone could.

21

She was being followed. She had known it for hours now, and she was convinced it was not her imagination.

Aisha Costard sat on the edge of the too-soft bed in her boxy hotel room. The room had screens on all four walls. She kept the screens off, for the most part, except for one screen on which she kept running a program that showed water running down rocks into a high mountain lake.

The sound of running water was supposed to be soothing. But she wasn't soothed. She liked to think it was because she knew the sound was fake.

But that really wasn't it.

She was so homesick that she could hardly breathe. She loved Madison, loved the university town with its isthmus and its lakes. She loved its history and the weather.

She loved the wind.

There was no wind in Armstrong, no wind at all in either of the domed communities she'd been to these last few weeks. All of the promotional materials she had found in this hotel room had told her that the Dome did its best to imitate an Earth environment.

Only they had forgotten wind and rain and humidity and snow, and that wonderful overheated sensation that came from too much sunlight.

Costard put her face in her hands. Being followed. Being

watched. Maybe since she had arrived on Armstrong, but certainly since she had gone to the Disappearance Service.

Were they following her to find out why she had turned them down? To see if she was some kind of authority?

She shook her head inside her hands, her breath warm against her palms. Maybe she was longing for Madison because she was longing for the innocence of that life, the way she could lose herself in the past, the fact that the only politics she had to pay attention to were university politics, and sometimes not even that because she had been a star tenured professor, a feather in everyone's cap.

What did it matter that she was a bit naïve, a little impolite, a tad distracted? Who cared that she didn't know the differences between Alliance laws and Earth guidelines? How would such esoteric things hurt her?

She had found out, of course. She had found out that what she considered esoteric was essential, and what she considered essential was esoteric.

She had never realized how very protected she had been until everything turned on her, until she had come to Mars. And now she was on the Moon, forbidden to go back to Earth until she was cleared by the Disty, and if Flint was right, she would never be cleared.

And now she felt trapped in this room. She wanted to see Flint, to make sure he would do the job even if she didn't disappear, but she was scared to go out. Scared that she would get followed to his office, scared that he would be angry because she brought someone who shouldn't be there.

Scared.

Homesick and lost and scared, all emotions she hadn't felt in a long, long time.

Not since her parents died. And even then, the emotions hadn't been this debilitating. Her blindness to the world around her made it possible for her to continue surviving—if she just focused on the past, on the bones, on history, everything would be all right.

Or it had been until she had traveled to Mars.

Before she left, she should have looked clearly at the situation, and she hadn't. Once she was there, she tried.

And now in Armstrong, things were even worse. She had to *see* everything around her, even the person (persons?) who was following her, and she couldn't. She could only rely on a feeling, little glimpses out of the corner of her eye, little details that were slightly off.

The SDHPD had warned her before she left that the Disty would monitor her as best they could in a non-Disty environment.

Maybe that was what bothered her the most. Maybe it was simply her conscience, worrying that some Disty spy had seen her go into the Disappearance Service.

She lifted her head out of her hands and flopped backward on the bed, sinking into the mattress. Around her, the sound of rushing water seemed so real that if she closed her eyes, she could almost imagine herself beside a brook.

But she didn't dare. Her imagination helped with her work—helped her visualize how someone died, just from their bones; helped her visualize how they might have looked in life; helped her even find corpses that were long missing—but it wouldn't help her here.

She had to get back to Mars. But first, she had to talk to Flint, to make sure he would continue working even if she hadn't disappeared. Maybe the person who had been following her had been him, just seeing if she had taken his advice.

To contact him, she would have to leave the hotel, and that frightened her for reasons she didn't entirely understand. If she contacted him on the hotel links, then the message would be public.

If she contacted him through her links, the hotel might be recording her part of the conversation.

She would have to leave sometime—even if it was just to go to the port to return to Mars.

Costard sighed, stood, and adjusted her shirt. She ran her fingers through her hair to comb it. She grabbed her purse but not a coat—it felt odd to go out without a coat, even now. Then she opened her door and stepped into the hallway.

The hallway was well lit with histories of Armstrong's greatest events running on the wall screens. Most of the events seemed to involve speeches and building things. She never stopped long enough to get a sense of what the history was all about.

On some level, she found that odd, considering how much she loved history. She used to say she loved human history, but she was beginning to discover that she only loved Earth history, and only then if it concerned humans. She had never thought of herself as narrow-minded until she had traveled so far from home.

She took the stairs down to the main floor, nodded at the woman who seemed to live behind that desk, and headed out the front door as if nothing were wrong. She would only go a few blocks, and then she would contact Flint, ask him for a safe place to meet.

He would know. He seemed like the safest person she had encountered since she left home—and he was the only one who had been rude to her, the only one who had made her mad.

She didn't think of the Disty as people.

And she certainly hadn't interacted with them. She had only heard their edicts from humans, people who seemed to know more about everything than she did.

She shivered, even though there was no wind and the air temperature was perfect. She longed for the coat, just for the sake of comfort.

The air still had that strange smoky electrical smell that Flint said came from last year's bombing. Costard looked around as she headed down the street.

A young couple walked toward a restaurant attached to the hotel. Two aliens—one with so many arms they looked like wings—appeared to be arguing across the street. A few more people hurried down the opposite sidewalk, as if they knew exactly where they were going.

Costard retraced the walk she had taken with Flint. She didn't know much about the neighborhood and she certainly wasn't going to go somewhere she hadn't been before.

The skin on the back of her neck crawled. But she knew bet-

ter than to turn around, knew that if someone was watching—
or following—he would do whatever he could to avoid getting
caught.

She hurried, finally reaching the end of the block. She
looked around again before crossing the street, and saw a
slightly different group of people. The aliens were still the only
ones on the street, still arguing.

No one appeared to be watching her.

She didn't know how far to go. Restaurants had to have
public links. Maybe if she just went into one and ordered a
salad, she would be able to contact Flint. It would be a quick
trip, and there would be people around her.

Maybe that was all that mattered.

Two of the nearby restaurants had sidewalk tables. She
wanted to avoid those. She didn't want to sit with her back to
the street. The closest restaurant looked like a café. She let out
a small sigh of relief and headed toward the door.

Someone grabbed her arm. The grip was so tight that she
gasped in pain.

"Keep walking forward," a man said in her ear. "Act calm."

She sent a help message through her links, but the message
was instantly blocked. She opened her mouth to scream when
another hand grasped her other arm.

"Try anything," the second man said, "and we will kill
you."

She took a shuddery breath, then closed her mouth. "What
do you want?" she asked.

"You to stay quiet," the first man said.

They propelled her forward. Her feet tripped against each
other, unable to keep the pace. The men lifted her slightly, carrying her between them.

No one around them seemed to notice that she wasn't walking.

"Please," she said softly, "I'll do whatever you want. Just
tell me what this is about."

"The Disty," the second man said. "They don't want you to
disappear."

22

Gavin Trouvelot folded his hands inside his robe. He stood inside the Disty-Human Chamber, designed to accommodate both species and, of course, accommodating neither. Seven Disty sat on the tabletop, their bare feet pressed together, their hands resting on their knees.

For the moment, all seven ignored Trouvelot. Apparently, they weren't ready for him yet.

The chamber was in the middle of the Liaison Building, which stood in that no-man's-land between the Disty and human sections of Sahara Dome. The Liaison Building served dual government functions: It became host for all the Disty-human meetings needed to run a two-tiered governmental system, and it also provided the courtrooms needed for infractions between cultures.

The chamber was on the top floor, with a view of the Disty section on one side of the room and the Human section on the other. Tables lined the walls. Chairs filled the spaces between the tables.

Trouvelot was a third-level minister, deemed just senior enough to meet with the leaders of the Disty Death Squad, but not too senior. No need to taint one of the main human liaisons by contact with the Death Squad.

He hadn't wanted this meeting at all. He had fought it, even though he had been the next minister up for a private meeting with the Disty. But Death Squad interactions sometimes led to demotions or banishment, and he couldn't afford either of those.

All his life, he had wanted to work with the Disty. He had been modified so that he was shorter than the average human, with slightly longer limbs. He couldn't gain as much weight as some short humans did, either, and his skull had been enlarged just a little.

In essence, he was as Disty as a human could get without exactly duplicating their physiology. To do that would insult them. So far, no Disty had even noticed his modifications.

He wore a robe for this meeting with the Death Squad just so that he wouldn't inadvertently touch anything he shouldn't. Even though he had spent his life in Sahara Dome and all of his education studying the Disty, he still wasn't versed in some of the more esoteric customs. In fact, he had avoided most of the death rituals simply because they were so tricky.

Now he wished he hadn't.

Seven Disty led the Death Squad. They sat in a semicircle on the table that was the longest in length, shortest in height. This group wore all black, with tiny reflective insignia on the fabric. The insignia was a silver flame, the symbol of the Death Squad.

Trouvelot wasn't sure if he had seen these Disty before. Individual Disty were difficult to distinguish: Their skin was the same dusky tan color, and they had no real hair to speak of. Their eyes filled the large sockets, and were uniformly dark.

The differences came in the length of their feet (long feet were considered a sign of beauty—which was why the Disty found shoes barbaric); the shape of their heads—some narrow and others rounder at the chin area; and the degree of depth in the cavity that formed their ears. Sex differences were impossible to determine without intimate contact. Humans had settled this issue by referring to all Disty as *it*. Age also emphasized a few features: The eyes tended to bulge the older a Disty got, and the mouth shrank in on itself.

Judging by the appearance of these seven, most of them were as young as Trouvelot was.

The center Disty, obviously the head of the group and the

only one who would speak, finally deigned to notice Trouvelot. It studied him for a moment, then gestured at the empty space before it. It was clearly offering Trouvelot a place on the table.

Already, a ploy. He hated these games. He wasn't sure how to play this. If he sat at the table, he had already conceded power to the Disty. If he remained standing, he might be perceived as rude.

He bent his head slightly. This case was a tough one, this meeting one of the most delicate ever held. He would do well to acquiesce to the Disty instead of antagonize them.

He shuffled forward, keeping his head down, his bare feet catching on the nubby carpet. When he reached the table, he turned his back to the Disty, according to custom. He placed his hands on the top, and pretended to elevate himself with his arms.

Actually, the table was short enough that he could have slid onto the top. To do so, however, would make the Disty feel inferior, something he wasn't willing to do.

When he settled on the tabletop, he spun around and pressed his bare feet together. Then he pulled up his robe just enough to uncover his feet and his legs.

One of the Disty pursed its lips, a sign of distaste. Even with all of the modifications, Trouvelot's feet were too short, and the arches made it impossible to press the feet completely flat. His skin was too thick and multicolored. His anklebones were too prominent, and his knees had too many joints.

"We prefer our own language," this Disty said in perfect English. English was the language of the Alliance, and technically should have been used in all meetings between alien species.

But Trouvelot was willing to concede a lot, just to be heard.

"I will do my best," he said in Disty, imitating the flat affect they used when speaking to each other. "I might have to use English words to convey some of my meanings. Please do not take this as an offense. Please consider it ignorance on my part, since I am not usually the one who deals with death matters in my culture."

"Then why are you here?" the Disty asked. "Why isn't the person who deals with death consulting with us?"

"She has been banned from contact with the Disty," Trouvelot said. "She is considered contaminated because of the skeleton found in Sector Fifteen."

The Disty divided their section of Sahara Dome into numbered sectors.

At Trouvelot's explanation, all seven of the Disty let out a quiet "Oooo." He had gained a point by understanding that his lack of knowledge would offend them.

"Begin," the Disty in charge said. Miraculously, they had agreed to see him without knowing the exact reason why.

Now, however, the difficult part began.

"At your request, our people have been excavating the contaminated area," Trouvelot said. "The work has created a problem."

His heart was pounding: The very idea of telling the Disty about this terrified him. But the council thought it best, and they thought it best to start with a liaison and the Death Squad, instead of a city diplomat talking to the Disty Ruling Class.

The council believed that the more ignorance they showed, the lighter the Disty response might be.

"First," Trouvelot said, sounding more confident than he felt, "I must tell you that I have not been to Sector Fifteen for a long time, long before the skeleton was discovered. In fact, I have not been in the Disty section of the Dome for quite a while. The Liaison Building is the closest I have come to your home section in three human months."

He had to establish before the conversation got too intense that he was not contaminated.

"We understand and accept your lack of contamination," the Disty said. "It was a condition of our meeting."

So the higher-ups hadn't bothered to tell him that. Lovely. A misstep, but a recoverable one.

Trouvelot pressed his knuckles against his chin and bowed his head slightly, a sign of respect.

"I am happy," he said, "to have met an important condition of the meeting."

They nodded in return.

Now the moment of truth. His mouth went dry. "In fulfilling the Disty request to make certain the area around the Sector Fifteen site held no more surprises, my people have spent the last few weeks digging."

"We are aware that you have been following the terms of our agreements," the Disty said. "The sooner you can certify the area free of trouble, the sooner we can begin decontamination procedures. Several thousand of our people are currently homeless. Most have moved in with relatives, but the conditions are crowded, and there is much unhappiness."

Trouvelot swallowed hard. His knuckles felt sharp against his chin. "I am sorry to be the bearer of bad news. We have discovered something horrible in that site, something so awful our language has no words for it."

All seven Disty closed their fists. That gesture could be interpreted as a sign of displeasure, a sign of warning, or a sign of imminent departure. Trouvelot, usually so good at reading the Disty around him, couldn't figure out what the unison gestures meant.

That made him even more nervous.

"We have found more bodies," he said. "They are human, and we believe them to be much older than the initial skeleton. They have been in the sand for many more years. They are not skeletons, which is, I don't know if anyone told you, an aberration for our people on Mars. We do not know how these new bodies died, nor do we know how long, exactly, they have been in place."

One of the Disty slid off the table. The Disty caught its foot on the table's edge and nearly slid off. Another Disty grabbed the first one's arm and held it in place.

The leader didn't move. "How many dead?"

"That's our dilemma." And the beginning of Trouvelot's tap dance. "We are unwilling to risk the new lives to work on the site, so we are only allowing the already contaminated from the skeleton discovery there. The work is slow. We have no numbers for you, and no studies. We have nothing in our records that indicate this is a death location, and we have no mention of many deaths occurring in one place in our histories."

He hoped he had dodged the question well enough.

The Disty looked at each other. One of them raised a hand, a request for private counsel, but the leader shook its head.

"How many dead?" the leader repeated.

Apparently, Trouvelot hadn't dodged the question at all.

"We don't know," Trouvelot said.

"How many have you uncovered so far?" the leader asked.

"We have uncovered nine," Trouvelot said.

All of the Disty gasped, except the leader. Its dark eyes hadn't moved from Trouvelot's.

"Uncovered," it repeated. "That is a strange term. How many bodies are at the site?"

"We don't know," Trouvelot said for the second time.

"You suspect an amount, however," the leader said, "and that amount is greater than nine, simply from your attitude. How much greater?"

After much debate, the council had told Trouvelot to answer that question accurately if the question was asked. The key, the councilors had told him, was to ensure the Disty never asked the question.

He had lost that negotiating point in the first fifteen minutes. Maybe he wasn't as good as he thought he was.

He pressed his hands together as tightly as they went, then bowed his head until it touched the tabletop. He hoped he wouldn't have to hold this position long because it always made him dizzy.

"Maybe a hundred, maybe more."

The table shook as the Disty jumped from it. He couldn't look up until they gave him permission, but he saw limbs flashing around him, heard a high-level chatter—a form of the Disty language that was forbidden to all but the most important Disty, a part of the language most Disty never learned. Humans would probably never learn it either.

It didn't even sound like regular Disty, so he couldn't pretend to understand it.

At least they were arguing, though. At least they hadn't fled.

Then he heard the door open. More chatter, and then the door slammed shut.

The back of his neck ached. The only sound he heard in the entire room was the echo of his own breathing, shorter and more rapid than it should have been. His face was flushed with blood.

He swallowed again, painfully against the dryness of his throat.

"Forgive me for speaking out of turn," he said in Disty, "but I thought I heard the door. I want to confirm that the meeting continues."

No one responded to his words. He remained in the subservient position, however, hoping that he was not alone.

He held his breath, heard nothing, and then counted silently to one hundred, just like he had been instructed to do in a situation like this. Instructed years ago, by a teacher who had worked on some of the toughest negotiations with the Disty.

You'll probably never have to use this technique, the instructor had said. *The difficult years are over.*

Trouvelot raised his head. He was alone in the room. He put his arms down for balance, feeling the dizziness rush through him as the blood left his face.

Alone. He wasn't hadn't even been near the site, and still the Disty had fled the room.

This was bad. It was worse than bad.

It was a disaster.

23

Staff applications. Position papers. The minutes of fifteen different meetings in which nothing got done.

DeRicci leaned back in the plush chair behind her desk. She had brought in the chair because she hated all the transparent furniture, but it still didn't make her feel at home. The desk looked like a pile of computer pads and blinking lights, not like a workspace. And she hated being able to see her knees through the desk's surface.

Most of the information had come through her new link, the one that was on a secured network, designed only for the security department's staff. Security memos—hundreds of them—scrolled on a continuous loop at the bottom of her vision. Even with her eyes closed she could see the damn things. Literally.

DeRicci resisted the urge to shut down the link. That had been her solution during her detective days, and back then, it had nearly gotten her fired. Now it was a matter of Moon-based security, and she could only shut off the visual part of the link if she planned to sleep.

She'd been told that some people got so used to this feature that they slept with the information crawling through their optic nerve, keeping one part of the brain active while the body slept.

If she did that, she'd be even crankier than she was now. And she was cranky. She wasn't designed for this kind of ad-

ministrative position. She wanted everything done and settled, the duties of the department delineated quickly so that
she could get to work.

At the last meeting she'd had with the Moon's Governing
Council, she had asked for a timeline, figuring if she had a
deadline for setup, she could get the interior meetings done
quicker.

We'll finish when we agree, the governor-general had said,
and with that had ended the whole debate.

As far as DeRicci could tell, they'd all agree when moss
grew on the top of the dome. Until then, she was going to be
in charge of a toothless agency, trying to determine its own
sense of purpose.

That was how naïve she and Flint were. They had thought
she could get something done here. Not even the greatest
politician in the universe could get anything done in this situation.

She was stuck, and it was her own damn fault.

DeRicci pressed on all three screens on the desktop. She
had devoted one screen to applications, another screen to public comments, and a third to private suggestions. As those
screens came on, a fourth rose behind them, its clear surface
blinking orange with more than a dozen urgent messages.

Of course, the urgency came from the media, whom she
had decided to ignore. The governor-general had questioned
that decision at the last meeting—*After all,* she had said, *the
people are the ones we're working for, and the only way they
hear about our good deeds is through the media*—but De-
Ricci had ignored that.

She hadn't done any good deeds yet, and after that terrible
piece Ki Bowles had run on her, she wasn't feeling particularly charitable toward reporters and their accuracy.

Or maybe she was feeling a bit persecuted. Nothing in that
report had been wrong—DeRicci had been a screwup in most
of her jobs, but not the kind of screwup who cost lives. The
kind of screwup who didn't play nice with others, who did
things to the best of her abilities, and often saved lives. The

kind who didn't suffer fools easily. That was the kind of screwup she had been.

DeRicci sent the screen back down and focused on the applications. What she really needed was a good assistant. Someone who kept the media at bay, who could learn how to take DeRicci's harsh statements and make them into something political.

In short, she needed a miracle worker.

And she wasn't finding one.

A knock on her door made her growl. But she had learned to ignore her staff here at her own peril.

"It better be important," she called.

Rudra Popova, DeRicci's de facto assistant, opened the door and leaned in. Popova had perfectly straight black hair that flowed like water whenever it moved. It went all the way to her waist, and never seemed messy or in the way. Her black eyes snapped with intelligence and a bit of condescension. DeRicci could feel Popova's thought whenever that woman's gaze fell on her: *I could do this job so much better than this uneducated cop can.*

"Well?" DeRicci had learned that she could do haughty better than almost anyone. She didn't like it, but it had its uses. Like right now, to get Popova out of her office.

"The media needs a statement," Popova said, with more than a touch of annoyance.

"Tell them we'll have the staff roster for them by the end of the month." DeRicci hoped that she wasn't lying. With a talent pool that covered the entire Moon, she would have thought that the applicants would have been at least competent.

"No." Popova's voice dripped with sarcasm. "They want a statement about the vengeance killing."

Obviously, this was something DeRicci should have known about. She was tempted to pretend that she was on top of everything, but when she had been an underling, she had always thought bosses who pretended they knew more than they did were especially stupid.

"What vengeance killing?" DeRicci asked. Then she held

up a hand. "And I don't want to hear chapter and verse. I want to know why the media is calling me instead of the police."

"Because the victim is a well-known criminal with so many warnings attached to her identification that she should never have been allowed into Armstrong in the first place. The media wants to know how we could let such a threat into the Dome."

"Oh, for God's sake," DeRicci said. "Hasn't anyone figured out that we have no enforcement powers? We have no powers at all. We're a figurehead agency until we finish our damn position papers and get all the mayors, all the city councils, and the entire government of the United Domes of the Moon to sign off on all of this stuff. Tell them that."

Popova slipped inside the room and pushed the door closed. "No, sir."

DeRicci raised her eyebrows. "No, sir?"

Popova flushed, but she didn't back down. "I want this department to work. I think it's necessary. If I give that response to the entire Moon-based media, I'm undermining everything we're trying to do here."

DeRicci sighed and shook her head slightly. "What kind of criminal was this person? Was she just some poor sap who crossed the Disty, or was she a threat to every dome she entered? And for that matter, was she Disty herself? Because they can bring their vengeance killings here. It's perfectly legal, and has been for as long as the Disty have been part of the Alliance."

"She was human," said Popova. "And I think it's time you study the issue. Shall I announce a press conference in an hour?"

"No," DeRicci said, mostly because she didn't want Popova making her decisions for her. "I'll look over the case and then decide whether or not I want to speak to the press."

"As you wish," Popova said with complete disapproval, and let herself out of the room.

Of course, she hadn't said a word about the case number or the people involved. She hadn't volunteered to forward a file, and she hadn't even tried to help DeRicci understand what was going on.

Not that DeRicci would ask—at least, not after that little encounter.

DeRicci sighed and turned on the main wall screen, going to InterDome's continuous news feed. If the media wanted DeRicci to make a comment, the vengeance killing had to be recent.

There had to be some kind of twist besides the victim's criminal history with the Disty—something so important that the story had route to Moon Security.

DeRicci didn't like the implications. And she didn't even know the facts.

24

She had never seen anything like it.

Sharyn Scott-Olson sat in front of the domed windows on the top floor of the Stanshut Government Office Building and watched the street below. She was surrounded by most of her coworkers, police officers she'd never seen, and a slew of government employees.

The Disty were fleeing the Dome.

All of the human taxis were booked, as well as the carts that wound their way through the Disty section. Entire Disty families packed their belongings in those carts and scurried alongside them, heading out of Sahara Dome in a panic.

Video, playing on the wall screen next to the window, showed the disaster at Sahara Dome's train station. Thousands of Disty crowded the platform, pushing, shoving, a few trying to climb on the side of the trains, only to be pulled off by human guards.

The Disty police weren't even trying to help. Rumor had it that the Disty officials had been the first ones out of the Dome.

The port was even worse. A split image showed the exterior of the port—filming inside it had been forbidden by the Disty—as hundreds of Disty shoved against the doors, trying to fit inside. Some of them fell and disappeared under the crowd.

Mercifully, the sound on the screen was off, so the screams

and hums that the Disty made when they were panicked didn't add to the live sounds coming from below.

All the humans in this building could do was watch. They couldn't leave—the Disty covered the entire street, from building to building—and doors wouldn't open. Even if they did, no human in his right mind would go down there. No human would dare get caught on the street.

The Disty's panic made them incautious. Their desire to get out of Sahara Dome made them ignore the threat of pain and death that a stampede could cause.

Scott-Olson let out a breath. She hadn't realized just how frightened she was until now. The worst-case scenario that she and Batson had discussed was coming true.

She supposed the site was the safest area in the Dome right now. The Disty were obviously terrified of the mass grave, terrified of the implications and the contamination. They wouldn't get near any humans, not even the ones trying to keep this flight from becoming something worse.

At least they weren't looting the area or burning down the homes. All the Disty were doing was trying to get out of here as quickly as they could.

"Where do you suppose they're going?" someone asked quietly behind her.

"Dunno," someone else said. "Probably anywhere that'll take them."

"Will other places take them?" Scott-Olson asked. "They've been living here, in the shadow of that grave. Aren't they contaminated?"

No one answered her. No one knew. This was a part of Disty culture that no human had delved into too deeply.

She leaned forward just a little, watching the tiny creatures run toward any escape they could find, some holding hands, others carrying children on their shoulders, even more clutching a handful of possessions against their concave chests.

Scott-Olson couldn't fathom that kind of fear—at least, not of something tangible. Dead bodies were dead bodies, nothing more. A part of life that had to be dealt with.

Not something to be feared.

She had lived in Sahara Dome for a very long time. She had thought she understood the Disty.

But as she watched them trample each other in their attempts to escape the now-tainted Dome, she realized she hadn't understood them at all.

25

Flint was in the basement cafeteria at Dome University's law school when he finally found information on Lagrima Jørgen.

The law school's cafeteria was busy year-round. It was also open all the time. Some law students seemed to live here; they were in the cafeteria every time Flint showed up to use a screen.

Although he'd heard that Dome University's Armstrong branch had one of the most diverse law schools in this solar system, he saw little evidence of it here. Part of the reason was that the cafeteria catered to human tastes. Coffee was free, as were sugary desserts. The food itself cost little more than a few credits, and wasn't even worth that.

But a student could survive for weeks on coffee and pastries made with Moon flour—and many of them did. The only aliens who seemed to come in here, aside from study partners, were the Peyti, who seemed to like the pastries (despite having to move their breathing masks to eat them), and the Sequevs, eight-legged aliens the size of a small dog.

Three Sequevs sat in the cafeteria this night, using the table as both chair and study area. The food had been pushed to the center, and the nearest Sequev reached out with the fourth limb, picked up a pastry, and brought the food to its mouth, while its multifaceted eyes studied the screen before it.

The other two Sequevs were whispering in English—

something that had unnerved Flint the first time he heard it, since the Sequevs sounded like small children when they spoke. He had since learned to ignore them.

Still, he sat as far from their table as he possibly could.

A single Peyti sat near him, using its long fingers to turn the pages of an antique book. Its breathing mask was squarely in place, but its skin looked a little too gray all the same. The poor Peyti had trouble with the oxygen atmosphere, but wanted all the perks that came from being in the center of the Earth Alliance. When he had been in the police department, Flint had worked on cases with the Peyti, but he hadn't enjoyed it. They were too logical and legalistic for him.

The remaining six people in the cafeteria were human. Two men sat side by side in a booth, flirting as they studied the screen before them. A woman sat by herself. The remaining humans sat at a group table, quizzing each other for an upcoming exam.

Their questions sounded incredibly easy compared with the legal issues that Flint had encountered over the years. He didn't come to the cafeteria as often as he would like, simply because he was tempted to approach group studies and ask them to ponder issues that still vexed him, years after the fact.

Instead, he kept to his private booth near the serving trays. The screen here had an extra backlight, and it didn't require vocal access. He could punch in one of the stolen identifications and work for hours without anyone noticing him.

Occasionally, he would open the order menu on his screen and have a tray deliver something to him. Those he charged to blanket university account that he had set up in the system long ago. He paid it anonymously every month, and no one seemed to notice.

This afternoon, he had ordered one of the pastries and some soy milk. He didn't plan on touching either—the pastries tasted like dried glue, and the soy milk had an oily texture that just wasn't natural—but he knew that ordering kept him off the cafeteria's recycling radar.

Flint had visited most of his favorite public network systems in the past few days, trying to track down Lagrima Jørgen without setting off any red flags. He hadn't found her or any semblance of her.

He hadn't even found an image of her, which he thought odd.

So when he came to the law school, he decided to focus on the Multicultural Tribunal Case, and see if he could find information about the various parties. He'd already done a lot of work on the M'Kri Tribesmen, so he started with BiMela Corporation—and that was where he had his luck.

BiMela Corporation bought the mineral rights from Arrber Corporation, whom Jørgen supposedly had worked for. Flint already knew that Arrber was probably a dummy organization. That seemed clear from the way they fought the suit. He would dig deeper there too, but that would take some time. People who excelled in corporate misdeeds knew how to cover their tracks.

BiMela was legitimate and had existed for fifty years before the case found its way to the Multicultural Tribunal. Flint scanned stock reports and earnings ratios, articles that examined the company's financial holdings, and a few indepth financial pieces about the heads of the corporation.

As far as he could tell, BiMela had been absorbed into another, larger corporate entity fifteen years ago, and had effectively ceased to exist. While the mineral rights on M'Kri had proven profitable, the loss of reputation from the case had put BiMela on an unsteady financial footing, which they were never able to recover from. Finally, new leadership had negotiated a deal with the larger corporation to take over BiMela.

At first, Flint had thought this another dead end. BiMela seemed legitimate, and once the Multicultural Tribunal case ended, the corporation had no interest in Lagrima Jørgen or her dummy corporation. He found no evidence of any communication between Arrber and BiMela, or between BiMela and Jørgen, in the two years between the end of the case and her death.

But the deeper he dug into BiMela, the more questionable business deals he found. All of the deals were with different corporations, and all of them had resolved in BiMela's favor before any court cases. The only case that ever went to court was the one with the M'Kri Tribesmen, and from public records, it was clear that the only reason it went to court was because the Tribesmen wouldn't settle.

Theoretically, corporate financial records had to be made public every quarter, so that stockholders could peruse the documents and make certain everything was in order. So many rules and regulations fell on these sorts of corporations that only the publicly traded ones followed these guidelines.

BiMela's reports were sketchy, and no one seemed to notice. Flint had been going through them year by year, when he finally realized he should try something else.

He looked up the merger of BiMela and the new corporation, Fortion Corporation. Because that merger went through Alliance channels, the financial records of both companies were detailed and in exquisite order.

Flint read BiMela's financial history as if it were a book.

He almost got kicked off the table. A student behind him protested, as the system reviewed the student's recent eating and ordering habits. Flint had gotten so engrossed that he hadn't noticed his pastry plate was missing, along with his soy milk. After a certain amount of time, the trays just cleared the old food.

He placed an order for a freshly made ham sandwich, and replaced the soy milk with the cafeteria's very bad coffee.

Then he returned to his reading.

What he learned as he went through was that fifty years before the merger, BiMela had had serious financial troubles. At that time, a new entity—a subcorporation, a group, he couldn't quite tell—had been formed.

Called Gale Research and Development, this arm of BiMela seemed to finance other, smaller corporations—farming out research and development money to "more creative organizations that will enhance BiMela's bottom line."

It took Flint nearly three hours to find that one of the smaller corporations that received funding was Arrber Corporation. And Arrber Corporation's funding started about the same time Lagrima Jørgen's name appeared in the system—

long before BiMela Corporation bought the mineral rights to the M'Kri Tribesmen's land from Arrber.

A tray came by with Flint's coffee and sandwich. He took both, leaned back in his chair, and thought. This discovery, which was a footnote to a footnote to a footnote in a report made years after the case closed, could overturn the entire case.

Or so it seemed to his nonlegal brain.

Because BiMela already owned those rights, if the financial documents were to be believed. Arrber was a subsidiary of BiMela, and as such had no need to sell anything to the parent company.

Arrber received funding through the end of the lawsuit, and then vanished off the books.

Flint sipped the coffee, ignoring its bitter, burnt flavor. If Arrber were a fake subsidiary, set up for a mineral-rights scam, how many other companies in the Gale Research and Development list were also fake?

He set the coffee down and started a new search, knowing it would take a while. First, though, he transferred all of BiMela's financial documents to one of his chips. He would store this information on his own system. It would take a lot of time to work through it, time he didn't want to spend at public terminals.

But he did look up each company. Only a few still existed. He examined those if they predated Lagrima Jørgen's death. Two did, but he found no Lagrima working for them, and no Jørgen either. It would take quite a while to see if a woman fitting her description had once worked for the company, but he would do it if he had to.

He just hoped he wouldn't have to.

26

DeRicci stood in the doorway of the small office. The stench of blood, feces, and rotting corpse made her stomach turn. She was noticeably out of practice at visiting crime scenes.

A body lay in the middle of the windowless room, legs and arms splayed, stomach carved open, and internal organs draping the room as if someone had decided this was a new form of decoration. The room's three chairs had been pushed against the wall.

The rookies who had found the scene hadn't been able to deal with it. They had gotten sick, outside, fortunately. The detective who had the case, a Bartholomew Nyquist, hung back as if the sight offended him.

DeRicci had seen too many Disty vengeance killings to find this one offensive. It stank worse than some, but not as bad as others. At least the body had been discovered fairly quickly. That was a small blessing.

DeRicci backed out of the doorway into the street. She hoped she hadn't gone in far enough for the stench to stick to her clothing. Nyquist closed the door behind her. She was grateful. That smell would travel otherwise.

The rookies stood on either side of her car, watching the roads. Several more officers guarded the perimeter, keeping the media and the gawkers back.

DeRicci had to come down here and see for herself what all the fuss was about. She wasn't sure what she hoped to find.

The owners of the building—a disappearance company—hadn't been allowed inside even though they were protesting, claiming they had a right to see what had been done to their office. They had been the ones who had gone to the media, complaining that their lives might be in danger from the Disty, and they couldn't even dig into their records to find out.

DeRicci agreed with Nyquist's decision to keep the owners out. She doubted this killing had much to do with the disappearance company. From everything she had seen, this vengeance killing was legal and justified.

The victim, Aisha Costard, had countless outstanding Disty warrants. She had gone to Mars, gotten herself involved in some kind of highly offensive murder, and then had come to the Moon.

Based on the location of the body, Nyquist had guessed that Costard had been trying to disappear. DeRicci agreed with that assessment.

The vengeance killing served as a dual warning: the first to anyone who was involved with Costard or the murder that had sent her fleeing here, and the second to disappearance companies for helping people charged with Disty crimes escape punishment.

The media had contacted DeRicci's office because Costard had gotten into Armstrong relatively easily. From what DeRicci had seen in the logs about the Costard case, Costard had been treated precisely the way anyone else with similar red flags would have been treated. She had been sequestered in customs for days and then released once the Disty were contacted. The Disty had confirmed that Costard was on a mission to clear her name, and was allowed a limited travel visa to meet with detectives and Retrieval Artists.

The warrants said nothing about Disappearance Services.

But it wasn't the security issues that had DeRicci intrigued. It was the hints that this wasn't a Disty killing at all.

DeRicci would have thought this killing completely Disty if she hadn't worked several vengeance killings. First, the location: Disty in this neighborhood, so close the old bomb site and near a Disappearance Service, would have been noticed.

Disty with a human woman would definitely have been noticed.

Second, early reports indicated that Costard hadn't been
seen with any Disty since she had arrived in Armstrong. The
records from her hotel showed her in the company of a few
humans, but no aliens at all.

Third and most important, many of the Disappearance Services had alarms that went off whenever aliens were in the
vicinity. Most of the alarms were sophisticated: They didn't
just set off a warning at police headquarters (or some other
designated place), they also brought down small cells that imprisoned the aliens, or the alarms activated locks and clamps
that made the office impossible to enter.

None of that had happened here.

Small things but important ones, especially for a
vengeance killing. Vengeance killings were usually for show,
designed to act as warnings for others who had violated or
thought of violating Disty law.

This almost felt too secretive. In the wrong location, no
Disty spotted nearby, and no immediate Disty claims of responsibility.

Something was wrong here, but it wasn't what the media
thought. There were thousands of people like Costard in
Armstrong, but Costard's death was a new twist, something
DeRicci didn't like.

Nyquist had stood silently, waiting for DeRicci to speak
first. She had liked him from the moment she met him. He
was broad shouldered and dark skinned, his thinning hair
bluish-black. He obviously didn't go for cosmetic enhancements, although she wondered if his muscular frame came
through artificial means as well as hard work.

"How many vengeance killings have you worked?" she
asked.

He shrugged. "Maybe a dozen, maybe a few more."

"Tell me about this one."

He glanced at the closed door, then over at the rookies
who still stood near DeRicci's car. They were street officers.
DeRicci would talk to them later and find out who had dis-

covered the body, if the owners of the business hadn't been the ones.

"It's not a vengeance killing," he said. "I'd stake my entire career on it."

"Why?" she asked.

"Details," he said. "You didn't go all the way in."

He looked pointedly at her shoes, which she had covered with borrowed evidence-collection bags. Then he let his gaze rise up her clothing until his look reached her face.

He obviously understood why she hadn't stepped into the gore.

"No, I didn't," she said, careful not to sound defensive.

"The Disty are precise. If they hang an entrail on the wall, it's a certain distance from the floor. The next piece hanging alongside is a slightly different distance. There's a pattern to the whole thing."

"As well as a pattern to the hanging," DeRicci said. So that was what bothered her. The pattern looked off.

"There is no pattern here," he said. "It's as if someone described a vengeance killing to a person who had never seen one, and that person tried to imitate it."

"You're sure of this?" DeRicci asked.

"If you doubt me, go look at the sides of the original incision. Whoever it was didn't use a Disty blade. This thing had ridges. The wound's edges are jagged."

DeRicci didn't like the implications of this. "Has everything about Costard gone to the media?"

"Everything we know at the moment, which isn't a lot," he said. "I haven't had time to do much more than call for backup, establish perimeters, and examine the crime scene."

"Where's your partner?" DeRicci asked.

"I'm between partners." His tone carried a familiar bitterness. DeRicci had often used that tone herself, when she was between partners. "I caught this case on the way home."

She nodded. "Have you contacted the Disty?"

"I sent word to headquarters," he said. "They've got some specialist now who contacts alien groups. I'm told not to expect too much. There's some kind of crisis on Mars. I haven't seen the feeds, but I guess it's got all the diplomats and Disty experts in some kind of tizzy."

"Great," DeRicci muttered.

"Honestly," he said, "I didn't expect you here. You missing the old detective work?"

She was missing it, more now that she was at the crime scene. She certainly enjoyed this kind of work more than position papers and incredibly optimistic resumes.

"The media is hounding me on this," she said. "I thought I'd come see the scene for myself."

"Hounding you?" He seemed surprised. "Why?"

"They seem to believe that Costard was a criminal who was a threat to the Dome."

His eyebrows went up, giving his entire face a comical look. "Aisha Costard? She's a well-respected crime scene analyst who specializes in human bones. Didn't you look her up?"

"I looked up the media reports and came right down here," DeRicci said. "I figured I needed some information about the vengeance killing before I looked at the victim."

"I don't get it," he said. "Why would they think she's a criminal?"

"The warrant from the Disty. Technically, she is a criminal."

"Technically," he said. "All she did was consult on some long-ago murder. It caused some kind of foo-fah that I haven't had time to look into. But she went to Mars to do it, and somehow angered the Disty. But they're the ones who let her come here."

"I saw that," DeRicci said. "This isn't making sense."

"Well, it would have made sense if this were a true vengeance killing," Nyquist said. "They let her here on a short leash, she tried to disappear, they're sending a signal to the others involved in the case back at Sahara Dome not to do this. Plus they'd done her a favor and she was screwing with it."

"Do you think she actually tried to disappear?"

He shrugged again. "Your guess is as good as mine right

now. We don't have evidence of much. All we have is an incident that would have made sense if it had been committed by the people who had the legal right to dish out the punishment. But this isn't Disty. No Disty would make the errors I saw in there. This is something else."

"Which makes it a crime," DeRicci said. "Where it wouldn't have been otherwise."

"You got it," Nyquist said.

"This has nothing to do with Moon Security." DeRicci couldn't keep the disappointment from her voice.

"I wish it did," Nyquist said. "You're the first person I've talked to in months whom I haven't had to explain each and every little thing to."

"I noticed that before I left the force," she said. "They're getting dumber, aren't they?"

"And less trusting," he said. "They simply don't believe that I have experiences that are of value."

"I don't miss that." But she missed the rest of it.

"You want to consult?" he asked.

She looked at him. "People are going to wonder. The media will follow my every step."

"But they're already on this case," he said. "So why not? I can use someone intelligent to bounce theories off of."

She grinned. "I'll do anything for a man who recognizes that I'm smart."

"Any man who doesn't," Nyquist said with an answering grin, "isn't smart himself."

27

Iona Gennefort stood in the control room high above the northern entrance to the Dome. Wells City had once been Mars' premiere destination, named for an Earthman who had popularized Mars in the human imagination. Wells had been as human as human could be.

Then the Disty took over.

They changed everything—the architecture, the street layouts—everything except the dome itself.

Gennefort wrapped a sweater around her shoulders and stared at the various monitors. Across her vision, warnings ran from a dozen different agencies. Around the periphery of her left eye's vision, she had five tiny images going, monitoring the crisis in the other cities closest to Sahara Dome.

The news reports were circumspect, the tone dire. Humans didn't want to offend the Disty, even now.

But the Disty were fleeing Sahara Dome in droves, and when she had contacted the head of the Disty government here in Wells, no one had responded. Finally, she reached a good friend, a male Disty whom she had known since childhood.

It's a mess, he said. *Our ambassadors are trying to contact the Alliance government. We need an immediate meeting. No one can talk to you.*

They have to, she said. *The bullet trains will arrive here within fifteen minutes. I need to know what to do with the passengers.*

He told her he would get back to her.

He never did. Instead, she found herself talking to the entire Disty Council. All fifteen of them were yelling at her in both Disty and English, reminding her that she had an obligation to them.

I don't know what the obligation is in this case, she had said.

Don't let them in! the Disty screamed. *They're tainted.*

But the trains, she said, *they have to go through the Dome.*

They had to go through the Dome. No tracks skirted the city.

The control room was in the center of the tracks and had a 360-degree view. The city was behind her, in Dome Twilight, and half a dozen tracks extended in front of her before the Dome wall ended and the Martian outdoors began.

On her right and left were the tracks, heading north and south, taking people away from her little universe.

Or bringing them into it.

She stood with two engineers and the Wells head of the train station. He kept telling her how many minutes she had left to make a decision, if she wanted to stop the trains.

The last number he had muttered was eight.

Eight whole minutes to decide some kind of future, one she didn't entirely understand.

Her right eye was the only one without extra images running across her line of sight. She concentrated on the equipment, the screens on the surfaces showing dozens of trains catapulting toward Wells. Dozens, on tracks not built to hold that many.

How unfortunate that this crisis had started in Sahara Dome, where so many of the train lines originated. Sahara Dome, the stop before Wells.

"Seven minutes," the train station head said. She hadn't been able to think of any of these men by name ever since she arrived here. That was one piece of information too many.

"How long can we keep the trains stopped outside the Dome?" she asked.

"And keep all the passengers alive? A few days, maybe," one of the engineers said.

"If they don't jump out," said the other. He claimed Disty who couldn't board the trains in Sahara Dome clung to the trains' exteriors as the trains hurtled out of the city, dying when the trains got outside the Dome.

"A few days," Gennefort repeated.

She was trying to accommodate the Disty inside her city, she really was. But she had no idea what she was facing—what caused the outflow, why the Disty here were so uncommunicative, and what would happen to her if she made the wrong decision.

Oddly, she was less afraid of the Disty than she was of the Alliance. She was a lesser official. She wasn't supposed to make decisions about Disty lives. The Disty ruled here; she didn't.

She could only think of one solution that accommodated the Disty and allowed the trains to continue moving south. "How long to build a track around Wells?"

"A track? You're kidding, right?" the station head said.

"No," she said.

"Even if we had the workers, which we don't—we have to import laborers and robots and supervisors—even if we had them, it would take a month minimum. The terrain out there is difficult. Add the dust storms and the rocks, and the fragility of this dome, and we're probably talking six months, maybe more."

Six months.

Her choices had narrowed. Do nothing and let this unfold as it may. Stop the trains between cities and let someone else handle the problem. Or let the trains through.

"Can these trains go through Wells without stopping?" She knew it hadn't been done in her lifetime. Wells had fought for the position of permanent stop on the bullet train route. Sometimes, she believed, that permanent stop order was the only thing that kept the city alive.

"They can," the station head said, "but it's not done."

"Why?" Gennefort asked.

"If something goes wrong, we'll have a major catastrophe on our hands."

"We already do," she said. "We can't accommodate any more Disty in this Dome. We can barely handle our own population. And once one train stops, they'll all want to. How many Disty are there in Sahara Dome, anyway?"

"None, according to some news reports," one of the engineers said. "At least none that aren't trying to leave."

"A lot more than we have here. Maybe ten times our Disty population," said the other engineer.

"My God," she said. Why weren't the local Disty handling this? Why had they left it to her?

She sent another urgent message through her links, only to get the same automated reply she'd been getting since the crisis began. The Disty were in a meeting and could not be disturbed.

"You have five minutes," the station head said. "Maybe less."

She gave him a look that she knew was filled with fear. Then she took a deep breath. One decision was better than no decision.

"Let the trains through," she said. "Don't let them stop."

"If they pile up . . ." the station head started.

"We'll have fewer deaths than we would if we strand the trains outside the Dome," Gennefort said.

"I don't see how you figure," the station head said.

"These trains aren't programmed for that kind of backlog. We have no idea how many more are coming, and from what I can tell, the Disty aren't acting rationally. Accidents outside the Dome will automatically kill those involved. They at least have a chance of surviving inside the Dome."

The nearest engineer shook his head.

"Besides," Gennefort said, "the safest action is to let the Disty through. Maybe by the time the trains reach Bakhuysen, the Disty there will have made a decision to stop this crisis, whatever it is."

"I hope so," the station head said. Then he looked at the engineers. "I'll send the messages to the floor, but you open the dome portals. Let the trains through and make sure none of them stop."

"Make sure none of them hit each other," one of the engineers muttered.

"Like that'll happen," another said.

"Give me a better idea," Gennefort snapped. "One that'll save lives."

No one answered her.

She folded her hands together and took a deep breath. "Let's do this thing."

28

About two hours after ordering his second coffee and sandwich, Flint moved to another table with a different screen and started using a different stolen identification. The law school cafeteria was filling up with students, most of whom seemed very intent on getting their food and finishing whatever project they were working on. A group of humans sat two tables over, arguing about the origins of the Multicultural Tribunals. Flint tried to tune out the argument, but at least two of the students were witty; he found himself smiling more than he thought possible when doing this kind of grunt work.

And grunt work this was. Corporate records, corporate finances, corporate regulations made his eyes cross. He was about to give up and move to a different line of research when he finally found what he was looking for.

A company that subcontracted to one of the subcorporations of Gale Research and Development had a single employee, a woman named Mary Sue Jørgen Meister. On most of the corporate records, she was listed as M. S. J. Meister, but on one he found her full name.

It hadn't shown up in his initial search because the company was so small that it was buried in the records. Still, Mary Sue Jørgen Meister made Gale Research and Development two hundred thousand credits in the space of a month.

She had acquired water rights for a small tributary in an Outlying Colony. She sold those rights to a subsidiary of Gale

Research and Development, who then sold those rights to Gale, who then transferred the rights to BiMela. Who then resold those rights to another corporation (not affiliated) for two hundred thousand more than Gale had originally paid for them.

Flint followed the lead all the way down to the tributary itself, which, it turned out, didn't exist. The tributary had dried up decades before, shortly after that nation in the Outlying Colonies settled a city upriver, but for some reason, mapmakers kept the tributary on the map. The owners of the land didn't mind selling the water rights for cheap, even though there was currently no water. They assumed that water would come back at some point, ignoring the dams that had been installed farther upstream.

But the hydropower corporation that had bought the rights from BiMela claimed fraud. BiMela claimed ignorance, and went all the way back down the chain, suing the company that M. S. J. Meister had founded. A company that had disbanded in the years it took the hydropower corporation to realize it had bought the rights to a nonexistent stream.

M. S. J. Meister had vanished as well. But Flint had names to work with: Mary Sue and Meister. He found various spellings and more scams, some connected to BiMela, some not.

Mary Sue had her fingerprints all over BiMela's corporate entity, but Meister didn't. That name ended with the hydropower case.

But the name began long before that.

A flashing red light caught Flint's attention. This table warned him with an obnoxious flashing sign that his free privileges were about to be suspended. He opened the food menu, ordered more coffee than he needed, and a plate of spaghetti that he probably wouldn't eat.

The law students behind him were still arguing. Another human had joined the Peyti across the room and was worrying about an interdome law exam. A handful of Dhyos pressed their long fingers together at still a third table, obviously arguing as well.

A tray piled with cake floated by. Another followed, this time with an entire pot of coffee, a new mug, and a plate of spaghetti covered with a sauce that was too orange.

Flint took the items, tasted the sauce, winced at its sour flavor, and went back to work.

Before Meister appeared in the corporate records, she had run individual scams all over the Outlying Colonies. Reading her history was like reading the development of a con artist. Flint would find variations of her name all over the news reports and records, mostly after she had left an area. Because the scams were small, the news rarely made it to the various nations inside the Outlying Colonies. Instead, the news was local and vanished as quickly as Meister did.

Over time, her cons got larger and more effective. She seemed to be gaining an understanding of the various legal systems and how much they confused the average human in the Alliance. No one knew, outside their own area, what was legal and what wasn't.

She took advantage of that.

The scheme that backfired on her and brought her to the attention of all the Outlying Colonies was her first large scam. She had targeted a group of families, most of whom had come to the colonies after surviving a hideous massacre on Mars.

Meister told the survivors that the Alliance owed them reparations for the illegal (and horrifying) deaths of their family members. She cited some case law that did in fact exist, which referred to compensation owed crime victims.

Unfortunately, that case law only applied to crimes committed on Earth. She had left that part out of her scheme.

Instead, she had told the survivors and their descendents that they were entitled to a lot of money. If they hired her as their legal counsel (at a significant cost per family), she would shepherd the case through the various courts.

She managed to collect a year's worth of fees from nearly a hundred families before someone looked up the case law for himself. The families confronted her, she made up some kind of fake story about the law being different now and she would get them the information, and then, that night, she fled the Outlying Colonies—with all of the survivors' money.

The news stories ran for nearly another year while the survivors searched for her. Reporters did human-interest stories on the financial burden she had placed on already overtaxed families. Some families lost everything because of her scam. Some family members lost jobs because of the time the members took to work on the case. A few of the older survivors died—a couple of them suicides, the rest because they could no longer afford the very basics of care.

Everyone else vowed revenge on Meister. And some of the younger members of the most devastated families promised they wouldn't quit looking for her until she was dead.

Flint leaned back in his chair and templed his fingers. Mars. Lagrima Jørgen, a.k.a. Mary Sue Jørgen Meister had been found on Mars, the victim of a murder complete with some kind of corpse mutilation. That showed extreme anger.

The kind of anger people who lost everything might display.

He had a hunch he found the incident that eventually got Jørgen Meister killed. But he still wasn't close to finding her family or helping the other contaminated people in Sahara Dome.

He let his hands fall to the tabletop. He wondered if Costard had disappeared yet. She hadn't really wanted to disappear anyway, and he was solving this faster than he expected. All it would take was a bit more work, and he would know if he could provide the humans in Sahara Dome with the names they needed to decontaminate their area.

Flint leaned forward, shut down the tabletop system, and then stood. He would go to Costard first, and if she had already left, then he would contact Sahara Dome himself.

For the first time in days, he felt like he actually had something positive to report.

29

Hauk Rackam, the incoming leader of the Human Governments of Mars, paced in his large office. Three advisors sat on straight-backed chairs, watching him as if he were some kind of new alien species.

He was terrified.

He stopped at the edge of his thousand-year-old Turkish carpet and whirled, his ceremonial robe flaring slightly.

"I don't have any real powers," he said. "I can't legally do anything."

"Sir." Wyome Nakamura stood. She was slight, her dark hair covering her like a gown. "I think we have to worry about legalities later."

She could worry about legalities later. It wasn't her neck on the line. She could always deny involvement: *Of course I gave him advice, but we all did. In the end, he was the one who had to take it.*

"You'll be the head of the Human Government next week," she said. "I don't think it matters much."

"According to the Disty Accords, it does," he snapped. "They'll only work with the actual head of government."

"Who happens to be in Sahara Dome," Nakamura said, "which makes him contaminated and unable to have contact with the Disty."

Of course, there was no second in command because the position really wasn't that important. The head of the Human

Governments was mostly ceremonial. Usually the main administrative duty was to inform all of the human mayors of the Domes about decisions the Disty had made or changes in human-Disty relationships. Nothing much. No negotiation. No difficult decisions. Just meals and hand waving and the occasional ceremonial summit.

Rackam had been looking forward to the state dinners and interstellar travel, all representing a not-very-united group of humans on a planet they didn't really control. He had expected two years of ceremonial acts that would only increase his visibility and make him a little more famous.

He liked the actual office itself. He'd used government funds to decorate it, down to the faintly citrus scent running through the environmental controls.

He hadn't expected anything like this.

"Sir," said Thomas Kim. Kim was a fusty little man, anal and precise. "I'm getting reports of hundreds dead."

Rackam had asked his assistants to monitor the news channels as well as any messages that came for him. He shut off all but a single link—his emergency family node. He needed to be able to think.

"Disty dead, I trust," he said.

Kim nodded. "In Sahara Dome, outside Sahara Dome, and now, they think, in Wells."

"Wells?" Rackam hadn't expected that. The trains had gone through Wells. The crisis was isolated, wasn't it? Half an hour ago, all the human heads of the Domes wanted to know was what to do with any incoming Disty. "Why have Disty died in Wells?"

Kim shook his head. "No one knows, sir."

Rackam wasn't a decision maker. That was the real problem. He needed someone who was, someone with the intelligence to handle widespread problems. When he'd gotten enhancements, he had focused on looks and charisma, not intelligence.

"We're still getting no response from the Disty," said Zayna Columbus. She was heavyset, oblivious to appearance and charisma, and the only one on his staff with real brains.

Rackam looked at her, but she didn't look at him. Her gaze was fixed on one of the screens, her mind clearly far away. He wondered how many images she had running across her vision, and decided he didn't want to know.

"All of the Disty or just the High Command?" he asked, trying not to let the panic into his voice.

"I've been trying every organization I can think of," she said, finally turning toward him. Her pupils were a kaleidoscope of colors, reflecting the various chips and implants she'd had installed.

"Even the Death Squads?" Kim asked.

She narrowed those strange eyes at him. "We can't go directly to the Death Squads. We have enough contamination issues as it is."

"Well, find someone who can," Rackam said. "We're in trouble here."

"Yes," Columbus said, "we are."

She glanced at Nakamura. The two women seemed to understand each other. But he wasn't understanding them.

"*I* have no power," he said. "I can't make any decisions. We need a meeting of the Dual Governments. The Disty have to tell us what to do."

"The Disty," Nakamura said as if she were speaking to a particularly dumb child, "are unavailable. What Disty we do see on our links—which you seem to be avoiding—are in such a panic that they don't seem to be thinking logically."

"There is a crisis, and someone has to solve it," Columbus said.

"Not me," Rackam said.

Kim stood up. His mouth was set in a thin line. "We'll figure out what to do and you'll do it. Agreed?"

Rackam wasn't sure he could agree. He didn't have the authority. Was he the only person in the room who understood that? He didn't have any authority at all.

"You're going to close the Domes to all bullet trains," Columbus said. "You're going to isolate those trains outside all of the Domes, and you're going to enforce this, with security teams if necessary."

The breath left Rackam's body. "We can't attack Disty."

"We're going to say we're protecting Disty," Columbus said. Everyone in the room was watching her. "Either there's some kind of virus going through that affects their mind, or some kind of group hysteria. Wells caught it after the bullet trains went through. The trains didn't even stop. So no Sahara Dome and Wells Disty can get into other Domes. Is that clear?"

No one had used that tone with him in nearly a decade. He bristled. "They'll shun me, or worse. They'll prosecute me, especially if somebody dies. This decision won't work."

Her expression, which had been flat, didn't change. "You'll stop the trains, and if the Disty question you, you'll tell them you were only holding the trains until someone from the Disty High Command got back to you and told you what to do. You could only act on the evidence before you, and the evidence was that something bad was happening to the Disty. You were only concerned for their lives."

"They won't believe that," he said. "They'll know it's not true."

"Stop worrying about them," Kim said. "We have to do something. Do you understand how this will cascade if we don't?"

Rackam was breathing shallowly. Cascade? What did they mean, cascade?

"No," he whispered.

Nakamura sighed. Columbus shook her head in disgust. Had they always thought of him this way? Had their respect been feigned?

He felt his cheeks heat.

Kim crossed his arms. "All the Disty from Sahara Dome will spread down southward. Now add the Disty from Wells. They won't go directly south. Some will go east, others west. None will go north because there isn't much beyond Sahara Dome. So let's assume this is a crazy-making virus. The large group of Disty will get into another Dome, then its Disty will start to flee. The Disty will keep infecting the Domes and moving until the entire planet is filled with Disty running from something none of us understand. They'll run out of places to go."

Rackam bit his upper lip. "But close the Domes . . ."

"Yes," Nakamura said. "It's our only choice."

"You should think of closing the ports as well," Columbus said. "The Disty need to stay on Mars until we know what's causing this."

Rackam shook his head. He had finally understood what his team was talking about, and he understood the implications.

"I won't close the ports," he said, "but I'll close the Domes to any on-world travel. Right now, all the Domes will be isolated *until we hear from the Disty.* Which better be damn soon."

He whirled again, feeling his robe swirl around him.

He could see the team reflected in the windows. He shook a hand at them.

"Go on. Begone. Get out of here. Get this done. And don't bother me until you hear from a Disty."

He could see the three of them glance at each other. Then they shrugged and left the room. Someone slammed the door.

Rackam sank into his favorite cushion, then placed his face in his hands. He had just ruined his own life. The Disty would never forgive him for this.

He would have to find a way to blame the advisors. Maybe he would find a way to modify the records, or take himself out of the discussion altogether.

I'm firing them, he would say to the Disty High Council. *They seemed to believe someone had to act, so they did. Without my permission. Maybe we can bring criminal charges against them for all the deaths. Would that satisfy you?*

Because it wasn't satisfying him.

All he'd signed on for was a ceremonial position.

He couldn't handle decisions that resulted in life or death. Particularly his own.

30

Flint stood in the lobby of the Domeview Hotel. A different woman paced behind the long desk; otherwise, the lobby was empty. Flint had his back to her as he used the automated network to contact Aisha Costard.

Like before, he couldn't find her listed on any of the internal servers. Unlike before, she didn't answer his page. If she had left within the last few days, the system should have shown her as checked out.

It didn't show her at all.

He wasn't quite sure what to do. He might have to ask for human help.

As he turned toward the woman at the desk, movement caught his eye. Two men in security uniforms headed straight toward him.

Flint tensed.

The men stopped in front of him. Both were larger than he was, and at least one had enhanced muscles. But Flint could outmaneuver them if he had to.

"Excuse me, sir," said the man with enhanced muscles. He had dark hair and even darker eyes. "You'll have to come with us."

"Did I do something wrong?" Flint asked.

"We're under orders to take you with us," said the man.

Flint stepped back so they weren't quite as close to him. "Are you police officers?"

"No, sir," said the guard.

"Then you have no right to take me anywhere. I walked into the hotel, looked up a patron's name, didn't find it, and was about to leave. That wasn't a crime the last time I checked."

They glared at him. How many hotel patrons didn't know their rights under Armstrong law? Probably most of them, just like Flint wouldn't have known what to do or how to behave in some of the alien cultures he'd heard about.

"I'm a former police officer," he said into the security guards' silence. "You can either tell me what's going on or let me leave."

The second guard glanced at his partner. The spokesman stepped just slightly in front of Flint.

"We've been asked to take you upstairs," the guard said.

"By whom?" Flint asked.

"The police."

That surprised Flint, but he didn't let it show. "Really? Why?"

"Apparently, you accessed a name involved in an ongoing investigation."

Now this was beginning to make sense. And the detective in charge was alone or with his partner, so that he had no one to send down to the first floor to get Flint. Instead, he let these amateurs handle it.

"Well, then," Flint said. "Bring the detective in charge down here."

"We can't do that," said the other guard, his voice rising with shock.

Flint shrugged. "And I can't go with you. I don't trust you. So I'm going to leave the hotel."

"Sir." The first man blocked his path. "If I send for the detective and have him contact you, will you go upstairs?"

"If he has a legitimate City of Armstrong identification code," Flint said.

The security guards glanced at each other. These two were so incompetent they obviously hadn't even checked that themselves. The first man kept his position in front of Flint, but looked down as he spoke under his breath into his own internal links system. An older, less expensive system that didn't have thought filtering. That didn't surprise Flint.

Security guards were poorly paid and had little job security. They couldn't afford their own upgrades, and the hotel wouldn't supply them—too many guards quit after getting better links.

After a moment, the guard nodded. "He'll contact you."

As the guard said that, a message ran beneath Flint's vision. It was a summons to Costard's room from a Detective Bartholomew Nyquist. The summons carried Costard's room number. Nyquist's City of Armstrong identification code wrapped through the message, almost like a taunt.

Flint sent that he'd be there in a moment, then shut down many of his own links. Nyquist had obviously gotten Flint's name and identification, as well as his link code, from the fingerprints he'd left on the screen.

Flint pushed past the guards. He took the stairs, hurrying so that the guards would have to work to keep up with him. Despite the enhanced muscles, the first guard wasn't in the best of shape.

As Flint climbed the unremarkable concrete stairs, he worried about the Armstrong Police's involvement. Had Costard done something wrong? Had the Disty rescinded her special pass to be in Armstrong in the first place?

The guards still hadn't caught up with Flint when he reached the door that opened onto Costard's floor. As Flint stepped into the hallway, he saw another open door at the other end, with a warning barrier sealing it off.

A warning barrier, made up of thin motion-detecting equipment and red light beams, letting anyone who tried to pass know that their presence was being monitored and would probably be recorded.

Something bad had happened.

Flint walked down the hall. No one stood guard outside the room, so his initial hunch had been correct. Nyquist was here alone.

The guards reached the floor just as Flint stopped outside

Costard's door. The room was smaller than he expected, and he didn't see anyone inside.

"Detective Nyquist?" Flint said to the empty room. "May I enter?"

Nyquist came out of the bathroom. He was square, with broad shoulders and a trim frame. He was shorter than Flint and probably older. His bluish-black hair was thinning on top, and he had real wrinkles in the corners of his eyes.

"Funny we never met," Nyquist said. "You hear how big the Armstrong P.D. is, but you never quite realize it, not until you run into someone who worked in the same department you did at the exact same time, and not only have you never met him, you've never heard of him."

Which pretty much summed up Flint's reaction to Nyquist as well.

"I've been off the force for a few years now," Flint said, determined not to establish a rapport.

"Yeah, well, I've been on it too long." Nyquist beckoned with his right hand, as if the room had been rented to him instead of Aisha Costard. "Come on in."

The lights went off for a moment, and Flint stepped inside the room. The room smelled of dust and cleanser, as if no one had been inside for quite a while. The bed was made. A familiar bag sat on the suitcase stand. Costard had brought that bag to Flint's office on that first day.

On one wall, a waterfall cascaded down some rocks. The sound had been muted, but otherwise the scene looked real enough. Flint wondered if Costard had set that program or if it was standard in the hotel.

The security guards arrived just then, and stopped.

"Thanks, guys," Nyquist said. "I think I've got it from here."

The guards glanced at each other, then shrugged. They left.

"Where's your partner?" Flint asked.

"I'm between partners." Nyquist's voice had a familiar tone. It took Flint a moment to identify that tone. It was a bitterness that reminded Flint of DeRicci.

"Yet they gave this case to you," Flint said.

"Lucky me." Nyquist shoved his hands in the pockets of his pants. He leaned forward ever so slightly as he paced around the small room.

"You gonna tell me where Aisha Costard is?" Flint asked.

"You gonna tell me you haven't linked up all day?" Nyquist asked.

Flint's stomach twisted. "I don't always follow the news," he said, taking a guess at what Nyquist meant.

"Must be the luxury of the unemployed," Nyquist said.

"Self-employed." Flint let himself step into that. He recognized Nyquist's technique—a little brash, a little tough, a little blunt. DeRicci liked that method as well.

"Right. You Retrieval Artists get to pick and choose your jobs. Lucky you."

Flint didn't respond to that. He clasped his hands behind his back so that he wouldn't touch anything. "Where's Ms. Costard?"

"Strange thing," Nyquist said. "Disty vengeance killing in a Disappearance Services office, if you can believe that."

Flint didn't move. He knew his expression hadn't changed because he had practiced keeping a straight face long ago. But the surprise had nearly knocked him over. He had to concentrate on the conversation. If he let himself feel anything, he would reveal too much to Nyquist.

"When?" Flint asked.

Nyquist shrugged. His shrugs were elegant. The one he'd used earlier had been larger than this one; this one was a slight movement that said timing was less important than the event.

"A day or so ago."

"Has departmental policy changed?" Flint asked. "I thought vengeance killings are open and shut."

"Usually," Nyquist said. "We have to confirm the Disty's involvement with the target and all that. You have anything to add on that?"

Flint wasn't sure how much he wanted to say. Technically, Costard wasn't a client any longer, but Flint didn't like to give away any information. Yet here he was, in her hotel, trying to locate her.

"Shouldn't be hard," Flint said, taking a gamble, "considering she'd just come in from Mars."

"So you do know her," Nyquist said.

"We met briefly."

"Did she hire you?" Nyquist asked.

"For what?"

Nyquist blinked. Maybe no one had ever questioned one of his questions before—and in the same tone, too.

"I don't know," Nyquist said. "To do whatever it is you people do."

For the first time, his banter seemed a little forced. Flint had thrown him off his rhythm.

"Retrieval Artists find Disappeareds," he said. "We're not Trackers. We don't always bring the Disappeared to face justice—if I can use that term for what passes for the law in some places."

Nyquist stopped pacing and looked at him sideways. "That's right. You people don't believe in the law."

"If that were the case," Flint said, "I'd never have joined the police force."

"But you left."

Flint nodded.

"Richer than when you arrived."

So Nyquist had done more than a cursory background check. That was interesting. Had he been surprised by Flint's appearance, or had he already marked Flint on his witness list?

"Actually, no," Flint said. "I made the money after I left the force."

Hours after, but after nonetheless.

"Always heard rumors about that," Nyquist said, contradicting his original banter about not even hearing of Flint. That didn't surprise Flint either. "Always heard you'd done something illegal. Decided the money was better than following the law."

"People always say things like that about Retrieval Artists," Flint said. "We're not very well liked."

Nyquist smiled sideways again. "Ever wonder why?"

"Nope. I understand it completely." Flint looked at the waterfall. The loop varied. Sometimes the water splashed and the droplets shone in the light. Sometimes the splashes were smaller and didn't reflect anything.

"This is really an interesting case," Nyquist said. "I have a woman who is considered a felon by the Disty, yet they let her come to the Moon on business. She dies in a Disappearance Service office, and the only person she has contact with, besides the hotel staff, is a Retrieval Artist."

Flint said nothing.

"I mean, she should know that the service isn't going to tell her if they disappeared a friend of hers, right?" Nyquist looked at the waterfall as if it could answer his question.

When Flint still said nothing, Nyquist turned. The technique was effective but familiar. Flint knew how this game was played. If Nyquist wanted to unsettle Flint, he was going about it wrong.

"If I understand how these things work," Nyquist said, "she wouldn't have gone to the Disappearance Service to ask questions on her own unless you turned her job down. But if you turned her down, what are you doing here?"

Flint could suggest reasons. They might have been friends in a previous life, coworkers, or maybe she was the Disappeared herself. But he said nothing. He wanted to hear Nyquist's theories.

"Then we have the Disty vengeance killing in the front office of the Disappearance Service. The Disty like to send messages. If I miss my guess, that message would be that people who try to disappear—or disappear and get caught—deserve this fate. Isn't that what you would think?"

"I haven't seen the crime scene," Flint said.

"Dismantled," Nyquist said. "The techs have been through it, the body's going through processing, we're investigating whether or not there's next of kin. Do you know if there is?"

Such a humane question, and one that most people would answer. But Flint resumed his policy of silence.

Nyquist raised his eyebrows and smiled again, only this

time the smile was real. "You know, I noted in your files that you used to be Noelle DeRicci's partner."

"She's a good woman," Flint said.

"She is." Nyquist glanced at the bag, sitting forlornly on its stand, as if to say that Costard had been a good woman too. "Yet I noticed that on one of Noelle's recent cases, you refused to work with her too. You were even a suspect in that case."

Cleared suspect. Flint knew that much. And he knew better than to be defensive.

"You'd think you'd work with your ex-partner."

"You'd think," Flint said.

"And yet . . ." Nyquist shook his head. "Were you always this uncooperative, or is that part of your new job too?"

Time to take some control of the interview. "You wanted me up here," Flint said. "You've told me that Aisha Costard is dead, something that I'm very sorry to hear. But I'm not going to dance anymore. I met her, I talked with her, I was coming to see her, and that's all you need to know."

Nyquist's playful smile faded. "I'll decide what I need to know. Why were you coming to see her?"

"I had a question for her," Flint said.

"And it was?"

"Personal," Flint said. "And, unfortunately, now it's unanswerable."

"Maybe we can help."

"The police don't help Retrieval Artists," Flint said. "Try that technique on someone a little more naïve."

"You should be more polite," Nyquist said. "You might be a suspect, you know."

"In a Disty vengeance killing? I don't think so," Flint said. "Unless it's not a vengeance killing."

"I didn't say that." Nyquist turned away.

"Yet you're investigating."

"You know the routine. Confirm before closing the case."

"Are you that unimportant in the department?" Flint asked. "Seems to me that a seasoned investigator wouldn't get perfunctory cases."

Nyquist's spine stiffened ever so slightly. Finally, Flint scored against him.

"There're a few questions about the case," Nyquist said.

"The Disappearance Service?" Flint asked.

"The sloppiness."

Flint couldn't tell if Nyquist inadvertently let that information out or if he intended it.

"The Disty aren't sloppy," Flint said. "It's a ritual."

"You see, that's my theory," Nyquist said. "But Andrea Gumiela—you remember her, right? The head of the detectives?—she seems to believe that some Disty here on the Moon don't get the same training as their Martian cousins. So she thinks they might have just been careless."

"I've never seen it," Flint said, deciding he could say that much.

"Me either. Which makes me wonder why someone would fake a vengeance killing. Got a theory?"

Flint sighed. He had a theory, but it required him to get involved. Still, he wasn't sure how much of Costard's recent history was public record. He didn't want to reveal too much, but he did want Nyquist, who seemed savvy enough, out of his way.

"If I were you," Flint said, "I'd see what Costard did to make the Disty angry in the first place. Maybe you'll find your answer there."

Nyquist peered at him. "You think so?"

It was Flint's turn to shrug. He made it a casual little shrug, as eloquent as Nyquist's were.

"I have no idea," Flint said. "Glad it's not my case."

He turned around and stopped by the lights that still flashed in front of the door.

"You know," Nyquist said to his back, "you don't seem overly concerned that she's dead."

"I'm sorry that she's dead," Flint said. "She was a nice woman."

"But?" Nyquist was still fishing.

Flint was going to end it.

"But I only met her a few days ago and only for a short

time. It's sad, I'm sorry, but I didn't know her well enough to grieve."

Nyquist didn't answer for a moment. Flint didn't turn around, nor did he ask for the warning light to go out.

"You're right," Nyquist finally said. "It is sad. I'm beginning to think no one knew her well enough to grieve."

Then the warning lights in front of Flint blinked off. He stepped through the doorway and into the hall.

"I may have more questions," Nyquist said to Flint's back.

"I doubt I'll have more answers," Flint said as he walked away.

31

The situation in Sahara Dome was getting worse.

Scott-Olson had returned to her lab. She saw no point in staying in the conference, watching the disaster unfold. She could see it a variety of ways—on a wall screen, through her links, or on one of the screens mounted on her main desk.

She kept the wall screen on—she had to stay informed; information had suddenly become a lifeline to her—but she shut down the news portion of her links. Having the information come through the links made it too personal. She didn't want to think about the disaster that was befalling the city in which she had spent most of her life.

The lab wasn't making her much calmer. Six of the mummified bodies were in her cooler. The skeleton of Lagrima Jørgen had its own table, the orange bones glowing in the lab's bright light.

Soon this place would fill with more bodies—some human from attempting to stop the fleeing Disty, and a whole lot of Disty. She doubted the local Death Squad even existed anymore, so she was gearing up her team to handle the Disty bodies as they got brought in.

She had already made up a bed for herself in the small side office, and told her assistants to do the same. Even if it were possible to get home—and at the moment, it wasn't; no one could safely step outside in Sahara Dome—she wouldn't leave. Not with so many corpses on the way.

Every time she looked at the wall screen, she saw a massacre. In some ways, it was as hideous as the one she'd found buried in the Disty section. Disty climbed over each other to get out of the Dome. They shoved each other aside, trampled each other, and some—abandoning the principles of Disty life—punched each other.

The train station was the worst. No new trains had entered the Dome, and no more were coming. Someone had ordered train travel to Sahara Dome to end.

The trains that originated here had gone, probably with Disty engineers at the helm. Even engines that had been in storage sheds for maintenance were put into service, probably causing disasters farther along the tracks.

But no one had told the Disty that more trains wouldn't arrive. The Disty crowded the edge of the tracks, pushing and shoving and arguing. More filled the station, and even more filled the streets outside the station, all of them trying to get out of the Dome.

They wouldn't, and Scott-Olson wasn't sure what would happen when they realized that. Would they pry open the Dome exits and flee? She'd already seen trains leaving with Disty clinging to the outside. Those Disty had to know they were going to die.

She had heard, but fortunately hadn't seen, that the Disty were taking enclosed dune vehicles outside the Dome. Those vehicles wouldn't get the Disty far—maybe to Wells, if they were lucky. Real lucky. She had even seen a report that a few Disty were driving aircars out of the Dome, something astonishing not just because aircars weren't designed for travel outside of a domed environment, but also because the Disty hated aircars. They hated the wide openness of human-designed vehicles, moving in human-designed areas.

It had to be hell for the Disty just to be outside the Dome. But to be outside the Dome in an aircar was as extreme as clinging to the outside of a train.

Scott-Olson washed her hands and started to scrub down her lab tables. It was all make-work. At this point, she didn't want to start an autopsy of the human remains. She wanted to keep the tables clear for the incoming disaster.

She hadn't felt this helpless in a long time. In some ways, she felt responsible. If she hadn't asked how to dig up the buried dead, the Disty might not have panicked. They might never have found out.

But as soon as she had that thought, she knew it was wrong. She had done the best she could with the knowledge she had. She had no idea that this entire incident would, essentially, drive the Disty insane.

She glanced up at the wall screen. Some human reporter had managed to get video of Sahara Dome's port. It didn't even look like the building Scott-Olson knew. The Disty were shoved against the doors, trying to get in.

From what she could tell, a trickle was getting inside, but that would create its own problems. The Disty section of the port was separate from the human section, just like the interior of the Dome itself. The Disty had their own space traffic–control monitors and their own regulations. They let humans work their side (following Disty rules) because so many alien groups were used to dealing with humans. It facilitated what little space traffic Sahara Dome got.

But Scott-Olson was certain the Disty in space traffic control and the port authority and space security weren't at their jobs. She had a hunch they had fled at the very first chance.

So a group of human controllers were trying to make sense of this mess, trying to make sure that ships didn't collide with each other as they took off, that the exodus from Mars was as orderly as possible.

Scott-Olson made herself focus on the lab. A lot of things could be moved to make extra space. She could even rearrange some samples so she could use part of her wall lockers for even more bodies.

Or body parts.

She was also going to have to triage. She knew without asking that the humans would want to know how each human victim of this stampede died. But she didn't know how to treat the Disty, where she should even keep their bodies, *if* she should even keep them.

She would have to ask the brass at the top about that, and at the moment, they were busy, so overwhelmed by not only the panicked Disty but also by the power vacuum the Disty had left as they tried to flee the Dome, that no one had time for niceties like how to handle the dead.

Handling the dead. The thing that had gotten all of Sahara Dome into this mess in the first place.

Scott-Olson closed her eyes and sank into a nearby chair.

She wished it were all over. Instead, it was just beginning.

32

After Flint left the Domeview Hotel, he walked toward his office. He needed time to reflect without dealing with public transportation or any problems that he might find once he got back to his side of town.

He had shut down most of his links. He wanted silence, not that he could get much inside the city. People talked loudly in the streets, sometimes standing by themselves, forgetting to speak softly as they used vocal links. Music blared from sidewalk restaurants, and aircars honked above him. Some cars simply honked to express displeasure, while a few buzzed by, perhaps hoping to upset pedestrians.

Flint couldn't get any more upset. He had been prepared for Costard's disappearance. He hadn't been prepared for her death. From all her accounts and from his own double-check of her information, her relationship with the Disty had reached a plateau. They had sent her here to find a way out of her predicament. They weren't chasing her.

That was one of the reasons he believed she could safely disappear. The Disty were trusting her. What they didn't know was how impossible it seemed for her to solve the Jørgen case. Other Retrieval Artists probably wouldn't have been able to. Flint's police training, combined with his data-recovery skills learned in his first job, made his research go three times faster than most people's, probably much faster than the average Retrieval Artist's.

Of course, he still hadn't solved the initial problem: He hadn't found any of Jørgen's family. He wasn't even sure if Jørgen had had any living family when she began her life of crime.

He had most likely found the reason for Jørgen's murder, and that was about it. If he had it to do again, he still would have told Costard to disappear.

He was shocked that she failed.

Flint made sure he walked around the area ruined by last year's bomb. Usually, that made this long walk easier. But nothing was going to make it easy today. Not even the part he had just reached, his favorite part of the walk, improved his mood.

This section, far enough from the university to attract a higher-end crowd yet close enough to bring in some students, had become the new Restaurant Row.

The restaurants in the new row were a mixture of cuisines, many of them from Earth, but some from the far reaches of the known universe. Buildings, many of them remodeled to accommodate a large clientele, had windows that faced the street, windows that opened at certain times of the day.

Before Dome Dawn was the best time: So many bakers plied their trade that the entire street smelled of bread and cakes and various sweets. But even this late in the day, the row had an odor all its own—a mixture of ginger, garlic, and grilled beef in the lower quadrant, and an equally tantalizing mixture of hot peppers, chili oil, and lemongrass in the next quadrant.

Often he stopped in this area for dinner, picking that night's place to eat based entirely on smell.

Only this afternoon, the cooking aromas didn't soothe him. They made him realize how queasy he had become.

The fact that Costard had been killed in the closed office of a Disappearance Service surprised him. No one should have caught up with her there. The service should have protected her.

He wasn't willing to believe that her death was random. The style of the death—the Disty vengeance killing, whether real or not—ruled out randomness. If Costard were just a victim of an unknown killer, the killer wouldn't have chosen this method of murder.

But the Disty wouldn't either. Costard's warrant said quite clearly that she was contaminated. The Disty wanted nothing to do with her. She hadn't been near any Disty since she had looked at Jørgen's skeleton.

No Disty would go near Costard, not even a member of the Death Squad, not even to exact vengeance.

The last few restaurants on the row gave off a honey–and–burnt sugar odor. The dessert restaurants, open from lunch until midnight, used to be his favorites. He felt a strange craving for a sugared coffee, but he let it go. He'd had enough coffee for one day, and it had been bad coffee at the university's law cafeteria. He didn't want to put something else on top of that.

Flint stepped down the curb and crossed the street, heading out of the row. He hoped that he had pushed Nyquist hard enough in the right direction. If Flint was right, someone else had killed Costard, probably someone human.

And he wasn't willing to guess who that human could be, except to acknowledge that the human had known about Costard's run-ins with the Disty.

The next block was filled with tiny shops, many of them so exclusive that they were open by appointment only. Flint didn't even bother to look at the windows displaying their wares. And he was glad that he had shut down most of his links. The irritating part about this neighborhood was that the shops could afford intrusion advertising—instant access to the links of anyone walking by, with a quickly chosen and usually appropriate appeal to the potential shopper's personal tastes.

Flint hurried past all of this.

This case wasn't over just because Costard died. He was being paid by the Human Government of Sahara Dome, not Costard. And there were people he needed to contact there.

He would probably be the person who let them know about Costard's death.

Flint sighed and stopped walking for a moment, leaning against one of those exclusive closed shops. He wasn't going to make that sensitive a contact on the streets of Armstrong.

It was time to get back to his office and focus on the work at hand.

If Costard were dead, then it stood to reason that the Disty might kill the other contaminated humans.

And Flint might have some of the keys to preventing even more deaths.

33

Someone had purged the records from her files. They weren't in the official history either.

It had taken Ki Bowles weeks to find the dirt she needed on Noelle DeRicci. The dirt came courtesy of one of De-Ricci's partners, a broken man named Jack Levenbrook.

At first, Bowles thought Levenbrook was dead. No one had seen him in years. But she had finally tracked down his last-known address, talked to his estranged daughter, and found him in Tycho Crater, living as far from Armstrong as he possibly could.

Then it took him a week to grant an interview.

Tycho Crater was one of the Moon's smaller colonies. Difficult to get to from any major port, it had little to recommend it, outside of some excellent agribusinesses that took advantage of the areas around the crater itself.

Bowles hadn't been to Tycho Crater before. She'd taken a bullet train there the night before the interview, and had been startled at how long the ride took.

Once she had arrived in the domed crater itself, though, she had been charmed. Unlike most Moon cities, Tycho Crater had used a lot of the natural landscape in its urban design. Actual rocks poked up through the permaplastic or were used as decorative items in lawns. Some of the Crater's dips became parks, without the addition of non-native plants.

The entire effect was eclectic and rustic, almost like a

moonscape with buildings and oxygen. She was finally beginning to understand why so many Armstrong residents retired here.

Levenbrook had. He had taken his pension at the earliest retirement date and fled Armstrong. Only his wife had come with him. His children had said good riddance and were happy to keep him away from his grandchildren.

His wife had died a few years ago, and the daughter who had told Bowles about Levenbrook had said the funeral had been the first time any of the rest of the family had gone to Tycho Crater.

The first and last time.

Levenbrook lived on a quiet street at the end of a Moon adobe development. His home was small but had beautiful paintings in a pale red and brown along its sides. Several rocks graced his yard, and other items, all of them decorative, made the entire place look welcoming.

Bowles hadn't expected that.

Levenbrook waited for her in a chair carved into one of the rocks. He was a tall man with a shock of pure white hair. His face was unlined, his eyes sharp. He'd obviously had physical enhancements to keep his bones strong, his spine straight, and the effects of aging at bay.

When he saw Bowles, he stood and put out his hand.

She hadn't expected the courtesy either.

"You're prettier in person," he said with a smile.

She smiled back. He had obviously planned to charm her.

"Thank you for seeing me," she said.

"I'd say it was my pleasure, but you'd know I'm lying." He swept a hand toward the front door. "After you."

She walked up a stone path that curved toward the door. The door was made of wood, which surprised her. Wood was an expensive and rare commodity anywhere on the Moon. In a place as remote as Tycho Crater, it had to be even rarer.

She pushed the door open and stepped inside. The air was cooler here, and smelled faintly of mint. The foyer was small, with rounded shelves built into openings in the wall.

"To your left," Levenbrook said from behind her.

To her left was a large room that was almost round. It had
an arched ceiling and more openings carved into the walls.
Many of the openings had a faint light that poured down from
above, illuminating the sculptures on the shelves.

The sculptures showed humans in a variety of poses. There
wasn't a single alien artifact in the room. In fact, Bowles had
a hunch that if she looked up the interior décor in the databases, she'd find that it came from some Old Earth culture,
one that had never heard of life outside the home planet.

Levenbrook pulled two wooden chairs close together. Both
chairs had hand-woven cushions in the same browns and reds
that had marked the house's outside.

"Not what you expected, is it?" he asked with a grin. "You
talked to my daughter, thought I'd be this cranky old coot who
didn't know anything about anything."

"Yes," Bowles said. "I'm sorry."

He shrugged. "Kids don't always get it."

But neither did Bowles. And she would have to if she
wanted to understand anything he told her. But she would
save the personal questions until his guard was down, until he
no longer tried to charm her.

"I'd offer you something," he said, "but then you'd have to
stay and finish it. I'd like this over as quickly as possible."

"You know I'll have to make a recording of this interview," she said. "There is a possibility that you'll be quoted in
my story on Noelle DeRicci."

"If I was doing deep background, you wouldn't be in my
house," he said. "You got my permission. If you need me to
sign something, just hand it over."

She did. The small pad she carried had a lot of permissions
contracts in its memory. She pulled up the least liberal one—
the one that allowed her a thousand uses of the interview—
and he didn't even protest. She wasn't even sure he read it.

Then he leaned back in his chair. "Ask away."

"First," Bowles said, "I've heard from my colleagues that
you've refused to discuss Security Chief DeRicci in the past.
Is there a reason you're speaking up now?"

"You just named it," Levenbrook said. "Security Chief

over the entire Moon. Even if I believed we should have a Moon-based government with security powers, I wouldn't want Noelle to head up any part of it."

"Because?"

"Because she's got serious problems. It's not a surprise that the first scandal she's getting herself involved in is with the Disty."

The twenty-four-hour feeds had been filled with talk about the Disty vengeance killing in Armstrong. DeRicci was coming under heavy criticism for letting a criminal wanted by the Disty into the Dome.

Bowles had been following the story for her own piece on DeRicci. Personally, Bowles thought the entire thing silly. After all, DeRicci had no real powers yet, and wouldn't have been able to stop the Costard woman from coming into Armstrong in the first place.

But the hostility coming at a woman whom the entire government had assumed would be a popular appointment had taken everyone by surprise. Even Bowles wasn't sure what caused it. DeRicci's personality? Or the new position? Or a combination of both?

"Why aren't you surprised about the Disty?" Bowles asked.

"Because," Levenbrook said, "it's because of them that Noelle got her first demotion and damn near got me fired."

"I haven't heard of any case with the Disty that caused a demotion," Bowles said.

"And you won't. It got hushed. Embarrassments to the department usually do."

Someday, Bowles would follow up on that entire phrase. But for the moment, she was only interested in Noelle DeRicci.

"So tell me about the case," Bowles said.

Levenbrook leaned back in his chair and folded his hands across his stomach. His smile, though small, was malicious.

"Make sure your devices are on," he said quietly. "I'm only telling this thing once."

*   *   *

The story went like this:

DeRicci had already gotten in trouble with her bosses. Early in her career, she'd been promoted to detective. She had a brain and she could solve cases, maybe better than anyone Levenbrook had ever worked with. A natural, able to see things most never saw.

But she also had a temper, and she wasn't afraid to show it to her superiors. Her favorite words were *idiot* and *stupid fool,* and she used them on anyone she felt deserved them.

Even her bosses. Even her bosses' bosses.

Levenbrook was more political. He'd already had twenty-five years of service behind him without a blemish. Ten years on the street, fifteen as a detective. When his partner retired, Levenbrook inherited DeRicci, to teach her manners.

That'd failed within their first year together. And to make matters worse, the brass thought she'd corrupted Levenbrook. Her constant anger at anyone who didn't understand—or didn't act like they understood—the difficulties of her job put her on a watch list, and made certain she and Levenbrook got the crappiest of crap jobs.

One of those came the January of their second year. The Armstrong P.D. got an arrest-and-deport order from the Alliance for a kid named Dalton Malone. Malone had grown up on Mars. There he'd somehow managed to teach a hatchling to speak English.

"A hatchling?" Bowles asked. She didn't know a lot about alien cultures, preferring to focus on human frailties. She only learned what she needed to understand her news stories.

Levenbrook nodded. "We didn't know about them either. Or maybe I didn't. Noelle, she knows a lot, but she doesn't always understand. Hatchlings are Disty offspring. They are the great secret of the Disty, and their great shame."

That seemed dramatic to Bowles, but she said nothing, preferring to hear his version of this.

"The Disty have three kinds of children—male, female, and hatchling. They're like gender-neutral, only how can you tell with the Disty? But the Disty can tell, and I guess it's a shameful thing to birth one. The hatchlings are kept inside the family home. They grow up to be glorified servants, never interacting outside the family, especially not with aliens."

Interesting that he chose the word *alien* to describe humans in this context. That showed a bias of his as well.

"So they never learned English?" Bowles asked.

"I got the sense they barely knew Disty. But I learned all of this at the same time as the case. Never could tell about Noelle. She might've known before."

"If the hatchlings aren't supposed to interact outside the family, how did this Malone teach one English?"

Levenbrook smiled. "Now you're getting it. Apparently, the kid grew up next to this family of Disty, and got to know the Disty children his age. He befriended the hatchling and taught the creature English, but nobody found out until years later, after the kid and his family had moved to Armstrong. The hatchling thing screwed up somehow and talked to somebody in English, understood some English program, read some English text. I can't remember the details. The important thing was that the hatchling, before it died—"

"Died?" Bowles asked.

"The Disty don't take kindly on anything that breaks their laws. I saw pictures of the thing. It was a vengeance killing at some gathering place. The parents got to see it, then take the image home to those trapped hatchlings, supposedly as a deterrent. It'd deter me, I tell you."

Levenbrook shuddered. Then he looked at her. Bowles hadn't moved. She hadn't seen a vengeance killing and could only imagine one. Apparently, her imagination wasn't as powerful as the real thing.

"Now, you gonna stop asking questions or am I gonna shut up?" Levenbrook asked.

"I'm sorry," Bowles said, working to keep the sarcasm from her voice. "I'll be quiet."

"Good," he said, and continued.

Before the thing died, it ratted out Malone, saying the kid— who wasn't even ten yet—had taught it how to speak and maybe even read the forbidden language. Levenbrook never understood the finer points of Disty law, and it wasn't his job to. He just had to execute the warrant, arrest the kid, and give him to the Disty representatives for deportation.

DeRicci didn't like any of it, and when she realized that she didn't have all the evidence in front of her, she liked it even less. First she argued that the Disty could have the wrong kid. Anyone would give up anything under torture.

Then she claimed the case was invalid, even thought it had gone through one of the Multicultural Tribunals. She liked the kid and didn't want to give him to the Disty.

Levenbrook tried to reason with her, showing her the entire warrant. The kid wasn't going to die for his crimes, just suffer exemplary justice Disty style. Since he'd committed cross-cultural contamination, a major crime in Disty-world, and had done it with his mouth, the punishment was simple: They wanted to cut out his tongue.

When DeRicci realized the deportation and mutilation was inevitable, she started talking about getting the kid an enhancement, regrowing the tongue when he got back. Levenbrook overheard that, and put a stop to it right there.

Exemplary justice, Disty style, meant that whatever happened was irreversible, even if the technology existed to reverse it. The kid had to be mute for the rest of his life.

Everything escalated to the point of screaming matches with the chief and a few lawyers. Levenbrook got the kid from DeRicci, but she managed to find him before Levenbrook could give the kid up. The Disty took the poor kid, screaming his lungs out, right from DeRicci's arms.

The Disty recommended punishment for Levenbrook and DeRicci, which the Armstrong P.D. took under advisement. Finally, they promised to reprimand Levenbrook and DeRicci in a human way, but a very public way.

Both got demoted. They got separated as partners, and Levenbrook, for protesting his sentence, was nearly fired.

DeRicci continued to fight for the kid. She said some horrible things about the Disty, some even worse things about upholding unjust laws, and got a suspension. She felt that alien laws had no place in human society, and she repeated that for countless folks to hear.

Levenbrook smiled at Bowles. "There weren't pretty reporters like you then, folks with brains and looks who really wanted to take on the whole basis for Alliance law. Good thing for Noelle. She wouldn't be so damn powerful if that scandal had become public."

Bowles waited for a moment. When it became clear that Levenbrook was finished, she asked, "I'm not sure I understand your problem with Security Chief DeRicci's new position. It sounds like she's very unsympathetic to aliens, which is, I believe, where the Moon's Governing Council believes our problems lie."

Levenbrook shook his head. "The Governing Council might believe that, but the people don't. That's why Noelle's in so much hot water, why she let in that human criminal the Disty wanted. Noelle doesn't believe in Alliance Law. She'll make the Moon a refuge for all of the criminals in the solar system, especially the ones whose cases sound minor to humans but really matter to some of our alien allies."

Bowles didn't believe that, but she wondered if others on the police force did. Maybe a few of DeRicci's other partners might have similar stories.

Bowles, of course, would research this whole thing and find out if it was true. If it was, she had a hook for her story on DeRicci, if she didn't find anything else.

Still, Bowles had one question to ask, one that she knew would anger her host, so she saved it until she knew the interview was done.

"Let me make sure I understand this," she said, putting on her best dumb-reporter act. "You believe it's all right to cut out a human child's tongue because he spoke English to another child from a different culture."

Levenbrook's face flushed. "What I believe don't matter. And it shouldn't've mattered to Noelle either. As police officers, we're supposed to uphold the law—whatever the law is, whether we believe it or not. There's reasons for those laws that other people have already thought out, and reasons we're upholding them, for a greater good than we probably know."

"But still," Bowles said. "A child. We don't usually prosecute children in our culture. Had anyone even told him that this behavior was wrong?"

Levenbrook's face grew even darker. "Does it matter? We were supposed to arrest and deport, not cause an interspecies incident. We could've ruined human-Disty relations if we hadn't upheld that law, and Noelle nearly did that singlehandedly. Did I like handing that kid over? Hell, no. He was smart and sweet as hell. But it wasn't my call. Dealing with the alien stuff is never our call. We just suffer through it."

He looked away from her as he said that last. Bowles frowned. She had expected more vitriol from him.

"Is that why you retired early?" she asked gently.

"What, the kid?" He seemed confused.

Bowles shook her head. "The injustice of having to enforce laws you don't believe in."

He stared at her for a long time. She stared back, unwilling to take back the question. After a few minutes, his right eyelid began to twitch. Finally, he put a finger against the corner of his eye, trying to stem the movement.

"I did my job," he said.

"I know." Bowles kept the gentle tone. "I'm just asking how it made you feel."

"Like a goddamn idiot," he said. "Just exactly what Noelle said I was. A stupid, goddamn idiot."

And then he stood and walked away, leaving Ki Bowles alone in his beautiful living room, designed in the style of Old Earth, without any alien artifacts, any hint at all that he lived in a multicultural world.

34

Bella Ogden climbed out of a very sound sleep. She blinked, feeling grit in her eyes. Two weeks of twenty-hour days made sleep an incredible luxury. She would need some enhancements to continue working this hard. She was sleeping too deeply to do her job well.

Her bed shook slightly, and a light grew brighter in the corner of the room. So something had awakened her. This gentle wakefulness came from her assistant. There was a crisis in the Alliance, one Ogden would have to deal with, but not something that required her to leap from her bed.

She at least had a few minutes to gather herself.

The light continued to grow brighter, and now a Mozart piano concerto started playing faintly on her sound system. Ogden glanced at the clock beside her bed, set to Earth time.

Only an hour after she had gone to sleep. No wonder she had so much trouble waking up.

And with the alarms going off this way, she knew she wouldn't come back to the bed any time soon.

Ogden sighed, got up, and crossed the large bedroom to the en suite bathroom. At least the facilities here in Earth Alliance North American Headquarters were luxurious. She wasn't sure she could work this hard in places as primitive as the North African Headquarters, where she had started her career. The building there had been under construction, and she had slept for two years on a cot with a paper-thin mattress.

Of course, she had been young then.

And a lot more naïve. Now she knew that with a summoning like this, she would have more work than any human could possibly do. She would have to make decisions quickly, and she would have to pray they were right.

She got into the shower and set the controls on cool, to wake herself up. The cold water hit her and sent a shiver through her system. She soaped off quickly, then rinsed and got out. By the time she reached her dressing room, one of her assistants had laid out the proper clothes for her meeting.

A long robe, no sleeves, no socks and no shoes.

Ogden cursed softly. She was going to deal with the Disty.

The Disty always tested her skills as the chief protocol officer for the Earth Alliance. They didn't like her height or her round figure. They objected to her round face and her relatively small eyes. They didn't like the way she spoke their language—her words were perfect, but her accent somehow offended them, in a way that she and her coaches could never quite figure out.

Ogden sighed, dressed, and sent a message through her links to make sure she had both coffee and some kind of healthy breakfast. No sugar for the next few days, no alcohol, and certainly nothing too heavy. She was going to have to stay alert as best she could without many stimulants.

Ogden double-checked her links for any messages about the possible crisis, but she got only a series of increasingly urgent summonses to a variety of meetings. Her assistant had clearly filtered through them, because many of the messages had been flagged. Ogden didn't care about the actual content. What she had learned in her early days working protocol was that words mattered a whole lot less than tone.

And at the moment, everyone's tone held an undercurrent of panic.

She let herself out of her apartment. The corridor had floor-to-ceiling windows on both sides—something her grandmother might have called a breezeway—which was one of the dumbest constructions in the North American Headquarters.

The headquarters were located on what was still known as the U.S.-Canadian border, sitting partly in Ontario and partly in Minnesota. Ogden didn't know her history well enough to know which part—Minnesota or Ontario—belonged to which former sovereign nation, and she really didn't care. What she did know was that this was considered one of the most isolated yet accessible areas on the continent, hence its choice for a headquarters.

The compound had been designed when the Alliance hadn't protected Earth space. Back then, attacks on Alliance buildings had been common. At first, the original headquarters had been placed in the Yukon, but after delegates got snowed in for one long and rather tense month, the Alliance had moved its headquarters to a less remote area.

This compound had been the Alliance's first headquarters. Now the meeting areas were spread all over Earth, with more than a dozen headquarters on each of Earth's seven continents rotating the title of "main." Only the headquarters on islands were left out of the rotation, and only the Executive Committee knew which headquarters would get the "main" designation next.

Right now, that designation belonged here.

Unfortunately.

Ogden hurried through the chilly corridor. Snow pressed against the windows, bathing everything in clean white. Some of the permanent staff of the facility loved the deep, cold winters, but Ogden hated them, particularly at times like this when she had to go barefoot just to fulfill her duties.

The marble floor felt like it was made of ice. She had been pressing for carpeting for this area for some time now, but she doubted she would get it before she moved to some other base headquarters.

Finally, she made it out of the residential corridor and into the main part of the building. Here the floors not only had carpet, but also the carpet was heated from below, just like the chairs were.

A real fire burned in the great stone fireplace at the end of the hall. One of Ogden's assistants, Sven Sorenson, stood near it, clutching a large information screen.

"Have you linked up?" he asked without any pretense at a greeting.

"I downloaded the last hour's news," Ogden said, reaching for the information screen, "but I haven't sorted it."

"Sort Mars," he said.

She did. The Disty were having some sort of crisis, fleeing Domes in the north and heading south. Someone had ordered the bullet trains stopped and the Domes closed. Only the ports seemed to be working, and not all that well. More than a dozen spaceship accidents had occurred, many during simultaneous liftoffs.

"What the hell?" Ogden asked. "How come we didn't know about this sooner?"

Sorenson shrugged. "Apparently, the news thought it was a Martian problem. No one paid a lot of attention until the ships started colliding."

"Good Lord," Ogden said. "I don't have time to sort everything. Do we know what caused this?"

"We don't, at least not accurately. The Disty believe they do. Number Fifty-six is inside, along with his team. I've never seen him so angry."

Ogden clutched the screen. She needed it for protocol updates made in the past hour that she might not have gotten or that might not, for reasons of clarity, have found their way into her personal systems.

She swallowed hard and glanced at the closed metal door in front of her. Number Fifty-six, the Disty's head delegate to the Earth Alliance, always intimidated Ogden. Unlike his previous counterpart, Number Eighty-eight, Number Fifty-six hadn't even wanted to reveal his gender when he first joined the diplomatic core. When told that would cause problems for a variety of species, not just the humans, he still didn't acquiesce. Only when most of the Alliance protested his appointment did he reveal what he considered private information.

The Disty were incredibly secretive about personal matters. That was one of the things that made them so difficult to deal with. The treaty between the Earth Alliance and the Disty Universal Government even stipulated that the Disty representatives not be required to reveal their names. Names were a form of currency on Amoma, the Disty home world, and to bandy them about casually, the way that so many other species did, offended the Disty so deeply that they felt they couldn't participate in most interstellar events.

Finally, an earlier chief protocol office had come up with the solution. On an interstellar scale, the Disty had to refer to themselves by number. They chose the number, and the number could not be repeated, for clarity's sake.

What concerned some members of the Alliance was that the Disty had started with high numbers—the first delegate to the Alliance was called Number Three Hundred, and gradually had worked their way down to Number Fifty-six. Some believed that the Disty would pull out of the Alliance once they hit zero.

"Anything else I should know?" Ogden asked.

"No one's talking around me," Sorensen said. "I just heard the shouts coming through the door, and I saw Number Fifty-six when he entered. The lines along his back had turned gray."

Ogden tensed. Disty showed emotion in a variety of ways, most of them hidden to the average human. When the emotion became visible, it was considered out of control. The lines in the back functioned like a human's face—the lines turned white, pale, or gray depending on the subspecies of Disty.

That Number Fifty-six was this out of control, especially when he had been trained to remain in control among alien races, was a very bad sign.

"I'm going to need the team," Ogden said. "I also want you to contact Disty experts and have them tell me their interpretation of the crisis. Feed me the information on my subvocal private link. I'm not going to be able to read anything or view vids. I'm going to have to observe every movement."

Sorenson nodded. "You want the other assistants on this?"

"I want everyone, down to the most junior intern," Ogden said. "If this has Number Fifty-six upset, then we are facing a major crisis. I want every tool available before I get in too deep."

"Done." Sorenson went to the door and grabbed the long metal handle. "Ready?"

"No," Ogden said, "but when has that stopped me?"

She nodded. He pulled open the door, and she stepped into the overheated conference room. This conference room was the smallest in the compound, with the lowest ceiling, designed with the Disty in mind.

Number Fifty-six sat on the blond wood table in the center of the room, his long feet pressed together. His team stood behind him, a breach of normal protocol.

Ogden had never seen anything like it.

Carly Ammer, the human delegate from Mars, sat opposite Number Fifty-six. She'd been genetically altered to look as Disty as a human could. Her legs and feet were proportionally too long, and her trunk too short. Her face was too narrow, and her eyes too large.

She had her feet pressed together as well, and her hands folded in her lap.

Three other humans hovered behind her. They all had higher rank than she did, but none of them were at Number Fifty-six's level. For that, the head human representative for all the Allied Human Worlds should have been in the room.

"Where's Roderick Jefferson?" Ogden sent along her link to Sorenson.

"His assistant claims that he can't be located."

"Well, go around the assistant," Ogden sent. "This is an emergency."

She walked deeper into the room, and bowed from the upright position. It wasn't the most polite move she could make—the most polite would have been to place her forehead against the tabletop—but she had learned long ago that she had to be invited to the table first.

"Rise," Number Fifty-six said. He was speaking Spanish, which meant that he was being extremely formal—using the dominant language of Earth rather than English, the required diplomatic language of humans.

Ogden stood up.

"Join us," Number Fifty-six said.

That was the invitation she needed. She walked to the table, put her hands on the underside of it, and bowed her head, touching her forehead to the smooth surface. The Disty had allowed humans to use that as their most polite gesture, since many older human bodies couldn't sit with feet pressed together, bend at the waist, and touch the forehead to a surface.

"Greetings, Chief Protocol Officer," Number Fifty-six said. The fact that he had acknowledged her in this way allowed her to stand upright.

She did so slowly, knowing if she moved too quickly she would get dizzy.

"You understand," Number Fifty-six said, "we did not send for you."

"I understand," she said, speaking as formally as he was. "However, when my assistant opened the room, he realized there was an imbalance in rank among you. Since you are using a public conference room, you must follow Alliance protocols."

"We have tried, Chief Protocol Officer," Number Fifty-Six said. "Your head of the Allied Human Worlds has rudely refused to appear."

"Forgive me," Ogden said. "I was informed that he was unavailable to my assistant only."

Number Fifty-six spread his long elegant hands in a somewhat gesture. "It is the same thing."

"Among my people, it is not," Ogden said, and mentally added *not always, anyway,* so that she wasn't telling a complete lie. "This is why a protocol officer should attend each meeting. Allow me to summon Mr. Jefferson. May we reschedule the meeting for a time that will allow him to attend?"

"No." Number Fifty-six startled her with the firmness of his denial. "We have an emergency and it must be dealt with now."

"I shall inform his people. They shall find him, wherever

he is." *And he'd better not be off-site,* she thought. She sent a complete message to her assistant, so that the message could get forwarded to Jefferson.

If he didn't show, she would have him stripped of his rank. It was one of the few privileges of her office: She could strip anyone of rank for not following procedures, particularly in an emergency. It was a power she couldn't use lightly, but in this instance, she would consider it.

"We shall continue without him," Number Fifty-six said.

Ammer looked at Ogden with undisguised panic. So the human representative from Mars believed she was in over her head. Then Ogden had to stall as best she could.

"Forgive me," she said again to Number Fifty-six. "I am the human with the highest rank in the room. If you feel you must continue, then I am afraid I must act in Mr. Jefferson's stead until he arrives."

"You are the protocol chief," Number Fifty-six said. "It is not allowed."

"I am afraid it is required," Ogden said. "Earth Alliance Protocol Code 20745.25, governing human-Disty relations, states—"

"Very well." Number Fifty-six clasped his hands together. He had already known that code, yet he had initially denied it.

Ogden felt her heartburn flare. Yet another enhancement that she didn't want. Her sour stomach was reflecting her moods too much these days—and this mood was barely contained fright. She knew Alliance protocols, but not the protocols for dealing with the Disty on an extreme level.

"Please," she said, "update me on the crisis."

"It is not a crisis," Number Fifty-six said with that same defiant tone he had used earlier. "It is a deception."

Ammer's expression became even more alarmed. The three humans behind her had bowed their heads, probably so that Ogden couldn't see their expressions.

Where the hell is Jefferson? She sent to her assistant.

We still can't find him, Sorensen sent back.

Then get his second here. Now!

"I am afraid I was awakened from a sound sleep and not

informed about the intricacies of this," she said. "I know that the Disty are in turmoil on Mars—"

"In turmoil?" Number Fifty-six switched to English, a language that the Disty were far more comfortable with.

If things got much worse, he might switch to his own language, and then Ogden would need an interpreter. She spoke thirty different languages, but she didn't have the nuances down for negotiation in all of them. She didn't trust herself in Disty.

"Your people have contaminated our lands," he snapped. "It has been going on for decades, and has, in the past few days, cost many Disty lives. The humans and the Disty can no longer coexist. Not on Mars. Perhaps not anywhere."

Ogden felt her breath catch. Ammer bowed her head, and Ogden felt as if she had lost her support.

"Contaminated?" Ogden asked.

"I cannot explain all of this to you," Number Fifty-six said. "You probably know of it. We believe your kind has planned this deception since our paths crossed, and it has finally come to fruition. What we need now is a clean area for our contaminated population to resettle while we figure out how to clean them. Then we must decide what to do with the Domes. We will not abandon them to the humans."

How could Disty-human relations have broken down so badly in the hour that she had been asleep? What had she missed?

The best thing she could do until Jefferson arrived was to keep Number Fifty-six talking.

"What do you propose to do with the Domes?" Ogden asked.

"We have limited choices. Unfortunately, we must find out from your leaders where the grave sites are before we can do anything, and we must trust your people to remove the bodies. Either that or we shall have to demolish the Domes, find someone else to dig up the land, and burn its contents. Perhaps we'll be able to rebuild. Perhaps not. The economic loss will be devastating. The loss of life has already been horrifying, and there will be more to come if you do not cooperate with us."

Send someone! She sent to her assistant. *Now!*

She did not wait for his answer.

"We shall cooperate," she said. "I am afraid I don't completely understand the level of disaster. May I take a short five minutes to review the emergency, consult with some human leaders, and see what we can do in this situation?"

Ammer kept her head bowed. The other humans hadn't looked up either.

Ogden wondered if she was doing something wrong.

Number Fifty-six continued to stare at her.

"I am sorry for your understandable anger, and I realize the need for haste. I must admit that I am out of my depth here, and uncertain about what my options are. I would like—"

"We do not care what you would like," Number Fifty-six said. "We have discovered criminal duplicity among your people. It's causing an unprecedented crisis among mine. *We might have to abandon Mars.* Have you thought of that?"

Of course she hadn't. She had no idea what he was even talking about. How could the Disty abandon Mars? They ran Mars.

"Please," she said.

He waved both hands upward, a Disty gesture of disgust. "Take your five minutes. A dozen Disty lives will be lost in that amount of time, but you humans have already shown that you don't care."

She didn't move. She wasn't sure if she should. His words gave her permission and took it away in the same breath.

"Go," he said. "Do not waste time standing here or I will know that you are part of this conspiracy!"

Ogden fled the room, forgetting the dismissal bow until she was already in the hallway. She put her hands to her too-warm face. Sorensen stood there, his eyes wide. He was chewing on his lower lip.

He had obviously monitored the meeting through her links. She didn't care.

"Did you find Jefferson?" she asked.

Sorensen shook his head. He sent, rather than said, *I think he's in hiding.*

"Son of a bitch." She had to think. Protocol. A grievance of one member of the Alliance against another. A serious grievance. Some groups liked to settle in public, but this sounded too extreme. If Jefferson wasn't here to deal with it, then she would need someone else to take over. "What about his second?"

"Not answering."

She sighed. She couldn't do much without them, and the Disty wanted immediate redress.

"All right," she said. "I need everyone from the delegation of the Allied Human Worlds. Get me Earth's ambassador as well. Mars's human representative is already inside. We'll need everyone we can get."

"They won't fit into that room."

"I know," she snapped. "Open a council chamber. And send security to find Jefferson. If he or his second are anywhere in the compound, I want them seized and brought to the chamber immediately. Do you understand?"

"It'll create an incident," Sorenson said.

Ogden nodded. "That's the least of our problems."

<u>35</u>

By the time Flint returned to his office, the news was all over
the nets: Something serious had happened in Sahara Dome
and the Disty were fleeing. The news reports were confused.
No one knew what had upset the Disty, nor did anyone entirely understand why even more Disty fled after a bullet train
went through Wells. Someone had called the problem a cascade, and it certainly seemed like one.

Flint locked down his office, muted the wall screen, but
kept it running news in several windows—all of them with
text scrolling along the bottom. He let his desk screens rise,
and had two of them run dummy files, filled with names and
crises long past. He configured the third so that it was no
longer attached to his internal network. Then he ran the most
sophisticated debugging program he had. He had to make certain no one was listening before he made his next few calls.

The work took him five minutes longer than he wanted it
to. He sat at his desk, a little sloshy from all the coffee he'd
had, and jittery as well. He wasn't sure if the jitters came from
the caffeine or the news he'd had: first, Costard's death, and
then the Martian crisis. Something was very wrong here.

Finally, the debugging program finished and he locked in
the new security protocols he'd designed. Then he sent
queries to the Human Police Department in Sahara Dome,
using Costard's name, and reminding them that they had
asked for a Retrieval Artist.

The queries bounced back to him instantly with this message:

> The human officials in Sahara Dome are dealing with a dome-wide emergency. Please monitor the nets and re-send your message when the emergency has cleared. If you are trying to reach a loved one, send your query to Sahara Dome Human Emergency Services, and someone will contact you as soon as possible.

Flint had been afraid of something like that. He had waited too long. Still, he went through every name in the police department. He kept his system cycling, then opened another window and checked the notes he had written in his own personal code after he had agreed to take the case.

He found names in there of the people Costard had worked with directly. Most of them belonged to the medical examiner's office. Generally, in a dome-wide emergency in Armstrong, the medical examiner and his staff would be in their lab. Flint might be able to get through there.

He double-checked his information, then sent his message through to the medical examiner herself, a Sharyn Scott-Olson.

To his surprise, she picked up. An image formed on his screen: a too-thin woman with age lines around her mouth and deep circles under her eyes. Behind her, shiny tables were barely visible, along with sinks.

Flint turned his own camera on visual. However, his was trained only on his face. No background views allowed. The camera's controls couldn't be changed through outside links. The person on the other end saw Flint's face against a black background. If that person tried to tinker with the view, the background absorbed the entire image.

"You're the Retrieval Artist that Aisha hired," Scott-Olson said. It was not a question, but Flint answered as if it were.

"Yes."

"You realize we're in hell here," Scott-Olson said. "I might lose contact with you at any time."

"Then I'll get right to it," Flint said.

"First, is Aisha all right? I haven't heard from her since she let us know about your hire and put the requisitions through for that rather exorbitant payment."

Normally, Flint would have explained the payment, but he felt the time pressure as well. "I'm sorry. Apparently, the authorities here haven't contacted you."

Scott-Olson seemed to lean in closer to her camera. "About what?"

"Aisha Costard," Flint said. "She's dead."

Scott-Olson closed her eyes. They remained closed for a good minute, as if she couldn't quite absorb the blow. Finally, she squared her shoulders, then opened her eyes again.

"How?" she asked.

"It looks like a Disty vengeance killing," Flint said.

"Looks like?"

He nodded. "From what she told me, the Disty wouldn't get near her, and the detective in charge says that the work on the killing was sloppy."

"Sloppy?" Scott-Olson sounded as if she couldn't comprehend the word. "You don't believe it's a vengeance killing."

"I don't know," Flint said. "Would the Disty hire out the killing if they couldn't do it themselves?"

"Normally, I would say no," Scott-Olson said. "But nothing is normal right now. You know what's going on here?"

"I know that the Disty are fleeing your Dome. I know nothing else," Flint said. "I'm not even sure of the cause."

"They're not just fleeing," Scott-Olson said, "they're dying. They're trampling each other and taking aircars outside the Dome—anything to get out of here."

Flint frowned. "I've never known the Disty to be irrational, at least not within the confines of their rules and culture."

"Me either," Scott-Olson said, "but they're overwhelmed."

"By?"

"The corpses. We found a mass grave that dates to long before the Disty came here. The Disty can't deal with the contamination. It's so bad, in their view, that they'd rather die themselves than stay here."

Flint rubbed his palms on his knees, feeling the dampness from his skin. He was suddenly nervous. "A mass grave?"

"You know of it?" she asked.

"I was contacting you because of Lagrima Jørgen," he said. "She's connected to a massacre in Sahara Dome."

"A massacre?" Scott-Olson asked.

So Flint told her what he knew about the massacre and about the scheme Jørgen pulled. "I figure her death might be connected."

"That explains it," Scott-Olson said.

"What?" Flint asked.

"We found the mass grave beneath the spot where we found her," Scott-Olson said. "I was going to tell Aisha, but I never got the chance. I didn't want to do it on an open link because—"

Her voice broke, then she shook her head.

"Because?" Flint prompted.

Scott-Olson gave him a rueful smile. "Because I didn't want the Disty to find out. I had no idea what they'd do."

"But they did find out," Flint said.

"Yeah." There was a lot of regret in that word. "Can you tell me who died in this massacre? Maybe we can find their relatives and get this place decontaminated."

"I can't tell you much. I just wanted to pass along this information. In fact, I was hoping you could tell me about it. My sources are pretty slim."

"I hadn't heard anything," Scott-Olson said, "but then, I didn't know where to look. The bodies were mummified, and we hadn't had a chance to date them before the craziness started here."

"I can tell you when they died," Flint said. "And I can research where the survivors are. I have their names from Jørgen's scam. I have to warn you, though. Most of them were in the Outlying Colonies when she found them."

"Great," Scott-Olson said softly. "We're never going to find a solution to this."

"You're closer now," Flint said.

"Send me what information you have," Scott-Olson said. "I'm trapped in this building until . . . until everything slows down here. I won't have a lot to do until the first bodies get brought in. Maybe I can see what we have in the official records."

"I'd try some unofficial records as well," Flint said.

Scott-Olson nodded. "It's not a coincidence that Jørgen's body was on that spot, you know."

"I know," Flint said. "That means someone in Sahara Dome recognized her, knew what she did, and killed her."

"Someone who truly hated her, I'd think," Scott-Olson said. "Perhaps a survivor?"

"Again, it might be easier for you to investigate that than me," Flint said.

Scott-Olson shrugged. "I'll do what I can. That building had been up for thirty years. Whoever killed Jørgen did so a long time ago, and might be long gone."

"Or long dead." Flint leaned forward and placed an elbow on his desktop, intrigued despite himself. "If we find the killer, will that be enough to stop the Disty?"

Scott-Olson's expression grew serious. She glanced over her shoulder, but no one else seemed to be listening.

"I don't know," she said. "Maybe it would have if we were only dealing with Jørgen, which was bad enough. But you have no idea how crazy it is here. We're not sure what's going to happen from one minute to the next."

"You're not in danger from the Disty, are you?" Flint asked.

She shrugged. "There's talk among some of the senior officials that the Disty might just destroy the Domes. They won't care if humans are inside when they do it. As far as the Disty are concerned, we're contaminated too."

Her voice shook at the end of that. She was obviously frightened, but trying to stay busy so that she couldn't think about it.

"Isn't there anything you can do?" Flint asked.

"Have you ever gone up against the Disty, Mr. Flint?"

"Yes," he said. And it hadn't been pleasant, not any single time it happened. Mostly because the Disty were so attentive to detail that they never committed any crimes. The Disty only prosecuted them, according to their laws.

Their very vicious laws.

"Then you understand," Scott-Olson said. "If I survive the next week, I'll consider myself lucky."

Flint nodded. He was about to sign off when Scott-Olson leaned even closer to her camera and lowered her voice.

"Do you have any idea why the Disty killed Aisha? They seemed to be cooperating with her when she left Mars."

"She was killed in the office of a Disappearance Service," he said, leaving out the fact that he had recommended she go there.

"Oh," Scott-Olson said. Her cheeks flushed. "I do understand. If I could, I'd hire one right now."

Flint wondered about the wisdom of saying that on a government channel. His side was secure, but he doubted hers was.

"Surely you don't mean that," he said, trying to cover for her.

She smiled, obviously understanding what he was doing. "It's all right, Mr. Flint. The Disty aren't listening, and even if they were, they wouldn't care. Right now, we're trapped here as effectively as if the Disty had designed it. They've taken all the trains, stolen aircars, and jammed the exits from the Dome. Even the port is overrun. There's no leaving Sahara Dome, even if I were courageous enough to wander out of this building."

"The port's jammed?" Flint asked.

"The Disty are trying to get out," Scott-Olson said, "but no one's working space traffic. It's a mess."

"Trying to go where?" he asked.

"I assume they're going to their home world." Scott-Olson shrugged again. "But I haven't been in a position to ask."

"Contact with a contaminated Disty creates other contaminated Disty, is that right?" Flint asked.

"Technically, as far as the Disty are concerned, any con-

tamination can be passed on. Apparently, breathing the air of
this Dome is enough. Any human from here could contaminate any Disty. It's ugly."

"And humans to humans as well?" Flint asked.

Her gaze met his. She was obviously quite sharp. "Only if
the Disty know about it. One should always make sure they
can't."

That was a warning to him. As far as the Disty were concerned, anyone who had contact with Costard was contaminated.

"Be careful," she said.

"I should say the same to you."

She smiled, and this smile was sad. "It's too late for that."

"Unless we can find some survivors," Flint said.

"And maybe even then." She nodded to him before he
could say anything else. "Thank you, Mr. Flint. We'll be in
touch."

And then her image winked out.

He captured the entire conversation, encrypted it, and
stored it in a special file. Then he cleared the links and leaned
back, unmuting the wall screen.

A dozen voices filled his office, all with a tone of urgency,
all sounding vaguely confused. A few of the reporters mentioned the mess above the ports, but he already knew more
about the events on Mars than the media did.

They were probably trying to get through in the exact same
way he initially had. And were, of course, having no luck.

He wondered if anyone had notified the Port of Armstrong about the possible Disty contamination problem. He
doubted it. And then he realized that the panicked Disty
wouldn't just come here. They might go to any available
port in the solar system. Armstrong's was just one of the
largest and the closest.

It was like a contagion. If the Disty arrived here, they
would contaminate Armstrong's Disty, who would then try to
flee. It would be the same kind of chaos that was occurring on
Mars.

If he contacted the port, they'd want to know what the reasoning was behind his argument, and he wouldn't be able to tell them. They might even ask for proof, and he couldn't give them that at all.

But he could contact DeRicci. She would trust him, at least enough to investigate.

And she was in a position to deal with the crisis firsthand.

36

Noelle DeRicci sat cross-legged on top of her desk, staring at her bank of wall screens. The crisis unfolding on Mars had a familiar aspect to it; she had toured the Moon discussing Dome evacuations two years before.

Each Dome on the Moon had its own evacuation procedures, but it would be her department's responsibility—if she ever got her orders together and the Moon's overall government actually gave her enforcement powers—to order an overall Moon-wide evacuation. She hadn't really understood the vastness of the problem until now.

Popova sent a message through her links: DeRicci had a visitor. Detective Nyquist.

DeRicci got down off the desk and turned her back on the wall screens. It would be nice to think about something else for a few minutes. She had Popova send him in.

Nyquist looked rumpled and tired. He moved with a rangy grace that seemed almost out of place on a man of his size. DeRicci wondered if anyone had told him he walked like someone taller.

Probably not.

She held out her hand and he took it. Neither of them shook. They just stared at each other for a moment.

Her cheeks warmed, and she let go first. "It's good to see you, Detective."

He nodded toward the wall screens. "Watching their crisis, huh?"

"Trying to learn from it," she said. "You have news on the vengeance killing?"

"Yeah," he said.

She moved a chair closer to her desk and indicated that Nyquist sit down. She started to go around to her large chair behind the desk and changed her mind. She didn't want that clear expanse between them.

Instead, she grabbed another chair and pulled it near his. Facing his, though, not beside it.

She still felt obvious.

"So what's happening with the case?" she asked, trying to focus her thoughts in another direction.

"I met your old partner," Nyquist said. "Miles Flint?"

DeRicci leaned back, feeling slightly lightheaded. Flint. What was he doing around a Disty vengeance killing at a Disappearance Service?

"Don't tell me," she said. "He has a connection."

"Costard met with him several times," Nyquist said. "I think she hired him, although Flint wouldn't confirm. He says that she'd have no reason to go to a Disappearance Service if she had hired him."

If he had been any other Retrieval Artist, DeRicci would have had to agree. But Flint was an unusual man. He had helped countless people remain disappeared a few years ago by bringing a reputable Disappearance Service into a police matter.

Still, she said nothing. She wanted to hear about the encounter before she formed an opinion. Besides, she wasn't sure if she could completely trust Nyquist, no matter how attracted she was to him.

"He's a strange man," Nyquist said, studying her. He was probably trying to see how she really felt about Flint. "I couldn't get a read on him."

"That's one of his skills," DeRicci said.

"He hadn't known about Costard's death. When he found

out it was a vengeance killing, he seemed surprised. At least that was how I read it."

"You told him it was sloppy?" DeRicci asked.

Nyquist nodded. "And that was when he gave me a suggestion. He told me to look hard into Costard's reasons for coming to Armstrong. He said I might find something there."

DeRicci's stomach flipped. Flint *was* involved. And for some reason, he gave Nyquist more than he'd ever given her on his Retrieval Artist cases.

"Did you?" she asked, trying to keep the emotion off her face.

"Oh yeah," Nyquist said. "That's why I'm here, actually. I found out that Costard was wanted by the Disty—"

"We knew that," DeRicci said.

"—but not in the way we expected. They felt she was contaminated because she handled the skeleton of a dead woman. Apparently, she was trying to find that woman's family so that some sort of ceremony could be performed, which would decontaminate not only Costard, but the others who had been near the corpse."

"Contaminated?" DeRicci asked, not liking the sound of that word. "Didn't she go through the decon chamber in customs?"

"Not that kind," Nyquist said. "We wouldn't even notice. It's a religious thing or some other kind of nonsense for the Disty. I don't completely understand it. But it means that Disty can't get near her for fear of being contaminated themselves."

"Then how did they kill her?" DeRicci asked.

Nyquist's eyes narrowed, and then he nodded. "See? I think that was the question your old partner wanted me to ask. And the answer is pretty simple. The Disty didn't get near her. They hired some humans to kill her. I tracked them down. I have records of the meeting and of the hire. I even know where the killers are."

"But?" DeRicci looked past him at the reports on Mars. They were running silently behind him, showing tiny explosions as someone recorded ships hitting each other from a distance.

"But," Nyquist said, "I have a dilemma."

That caught her attention. Her gaze met his, and she thought she saw disappointment in his eyes. Because her attention had wandered for a moment?

It had wandered because she was moving beyond her old position. She wasn't a detective anymore, no matter how much she missed it. She was the Moon's security chief, and something about this Mars stuff bothered her. On a deeper level than simple planning.

Something—

"Do you care?" he asked.

That snapped her back to him. "I'm sorry. I do."

"I thought I could talk about this with you," he said. "I don't want to bring it up in the department until I understand everything. If I'm disturbing you—"

"No," she said. "It's all right. I'm sorry. This Mars stuff is distracting me."

"You and everyone else," he said.

"Your dilemma," she prompted, wondering if she had hurt the fledgling feelings between them. That wouldn't be the first time she had screwed up something delicate in the early days of a relationship.

"My dilemma is this," he said. "If the humans are hired to carry out a legitimate Disty vengeance killing, a killing in which the Disty are physically unable to touch or even go near the object of the killing, have the humans broken the law?"

That did catch her attention. "I don't know."

The words bounced out of her before she could consider them. But she didn't know.

"See, I'm not sure if it's a murder for hire, since the humans have no cultural imperative to kill, or if it's just an executioner carrying out a ritual for a particular government," Nyquist said.

DeRicci let out a breath and stood. She hated these kinds of questions. The cross-cultural implications were always difficult. "Is the killing justified?"

"I can't reach the Disty to get their files," Nyquist said. "But I got someone at the Disappearance Service to tell me, off the record, that Costard had been in their offices a day or so before she died. She hadn't signed up, but that's not unusual. Apparently, people come back two and three times before they chose to dump everything they know and run."

"I thought that was dangerous," DeRicci said.

"The whole thing's dangerous." Nyquist folded his hands across his flat stomach. He was in good shape for a man who seemed to avoid enhancements.

DeRicci turned her back on the wall screens. She didn't want to think about the Mars crisis at the moment. Instead, she looked out her window at the crater left by last year's bomb.

"Let's say it is a legitimate vengeance killing," she said. "Then you have a real problem. I'm not sure this has ever been adjudicated. Have you talked to a lawyer? The city attorney might be able to advise you."

"Have you ever talked to those people?"

She had worked with them, and mentally cursed them the entire time. One of the last alien negotiations she had done, the city attorneys had nearly ruined everything. DeRicci had known more about the law than they had.

"Yeah, sorry," she said, and faced him. He was watching her, those sharp eyes taking in every movement. "I forgot what idiots the city attorneys can be."

He smiled. She liked his smile. It was gentle. It softened his features, made him seem a little less intense.

"You're right, though," he said after a moment. "I should talk to them."

She shook her head. "Not yet."

She returned to her chair and sat down, leaning forward as she spoke to him.

"This is what I would do," she said. "Since you can't reach the Disty for somewhat obvious reasons—"

And she indicated the wall screens. Nyquist nodded without looking at them.

"—then you've got to act on the assumption that the Disty had the right to do the killing."

He frowned. Hadn't he thought of that? Probably not. De-Ricci had learned long ago that her cop's brain worked differently than every other cop's brain.

"And if they had the right to do the killing, then it stands to reason that they had the right to carry out that killing, no matter how they did it."

"But that's my point," Nyquist said. "We don't know that—"

"Exactly." DeRicci spoke softly but with force. She didn't want this discussion to go on too long. "Right now, you know where the actual killers are, right?"

"More or less," Nyquist said. "I could have them arrested in the next hour."

"Then that's what you do. Let the lawyers worry about the law. You make sure you have a solid case against them. Count it as murder, make sure you have them in custody, and if you're wrong, who's going to blame you?"

"Gee," he said with a lot of sarcasm. "I don't know. The chief, maybe?"

That was how DeRicci got into trouble. But sometimes her take-charge attitude worked. And ultimately, she did get this goofy promotion because of her unusual way of thinking.

"No, she won't," DeRicci said. "Not if you write it up right. If you ignore the cross-cultural implications, claim that only the Disty have the right to carry out a vengeance killing, and state Armstrong law, which is pretty clear. Humans do not have the right to take another human life, no matter what the reason."

"Self-defense," he said.

"Even that's an iffy proposition," DeRicci said. "It's up to the lawyers to prove that an instantaneous cry for help along all of the victim's links wouldn't bring anyone in time to prevent serious harm."

He shook his head. "I hate that law."

"Me too," DeRicci said. "But it's the law, and it's one you know. So act on it. Clearly, if this Costard was attacked by more than one person, then the group wasn't acting in self-defense. If anything, Costard had the right to hurt them, not the other way around."

Nyquist let out a pained sigh.

"So you hold these killers and let the lawyers battle it out. You put that in your report. Claim that you couldn't risk letting killers go free—where would Armstrong be if we were filled with killers for hire, even if they have a legitimate right to do their job?—and plead communities' rights. The way that everyone's been feeling since the bombing, you'll definitely get away with it. And no one will think less of you for it."

He had leaned away from her as she spoke, and his expression was closed off. "You'd really do that?"

She nodded.

"Amazing," he said. "No wonder they gave you the cases that weren't straightforward."

"You don't approve." She tried to say that lightly.

He started to answer, but her links flashed red. She held up a hand, stood, and turned away from him.

What? She sent, not sure she could go to full vocal.

"Noelle, it's Miles." Flint's voice sounded self-assured. "Something important's come up."

"And it can't wait?" DeRicci figured she could ask that question aloud. That way, Nyquist would know she wasn't pretending a link communication to shut off the discussion.

"No," Flint said. "In fact, we may have already waited too long. You watching this Mars thing?"

"Of course." DeRicci glanced over her shoulder at Nyquist. He had his head bowed. He was staring at his folded hands as if they were the most fascinating things he had ever seen.

"I just got done talking to the medical examiner in Sahara Dome," Flint said. "She told me some of what's happening there, and it's scary, Noelle."

"I could figure that out on my own. And how did you get ahold of Sahara Dome? People have been trying to do it from here for more than an hour."

"I was too, but I stopped going through official channels. I had some back-contact information and I used it. That's not important. . . ."

Nyquist stood. He touched DeRicci's arm, making her lose her train of thought.

"Thanks," he mouthed. "I'll talk to you later. You clearly need to work on this."

She found that she didn't want him to leave. "If you don't mind waiting—"

"I've got some thinking to do. I have a hunch you're right. But I want to go over this." He smiled at her. "Thanks for taking the time."

He sounded formal. Formal was always a bad sign. She had offended him. Or maybe he was one of those shallow people who always thought of their career before they thought about what was best for the case and best for the Dome.

". . . Noelle? Have I got you at a bad time?"

She realized Flint had been talking while she was saying good-bye to Nyquist. He was heading out the door and he didn't turn back, so that she could catch his eye.

"Sorry," DeRicci said. "I had someone in my office. He's gone now."

The door clicked shut, and she sighed as inaudibly as possible.

"I missed that last," she said. "You were saying you talked to the medical examiner in Sahara Dome? Why in God's full universe would you do that?"

"Some questions I can't answer, Noelle," Flint said.

It was a case then. Something to do with Costard?

"But the examiner told me that they had discovered a mass grave in the Dome, which frightened the Disty. Somehow the presence of that grave made the Disty feel contaminated—"

There it was again, that word. Twice in the last half hour. DeRicci didn't like the coincidence.

"—and that's why they're fleeing. You've been watching this, right?"

"Yes." Hadn't she already answered that? She felt off balance, first because of Nyquist and then because Flint had gotten into the middle of everything, like he seemed to have a talent for doing.

"Then you've seen the accidents in the space over the ports."

"So?" DeRicci asked.

"Have you thought about where the Disty will go if they get out of Martian space?"

She hadn't thought about it. She'd been thinking of everything but that. She'd been thinking about how she would handle such a crisis, but she hadn't realized that the closest non-Martian port that could handle vessels of all types was hers.

She swore. "You think they're coming here?"

"I think they're going anywhere and everywhere. What isn't in the coverage is that this contamination thing makes the Disty act insane. A bunch have already died in Sahara Dome just trying to escape, and the medical examiner thinks there are going to be more."

"We're going to have a refugee crisis," DeRicci muttered, more to herself than to Flint.

"It's worse than that," he said. "Listen closely: If the Disty come into contact with anyone they believe to be contaminated, then the Disty will become contaminated. Do you understand me?"

DeRicci frowned. He was saying this as if it related to the refugee crisis. She understood that concept in respect to the vengeance killing that Nyquist had been discussing. But in terms of Armstrong and the port, she wasn't sure she got it.

"Are you saying we'll have to isolate them when—or if—they arrive in Armstrong?"

"No," Flint said. "I'm saying you can't let them in at all. To any Moon port."

"Why not?"

"Because of Wells," he said. "The bullet trains went through without stopping, and now the Disty are fleeing Wells."

She got it finally. And she didn't like it.

"You're saying that even a hint of contact—like a space

yacht landing inside the Dome—is enough to make our Disty act like the crazy Disty on Mars?"

"Yes," Flint said.

"Is it a disease?" DeRicci hoped not. She'd had enough of disease to last her an entire career.

"The M.E. didn't know. But she didn't think so. She thinks it's religious or cultural, which makes it worse in some ways. It's irrational, and it'll spread."

DeRicci walked to her windows. Nothing had changed outside. The aircars floated past, the buildings looked impenetrable, people walked along the sidewalk.

But she had the beginnings of a headache, and she wasn't sure what caused it—watching the wall screen, talking with Nyquist, or this conversation with Flint.

"You realize that I'll have to verify all of this," DeRicci said.

"Make it quick," Flint said, "because if any ships got out of Mars's gravity well, then they're headed somewhere, and God forbid that somewhere is here."

DeRicci knew Flint didn't call on God—any god—very often. He didn't seem to believe in any. Even hearing a deity's name on Flint's lips made the situation seem dire.

"You think they're coming here, don't you?" she asked.

"I don't think they're thinking," Flint said. "So that means they're getting into ships with no planning or preparation. They may initially be heading to Amoma or somewhere in the Disty home system, but they'll soon discover they don't have enough fuel or a ship with the right distance capabilities, or enough food or anything. And that means—"

"They'll come here. Got it." DeRicci leaned her forehead on the thick plastic. It was as warm as she was. "Thanks for the heads-up, Miles."

"Thought you needed to know," he said, and signed off.

Thought she needed to know. DeRicci sighed. As if she could do anything about it. She had a title and no powers. She couldn't even shut down Armstrong's ports.

If Flint was right, someone would have to act. DeRicci would just have to figure out who that someone was.

37

The conversation with DeRicci left Flint disturbed. She had sounded odd. And it wasn't like her to lose focus as she had in the first part of the conversation.

Still, he had done all he could. Someone had to be warned about the impending disaster, and the only someone he could guarantee would pay attention to him was Noelle DeRicci.

For better or for worse.

Flint shut off his external links again and continued researching on his center screen. The coding information scrolled on the screens beside him. He set up yet another security perimeter in his networks, figuring someone might have monitored his conversation with DeRicci, no matter how hard he worked to keep it quiet.

He shut off his wall screens, preferring not to see the crisis unfold. He set up his interior links so that he would only get breaking news, and he made sure the news was filtered, so that it would only be the real stuff, not the things the reporters made up for attention.

Then he got to work.

He had a list of survivors' names from the lawsuit they had filed against Mary Sue Jørgen Meister. The names came with addresses and identification codes, but all of that information was more than fifty years old. He couldn't immediately get a listing of the survivors' ages, but he would have guessed that most of them were—at the youngest—thirty- to forty-year-old adults at the time of the filing.

Humans lived more than a hundred and fifty years on average now, but that was a true average. Some died quite young; others lived an extra fifty years beyond that.

He had no idea if the survivors who filed that suit were still alive, or if they had children.

And then there was the issue of the Outlying Colonies.

The Outlying Colonies had acquired the name long ago, when the name had been accurate. Since then, the known universe had grown around them. The Outlying Colonies probably should have been renamed the Center of the Known Universe, but not only was that pretentious, it also didn't give an adequate picture of the colonies themselves.

And now he had to search ancient data files to see if he could find anything from those places. Such a search could take weeks and a lot of credits, paid to a variety of people who claimed to have knowledge, some of whom wouldn't have any. He had to make that same search in the space of hours, maybe even minutes.

He would have to outthink the colonies—and outthink the survivors, many of whom probably went there in order to escape whatever it was that had gotten the rest of their families killed.

Some of the survivors had to be nearby. Someone had even returned to Mars, if indeed one of the survivors had killed Jørgen. There had to be some survivors in this solar system.

He just had to find them.

He just wished all of this wasn't placed on him. And he wasn't even sure if his work would be valuable. No one had talked to the Disty since this crisis began. Scott-Olson was guessing that the survivor ritual would work, just like Flint was guessing.

He was shooting in the dark. And he couldn't quite shake the feeling that even if he succeeded, he would be doing too little much too late.

38

Roderick Jefferson was dreaming of Tahiti, sun beating on sand, the ocean lapping against his feet, warm and inviting. Tahiti and some cold pineapple drink, and a woman he didn't know on his arm. A soft woman, a beautiful woman, a woman who—

Suddenly, he was being dragged across the carpeted floor of his apartment, people—humans?—holding his arms, pulling him into the bathroom and tossing him into an ice-cold shower. It took him a moment to realize this wasn't part of the dream. He was awake, he was naked, and he was freezing.

"You've been summoned, Mr. Jefferson," a man the size of a gorilla said from outside the shower. Barely outside. Two men stood in the bathroom, blocking Jefferson's exit. But they hadn't closed the glass shower door either.

They were staring at him as if they'd never seen a naked diplomat before.

He had a headache, his mouth tasted of sour beer, and his message storage links were pinging. With a single thought, he shut off that internal sound. But the pinging continued.

Emergency links? He shut those down too. He'd given instructions, and no one was paying attention. Dammit.

With one fist, he slammed off the shower, then rubbed the water off his face.

"I told everyone that I was taking the next two weeks off.

I was not to be disturbed. I'm leaving in"—he checked his internal network—"four hours. I'm going somewhere warm and tropical with lots of naked women."

He had no idea where these two thugs had come from or how they managed to get into his apartment, but they had no purpose here, no matter what they were told.

"Sir, there's a crisis—"

"There's always a crisis. And this time, Layne Naher can handle it. I need time off."

Doctor's orders, in fact. Jefferson had been working too hard. His own psyche was breaking down with all of the internal communications, the stress, the sheer make-or-break attitude of dealing with aliens, aliens, aliens—always different, and always dangerous.

"We were told to bring you, sir, no matter what. We will arrest you if we must."

Jefferson stared at both men, then realized there were at least three more in the bedroom. They were wearing black, the standard outfit of human security in the Alliance.

"Who the hell are you?" Jefferson snapped, realizing in all of his confusion, he hadn't asked.

They both touched the backs of their wrists, and the ID tattoos in their cheeks lit up. They were Alliance Security.

Something was seriously wrong.

He sighed and grabbed a warm towel from one of the racks. His head felt like it had had a run-in with a wall. What brand of idiocy had made him think that an old-fashioned hangover would be fun?

With his tongue he pressed the chip on the roof of his mouth, sending endorphins into his system. He followed those with a mild painkiller and some detoxing agents. Then he had his links purify the oxygen in the room, making it just a little richer.

All the tricks a high-level ambassador learned so that he could stay awake and alert, no matter what the crisis.

"How long do I have?" he asked.

"You need to be there in"— the security man paused, as his

own links informed him of the time—"in less than three minutes, sir."

"What the hell?" Jefferson snapped. "Someone want to explain to me what's going on?"

He toweled off as quickly as he could, then pushed past the men to his bedroom. It was dark, and the bed was rumpled. He longed to climb back in it, but he made himself turn toward his closet. The three other men moved toward the living room, still watching.

"Someone want to answer me?" Jefferson asked, wondering if these men could talk and move at the same time.

"Sir, you have a message from Chief Protocol Officer Ogden. She suggests you download it and place it into your speed-enhanced learning system. You have quite a bit to catch up on."

Speed-enhance. He hadn't used that since the Ssachuss had joined the Alliance two years before. The system had left him full of Ssachuss customs and language, and with a headache that hadn't broken for three days.

Wonderful. Speed-enhance, an emergency, and a hangover. Could things get any worse?

"At least tell me what I'm dressing for," he said.

"A meeting with the Disty in the council chamber," one of the men said.

Jefferson leaned his head against the closet doors, feeling the wood gouge into his skin. He shouldn't even have had that thought. Things could get worse. They just did.

He loathed the Disty. All their rituals, the stupid table sitting, their horrible superiority and unwillingness to listen.

And they loathed him too, believing him the worst kind of human—stubborn, small-minded, and weak.

"This is bad, isn't it?" he mumbled into the door.

"Yes, sir," one of the men said. "Chief Protocol Officer Ogden said to tell you, if you weren't moving quickly enough, that right now, the Disty are a half a heartbeat away from declaring war."

39

Sharyn Scott-Olson sat at her desk, her fingers playing the screen in front of her as if it were a musical instrument. She had gone through the files the Retrieval Artist from the Moon—Flint—had sent her, finding them shocking in their lack of concrete information.

But at least they were a place to start.

She had moved her desk so that it faced the door to the lab. Her assistants were still cleaning, preparing for the onslaught that they knew would begin.

Scott-Olson had stopped monitoring the wall screens. In fact, she had shut hers off when some Dome camera showed a pile of bodies at the doorway of one of the Disty's buildings. The bodies were Disty, but not a kind she'd seen often.

Hatchlings. They'd tried to get out of the building, but had either been trampled as the regular Disty went through the doorway, or had died from some other means. Scott-Olson had heard that the Disty had ways of dealing with hatchlings in a crisis. At one of the M.E. conventions in Noachian Dome One, one crusty old doctor who had claimed to have seen everything said the Disty had installed some sort of poison in the hatchlings that would be released if they were ever threatened.

She had ignored the story then, but seeing those small bodies, their limbs twisted and mangled, she wondered at its truth now. And then she had to turn away, feeling the full impact of the day for the first time.

In the main lab, she could still hear the cacophony of voices as various announcers tried to make sense of everything. Her lab assistants were also contributing to the noise, their tone slightly shrill, as if they couldn't control their own panic.

She was trying not to think of hers. She already knew the various options the Disty had. Once some Disty in some faraway place came to its senses, all of Mars would change.

And Sahara Dome would go first.

She shivered and returned to her research. The massacre made no sense to her. She wasn't sure how it had stayed out of the history texts.

But it seemed to. When she had done her initial research, before she had heard from this Flint, she and her assistants had looked for massacres, mass graves, cemeteries, anything in the history that would tell her what had happened. She had found nothing.

So she didn't duplicate that work again. Instead, she looked up the names of the families that Flint had given her, and was surprised to find none of them in Sahara Dome and, indeed, none on Mars itself.

She sat back, blinked, and thought about it, her fingers off the screen for the first time in hours. Of course it made sense: If these people were survivors of a massacre, they would go as far from Mars as they possibly could. They would leave nothing to chance, and if they returned, they would do so under false names.

If she had time, she would have looked through other databases to see if there were unexplained murders, maybe in groups or of groups. But she didn't have that kind of time.

Instead, she searched through historical files for the entire solar system, and looked by name. Perhaps these survivors wrote accounts of their experiences. Or maybe recorded something or produced some sort of entertainment based on it.

To go through that much data required time, which she

didn't have. She couldn't eyeball everything, so she had to trust her system to do it.

She set up her search perimeters, then started searches in several windows on the network. The system scrolled through information so quickly that the various windows became a blur of activity.

For a few minutes, at least, she had a reprieve. She stood, stretched her arms, and walked into the lab.

It was always clean, but it had never sparkled before. Her assistants had scrubbed everything down. They had moved in nearly a dozen tables, so the room seemed cramped. The back storage area had been cleared out, and information pads had been placed with the other equipment near the first three autopsy tables.

Her assistants were leaving nothing to chance. Even though they would all visually record the autopsies they did, there was always the risk of recording failure. With the pads there, the assistants had provided for an automatic backup.

"I'm not sure what we're going to do," Nigel said. He looked small and lost as he leaned against one of the countertops. In his work as an intern, he had had trouble with routine cases. Shortly, this day would become anything but routine.

"We'll just do the work," Scott-Olson said.

Nigel nodded at one of the wall screens. "Someone just said there were at least two hundred casualties at the eastern exit to the Dome."

"And that's *human* casualties," said Mona Browning. She was Scott-Olson's most experienced assistant. Scott-Olson relied on her now to keep everyone else calm. "We have no idea how many Disty."

"I think we should deal with the humans first," Evan Shirkov said. He was always organized, but sometimes he missed the interpersonal parts of the job.

"How would you propose to do that?" Scott-Olson asked. "If these bodies are truly trampled, we're not going to be able to tell where some begin and others end."

Nigel grimaced. "Maybe we shouldn't do any autopsies.

Maybe we should just take names and identifiers, and leave the bodies for later, when we know what's going to happen."

Scott-Olson stared at him. Nigel's cheeks grew red.

"What?" he asked after a moment. "Isn't that practical? I mean, it might end up that no one'll care what we do."

The team looked at Scott-Olson. Apparently, no one else wanted to respond to that. She didn't either.

"There's that chance," she said quietly. "But what if everyone's dying of something we can't see? A toxin in the air, or something that drives the Disty insane? What if it shows up in our scans and tests? We might be able to do something useful, and maybe even stop this thing."

"You don't think that's what's going on?" Nigel asked, with just a thread of hope in his voice.

Scott-Olson shook her head. "I'm pretty sure we know what's causing this. But I've been wrong before. I try to keep an open mind."

And then she went back to her office, mostly to cut off the debate. One of the windows on her desk screen blinked. She touched it. The system had found a memoir by Allard da Ponte. Da Ponte had died just recently, and this memoir was published by his family after his death. He had lived in the Outlying Colonies.

Scott-Olson sank into her chair, reading as she did so. Da Ponte had survived the massacre. He had been four at the time.

And the account he left was as chilling as anything Scott-Olson had seen all day.

40

Ki Bowles had gotten the earliest news reports before she left Tycho Crater, but she hadn't understood the urgency of the situation until she returned to InterDome Media's offices in Armstrong. InterDome had one of the largest buildings in the city, and the complex spread for two full blocks.

Because Bowles was one of InterDome's best-known reporters and she had a lot of seniority, she could go anywhere in the complex. So when she got off the bullet train from Tycho Crater, she headed immediately to InterDome's live-feed monitoring chamber.

The monitoring chamber had no windows. The walls were screens, but the screens were unlike those found in the average building. These screens had high-resolution imagery, and everything shown on them was life-sized. Multiple images did not run in the chamber. Instead, one large image covered the entire room, so that the person who monitored this particular story could feel as if the story lived and breathed and surrounded him.

Bowles usually stayed out of the chambers, preferring to experience the story herself through live reporting. But this time, she couldn't. So she went through a series of image rooms, each worse than the last—starting with the images coming out of Sahara Dome, and ending with the space around Mars.

The bodies disturbed her, as did the panic in the various

Domes, but the scope of the crisis became clear to her as she stood in the center of the last room, the blackness of space around her, Mars a red presence in the foreground, and ships coming off it like fur off a cat.

So many of these ships collided, exploded, or simply lost control and flipped end on end that it seemed as if no one were piloting them at all.

Maybe no one was.

Bowles had seen things like this before in her history classes. She had studied mass exodus when she was dealing with Etae last year. But she had never personally witnessed this kind of panic.

She burst out of the room and headed past the imaging chambers to the main offices. Her boss, a shy, sensitive man named Thaddeus Ling, had the largest office on the floor. He was also shielded by a bevy of security codes, links, and real-life assistants, all of whom were supposed to keep people out.

Bowles pushed through the doors without sending a message in advance, as was the desired custom, startling three assistants who were lounging at their desks.

"I'm seeing Thaddeus," she said as she continued toward the large plastic doors he had painted a bright yellow, just because he could. Her own links were screaming; the security worked in the form of high-pitched blasts to the inner ear.

The assistants were scrambling after her, demanding that she stop. At least that's what she thought they said, because she couldn't hear a thing. The instant headache she got for her troubles made her vision blur. But that yellow door was hard to miss.

She hit it with both palms and it bent open, as if it were expecting her.

Maybe it was.

She stepped inside Ling's office, and immediately all sound ceased. She wished the headache had as well.

"This is really unorthodox, Ms. Bowles." Ling was standing beside a jade sculpture of one of his ancestors, a slender woman who had a pleasant face. Ling's face wasn't pleasant. It was too thin and had frown lines that enhancements couldn't tame. They made his golden skin look chapped, and over time, his eyes had stretched until they seemed too large for the sockets. Apparently, no one had ever suggested repairing that.

"Have you been to the imaging chambers?" she asked.

He was rearranging some tinier jade sculptures on a shelf built into the wall. Plants she didn't recognize rose around the shelves, the green leaves looking alien against the brown backdrop. The only thing that looked natural, oddly enough, were the jade sculptures on every surface. There was even a life-sized dog next to his desk.

"I've been thinking of getting rid of those chambers," he said, moving a sculpture the size of his thumb up two shelves. "They're a waste of space."

"They help put things in perspective," Bowles said. "Come with me."

He peered around yet another sculpture. This one was a simple obelisk as tall as Ling was, with writing in a language Bowles didn't recognize running up the side. "You barged in here so that I would accompany you to the imaging chamber?"

"You want a larger office?" she asked. "Maybe a little more power with InterDome? Haven't I heard you mention that you'd like to be in charge of the expansion to Earth?"

"We're not going to expand to Earth in my lifetime," he said bitterly.

"Stop it, Mr. Ling," she said. "We've got a story here."

"Is it that security chief story you were nagging me about?"

"It might be," Bowles said. "Come with me."

Then, without waiting for his reply, she grabbed his arm and pulled him away from the sculptures. He bumped into the obelisk and for a moment, it looked like the entire thing was going to tumble. Bowles caught it with one hand and pushed it back into place, surprised at how heavy it was.

"Violence doesn't solve a thing, girl," he said.

She narrowed her eyes and kept pulling him forward.

When they reached the doors, she said, "Shut off the damn security. My head can't take more of those tones."

He smiled. "You're the only one who has ever gotten through them."

She took that as a promise and pulled him out of the room. The assistants watched gape-mouthed but did nothing to stop her. When she hit the corridor, she kept her grip on Ling, but noticed that she was no longer pulling. He was keeping pace with her.

"I have to inspect these rooms anyway," he said. "I've been promising the unit manager that I would give him a report on the chambers within the week. Everyone believes they're not worth the funding—"

"Everyone except the writing staff, the reporters, and the researchers," Bowles said. "Of course, you never bother to check with us."

"Sarcasm won't put me in a mood to help you, Ms. Bowles."

"I'm not bringing you here to help me," she said. At least, not exactly. "We have the story of the century here, and we have to figure out how to cover it."

"You could have explained it in my office," he said.

"Not like this."

She pressed a hand on the lock that opened the first imaging chamber, and walked inside. The images coming from Sahara Dome were still devastating.

Ling gasped.

She took him from room to room, showing the ever-expanding crisis on Mars, until they reached that last room. The images were as amazing as ever: the blackness, the pin-pricks of burning light against a red planet, the sheer volume of free-floating ships.

"My God," he breathed. "Have they all gone mad?"

"They're afraid of something and they're running," Bowles said. "Everyone thinks they're crazy, but I downloaded some Disty histories. I found a lot of evacuations. Do you know how they discovered our solar system in the first place?"

"No," he said, without looking at her. He was watching the tiny ships whirling away from the surface.

"Some Disty were fleeing a death ritual gone awry. An entire town had been destroyed, but before that happened, several dozen Disty got into distance ships and fled. They ended up here. Other Disty followed—their death leaders, whatever they're called—"

"The Death Squad," Ling muttered, still watching the ships.

"And took care of the escapees. But then they reported back to Amoma, and someone sent scout ships. Humans met them near Titan. The rest you know."

He nodded absently. "So?"

"So," she said, "the point is that the Disty have a history of running from places where something has gone wrong."

Ling turned toward her. She finally had his attention. "Wrong how?"

She shrugged. "Something to do with ritual and ritualistic banishment. I don't entirely understand it, but you have to understand, I've only processed about five minutes of information. I'll have it all within an hour or two."

"This is a Mars story," he said. "InterDome on Mars probably has feeds going all over the solar system."

"They do," Bowles said. "But it's a Moon story too."

She swung a hand toward the red planet, looking too bright against that black backdrop. "Where do you think those ships are going to go? They're so panicked, most of them don't have real pilots. The ones that do won't be able to make it all the way back to the Disty system, not right away. They're going to need fuel and maybe some money, and maybe even some contacts. Where're they going to go?"

His frown lines softened as he realized what she was saying. "They're coming here."

She nodded. "We've had refugee situations in the past, but nothing this overwhelming. If the figures I'm getting from research are correct, the number of Disty coming this way will double Armstrong's population within a day. If all the Disty make it and somehow end up here, we won't have room for them in any of the Domes."

"They won't all come here," he said, but he didn't sound like he believed it.

"They might. Refugee situations are dicey. They go to the nearest place, and they don't care if there's no room. We don't just have room factors. We have food and strain on the old Domes, and maybe even problems in the ports."

Ling glanced over his shoulder. The redness from the image of Mars made his skin seem copper. "Everyone'll be covering this within a few hours. Why bring me here?"

"I just got back from Tycho Crater," she said. "I just saw Security Chief DeRicci's ex-partner from the police force. He gave me a story about her, one that shows how much she hates the Disty."

Ling's eyes narrowed, reaching almost normal size. "You think she's going to deny them entry."

Bowles nodded.

"Oh, my . . ." He didn't finish the thought. "She can't do that. Thousands, maybe millions will die. She has to take in at least a portion. That's what governments do in these kinds of situations. They provide as much humanitarian aid as possible."

Bowles just stared at him, letting him reach the conclusions she'd been thinking about for a while now.

"She doesn't have that kind of power, does she?" he asked.

Bowles shrugged. "That's why she was hired. For exactly this type of emergency. No one ever anticipated the scope."

His eyes were sparkling. He was seeing awards and classic stories and life-changing reporting work. He was seeing the story that would open the doors to Earth for InterDome, and all the promotions he ever dreamed of.

Bowles knew that as well as she knew her own reaction. She'd worked with Ling long enough to understand what interested him. It wasn't news. It was advancement.

This story would advance all of them.

"What are you thinking?" he asked.

"I need a team," she said, "from all over the Moon. I need

researchers and people who specialize in Disty, and maybe even a Disty or two if we can get them. I need a secondary live face—I'll be primary—and I need total control. This entire story, from the crisis on Mars to the refugee situation on the Moon, is mine from start to finish."

"And?" he asked.

"Do your best to get me unlimited access to the United Domes Government. Most of all, I want to be there when Security Chief DeRicci makes her fateful decision. I want it all recorded, and I want to be the reporter of record."

"I may not be able to do that last," he said.

"We need it," she said. "It's the heart of the piece."

"You got the ex-partner recorded? We have the history of her hatred of the Disty?"

"We have it," Bowles said. "And I'm going to play it front and center, the minute she closes our borders."

"You're convinced the borders will close."

"Yes," Bowles said.

"And that the chief will do it."

"If not," Bowles said, "she'll be the one recommending it, and right now, they'll listen to her. She's handled two crises. She's the experienced one. They don't realize how this'll backfire."

"The Disty will blame the Moon."

Bowles nodded. "The entire Alliance might be ending, right here. Right now."

"My God," he whispered. "And we'll have the evolution of that collapse on every link the moment it happens."

"As it happens," Bowles said.

Ling frowned, looked at the ships again, and rubbed a hand over his chin. "This doesn't frighten you?"

"The story?" she asked.

"No," he said. "The real-life implications."

His body was silhouetted against that planet, the exploding and drifting ships. If she told him the truth—how this whole thing felt like the end of everything she knew and understood, and that it terrified her more than she could say—he would take the story from her. He would think her unable to be log-

ical and cold about it, when logical and cold was her only
refuge.

"It's not my job to worry about the implications," she said.
"I'm just supposed to report them."

He put a hand on her shoulder, startling her. It was all she
could do not to jump in surprise.

"We're lucky to have you," he said. "Now, get to work."

41

DeRicci sat at her desk, marshalling information as if she were the governor-general instead of an ex-cop who had been promoted above her competence level. She had one of her assistants searching for those backdoor links Flint had talked about, the ones that would let her talk to someone in Sahara Dome. And she'd assigned Popova to organize a meeting with the governor-general and the council for the United Domes of the Moon, stressing the importance of having that meeting within the hour.

Popova doubted everyone could make it, and DeRicci had told her in no uncertain terms that everyone had to be there, even if it was on vid link on a secured channel.

So far, no one had mentioned that DeRicci lacked the authority to do any of this. But, she supposed, before the day was out, someone would remember. She only hoped they would already know what the plan was.

She certainly didn't. Flint had spooked her. A cursory search of the Disty on Mars had never shown behavior like this before. The Disty ritual list was so long that Disty would never have time to go through it, and she found nothing about contamination, but she really didn't know where to look.

What she needed was some kind of Disty guide or an authority on the Disty. She didn't know any Disty personally—not that she'd ever wanted to; the creepy little creatures bothered her on an almost instinctual level—and she had never cultivated authority on anything.

She only had two assistants, and she felt they were already doing important tasks. So she'd gone blindly through Dome University records until she found someone home in alien studies. Then she'd asked who specialized in the Disty.

The name she got was Coral Menodi, along with a private link. When DeRicci tried the link, she initially got no response. She was going to look for someone else when she remembered how people used to get through to her when she kept her links off. She turned on every alarm and red light and flasher available through the links, and sent those along with a request for contact to Menodi.

Menodi picked up with both audio and visual. DeRicci downloaded the image from her links to her desk screen.

Menodi was tiny, with black hair and skin the color of Flint's. DeRicci had never seen that combination before.

"Forgive me, Professor," DeRicci said after introducing herself. "I understand you specialize in the Disty."

"No one specializes in them," Menodi said. Behind her, someone moved. There was a lot of flesh, and a rumpled bed. DeRicci had clearly interrupted something. "They're too private for that."

"But you understand them."

"No, sir. I try to. I figure this will be my life's work."

"Have you caught the news today?"

Menodi glanced over her shoulder, made some sort of gesture that her visual link didn't pick up, and then turned back. "No. Should I?"

DeRicci suppressed a sigh, beginning to understand people's old irritations with her. Willful ignorance made things difficult all the way around.

As quickly as she could, she explained what was happening on Mars, and then she mentioned Flint's theory, not using his name but letting Menodi know the idea had come from Sahara Dome.

"First," DeRicci said, "is this idea of contamination correct?"

Menodi's skin had turned even whiter. "Oh yes. I don't know how severe the Disty believe this contamination is— obviously they think it drastic or they wouldn't be doing this—but the situation could be so out of hand that our own Disty population, which is quite large, you know . . ."

DeRicci didn't know. She knew that there was a Disty section in Armstrong, and she had avoided it ever since her first run-in with the Disty. She'd tried to avoid them as well.

". . . Our Disty might think that having the Contaminated Ones in our ports might be enough to contaminate the Moon. I don't know without knowing the exact nature of the contamination."

"If I get that information for you, will you be able to help me?" DeRicci asked.

"It would be guesswork," Menodi said. "Normally, I'd contact some friends of mine in the Disty community, but I don't think that would be wise in this instance."

DeRicci thought this would be the perfect time. She would be calling Disty if she knew them. "Why not? Don't we need their advice?"

"Have you had contact with any of these fleeing Disty?" Menodi asked.

"No," DeRicci said.

"Have you had contact with anyone who has had contact with those Disty?"

DeRicci felt like she was suddenly on trial here. "No."

"How about contact with anyone in Sahara Dome?"

"Human or Disty?"

"Yes."

"No," DeRicci said. "I haven't."

"Have you had contact with anyone who has talked with someone in Sahara Dome during this crisis?"

DeRicci almost said no, and then she remembered Flint. "A colleague of mine. He's the one who warned me about this entire situation."

Menodi cursed softly.

"I'm only guessing here," she said, "but considering the

Disty's reaction to whatever this crisis is, they would consider you contaminated."

DeRicci leaned away from her screen. "How could I be contaminated? I haven't gone near a Disty, and my friend told me via link."

"Doesn't matter," Menodi said. "The Disty react to severe contamination as if it's virus spread from brain to brain, not just by physical contact, but by breathing the same air, inhabiting the same environment, or sharing the same conversation. My understanding is that this is an old ritual, one that predates science, in which the Disty—trying to avoid real-life contagions, especially lethal ones that caused horrible deaths—set up this system, based it in their religion, and have not departed from it. Ever. It's one of the rituals that they take the most seriously. And believe me, the Disty take all of their rituals seriously."

DeRicci didn't like it. She didn't even really understand it, but she had learned in previous interactions with aliens that understanding wasn't necessary. In some cases, it wasn't even possible. All she could do was deal with the problems created by those beliefs.

"What do you suggest I do?" she asked.

"First," Menodi said, "don't tell anyone else about your conversation with a Contaminated One. Human or Disty. Don't let that information out. I certainly won't."

Menodi twirled a strand of hair around her forefinger. She didn't even seem to be aware she was doing it. She hadn't fidgeted before. Before she had been merely curious, not quite as nervous as she was now.

"Second," Menodi said, "don't let those contaminated Disty anywhere near Armstrong. We'll have the same kind of riot on our hands that Sahara Dome is having. It'll be a mess. The more contaminated Disty, the more they'll try to flee, and the more they try to flee . . ."

She didn't finish the sentence. She didn't have to. DeRicci was already aware of that problem.

"Is there any solution for this? I mean, the Disty can't always run from death," DeRicci said. "They wouldn't be able to have a society."

"They have cleansing rituals, involving family members of the deceased. If there is no family, there are other rituals, often involving the Contaminated Ones themselves. Those rituals are conducted by a Disty Death Squad, and often—usually— the cure is worse than the actual problem. Few contaminated Disty survive that ritual. Humans never do."

"Wonderful," DeRicci muttered.

"And that doesn't solve the problem of place," Menodi said. "If a place is contamined, like Sahara Dome, the Disty do their ritual thing with the families—something I have never seen written up or filmed. We have no records of how this works, so I can't tell you what they do. Only that there is no death rate with the family rituals."

"Good to know," DeRicci said.

"But if there is no family, then the Disty do something that would be very familiar to medieval humans."

DeRicci knew more about the Disty than she knew about medieval humans. "What would that be?"

"They cleanse with fire. If all of Sahara Dome is, by definition, contaminated, it'll have to be destroyed. All of its interior will be burned, and the exterior—the dome itself—leveled. The ground might stay contaminated for years after that. Rebuilding might be forbidden for decades, maybe even centuries."

DeRicci let out a small breath. "Would this happen in Wells too?"

"The one the train passed through? Yes, if the Disty are fleeing it."

"Could it happen here?"

"Yes," Menodi said.

That shiver went through DeRicci again. "You're sure about this? You don't have to check files or talk to colleagues?"

"I'm sure," Menodi said.

DeRicci's head was spinning. "None of this makes any sense."

"To us, maybe. We don't have the subcultures that deal with all the death rituals like the Disty do. They have strata upon strata upon strata. There are members of Disty society that aliens never see. Disty diplomats who deal with aliens are the same societal level as the Death Squads, simply because the Disty believe all aliens are peripherally contaminated by death within their culture. The diplomats have to go through some major cleansing procedure just to interact with regular Disty. It's very complicated."

More complicated than DeRicci needed. "How quickly do I have to act?"

"How close are they to coming here?" Menodi asked.

"Ships have left Mars."

"Then you better stop talking to me," Menodi said. "Send me what information you have. I'll see what I can dig up."

"Thanks," DeRicci said, and signed off. She sent a message to Popova, asking her to download to Menodi whenever she got the chance all the nonclassified information. Right now, research wasn't what DeRicci needed.

She needed to take action.

She got up from the desk and walked to her door, pulling it open. Popova was at her desk, working several screens. Her mouth was moving as well, which meant she was subvocalizing on a link.

"How soon to that meeting?" DeRicci asked.

Popova shrugged and shook her head. She wasn't getting any cooperation.

DeRicci closed the door and unmuted the sound on her wall screen. Some reporter informed her that some ships had finally made it through the mess that surrounded Mars's northern hemisphere.

Ships were on their way. Maybe some had escaped earlier and no one had reported it.

She probably had only a few hours before the first ships arrived in restricted Moon space. And it would take at least two hours for the shutdown order to penetrate.

Not to mention however long it would take for the meeting with the various authorities, and that didn't factor in the time it would take to convince everyone. The very thing De-Ricci was terrible at.

She tapped a finger against her teeth, noting her own nervous gesture. She was worried too. She clasped her hands together, trying to keep them still.

No matter what decision she made, it would be bad. If she did the political thing and tried to get everyone on board, then she might miss the opportunity to keep this problem from spreading to the Moon. Flint had called nearly half an hour before. He had already been convinced, and she trusted him. Still, she had to search for her own expert, get her own information, before she believed it.

Powers or not, guidelines or not, it was all up to her. She was going to have to take action just to save lives. She'd deal with the consequences later.

Rudra, she sent to Popova, *I need you in here now. Put someone else on the meeting. Make sure they tell the governor-general it would be best if she comes here in person.*

I'm in the middle—

Now, Rudra, DeRicci sent, and signed off.

She walked to those windows, looking out at the calm street. People still walked by. Aircars went about their business. The Dome had changed color ever so slightly as it moved its way toward evening.

No one else had figured out the problem. But then, why would they? As Menodi said, the Disty were hard to know. Even the experts were uncertain.

"Yes?" Popova said from behind her.

DeRicci turned, surprised she hadn't heard the door open. But she'd been so lost in her thoughts. . . .

She squared her shoulders. Popova was the first test.

"In the next fifteen minutes, we are issuing two orders Moon-wide," DeRicci said. "In the first, we close every single port to space traffic. No one lands, no matter where the ship is from."

"We can't—"

"Next," DeRicci said, not letting Popova state her objection, "we send up security teams from every city with a space traffic control. We extend our restricted space above the Moon, and we defend it."

"What?" Popova said.

"You heard me," DeRicci said. "This is a serious crisis. I don't have time to explain it to you, and yes, I know we don't have the authority to do this. I'm not even sure the governor-general does. I'm going to bluff my way past every mayor and local police chief, if I have to. No one knows what's going on with this office, and we're going to use it to our advantage, do you understand?"

"Um, no, actually. How can we—"

"I'll teach you," DeRicci said, sounding more confident than she felt. "I'll show you how to do this if you're willing. But if you feel that law is more important than saving lives, get back on your links and set up that meeting. I'll do this alone."

Popova stared at her as if she hadn't ever seen DeRicci before. "This is the Disty thing?"

DeRicci nodded.

"It really does move from Dome to Dome?"

"And world to world," DeRicci said, not exactly lying.

"Oh, my God." Popova bit her lower lip, obviously considering all that DeRicci had told her. "Oh, my God."

"We'll panic later," DeRicci said. "Right now, we have a small window in which to take action. I need you beside me. If you can't do it, I'll go alone. What do you say?"

Popova blinked, then nodded.

"Okay, boss," she said, looking more ruffled than DeRicci had ever seen her. "Tell me exactly what to do."

42

Flint had been researching the massacre survivors for more than an hour. He had his network search for information by family name, starting with the names and addresses listed in that lawsuit against Jørgen. He let the system work on separate screens, tracing family trees, following the public records from person to person to person.

But he handled the details. First, he went through the court records and determined which survivors were descendents of people who had died and which ones were actual survivors. He set the descendents aside, letting the network trace them.

If he could get an actual survivor, one who was related to other victims, he figured that was a lot more powerful than some great-great-grandchild. He figured there had to be a number of actual survivors out there. Somewhere in the body of the case, the text mentioned that children beneath the age of four were taken from their families and sent away before, as, or after the massacre happened. Unfortunately, the record wasn't too clear on that part.

And Flint couldn't think about contamination of the survivors. He assumed that because the Disty used family members in their decontamination rituals, the actual survivor contamination didn't matter.

But he couldn't be sure. He was all in a knot, thinking about a ritual he didn't entirely understand.

Still, he felt the actual survivors were the way to go. And

all of them would be between the ages of 100 and 104. Not all of them would still be alive, but some of them would.

Public records, especially from places as far away as the Outlying Colonies, were a mess. Names flitted in and out, identifying data changed, identifying numbers varied from colony to colony, world to world. Flint was dealing with records so old that many of them were encrypted in a fashion he hadn't seen since his early days as a computer tech. He didn't have the time to decode, so he didn't.

Instead, he took what he could, used it as best as he could, and skipped over the gaps in information. If this were a case in which he had months or years instead of hours, he would make a detailed month-by-month account of each survivor's life.

But he didn't have that kind of time. Instead, he had to be happy with year by year, and in a few cases, settle for decade by decade.

And even in those cases, he would have holes—several missing years or an inexplicable jump. At one moment, the survivor lived in the Outlying Colonies; at the next, he was back in this solar system. Flint had found a few like that, and they were all dead ends.

At some point—and he wasn't sure when that was—he would simply have to give all the information he had to Scott-Olson or DeRicci or someone in the Alliance who had contact with the Disty.

At some point, Flint would have to declare this investigation done, and let the experts handle it: Let them send a search team to the Outlying Colonies to bring the descendent of a survivor back for some weird ritual that might mean nothing at all to the descendent. Flint certainly didn't have the authority to do that. He wasn't sure anyone had.

But that wouldn't be his problem. His problem right now was filtering the wealth of information before him, and making it useful as quickly as possible—a problem he wasn't sure he would ever really solve.

43

Roderick Jefferson sat on a tabletop in a conference room that had been modified to satisfy the Disty's need for weird protocol. The room was stair-stepped upward, and had been designed with long tables that curved toward a main table at the base of those stairs. Behind the tables sat the chairs preferred by most Alliance members. This was a general session room, designed for a hundred delegates or more, all of whom would be discussing one issue. At each place were nodes that allowed the delegate to listen to the debate in his own language without the delegate having to filter the information through his own personal links.

Jefferson loved the formality of the general sessions. He believed in diplomacy, he truly did. It was his one true religion, the thing that kept him going, the thing that made his life worth living from day to day.

But that wasn't to say he found it easy.

Number Fifty-six, a wily old Disty, sat across from him. Jefferson had had run-ins with Fifty-six before. To most humans, Fifty-six looked no different from other Disty. But Jefferson had been around him long enough to recognize the particular bend of his long fingers, and the strange, almost invisible markings along the inside of his arms. Fifty-six also had a particularly raspy voice for a Disty, something Jefferson learned years later came from some sort of accident or handicap, a defect that other Disty found repulsive.

Jefferson's headache was worse. He hadn't entirely gotten rid of his hangover—or perhaps he had, and the fifteen minutes he had spent with his forehead pressed against the table while he waited for Fifty-six to arrive had given him an all-new headache.

Or maybe it was just the damn negotiation. Jefferson had no idea how he was going to resolve this.

Ogden had abandoned him. Once she had set up the room—removing all of the tabletop items in the first six rows, roping off the chairs so no human accidentally sat in them, and letting all the parties know that this session would be doubly backed up for posterity, she had vanished. She hadn't even said good-bye—which had been a bright move on her part, because Jefferson would have begged her to stay.

She seemed to be the only competent member of his species who was involved in this mess.

Behind him sat the human representative to Mars, a flaky woman who seemed to believe that diplomacy was about genetic modification, not actually learning the culture. Behind her sat other human representatives, most of whom Jefferson did not know and did not care to know. All he had done after shaking their hands was instruct the group to remain quiet. He would do all the talking for the human populations of the Alliance, just like he had been hired to do.

But it wasn't easy. The Disty were angrier than he had ever seen them. Number Fifty-six was managing to remain calm—at least superficially. But the Disty behind him—representatives of at least two major Disty corporations based on Mars, and the Disty representative from Amoma, the Disty home world—seemed so furious that they refused to sit on the tabletop.

Instead, they stood behind Fifty-six and stared down at Jefferson, something considered beyond rude in Disty culture. He ignored them as best as he could, not sure if that was the right tactic. But no one commented on it, so he supposed he was doing well.

It seemed to be the only thing he was doing well. He had started with denials—the wrong thing to do, apparently—

claiming the humans had no designs on Mars and certainly weren't trying to toss out the Disty.

That just made the Disty even more hostile, and one Disty, whose position Jefferson never did get, stomped out of the room.

Fifty-six then calmly told Jefferson that negotiations would be over when Fifty-six was the only Disty left.

"I cannot control them," Fifty-six said with complete disingenuousness. Jefferson knew that Fifty-six had planned this strategy.

At that point, Jefferson decided that truth was his only weapon. "I have no idea where those bodies came from," he said. "I've got no information on other grave sites on Mars. I don't know if some human group a century ago did this in protest to the growing Disty control of what had once been humancentric Domes. I'll do my best to find out."

That caught Fifty-six's attention, and actually made the remaining Disty climb on the table and sit down. The table shook while they all took their places

"You acknowledge that this could be a human plot?" Fifty-six said.

"I think anything's a possibility at this point," Jefferson said. "But I can unequivocally state that the humans currently represented by the Alliance had nothing to do with this, and actually prefer Disty control of Mars."

Prefer was probably too strong a word. There was always talk, particularly among Earthbound humans, that the Disty were too close, that their control of Mars was unnatural, and that they had used superior economic power to steal the planet, one Dome at a time.

But that was talk, harmless talk. At least, that was what Jefferson used to think. Now he wasn't so sure. As one of his personal links kept the disaster unfolding image by image on a window in the upper corner of his right eye's vision, he wondered if someone had known all along that this kind of thing would cause the Disty to go crazy.

Jefferson chose to believe that mass grave was unconnected to human-Disty politics, and probably had something to do with humanity's long history of violence against its own kind.

Fifty-six acknowledged that could be possible as well, and finally the negotiations reached a more cordial level. That had been a half an hour ago, and what had seemed like a real breakthrough now seemed like the only breakthrough the negotiations would have.

And then word came through the news that the Moon had decided—unilaterally—to close all its ports and close its space to incoming vessels.

Jefferson sat up straight, almost committing a major faux pas. It would have been very serious if Fifty-six had noticed it, but he hadn't. He was looking off in the distance as well.

He had also gotten the news.

Jefferson sent half a dozen messages to various sources, demanding to know why he hadn't been informed of this before the media had found out. He ended each message with: *It's probably ruined my negotiation with the Disty,* and that wasn't far from the truth.

If the Disty wanted to declare the humans uncooperative, now was the time to do so.

Fifty-six turned his shiny gaze onto Jefferson. "So this entire meeting," Fifty-six said in his own language, "has been a ruse to cover your duplicity over the Moon situation."

In a normal meeting, Jefferson would have feigned ignorance. But the closing of the Moon's ports had already hit the news, and Fifty-six knew that Jefferson was monitoring his links. They had established that open lines were all right, within diplomatic perimeters, at the beginning of this meeting.

Jefferson wasn't used to truth. Telling it made him more nervous than lying did.

"No," Jefferson said. "I just found out about it. I can send you a copy of the message I just sent to dozens of my colleagues."

Minus the last sentence, of course.

"I am here in good faith," Jefferson said. "I truly don't know what's going on."

His Disty was weak, but he seemed to make himself understood. He wanted to beg that they return to Spanish or English or almost any other language that he knew, but he didn't. Right now, he was at an extreme disadvantage in this meeting, and he knew it.

"Yes," Fifty-six said. "Send me that memo."

Jefferson did, and at the last second, decided to leave the final sentence on. Fifty-six tilted his head as he received it, his eyes widening ever so slightly, a sign of pleasurable surprise.

Fifty-six pressed his palms together, then brought his hands to his face. His forefingers touched what little nose he had, and his thumbs rested below his chin. He stared at Jefferson as if he were trying to see through him.

Jefferson met his gaze and didn't flinch. Sometimes negotiation was that simple. Staring each other down to see who had courage and who did not.

In this instance, Jefferson knew he would be the first to look away. He was the one on weak ground. He was the one being undercut by his own people.

But he kept staring for a moment longer. And then, to his surprise, Fifty-six nodded.

"Your people on the Moon have made the right choice," he said in English. "You must notify the other worlds in this system that they cannot accept the Disty craft either."

Jefferson was glad that Fifty-six had spoken English. Even so, Jefferson was still afraid he hadn't understood. Jefferson couldn't believe Fifty-six was calling for the death of his own people.

It actually took Jefferson a moment to figure out how to phrase his next question without causing offense.

"I'm sorry," Jefferson said. "I must not have heard you correctly. Did you say the Moon should remain closed?"

"Yes," Fifty-six said. "These Disty are contaminated. We have no way of decontaminating them. We could lose every Disty in this solar system if things do not go well."

"But if the Moon doesn't accept them and Io doesn't and Earth doesn't, and . . ." Jefferson just stopped speaking. Then he frowned. "Your people will die, sir. I'm sorry, but if they can't land anywhere, they'll run out of fuel, and drift. We'll be condemning everyone who leaves Mars to death."

Fifty-six kept his hands in front of his mouth, but he leaned forward ever so slightly, placing himself at a subservient position to Jefferson.

That surprised Jefferson even more.

"I understand the implications," Fifty-six said. "Nonetheless, I make this request, followed by one other."

Jefferson nodded, his heart pounding.

"I request that we find a place within this solar system, a place with no Disty, where my people can land for a short time, until we get this problem resolved."

"A place with no Disty?" Jefferson asked. "What do you mean no Disty? There are Disty all over the solar system."

"A place where these Contaminated Ones can go without contaminating others," Fifty-six said, as if his logical were obvious.

"I understand the requirement," Jefferson said. "I'm just not sure how far away the other Disty have to be."

"Best not to have them in the hemisphere—those in the southern hemisphere of Mars are all right for the moment."

"The Moon doesn't have hemispheres," Jefferson said.

"Just so," Fifty-six said. "So small places will not work for us, except, perhaps, if there are no Disty at all."

Jefferson shook his head. "I'm not— I— you—"

He had to stop himself. He had never stammered in a negotiation before. He had never been faced with something like this before, either. A diplomat suggesting the relocation of thousands of his people. Immediately.

"Do you know of such a place?" Jefferson asked.

"If I knew of one, I would suggest it," Fifty-six said. "My people are already working on this. Perhaps if our groups join forces with the rest of the Alliance, we might find a place that no one has thought of."

"Perhaps," Jefferson said. "Or maybe some other solution."

"There are very few solutions," Fifty-six said, "that do not involve large casualties."

"I'm beginning to realize that," Jefferson said. "But at least we're working together now."

Fifty-six let his hands drop. "I would not go that far. Your people have much to answer for."

He got off the table, then bowed once, a sign that the meeting was over. Still, he said one more thing:

"We shall meet here again within the hour. Use this time to implement our plan."

And then he left, followed by the other Disty.

Jefferson remained seated. He bowed his own head slightly, and realized the headache was gone. Adrenaline— natural adrenaline—did that sometimes.

And he was filled with adrenaline—caused not by this so-called solution, but by fear. The Disty were savvy and unforgiving. And Jefferson didn't know if he had just lead his own people into a trap.

44

Ki Bowles had scored her own broadcast booth at InterDome Media. Thaddeus Ling felt her story was important enough to give her control over where and when the story went out, and how many of the one hundred different types of media controlled by InterDome would carry the piece.

Bowles sat at the booth controls, a tiny angled desk with a dozen glittery chips, designed more for looks than for practicality. The room was dark and too hot. The wall screens around her actually put out a little heat.

Ling had believed in this story, but he hadn't given her the one of the state-of-the-art booths. She still had a lot to prove to him.

And she would do so. She was running the story on a dozen levels, following every angle she could think of. She had a few beat reporters handling the Armstrong part of the tale as well as the port. But her coup had been a chance hookup with two freelancers who had messaged her because hers was the only name they knew.

The freelancers had managed to get a ship off Armstrong before the port closed, although the freelancers were claiming only incoming ships were banned; outgoing could leave at any time. Bowles wasn't reporting that. She hadn't told anyone for fear they might seize on her idea.

Well, actually, the freelancers' idea. They had recording equipment all over that ship, and they took it out of restricted

Moon space. They were going to interview Disty ships that were turned away, as well as get footage of those ships as they left.

If things worked out as both Bowles and the freelancers expected, they'd get some internal footage from the ship itself —face-to-face contact with whomever passed for the captain of the Disty vessel being turned away.

Personal touches were so crucial on a story like this. Most people didn't realize that these ships contained dozens of lives. No one seemed to understand that those little pinpricks of light above Sahara Dome's port had meant that Disty were dying at an alarming rate.

Bowles had been appalled at DeRicci's order to close the ports. DeRicci's action had confirmed her bigotry. She clearly didn't want more Disty here, even if it cost thousands of lives.

Bowles wasn't sure Ling had believed that side of the story until the order came through. He had a hunch that DeRicci's old partner was only saying these things out of jealousy or misguided hatred.

Noelle DeRicci was a popular public figure, and Ling thought she deserved softer gloves.

Until this.

Until the calls from someone in the Port Authority, questioning DeRicci's rights to restrict entry into Moon space and to close down the port. And then there was that little message of protest from the train lines, again about DeRicci, wondering if she truly had the right to ask that no Disty be carried from Dome to Dome unless those Disty could show they had been on the Moon for the past week.

Other InterDome offices all over the Moon were getting those kinds of calls, mostly because no one knew exactly what DeRicci's authority was. Apparently, a few of the port administrators had tried to refuse the order, only to be told that they would breaking the law.

Bowles had an intern investigating which law applied. There were still very few Moon-wide laws. Generally, each Dome ran its own port and its own transportation system. And each Dome took care of its own citizens.

This was a mess, and Bowles was relishing it.

All except one part.

It had been relatively easy to think of the dying Disty in the abstract while the crisis had been confined to Mars. Then Bowles had prepared herself for the refugee story, willing to wade into crowds of Disty at the port, asking them how they would deal with the dislocation in their lives.

She had covered refugee stories before. They were always emotionally wrenching—children who seemed lost because they'd never been away from home, adults who were so frightened they could barely speak, and authorities who were just as frightened as they tried to figure out what to do with the influx.

She'd seen tent cities. She'd seen horrible overcrowding. She'd seen violence like none other in one of the refugee camps on Io during her days as a cub. But she'd never ever heard of a world unilaterally denying access at each and every port. Funneling people into one area, yes, she'd seen that. Creating ghettos for the refugees that had their own problems of air, sanitation, and privacy; she'd seen that as well.

But condemning dozens, maybe hundreds, to die in space, unable to land? She'd never seen that.

She knew Earth wouldn't take them. Getting into Earth had been difficult for centuries now. The Disty might request refugee status on Earth, but they wouldn't get it. Earth often didn't let legitimate non-Earthlings onto the planet, humans with relatives there, Peyti with student visas, or Rev with work permits. Disty who had little or no identification, their only possessions what they had carried out of their homes, would have no chance.

That was why the Moon had become so popular with aliens and itinerant travelers, why the Moon's universities were getting interstellar acclaim. The Moon hadn't had that overarching central government that made silly unilateral decisions.

This change, which seemed to have snuck up on everyone, boded badly for the Moon's Domes. All that progress, all that tolerance the Moon prided itself in, had just vanished.

At the cost of hundreds of lives.

Bowles would report that. But she wasn't going to look at those ships more than she had to. And when the footage came in from the freelancers, she wouldn't look at the faces of the Disty trapped outside the Moon's restricted space.

She knew from past experience that the dead stayed with her. She saw them in her dreams—the people she hadn't been able to save, the people her job forbade her from touching, from helping. She could report, but she couldn't become part of the story herself.

She could focus the story and point it in the right direction. Noelle DeRicci was the focus of this story, not just her inexperience, but also her ignorance. Combine those two things with unbridled power and a willingness to use it, and the result was visible on everybody's news links.

Ships hurtling toward the Moon's space, ships that wouldn't get in. Ships that might hover there, waiting until someone took pity on them, or might go from place to place until their fuel ran out.

Either way, the occupants would simply be waiting. Waiting to be set free or waiting to die horribly, homeless, in the darkness of space.

45

Flint finally found several enclaves of survivors who had moved back into this solar system, apparently trying to get as close to their former homes as possible.

From the interviews he scanned, the messages that had somehow made it onto public boards, vid blogs that a handful of the young had done, the survivors believed no one remembered the massacre here, and they might actually have a chance at living a peaceful life.

Not everyone felt that way—he still got an undercurrent of killing anger from much of what he saw—but enough had to venture within easy travel distance from Mars.

His office was dark except for the lights from various screens. He had turned the environmental controls on cold because he was having trouble focusing in the warmth of the afternoon. He had the sound off—the various reports coming in from Mars only added to his tension. His own links were down as well; all he had on were the emergency links.

The largest group of survivors was on Europa. They had come back to this solar system together after some kind of conflict in the Outlying Colonies. Something about this group of people seemed to anger the already established settlements —which was very unusual in the Outlying Colonies. Usually, they were tolerant of differences.

The Europa survivors hadn't lasted long as a group. After a few years, many of them went their separate ways—some to different cities on Europa, others back to the Outlying Colonies, and a few into deep-space travel—going as far away as they could.

But then Flint found a note that intrigued him. Five survivors had come to the Moon. They had scattered, none going to the same city. He felt a surge of pleasure at the discovery, even though the move had taken place more than three decades ago.

Before he traced them, he looked at the other data his system had accumulated. There he found twenty more survivors or survivors' descendents who had ended up on the Moon. Most of the arrivals were within the past fifty years—and only one, a great-great grandson—had been within the last five years.

Flint didn't care about the descendents, so he selected his perimeters to remove them from his current database. Of course, he kept the information in case he needed it. Then he redesigned the searches on his other networks, seeing if he could trace the addresses of the fifteen remaining real survivors of the massacre who, at one point or another, had lived on the Moon.

Two more hours later, he had the information he needed: An even dozen survivors of the massacre still lived on the Moon as of last year. He verified names and addresses— making sure that private records didn't show other changes, such as deaths, incapacitation, moving to some sort of care center, or selling a home to a relative.

Within a few minutes, his list was complete.

His heart pounded, and he realized he had been breathing shallowly. He downloaded the survivor list into one of his unlinked information chips, then closed his eyes for just a moment. Step one—the hardest step—was done. The rest wouldn't be up to him. Someone else would have to convince these people to return to the scene of the most hideous event of their lives. Someone else would have to do the talking, and make sure that these people trusted them.

And someone else would get to ferry them to Mars.

Flint opened his eyes. On the wall screens, various images

of ships superimposed over other images, all of the windows bleeding together thanks to the dark backdrop of space. Only a few of the news reports showed Mars at all.

His stomach twisted, and he realized he hadn't eaten anything in hours. He wasn't sure he wanted to know how the crisis had expanded. He would take care of this, then maybe get back into the moment-by-moment details of the entire thing.

He used his most secure link to reach Sharyn Scott-Olson in Sahara Dome. She might be able to use their channels in Sahara Dome to put him through to people who could actually do something with these survivors.

But no matter what he tried, he kept getting the message he had gotten from the public links earlier: The links were unusually jammed, and he should try again later. One link actually told him that communications were down in Sahara Dome. He wouldn't doubt it, with everything going on.

But that didn't settle his problem. He now had a list of people who might be able to solve the Disty crisis, and he had no one to give the list to.

He had to find someone who could take action—and he had to do it fast.

46

It took the governor-general three hours after receiving the emergency communication from DeRicci's staff to come to Armstrong. The council members for the United Domes of the Moon were on standby, waiting for the governor-general, who insisted on a personal meeting.

DeRicci no longer cared. She had spent the last three hours issuing orders, answering queries from mayors of various cities, and fretting about how to enforce the restricted space law. Bluffing her way through the hierarchies of all the Domed governments had been easy; the problem she now had was that the United Domes of the Moon had no police force, no security team, and no military.

If she wanted to keep those Disty vessels out of Moon space, she would need the cooperation of every Domed city with a port. Their own space traffic control teams would have to take on the Disty vessels.

The Domes had agreements about which port controlled which section of Moon space—and even had agreements for sharing burdens, should something go out of control. But no one had set up a fleet of ships that belonged entirely to the United Domes of the Moon.

So when the governor-general swept in without even an announcement of her presence, she found DeRicci staring at the wall screen, praying that none of the Disty ships would test the restrictions placed on Moon space. Usually, DeRicci didn't believe in prayer.

At the moment, she thought it the only hope left.

"What is the meaning of this?" the governor-general snapped. Her delicate frame always surprised DeRicci—not because the governor-general was so tiny, but because she carried so much force. She wore dark pants and a black shirt, casual clothing by the governor-general's standards.

She put her hands on her hips and looked up at DeRicci. "You have no authority to do anything. You should have cleared this with us—"

"I tried." DeRicci said.

"Tried isn't good enough. You weren't given this position so that you could take over the Moon."

DeRicci made herself take a deep breath. If she lost her temper, she would never get the opportunity to make her case.

"You appointed me to keep the Moon safe," DeRicci said. "This Disty crisis is worse than you think: It's going to spread like a disease, and if it gets on the Moon, we're going to have the same kind of problems that Mars has."

The governor-general took a step toward DeRicci. She tried not to sneeze at the sudden overwhelming scent of the governor-general's vanilla perfume.

"I've been following the news on my links. I'm as informed as you are. Maybe more informed." The governor-general nodded toward the wall screens. "I've heard nothing about anything except some kind of refugee crisis. My aides have heard nothing except the refugee crisis, and the other officials in the United Domes have heard nothing except the refugee crisis."

"Have you spoken to the Disty?" DeRicci asked. "Or Sahara Dome? Or anyone connected with either? Because I have been gathering information and—"

"Save it," the governor general snapped. "All I've been hearing is your hatred for the Disty, and how you'll do anything to keep them off the Moon. And that's becoming quite apparent."

DeRicci felt like she'd been slugged. "My what?"

"Your hatred of the Disty," the governor-general said. "Don't deny it. I've seen the interviews, and actually went through the details of the case."

DeRicci felt like she had stepped into another world. "Case? Interviews? What are you talking about?"

"What everyone on the Moon is talking about, Noelle. You tried to prevent the Disty from disciplining some poor boy, and when that failed, your hatred of the Disty was cemented, proven, perhaps, by the way you handle other cases. Certainly proven by the way you've handled this crisis."

DeRicci had no idea where any of this was coming from. She wasn't sure how to deal with it.

"I honestly don't know where you're getting your information," DeRicci said. "I've been talking to Disty experts here and in the Alliance. What I'm understanding is that the crisis in Sahara Dome started with something the Disty call contamination, and it's not an easy concept to grasp. What happens is—"

"It doesn't matter," the governor-general said. "What matters is that you've created an out-of-control mess. I'm going to reopen the ports and—"

"No!" DeRicci grabbed the governor-general's arm, her fingers slipping on the silk sleeve. "You can't."

The governor-general looked at DeRicci's hand, then looked up at DeRicci's face. "You want to rethink this moment, Noelle?"

DeRicci didn't move. "You're going to have to listen to me. I don't know what kind of garbage you've heard about me. What I'm doing is protecting the Moon, which is what you've asked me to do. Yes, I know I've acted without authority, but someone had to. I told you this was an emergency three hours ago. The other members of the council have been standing by for the last two hours and forty-five minutes. If you'd had the courtesy to contact us, maybe all of this could have been avoided, or maybe you could have acted on this as a unit. But I had to do something before Disty ships got into

Moon space. There is a chance if they even enter Moon space, we could be in trouble, and—"

"Let me go, Noelle." The governor-general's cheeks were flushed.

"No," DeRicci said. "You can call for help on your links all you want, but I'm not letting go until you give me an audience. We have to protect these Domes, and we're going to do it. You hired me because you believed in me, because you thought I would do the right thing. I am doing the right thing, even if I had to use unorthodox methods. Just give me the chance to explain before you jump to conclusions."

"The evidence they have against you on InterDome Media is pretty damning," the governor-general said.

Ki Bowles. Dammit, she found something and she was twisting it.

"No one ever contacted me," DeRicci said. "So right there, you can assume the reporting is biased, if I haven't had a chance to respond to the charges. Besides, hasn't anyone ever accused you of something you didn't do?"

The governor-general's head moved ever so slightly. DeRicci had scored a point with that comment.

"All right," the governor-general said. "You will tell me and the council why you have pitted us against the Disty, and you will do so succinctly. We have to have time to rectify this situation."

"By the time I'm through," DeRicci said, "I'm pretty sure the only changes you'll need to make are ones that give us some firepower at our spatial boundaries."

"Firepower," the governor-general repeated. "You actually think we'll shoot defenseless Disty ships?"

"This is life and death, Celia," DeRicci said, using the governor-general's first name as a weapon, just like the governor-general had used DeRicci's. "We're going to do what it takes to protect every single life—human, Disty, Peyti, Rev, it doesn't matter. Every single life on the Moon is our responsibility, and we have to take that responsibility very seriously."

The governor-general shook her arm slightly. DeRicci let

it go. The governor-general ostentatiously rubbed the skin with her other hand.

"Call your meeting," the governor-general said. "You have exactly fifteen minutes to convince us you're right."

47

Sometime during her examination of the work in front of her, Sharyn Scott-Olson shut the door to her office. As she went through Allard da Ponte's memoir, she almost felt like she was examining a forbidden document.

She kept her wall screens and news links off. But she had her personal communication links open. She expected to be summoned into the lab at any moment.

The deeper she got into da Ponte's work, the more she wished someone would summon her. She was beginning to understand why this incident had been left out of the history of Mars.

Da Ponte's memoir was a work of art. He compiled still photographs, drawings, composite vids, and other information throughout the document. He linked to various blogs and partial histories, and even made several vids of himself recollecting events—once under some kind of regression.

And he researched everything he had lived through, citing other sources, news reports, historians, and once-live feeds to document his claims.

After two hours of watching, reading, and following links, she was able to piece together something of a story:

A hundred years before, Sahara Dome was a closed society. Founded by humans who mined the polar ice caps and shipped the water to new developments on Mars, Sahara Dome had become a thriving community of the miners' families and descendents, one that was surprisingly uniform in its looks, religion, and beliefs.

But the Dome's leaders believed that the Dome had to expand, and expansion required new capital. The only way to bring in new capital was to bring in new industry, which it did. Suddenly, Sahara Dome had money, and actually started expanding the Dome itself. Before the residents completed that job, however, they opened their port to off-world traffic.

That had been their first mistake.

Their second was failing to establish some kind of customs system.

A group, recently expelled from Europa for attempting to "grow" democracy in alien societies that couldn't understand the concept, needed a new home. Their leader, one Jorge Bouyzon, somehow located Sahara Dome, targeting its export business and its new industries, believing that his group could take over the growing government there.

Bouyzon's big mistake was announcing his intention the moment he and his band of two hundred settlers arrived in Sahara Dome. The settlers took over an abandoned church at the far end of the Dome, and began buying property in the as-yet-unexpanded section of the Dome.

Scott-Olson skipped through the year of back-and-forths. What became clear, as she looked, was that Bouyzon refused to negotiate. When he needed something, he cajoled, threatened, or outright stole it.

The citizens of Sahara Dome hated this new group, and soon worried that the group would overtake the Dome. Bouyzon's people called that democracy—asking for free and fair elections, knowing that their large numbers would at least gain them a few seats on the growing council.

But as the elections were being held, a number of citizens were attacked. Others "lost" their children for a few days, only to have the children returned with a message. Still others were directly told not to register to vote.

It became clear that the "free and fair" elections would go to Bouyzon and his cronies in a landslide.

Allard, in his memoir, tried to dispute this. He claimed this part of the record was a distortion—that his family and his people were good people with only the best intentions for Sahara Dome, that Sahara Dome's government was corrupt, and that the beatings came not from Bouyzon and his friends but from the Dome's own government.

The truth was lost somewhere in the middle. Scott-Olson didn't have time to ferret it out.

But what she did discover was that Sahara Dome's original population decided to take matters into their own hands.

In a secret meeting held late one night, Sahara Dome's council approved a vigilante committee to "take care of" Bouyzon and his group. Some on the council objected strenuously to the use of violence, and the fact that children were involved. So the new committee and its leaders brokered a truce within the council: Children four and under would not be harmed. Instead, they would go to a foster home and then be farmed out to relatives off-world. The leftover children— those without family elsewhere—would go to a mission off-world and be raised with the stipulation that they could never return to Mars.

Somehow this satisfied the council, many of whom did not want to know what exactly the vigilante committee was going to do.

Da Ponte claimed that the vigilante committee lied to the council, knowing that no one would approve the real plan. The real plan was simple: They took families from the Bouyzon group one at a time, under guard, to a pre-dug hole at the edge of the Dome. The hole was deep, da Ponte said, because that way the good citizens of Sahara Dome wouldn't smell what hid beneath the sand.

The vigilante committee made entire families stand inside that hole, then shot the family members one at a time, from oldest to youngest. Sometimes parents would crumble, clutching a still-breathing baby in their arms.

The vigilante committee would then go into that hole and remove the living children, not bothering to wipe the blood from them as they took the children to the so-called foster home.

My older brother—he was six—stood next to me, Allard said in one of his vid interviews, his lower lip shaking. *He took my hand.*

Already they had killed more than a dozen families— people we all knew. They were lying in the orange dirt, most of their middles gone. The committee's weapons were designed for maximum hurt. The wounds weren't small like those made from most laser weapons. They blasted holes in the center of people, covering everyone around them in warm, sticky goo.

My sister—she was ten—she screamed at them to stop, stop! as first my father, then my mother fell to the ground, covered in their own blood.

Da Ponte had paused then, put a hand to his mouth, and closed his eyes. When he opened them, he looked down, unwilling to stare at the camera any longer.

It was that motion, more than any other, that convinced Scott-Olson this elderly man was telling the truth.

They shot and shot and shot—my sister went down screaming at them—and then they turned the gun on my brother. He wet himself—I could smell it—but said nothing. His fingers dug into mine. They shot and—

Da Ponte's voice broke. He shook his head, and the vid cut off there. Later, all he added was:

For the longest time, they thought I was dead too.

A little boy, less than four years old, his family dead around him, surrounded by maybe fifty other bodies of friends and adults he had known all his life, lying in the sand, clutching his dead brother's hand.

Scott-Olson stopped there. She couldn't take any more.

She didn't know how long she sat there before Nigel opened her door.

"They're starting," he said.

It took her a moment to understand him. She was thinking of a vigilante committee and humans so intent on protecting their little piece of ground that they had murdered children.

"Doc?" Nigel said. "Did you hear me?"

She nodded, then realized what he was talking about. The bodies were coming in. From the latest disaster.

There'd be dead children here, too.

She stood up. She was shaking as badly as da Ponte had been when he recorded that remembrance. How did anyone clean the stain of that from his soul?

Maybe the Disty were on to something. Maybe some events did contaminate a place forever.

She stepped out of her office. A dozen techs carried bodies inside. Male, female, human, Disty, adult, child.

Her work had finally begun.

48

The hour had come and gone, and they had no solution. Jefferson sat on the tabletop in the session room, surrounded by Disty and humans, and a handful of other top officials in the Alliance—Peyti, Nyyzen, Ebe—none of whom seemed to follow the Disty protocol, with bare feet and table sitting.

He felt like a fool. He had felt like one ever since Number Fifty-six had had his apparent change of heart—supporting the Moon boycott, a boycott that had spread to Earth (not that that was any surprise—no one expected Earth to welcome Disty refugees).

Number Fifty-six sat across from him, looking less perturbed than he had when Jefferson first arrived—if, of course, Jefferson was reading Fifty-six correctly. The Disty were being as mysterious as ever, but it felt like they were working together.

The temperature in the room had risen, and Jefferson's feet weren't as cold as they had been. His stomach started growling an hour before and he longed for food, but knew better than to eat in front of a Disty.

The negotiation looked like it would never end.

Jefferson set an information pad in the middle of the table. Then he took his hand off the pad, so that he wasn't touching it or the screen when Number Fifty-six picked it up. That would offend the Disty outrageously.

Jefferson nodded at the information he called up. He said

in English, "We can't find any available land anywhere in this solar system. Not that's big enough or free enough of Disty to take on this refugee crisis."

"Our information is the same," Number Fifty-six replied in the same language.

"Then we started looking for empty space stations," Jefferson said, "even some old, still-working generation ships that we could supply with food and other needs for your people. We have found no one thing big enough, but there are a few combined—"

"How would you propose that we transfer our people there without contaminating anyone else?" Fifty-six asked.

"It would have to be an in-space transfer. The generation ship, for example, would be towed to your people's location, then left there. They'd have to transfer on their own."

"Most of these Disty have no space experience," Fifty-six said. "This is a tricky maneuver."

"I know." Jefferson nodded to the pad again, trying not to point. Pointing was also considered rude. "We could just fill some ships with supplies, and transfer them over until this crisis ends."

"Thereby contaminating those ship's crews," Fifty-six said.

"We could use some automation," Jefferson said. "It might work. We have—"

"As I said." Fifty-six spoke curtly. "Most of these Disty have no space experience. They won't know how to get the supplies out of the airlock without risking their own lives. We prefer a single transfer to a safe place, which would then allow us the leisure to settle our differences with you, and solve the problems on Mars itself."

Jefferson didn't like the phrase *solve our differences with you.* He kept hoping that those differences were small enough that Fifty-six wouldn't focus on them, but as this meeting progressed, Jefferson realized that the differences weren't small. He might have temporarily avoided any kind of violent conflict, but there was no guarantee this so-called spirit of cooperation would continue.

"I have only one other suggestion," Jefferson said. And it really wasn't his. It had come from the Peyti, who were good at brokering arrangements. But the Peyti representative, who had approached him during that hour-long break, warned him to make sure each idea sounded like it came from a human source.

Right now, the Peyti said, its voice distorted through its breathing mask, *the Disty are looking for all ways to blame humans. The Disty will condemn you all if you do not find the solution yourselves. Even then, it is a risk. We have seen this in the past. The Disty are not forgiving.*

"Your solution?" Fifty-six asked.

"We take an existing space station, like one of the ones orbiting Earth, and evacuate it. The various species who live on that station are not contaminated, so they can go anywhere. We can provide them temporary shelter."

Number Fifty-six templed his fingers. Jefferson was beginning to see that as a quirk: Fifty-six did that only when he was intrigued.

"Go on," Fifty-six said.

"When the station is empty, we open it to the Contaminated Ones, letting them live there until this crisis is resolved."

"If it is not resolved?"

"Then we abandon the station to them, I guess, and have robotic missions service them."

"That last is unworkable," Fifty-six said. "But we might get around it. There is one great problem though."

"What's that?" Jefferson asked.

"If we have to, we might decide to destroy the station and the Contaminated Ones. That would be difficult in Earth's orbit."

Jefferson felt his breath catch. Number Fifty-six spoke of mass murder as if it were a simple problem of logistics.

Maybe to him it was.

"Um," Jefferson said, feeling reduced to an attaché at his first posting. "Ah, if we displaced hundreds of people on an emergency basis—people of all species—we'd have to do so with the understanding that their home wouldn't be destroyed."

"If we can't resolve the contamination," Number Fifty-six said, "we would have no choice."

"We would," Jefferson said, feeling his cheeks heat up. "Many non-Disty might choose to live with the problem."

"And be forever banned from interaction with the Disty? They wouldn't even be able to go to cities in which there were Disty. It would be more than an inconvenience." Number Fifty-six glanced at his colleagues, all of whom watched the proceedings with great interest. "Of course, we would pay for any loss of property."

"We wouldn't be able to get people to agree in the first place," Jefferson said. "We'd be doing this for humanitarian reasons, and you would negate those reasons with—"

He almost said *murder,* but he managed to stop himself just in time.

Number Fifty-six seemed to know where the comment was going anyway. He tilted his oblong head as he looked at Jefferson. Fifty-six's eyes were glistening in the diffuse artificial light.

"That word, *humanitarian,* is so very interesting, isn't it?" Fifty-six said. "Its cultural assumptions, its biases, are all there in the first five letters. Honestly, we Disty don't care to be humanitarian. It is not in our nature."

Jefferson felt his cheeks grow even warmer. "I wasn't implying that you would be making any humanitarian moves. I did say, however, that my people would be acting from that impulse. They might find it offensive to our cultural values to make a humanitarian gesture, only to see that gesture result in destruction."

He gave himself points for not sounding too defensive, and for managing to avoid the word *murder* yet again.

"You are saying that unless we follow your rules in receiving your help, we will cause a great cultural disruption among your people."

"Yes," Jefferson said.

"Yet you tell us often that humans have no unifying culture. You have many cultures and are quite proud of that fact. You claim diversity is your strength."

"Some things are universal."

"Yet the cause of this crisis seems to be a lack of humanity," Number Fifty-six said.

"Excuse me?"

"A mass grave. My sources tell me that the bodies within it died at the same time, a time when there were no Disty on Mars. So perhaps some other alien group came into Sahara Dome and destroyed a hundred humans in a single angry gesture, or the humans did this to themselves."

Jefferson took a shallow breath. It took all of his strength not to look at the diplomats behind him or at the Peyti sitting one step up. He couldn't give Fifty-six this point. It would undermine every argument to come, particularly if the Disty wanted to use some space station as a short-term solution.

"We are not responsible for those deaths," Jefferson said. "Whatever conspiracy theories your government is developing are wrong. We had no knowledge of those bodies until this turned into a crisis."

"Someone did," Fifty-six said. "Someone used a disgraced corpse to call attention to the mass grave, knowing the Disty would be forced to look through the land before declaring it clean. Someone knew. And if the deaths were caused by humans acting against humans, then that someone was human."

Jefferson was out of his depth. "We are trying to save lives here. If you persist in blame and squabbling, your own people will die."

"You imply we should then take the fault," Number Fifty-six said. He slipped off the table. "They might have to die anyway. This contamination is the greatest we have seen in hundreds of years. If we cannot effectively decontaminate, the Contaminated Ones will have to die before they can infect anyone else. You seem to think this does not move me. It does. But I know the risks to my people. Do you know the risks to yours?"

Jefferson wasn't sure how to take that. Was it a threat?

"This will get resolved," he said.

"Another human trait," Fifty-six said. "Unrealistic optimism. Just because you believe it does not make it so."

Jefferson had had enough. "That's a strange thing to tell me, when there is nothing physically wrong with the Disty you're planning to slaughter."

The diplomats behind him gasped. The Peyti raised their fingertips in a sign of displeasure. The Ebe closed their eyes, and the Disty—all but Fifty-six—left the room.

"You are so certain there is no physical consequence to us from this contamination?" Fifty-six asked.

Jefferson had already fumbled. He saw no reason in trying to make up for it now.

"Yes," he said. "If there was physical contamination, you would have had signs of it long before the bodies were dug up. Your people would have been ill for decades—every single one who lived in that section of Sahara Dome."

Number Fifty-six seemed small as he stood beside the table. "Your ignorance astounds me. And it should not, considering I have spent most of my adult life among your people. I have thought, in my years in service to this strange dream of allying with cultures that are so foreign from mine as to be unintelligible, that eventually some would learn. *You* would learn. But you do not. You believe what you see and feel, and deny everything else."

Jefferson felt the rebuke but didn't understand it. Was Fifty-six saying they were physically contaminated? How did that work, then?

Number Fifty-six templed his fingers, bowed slightly, and started to leave. Then he stopped.

"Because you are wondering," he said, and then he paused, tilted his head again, and let his eyes glitter. That seemed to be the Disty equivalent of a polite smile.

Jefferson didn't move. He wasn't sure of the damage he had done.

"And I know you are wondering," Fifty-six said, "because I have made it a lifelong mission to understand all I can about the aliens that surround me. Because you are wondering, I will tell you this: My people *are* ill because of this contamination. They have a sickness of something you might call the soul, although that wouldn't be quite accurate."

Jefferson opened his mouth to ask a question, but Fifty-six held up a hand. It was a startlingly human gesture, and it made Fifty-six seem even smaller.

"Were there signs of this sickness?" Fifty-six asked, as if neither he nor Jefferson had moved. "No. Of course not. Such a sickness only occurs when what has been buried has been revealed. The contamination becomes real and must be dealt with immediately."

"Which we are trying to do," Jefferson said.

"*We* are trying nothing," Fifty-six said. "Your people have no understanding of this, and think it a foolish overreaction. My own people are trying to stop a crisis from spreading first, and then we shall deal with the contamination's source. But at the moment, no one is doing that. No one is trying to clean up the source."

"So your people would have stayed fine if this grave had remained buried," Jefferson said.

Number Fifty-six shook his head slightly. "Not fine. Better than they are now, but not fine. You have not listened to me."

"I have listened to you," Jefferson said, "and I am hearing a fundamental difference between our peoples. We believe that revealing problems—opening them to the light—is the first step in solving them. You seem to think revealing problems makes matters worse."

"Once again, you see only through the prism of your own experience. Someday, Mr. Jefferson, you should try to live in a completely nonhuman environment and see what kind of perspective you will gain. Until then, I think you a poor advocate for your people."

Number Fifty-six turned back toward the door, and started to leave.

"Wait!" Jefferson said. "What about finding a solution?"

Number Fifty-six stopped but did not face Jefferson. "I believe we have just discovered that there is no solution, at least not one we can find together. We shall take care of our own. I suggest you do the same."

And then he left.

Jefferson bowed his head. He had never failed so spectacularly before—and had never done so with so much at stake.

The rift between the Disty and humans had just become insurmountable.

49

Flint went through his entire list of contacts. He was unable to reach the governor-general, the mayor of Armstrong, and Armstrong's representative on the Council for the United Domes of the Moon. He couldn't reach any of the city council members either, and the chief of police responded to his link with a pointed message: She didn't talk with Retrieval Artists.

He even tried to reach the Alliance, but got only an invitation to leave his message on a board and wait for a response that would arrive "within a few days."

Flint was feeling lightheaded and desperate. The office had gotten hot again. He would have to realign his environmental controls—something he had to do, it seemed, monthly. He wiped the sweat off his forehead.

He hadn't wanted to contact DeRicci. He knew she was already overwhelmed with the refugee situation. But he had no choice.

He used her emergency links.

She responded audio only: "Can this wait?"

He heard the annoyance in her tone and almost smiled. Noelle DeRicci was under a lot of pressure and wanted less information rather than more.

"No, Noelle, it can't. I may have a solution to the Disty crisis."

DeRicci cursed, which wasn't the reaction Flint expected,

and then told him to hold on. The link went so silent that he had to check the function to make sure it wasn't dead.

Then she appeared, full audio and visual, which he routed to his main desk screen. Seeing a tiny DeRicci on a vision screen made him nervous.

"Make this fast." DeRicci's face was set in harsh lines. "I'm talking to the governor-general right now, and she's not happy that I closed down the ports."

Obviously, DeRicci had gone outside politics to do her job. That didn't surprise Flint, but he couldn't ask about it at the moment. He recognized DeRicci's expression. She was so stressed that she would cut him off if she felt he was wasting her time.

"I have found a number of survivors of that massacre," he said.

"So?"

"So," he said, "the Disty can use them to decontaminate their people and the Domes."

DeRicci's eyes narrowed. "I *know* that. Why should I care about these survivors?"

"Because a dozen of them are on the Moon."

The color left her face. Then her mouth opened slightly and she shook her head. She understood exactly what that meant. It meant a solution. It meant that the crisis would end.

"I've been trying to hand these names off to someone, anyone, but no one was taking my calls."

"Except stupid ole me," DeRicci said, and actually smiled. "Can you send me that information? Encrypted."

"Doing so as we speak," Flint said.

"You're sure all the information is accurate?"

"Most of it to the day, a few to the month. Good luck with this, Noelle."

"Thanks, Miles. You have no idea what you've done." Then she signed off.

He clasped his hands behind his head, leaned back in his chair, and let out a huge sigh of relief. He had done what he could. He had served his clients in Sahara Dome, and he might have stopped a crisis—provided DeRicci could make timely use of those names.

Having the governor-general in DeRicci's office made the likelihood of success all that much greater.

Flint stood. He deserved a good meal and a long rest. If the crisis settled down—*when* the crisis settled down—he would send a final bill to Sahara Dome.

And then he would consider this case closed.

50

It took DeRicci nearly the full fifteen minutes to explain everything to the governor-general. Getting the governor-general to understand that family members could somehow help with the decontamination process took the most time.

Finally, DeRicci had the governor-general talk to Menodi at the University of Armstrong—after warning both of them to keep the conversation short.

Then, without telling the governor-general where she had gotten the information, DeRicci told her that there were a dozen such survivors—real members of the families that died—on the Moon.

The governor-general's eyes lit up. "We can actually solve this? We can use our Disty to perform some sort of ritual when these ships land?"

"I don't think so," DeRicci said, and wished she hadn't limited the conversation with Menodi after all. "I think we're better off contacting the Alliance, and letting the Disty High Command take this over."

The governor-general studied DeRicci for a moment, then sighed. "I suppose you're right. Let me make the contact and see what we have to do."

She walked to a far corner of the room so that she could have some privacy while using audio and visual links. DeRicci let her have the entire office.

DeRicci went into Popova's office, where she had initially

taken Flint's call. Popova was at her desk, placating various people, from the UDM councilors who were still on standby for a meeting that might never happen to mayors of the port cities who were beginning to get nervous about the growing number of Disty vessels hovering outside the restricted space.

"How many ships are there?" DeRicci asked.

"Fifty at last count." Popova nodded toward the wall screen. Vessels floated against an invisible line, following the requests of the various Moon governments.

"Have any tried to cross?" DeRicci asked.

"Not yet," Popova said, "but it's only a matter of time."

"How many more are coming?"

Popova shook her head. "It looks like they solved the issues with the space traffic control near Sahara Dome, so a lot of ships have taken off in the last few hours. No one knows how many because Sahara Dome isn't talking to anyone. And other Disty are fleeing from southern cities on Mars—only no one thinks those Disty are contaminated. They're just scared."

"Lovely," DeRicci said.

The governor-general summoned her along the links. De-Ricci sighed and went back into her office.

The governor-general was using part of DeRicci's wall screen as a personal viewing screen. A woman DeRicci had never seen before peered out. In the corner, an Alliance logo marked the transmission.

"Can you assure me—us—that these names are legitimate?" the governor-general asked.

"Yes," DeRicci said. She trusted Flint. He wouldn't have contacted her otherwise.

"You got them how?" the governor-general asked.

"I put a researcher on this the moment I heard of it," De-Ricci said, hoping she wasn't lying too badly. "It took some time and some luck, but I got this information in return."

The woman on the screen nodded. "My sources tell me we have to get those survivors to Sahara Dome. I'll talk to one of the Disty here and make sure of procedure. You get those survivors ready to leave the Moon."

"Will do," the governor-general said.

"I'll be back in touch with instructions shortly," the woman responded, and signed off. For a moment, the Alliance logo filled the screen, and then the news reappeared, tiny images of Mars with even tinier ships coming off it like dust in a windstorm.

"You heard her," the governor-general said. "Round these people up."

"That's a problem," DeRicci said. "These survivors are scattered all over the Moon. We don't have a Moon-wide security force to handle this. We'll need the cooperation of all the mayors."

The governor-general sighed. "I'm sure they will when they understand."

"And," DeRicci said, "if these survivors have to leave the Moon, how do we get them out of here? The United Domes has no fleet."

"I guess we commandeer a private ship," the governor-general said. "We'll bring them all to Armstrong and leave out of this Dome."

"We don't have the authority to commandeer a ship," DeRicci said. "We could hire one, but I worry about attracting media attention. If they hear anything about this, they'll be all over it, and I think we need to keep this quiet."

"Agreed," the governor-general said.

"We also have a problem with the pilot, whoever it's going to be," DeRicci said. "We need someone experienced who won't buckle under any kind of pressure."

"See what you can do about that," the governor-general snapped. "I'll handle the mayors."

"We need those survivors as quickly as possible," DeRicci said.

The governor-general glared at her. "I am aware that this is an emergency."

"Good," DeRicci said. "Because there's still a lot that can go wrong."

51

Jefferson stepped through the tiny square door, feeling like he was visiting a child's playground. He'd never been to the Disty section of the compound before. He felt uncomfortable going there now, but Fifty-six wasn't going to come to him.

They were going to meet on Disty turf.

Jefferson had sent a dozen messages since he received word from Armstrong that survivors of the massacre had been found. Half a dozen Disty specialists on the human diplomatic team had assured him this would solve the problem.

He wasn't sure how, but this time, he was smart enough not to ask.

He only wished he had been smart enough not to lose his temper with Fifty-six in the first place.

Number Fifty-six had clearly lost his temper with Jefferson too. Fifty-six hadn't taken any of his messages. Finally, one of the Peyti delegation had intervened.

Jefferson still didn't understand how Fifty-six's pride was more important than the death of hundreds of his people, but then, Jefferson had come to realize he understood next to nothing about the Disty.

Certainly, he didn't understand how they lived. He had been warned that the quarters would be cramped and claustrophobic, but he hadn't realized how very tight they were. He had to walk while crouched, and it took only a few moments for his back to protest.

The lighting was thin, and the walls were so close together that they brushed his shoulders. There was only room for one human in a passage, although ahead of him he saw two Disty pass each other. Fortunately, neither Disty came his way, and he had the corridor all to himself. If he hadn't downloaded an area map and hadn't placed it in his vision, he would have been lost a long time ago.

The entire area smelled vaguely of unwashed skin and old wood. Other lingering odors—he assumed (he hoped) they were cooking odors—caught his nose whenever he reached a cross-corridor, and that was most of the time.

Finally, he reached the set of rooms that belonged to Fifty-six's delegation. The door at the end of the corridor was open, and a Disty bade him to come inside.

Jefferson had no idea if that Disty was one he'd seen before or not. He was still having trouble with all but the largest distinctions among them. He hoped none expected him to remember them.

The interior of Fifty-six's rooms weren't quite as cramped as the corridor. Jefferson could stand upright, but his head brushed the low ceiling. He wouldn't be able to sit on a table-top here, not that he saw any. The furniture was built into the walls—seats like boxes came out squarely and folded against the floor.

In a far room, he saw a Ping-Pong table, but it wasn't being used. The Disty had adopted few human things, but Ping-Pong was one of them. The other was the game Go, which had always worried Jefferson. Go was a game of strategy. It suited the devious mind.

The Disty who had let him in led him to a chamber toward the back. Its walls were covered in red velvet, and the place smelled of a mixture of lilac, tobacco, and incense. Jefferson's eyes watered, and he had to use all of his personal strength to hold back a sneeze.

It took him a moment to see Fifty-six. Fifty-six was wearing a red velvet robe, which looked five sizes too big on him, and he sat on a carpeted mound in the middle of the floor.

"This is our negotiation room," Fifty-six said. "We redesigned it with humans in mind. We can be on a platform, but you won't have to bend quite so much."

"Thank you," Jefferson said, uncertain how else to respond.

"I am told by a reliable source that you beg forgiveness for your crude and insulting remarks earlier," Fifty-six said, as if that were a foregone conclusion.

Jefferson would never beg forgiveness of anyone. He had negotiated his way out of delicate situations in the past, but he had never done so by placing himself so squarely in the wrong.

This time, apparently, he had no choice.

"Yes," he said. "I am sorry."

Then he bowed his head, hoping he was contrite enough.

"Sit," Fifty-six said. "Tell me your proposal."

Jefferson sat on the platform, surprised at the bit of cushion beneath. He almost forgot to bend and touch his head to the top of the platform. He hoped that Fifty-six wouldn't take offense at the momentary lapse.

Jefferson kept his forehead down until Fifty-six told him to sit up. "Through extensive research, we have found survivors of that massacre. Most are in the Outlying Colonies and cannot be here in any swift amount of time. But twelve are on the Moon."

Fifty-six templed his fingers and raised them. "I thought no one knew of this event."

"Apparently, there are records of it in the Outlying Colonies. The woman who was killed—whose body we initially found—had tried to steal money from the survivors, and her body was placed there as some sort of sign."

Fifty-six waved one hand in dismissal. "I am intrigued by these survivors. Are they descendents?"

"Immediate relatives," Jefferson said. "We searched for those first. These people were actually present at the massacre and managed to escape."

Fifty-six folded his hands back together, then bowed his head. He said nothing for a very long time.

Jefferson wasn't sure what Fifty-six was doing. He had no

idea how tightly the Disty were linked or if there was even any kind of network among them. He didn't know if Fifty-six was just thinking, meditating, or communicating.

Then Fifty-six raised his head. "You are certain these are the survivors, the actual survivors?"

"Positive," Jefferson said.

Fifty-six pressed his templed fingers against his face.

"There is hope then," he said with something that sounded like relief. "There is finally hope."

52

The governor-general was still using DeRicci's office as if it were her own private conference center. She sat in the center of the room, looking like a wizard as she worked the screens above the see-through desk.

DeRicci left, glancing at Popova. She had dozens of people on her personal screen, and several assistants, some De-Ricci hadn't seen before, crowded the front office, trying to cajole, convince, and coordinate the various aspects of the survivor roundup.

DeRicci couldn't find privacy anywhere. She had been thinking about the pilot situation and she could come up with only one solution. But she didn't want anyone else to know about it.

She avoided the elevator and took the back stairs to the third floor. There she found offices still under construction. She took the office in the very back—one with no windows —and hoped it had no surveillance equipment either.

She sat in the middle of the floor and contacted Flint. It took him a moment to answer. Behind him, she heard the rumble of voices.

He wasn't alone.

"Where are you?" she asked.

"Stefano's Restaurant," he said. "Why?"

"I need to talk to you in private."

"You want to come to my office?"

"There's no time," DeRicci said. "Go somewhere and call me back."

Then she signed off. She waited five minutes and was about to call him back when her link chirruped. She answered and saw Flint's pale skin and startlingly blond hair fill the tiny screen she had raised in her vision.

"What's going on?" he asked.

"Is this private?" she asked.

"Yes. I've secured my line and encrypted as much as possible. Have you?"

She didn't know. All of that level of tech was beyond her.

"You haven't, have you? Let me." He did something. His image bounced, floated into bits, and then returned. "That's the best I can do from this distance."

She didn't want to know what he had just done. His ability with computers and links and chips always disturbed her.

"What's so important?" he asked.

"Do you still have your ship?" she said.

"Yes," he said.

"I need to hire it. I'll pay you out of my own discretionary funds. I can't track this."

"What's going on, Noelle?"

"We don't have a way to get the survivors to Mars. I'd like to hire you to do it."

He let out a small sigh. "I'm not in the police business anymore, and I'm not for hire as a pilot."

"Miles, we have no one else. I either hire you or some unknown company, and I'm afraid to do that. First of all, you know the risks. Second, you've handled delicate situations in space when you were with Space Traffic Control. Third, you know how to dodge the press. And finally, I trust you, Miles. I'm afraid to give this one to anybody else."

"You realize that the Disty consider me contaminated," he said.

"We don't know that for sure," she said, not because she was convinced of it, but because she had forgotten. If Flint couldn't do this, she didn't know what she would do.

"I'm pretty sure of it," Flint said.

"Well, don't tell anyone," DeRicci said. "I'm certainly not going to bandy your name about."

"If it comes out that you hired me, you could get into a lot of trouble."

"So be it," she said. "I'm already being called a bigot. It's all over the news that I'm not letting the Disty in because I hate them."

His expression sobered. "I know. I'm sorry."

"It's not your fault. You weren't the offending partner."

"No one should have said that. I don't care how jealous he was."

She grinned. "That was my take on him too."

"But bad press is one thing, Noelle. The chief of police wouldn't take my call today because she doesn't want to be in contact with a Retrieval Artist, even one that used to work for her. Hiring me could cost your career."

"Like I care," she said. "People are dying."

Flint smiled. "You're never going to be a politician."

"I could have told you that. In fact, I think I did."

"What do you need me to do?" he asked, and she felt herself relax.

"Get to the port and wait for instructions," she said. "I'm sure I'll have some for you soon."

"How many survivors am I taking with me?" he asked.

"All of them," she said. "We hope."

"I'll be ready," he said, and signed off.

DeRicci buried her face in her hands. She was shaking. She had lied to Flint. She did care about her career. It was just out of her control now.

So she would do what she always had. She would do what she thought best—until someone, or something, proved her wrong.

53

Flint got to Armstrong's Space Port in record time. The port was unusually empty, since no flights were landing at all. He saw no one he knew as he made his way to Terminal 25, where the *Emmeline* was housed.

The *Emmeline* was named for Flint's daughter. He wished he could find a way to give her a more permanent memorial; naming a yacht after his child seemed like something the idle rich did. And while he was rich (and having trouble remembering it), he was not idle. He was just beginning to think he was the only person who remembered his baby girl.

The survivors might wonder why they were being dragged into this part of the port. In fact, so might the authorities that brought them here. Terminal 25 was the largest terminal, partly because of the size of the vessels that docked here. They were all owned by the very rich, and were all oversized.

That was probably another reason DeRicci had contacted him. She knew his yacht was large enough to carry twelve people in comfort.

She also knew he had enough weaponry aboard to blast his way through the Disty perimeter just outside of Moon space, or anything else he might run into. He constantly upgraded the *Emmeline*. If a new weapons system came out, he installed it. If an improved drive came out, he installed that too. He also added things that he had become used to during his turn as a Traffic cop: a brig, hooks on the sides of chairs for handcuffs, and redundant security systems that weren't linked to each other, so no one person could easily take over the ship. He also had handheld weapons in the cockpit and in his private quarters. The weapons were concealed, and were keyed to his palm print.

The outside of the ship had no identifying markings. It was black and sleek, built for speed, shaped like a bird with its nose pressing slightly downward. There were other yachts in Terminal 25 that were bigger, many that were more impressive, but none had the speed, agility, and security features that the *Emmeline* did.

Flint sat outside the ship, on the dock itself, and waited, just like he had been instructed. He had no idea how he would take all of these disparate people to Mars—the site of the greatest tragedy in their lives. How had DeRicci convinced them to donate their time—and perhaps their future—to rescuing the descendents of the very people who had murdered their own families?

Flint hoped the flight would be as easy as DeRicci seemed to think it would. This was a level of involvement he didn't want—one he was only doing for his friend.

Although that wasn't entirely true. As she had said, he knew what was at stake, and he knew that few others would help or have the skills to do so.

He was beginning to realize that no matter how hard he tried to stay out of things, he would fail. Somehow he always found himself in the middle of a crisis, and he never could walk away.

No matter what was at stake.

54

Jefferson stepped out of the tiny door that marked the Disty wing of the compound, and stood upright for the first time in hours. His back ached, his head ached, and he was covered in sweat. He was also shivering; the air in the main corridor was thirty degrees colder than the Disty kept their wing.

Several assistants, the lower-level human-Disty ambassadors, and Chief Protocol Officer Ogden all met him. They were waiting by the floor-to-ceiling windows, silhouetted against the backdrop of snow that seemed to extend forever.

"Well?" Ogden asked. "What do we have to do?"

"We have to get the survivors to Lowell. It has the largest Dome on the southern hemisphere of Mars. From there, the survivors will be taken to some smaller Dome, where they'll conduct a ceremony with the Contaminated Ones. It's going to take time to get them to Wells and Sahara Dome. We're going to have to compensate these people and their families somehow. I'm not sure we can justify this otherwise."

He wiped the sweat from his face. He felt like he had been up for three weeks.

Ogden put a gentling hand on his arm. "Are you all right?"

He looked at her, blinked, and realized he hadn't really seen her at all. Her face was pulled into an unusual frown, the shadows under her eyes deep, a line across her forehead looking new. He had never had much feeling for her; he had al-

ways thought her job dull but necessary, and felt that only a
fussbudget could perform it well.

"No," he said, and staggered toward one of the chairs in
the hallway. He sat, then leaned against the back, feeling cold
seep in through the windows.

"Is it physical?" Ogden asked as she followed him. "Must
I notify someone?"

He shook his head. The human representative to Mars
watched him, as did the other human representatives to the
Disty. They all probably thought they could have done better
than he had.

"They want a Death Squad to meet the ship in orbit. The
Death Squad is going to take the survivors to Lowell."

He closed his eyes for a half second, felt dizzy and weak,
and opened them again. Everyone was still staring at him.

"I agreed to it," he said. "And I have no idea what a Death
Squad is."

The silence that followed his words was profound. Maybe
they felt that he was stupid, but they hadn't been in that red
velvet, overheated room, with Disty all around, their little bodies pressing against the platform, their oblong eyes watching
his every move.

"It's their version of an undertaker," the Mars representative finally said. "And more."

"Combined with assassins," one of the other representatives said. "They're the ones who do the vengeance killings."

"Only because they handle everything to do with death.
This has to do with death. I'm sure that's why they're in
charge." The Mars representative rubbed her elgonated hands
together.

Jefferson didn't trust the movement.

"You're afraid you've killed them," Ogden said, so softly
that only he could hear. "That's why you spoke of familial
compensation."

"Fifty-six had me in a corner. He agreed on the record that
his people will stop blaming us if we let them handle the survivors their way."

"Stop blaming us?" said the second representative, another young woman. "What does that mean?"

Jefferson looked at her. He apparently had been speaking loud enough to have been overheard.

"If the Disty stop pursuing this massacre as an act done only to take the Disty off Mars, then we actually have some basis for discussions. We'll probably have to make even more concessions to them—after all, it's their people who are dying—but we won't have economic and physical liability. Which is a good thing, in this current economy."

"I thought Alliance members can't sue each other," the Mars representative said.

"The countries can't. The representatives for various governments can't. But the corporations can and individuals can. It would have gotten ugly, and not just on the legal side. We might have lost our entire claim to Mars."

He leaned his head back, feeling the cold glass against his scalp.

The representatives still stared at him as if they couldn't understand what he had done, agreeing to something involving a dozen human lives, something he hadn't entirely understood.

"We're not well liked within the Alliance," he said. "We think we are—what Fifty-six calls the infallible human optimism—but we are mostly hated for our intolerance and our lack of understanding about other cultures. If the Disty had declared war on us, a war that they would have been able to justify, a *culture* war, we would have found ourselves alone against former allies. The destruction would have been unimaginable."

"Yet you imagined it," the second representative snapped. "And paid for it with twelve lives."

He closed his eyes. "Probably," he whispered. "Probably."

55

They looked terrified and somewhat sick, the seven people who sat in the game room of the *Emmeline*. They were scattered on the couches, not touching the screens in front of them, ignoring the food the serving 'bots kept circulating.

Seven people who, hours before, had been going innocently about their lives, and would have continued to do so if Flint hadn't found them.

They looked different than he expected. He had expected them to have a similar appearance, perhaps because they were all about the same age and had gone through the same horrors in their childhoods. But the three women, all of whom sat on the same side of the room, varied from portly to thin, from gray haired to hair an unnatural blue, from middle-aged features to features so clearly enhanced that they seemed not quite human.

The four men were just as different. Two were rangy, with the unnatural thinness that suggested too much time in zero-G—perhaps space work, perhaps terrible travel conditions back when they were children. The other two looked a bit too comfortable. One had the round body so preferred in the Outlying Colonies—fatness as a sign of wealth. The other seemed so normal that Flint would not have noticed him on the street—brown skin, brown eyes, brown hair, a softness to his body that suggested a lack of exercise, a way of disappearing in a room filled with people.

The private security team that had brought them to the *Emmeline*—a team hired from one of Armstrong's best and most discrete firms—had told Flint that the remaining five survivors had refused to come. Even though the officers who had found them mentioned imprisonment, the five who had stayed behind claimed they would have preferred anything— even death—to returning to Mars.

Flint had a hunch that, in their shoes, he might have made the same choice.

He had spent the first hour of the flight getting the *Emmeline* out of the Moon's restricted space. There had been a difficult moment when he had gone past a group of Disty ships still hovering outside the boundaries.

DeRicci had told him, as she gave him his final instructions, that these Disty were waiting. Apparently, someone had told them that negotiations were underway, and any impulsive actions on the part of the Contaminated Ones would go badly for all involved.

Flint wondered how long that truce would hold.

DeRicci had also told him that he wasn't going to land on Mars. Instead, a Disty ship would dock with his and take the survivors to Lowell.

Flint hadn't informed them of that yet. He hadn't said much of anything.

In fact, while he had been in the cockpit, alone, negotiating the ship through the rough section, he had opened the communication system to the game room and listened to the survivors. Their conversation had been perfunctory, conducted almost as if speech were required. The introductions had a tinge of sadness, or perhaps it was the sentences that followed:

I remember you.

I haven't seen you since that night.

I had no idea what happened to you.

And on and on, until Flint wanted to shut off the conversation. Then it switched to the ways they were brought to the ship:

They told me they'd take my children if they couldn't take me.

They told me I would be imprisoned if I didn't come.

They told me I'd be killed.

They told me. They told me. They told me. And Flint had become the representative for "they." Had DeRicci known how these people were picked up and convinced to go on this mission? Would she have asked him to participate if she had?

When the ship was safely away from the Moon, he put it on autopilot, linked it to his own personal network, and left the cockpit. He walked down the carpeted halls, past the large, fancy galley that came standard on this version of the yacht, past the sitting area and the main dining area, to the game room.

He didn't play games and he had asked to have the room converted into something else. The manufacturer had toned down the games, but convinced Flint to keep part of it, saying that his guests would appreciate the opportunity to do something fun on long voyages.

He never thought of this yacht as fun, nor had he ever expected guests. Still, he must have had a vestige of that conversation on his mind when he placed the seven passengers in here, after showing them each their separate quarters.

The game room had an unused air, even now, when it was filled with people. The room smelled faintly of musky perfume and garlic—the serving 'bots were carrying around some sort of beef-and-garlic concoction they had pulled from his stores. The concoction was wasted on this group; no one was eating.

All seven looked at him when he came in the room and leaned against the stylish black wall. He had decided, as he had walked here, that he had nothing to lose in disassociating himself from the various government agencies that had rounded them up.

"I overheard your conversation." He nodded at the small systems panel near the ceiling, just so that they knew he hadn't hidden the sound system capabilities from them. "We can turn back if you want. I'm not any kind of authority. I'm just a pilot they've hired to take you to Mars."

"You'd take us home?" asked Hildy Vajra. She was the youngest survivor, barely four months old when the massacre happened, yet she looked the oldest now. She clearly hadn't had any enhancements. Her eyes had laugh lines in the corners, and her skin was beginning to get a patina of age.

"Yes," Flint said. "I can't vouch for what would happen to you after you arrived, but I would take you back to Armstrong and try not to call attention to your arrival."

"Meaning what?" Kiyoshi Stewart asked. He was the oldest, and had come the farthest that day. His home was in one of the small, remote Domes near Tycho Crater.

"My yacht docks in Terminal 25," Flint said. "One of the privileges there is that the port doesn't have to report my comings and goings to Space Traffic. If they don't notice us, then we'll have gotten in easily."

"Only no one can get onto the Moon right now," Elwin Wilson said. He was the soft one, the one who blended into the background. Flint was surprised he had spoken up at all.

"I know some people. We could probably land," Flint said.

"Which would call attention to us," Juana Marcos said. Her beauty was so perfect that it looked fake—the high cheekbones, the almond eyes, the smooth skin. Her eye and hair color matched perfectly, and the color of her cheeks picked up the pinks in her blouse. Her legs, covered in cropped pants, were crossed at the ankles and swept to the side as if she were at a party instead of riding away from her home.

"It might," Flint said. "It might not."

"What'll it cost us?" Wilson asked.

"Nothing," Flint said. "I'm not doing this for the money."

"Then why are you doing it?" the last woman, Eugenie McEvoy, asked. Her blue hair looked like an affectation. All of her clothing did as well. It didn't quite fit, and seemed like something someone else had picked out for her.

"Because Mars is having a crisis, and we're going to have

one, if this doesn't get solved. From what I understand, you people are the only solution."

"The massacre," Salvatore Weiss said. He was the fat one, his voice as sculpted as his body.

"Yes," Flint said.

"They expect us to go back and save the people who killed our families," Weiss said.

"Maybe their descendents," Flint said. "But there are a lot of others there. Innocents who had nothing to do with that massacre."

"So?" McEvoy asked.

"So it's your choice," Flint said. "But no matter what happens, the news of the massacre is finally out. That's some good which has come of this."

"As if that brings our families back."

Flint looked sideways. The last survivor, Glen Norton, finally spoke up. He had been lounging in the corner, his long legs extended. His eyes, hooded and tired, met Flint's.

"Of course it won't," Flint said.

"But you said that as if it would, as if we should care that the universe finally knows about our little tragedy. So what if the Disty are having one? So what if humans die because of some weird cultural difference? I don't care."

"Then why did you come?" Marcos asked him.

Norton moved his head ever so slowly toward her. His gaze ran the entire length of her, from cropped pants to perfect cheekbones, and Flint got the sense that Norton didn't approve of what he saw.

"I had no choice," Norton said curtly.

"I'm giving you a choice," Flint said. "You can go back."

"Do we vote?" Norton asked. "What if six agree and one doesn't? Then what do we do?"

"I don't know," Flint said. "I'm just the pilot. You're the ones who are probably going to lose a week or two helping folks you don't know."

He wasn't quite sure why he had phrased it that way; maybe because Norton had annoyed him. Maybe because

Flint didn't really want to turn back. He wanted this crisis solved, and the seven of them had the power to do so.

"People helped us," Vajra said quietly. "Took us in when they didn't have to."

"People also slaughtered our families." Norton's voice had a sarcastic strength. "If we follow your logic, we could be saints or sinners, depending on how we choose to see our past."

"I think that's exactly right," Stewart said. "We could hate or we could choose to be different. I've always chosen to be different."

"I'm rather fond of hate," Norton said, and crossed his arms.

Everyone stared at him.

Then Flint said, "If you make the passive decision, you will end up on Mars. I think you're all better off to make an active one."

"They rounded us up like animals," Weiss said.

"It was like the past all over again," said Wilson.

"I have only been that scared once before," Marcos said.

Flint nodded. "That's why I'm giving you a choice."

Vajra sighed. "What do we become if we don't help? Will this get fed to the media?"

"I have no control over that either," Flint said. "I can get you there or not. It's that simple."

"I say we go," Stewart said. "It's the right thing."

"The right thing." Norton shook his head and closed his eyes.

"Don't you have a vote, Mr. Norton?" Vajra asked.

"I think we know how he stands," Marcos said coolly, obviously still smarting from that appraising look he had given her.

"So let's find out how the rest of us feel," Weiss said. "If you don't mind, mister, can you leave us? And maybe shut off that intercom in the control room for a little while."

Mister. Flint hadn't realized that he had failed to give them his name. "Sure," he said.

He nodded at them, then eased out the door. He wasn't

about to shut off the controls. He wanted to know at all times what the people on his ship were doing.

But he would give them the illusion of privacy.

Just like he was giving them the illusion of choice.

when the ports in his ship were closing.

This, he would give them to medium a severity
just like he was giving them the most punishment

56

Hauk Rackam watched the wall screens in his office, staring at the hundreds of ships still leaving Mars's orbit. Hundreds of ships, all because he hadn't closed the ports. His assistant, Zayna Columbus, kept reporting the Disty death toll to him, mostly to rub it in. She had disagreed with him all along. He had made one executive decision, and she hated the fact he hadn't taken her complete advice.

He had no idea how many dead there would have been in the ports if he had closed them when she had suggested, all those hours ago. He knew quite well that the colliding and exploding ships were his fault, just like the saved lives—the fact that only Wells and Sahara Dome were affected—were also his fault.

And Columbus's idea.

Rackam closed his eyes, rubbing them with his thumb and forefinger. When this was all over, he was going to resign as incoming leader of the Human Governments of Mars. He had thought it a ceremonial position—he had even checked the bylaws: It *was* a ceremonial position, except in the unlikely event of a governmental vacuum.

Which had happened. He made sure he had recorded everything: the unavailability of the Disty High Council, of the Death Squads, of anyone who could give him advice. He even had Wyome Nakamura collate everyone's notes on the events of the past day, so that when the inevitable trial came—and it would—he would have evidence to present that someone had to act, and his assistants convinced him that someone should have been him.

That knowledge didn't help his conscience, though. He had a feeling that if he had been smarter or perhaps less focused on his own fear, he might have made a better choice.

He hadn't been made for this kind of decision. He had no training for it, no mind for it, and obviously no stomach for it.

It would haunt him for the rest of his life, even if no one brought charges against him for all these deaths.

"Sir?" Columbus was at his door again. She seemed even more grotesque to him, with her lack of concern about her appearance, her too-intelligent eyes always seeing everything, that narrow and disapproving mouth.

"What is it now?" he asked, letting the weariness he felt into his voice.

"We've finally heard from the Disty."

A drop of sweat ran down the side of his face and settled on his chin. "And?"

"They have a solution, sir, and they want us to make the arrangements with the governments of Wells and Sahara Dome. They'll take care of their own people, but there are humans to be decontaminated as well."

Solution? Humans? Decontaminated? Could he be so fortunate?

"What do we have to do?"

"A Death Squad will arrive in Wells in two days. The squad will use its own ritual to decontaminate the Dome as well as the humans inside it." She tapped a chip on the back of her hand. "I have a list of instructions. The humans of Wells are supposed to do all these things to prepare."

Rackam wiped the sweat off his chin. "What about Sahara Dome?"

"It's more complicated for them. The Disty want several members of Sahara Dome's human government to go to Wells for decontamination so that they can then meet with some of the ranking Disty. Apparently, what has to happen in Sahara

Dome is long and involved, and the Disty don't trust the news of it to a go-between."

Rackam stared at her for a long time, parsing her words. He was to make sure everything happened in Wells, and then it was out of his hands. "Did they say anything about us? About culpability? About the ports?"

"No," Columbus said, "and I'm not about to prompt them. So much has happened, they might ignore some of the smaller things."

Lost ships and lost lives were smaller things?

He knew sometimes the Disty didn't care about their own people at all. He had just figured that was the Disty's business. Now it had an effect on him.

Everything had an effect on him.

He sighed and looked at those ships, still leaving the ports.

"Fine," he said to Columbus. "You talked to the Disty, you may as well talk to Wells. Tell them what they have to do. Make sure they do it. Okay?"

"You don't care what 'it' is?" Columbus asked.

He didn't look at her. "Am I ordering more death?"

"Not from what I understand. This is actually a solution."

"Then I don't care about their damn rituals. I just want this whole thing to end."

"It looks like it will, sir," Columbus said. "Barring unforeseens, of course."

Rackam shuddered. Unforeseens. This entire event had been unforeseen. He didn't want to think about any more unforeseens.

"Just see that this gets done," he said to her.

"Yes, sir." She bobbed once, then left the room.

He folded his arms on the table and hid his face in them. Someone else was going to handle everything from now on.

He just wished he knew a way to forget the past twenty-four hours. Forget them for the rest of his life.

57

Flint sat in his cockpit, arms crossed, listening to the vote. At first, he tried to count the voices weighing in, but he couldn't. He wasn't familiar enough with them. He wasn't sure if Norton voted at all. Since this wasn't a formal vote, no one had made little ballots or asked people to raise their hand.

Instead, they simply declared themselves, all of them—to Flint's surprise—in favor of going. Then they discussed how difficult the next few weeks would be on themselves and their families. Vajra suggested that this might help them deal with the massacre itself. The others quietly agreed—all except Norton.

He let out a small bark of a laugh. "You think you'll ever get over that? It's not something people recover from. We'll wear its stain for the rest of our lives."

"Maybe we'll be able to deal with it better," Vajra said.

"You mean bury it, don't you?" Norton asked.

The others shut him down, but Flint shuddered, just a little. The man told enough truth to make him difficult. Flint hadn't liked him. Having him in the same room during this decision process had probably been hard for all of them.

When the group elected Weiss to tell Flint their decision, Flint shut off his overhead speakers. He kept monitoring the conversation on an internal link.

It took Weiss a while to find the cockpit—a good sign, Flint thought. These people weren't as familiar with ships as

Flint had worried they were. That gave him an advantage too. Ever since he'd discovered that they'd been coerced into coming here, he had worried about them. He didn't want them to take out their anger and frustration on him.

Weiss knocked on the open cockpit door. Flint swiveled his chair as if he were surprised at having a visitor. Weiss seemed even rounder as he stood there, his arms folded across his jutting stomach.

"We're going to do this thing," he said.

"Good." Flint didn't invite him in. He wanted the cockpit to remain his alone. "I think it's the right decision."

"It's the right decision for us," Weiss said. "But we are worried about how this'll go. Will you be staying in case we need to leave?"

"No," Flint said. "I'm just supposed to deliver you."

He almost told Weiss that the *Emmeline* wasn't even going to land on Mars, but then decided against it. The less they knew, the easier the trip would be.

Weiss sighed, his rounded shoulders going up and down, although the rest of him didn't seem to move. "That's going to be difficult. What're we going to do if things go wrong?"

"There are humans on Mars," Flint said.

"Will we be dealing with them?"

"I don't know." Flint held up a finger, then turned toward the console in front of him. He downloaded some background files on Mars into the game room.

Then he swiveled his chair toward Weiss again.

"The only onboard computer systems you all can use are in the game room." Flint had locked them out of the more elaborate systems in the bedrooms. He didn't want to go through the hassle of limiting access and worrying about what they were doing behind locked doors. "But you should be able to find the names of all the major human representatives on Mars. I'd suggest you each download that information into a chip, so that you have backup help. I also suggest that the seven of you network together, in case you're separated."

"What're they going to do to us?" Weiss asked.

"It's some kind of ritual. Apparently, Disty family members go through it all the time after someone dies, so it can't be too strenuous."

Weiss frowned. "They're not built the same way we are."

Flint knew that. He wished these people weren't so good-hearted. He hated fudging information. "They're as fragile as humans, though. Maybe more fragile, given their small size. If they can go through this easily, we probably can too."

The *we* was disingenuous. He wasn't going to go through anything.

Still, the words seemed to comfort Weiss.

"You've been pretty nice about this," Weiss said. "And this ship is absolutely amazing, not to mention expensive. You say you're not getting paid. This is your ship, right?"

Leave it to the man who wore his wealth all over his body to notice the traces of money around Flint.

"Yes," Flint said. "It's my ship."

"I can't believe you're doing this out of the goodness of your heart."

Flint gave him a slow smile. "You are."

"After they more or less arrested me. Did they do that to you?"

Flint shook his head. "I knew one of the early victims of this whole mess. It started small—the discovery of a skeleton above the mass graves, someone not related to the massacre —and I was helping figure out who that skeleton was."

"Out of the goodness of your heart?" Weiss's question didn't seem pointed. Only confused.

"No," Flint said. "I used to work in computers, and I have a background with the police. I had the needed skills, and I was getting paid for that job."

He didn't want it to sound like he simply did people favors for no reason. Over the years, he'd learned that people distrusted others who did a lot of things for free.

"I don't understand how that connects to this," Weiss said.

"I found myself in possession of a lot of information other people didn't have. I let a friend of mine in authority know, and here I am."

Weiss nodded. He took a small step away from the door, then he stopped.

"You tell your friend in authority, whoever it is, that we might have been a lot happier if we'd had a choice. This strong-arm stuff, I think that's what scared most of us. We've been hauled out of our homes before and lost our entire families. The police brought that all back. You tell everyone that, okay?"

"I will," Flint said, although he didn't know what good it would do.

"Thanks," Weiss said, and walked down the corridor.

Flint didn't move for a long moment. Then he sighed and turned toward the console. He would turn on the overhead sound as soon as he knew that Weiss was out of hearing range.

"My, my, my, aren't we just the *nicest* people."

Flint jumped and turned.

Norton had come all the way into the cockpit. He seemed bigger than he had in the game room. He was taller than Flint and broader too, but his thin arms told Flint he was weaker. If Norton's arms were any indication of the length of his space travels, his bones would either be elastic (if they'd been modified) or they would be brittle from a lack of proper weight-bearing exercise.

Still, Flint's heart pounded.

"May I help you, Mr. Norton?" Flint asked.

"It was just like I said." Norton leaned against the door in such a way that his body blocked anyone from getting in—or Flint from leaving. "Six voted to stay and one voted to go."

Flint couldn't argue with him without letting Norton know that Flint had been listening.

"I thought it was unanimous," Flint said. "Mr. Weiss seemed to think so."

"Of course he did," Norton said. "Because they decided that I was unimportant. I was too cynical, too mean. I'd come around."

Had they had that discussion while Flint was talking to Weiss? He didn't remember those words. But then, Flint was beginning to wonder how reliable Norton was.

"I overheard you telling that pompous ass that someone had found a skeleton on the massacre site. Did you ever find out who that skeleton was?"

"Yes," Flint said.

Norton nodded. "Then you know that this massacre is the gift that keeps on giving. First we lose everyone, nearly get murdered ourselves, get thrown out of our homes and the Dome itself, and then sent to places we never even imagined—"

"I know the story, Mr. Norton."

"It's not a story." He peered at Flint. "The story, as you call it, has lots of personal twists and turns, which I'm not going to tell you. Let's just say that our new mummies and daddies weren't always vetted well."

Flint wasn't in the mood for a sob story, but he didn't know how to easily shut Norton down.

"Then this lovely woman walks into our lives. Not all of our lives, but enough of them. She tells us how much money we can get from the Martian government, how the laws had changed, and how the Multicultural Tribunals favor people like us, people who've suffered for no apparent reason. All she needed was a little money to get the case prepped."

Flint stared at him. Norton let his arms drop.

"You know how this ends, right? How she took our money?"

"I don't know what it has to do with me," Flint said.

"Yes, you do." Norton started to cross his arms and then stopped.

The movement put Flint on alert. Norton was going to try to something. This close to the cockpit, he was probably going to try to take over the ship.

"You said you know who she is," Norton said, "and if you know that, you know why she was there. Do you know why she had no flesh on her bones?"

A shiver ran down Flint's back. Norton knew how Jørgen died.

Flint leaned his chair until the back hit the console. He hoped the move seemed natural. "No, I don't know why."

Norton smiled ever so slowly. That smile had probably been the last thing Jørgen had seen before she died. "She took everything from us, coming back over and over again with new petitions, seemingly real refiles of the case, court documents that seemed to pertain to us. And we paid each time, her fees, just to keep her going."

Flint's left arm wasn't in Norton's view. Flint slowly reached back under the console.

"She skinned us clean. I thought it only fair to do the same to her." Norton spoke calmly, as if everyone killed and then desecrated the corpse.

"Why are you telling me this?" Flint made himself sound nervous. Norton wanted him to be afraid, so Flint pretended to be afraid.

"So that when I ask you to turn this ship around, you'll do it."

"And then what?" Flint said. "You know what you just told me, right?"

Norton shrugged. "No one's going to pay attention. No one cares. It was thirty years ago, she was a crook, and I can confess all I want. There's no evidence. I cut it all off."

Flint's fingers found his laser pistol. "A confession counts."

"And now you'll tell me that the cockpit's system recorded it, and that the courts can use it against me." Norton smiled. "So? They have to arrest me first."

He took a step toward Flint. Flint raised the laser pistol. "Stay back."

Norton stopped. He raised his hands.

Flint stood slowly. He felt the top of the console, pressed the intercom button. "Would you all come in here, please? I need help with Mr. Norton."

"They can't do anything," Norton said. "Especially since I'll have control of this ship by the time they get here."

"You know what I wonder?" Flint said. "How did they find you, of all people? I would have thought you would have been the hardest survivor to find."

Norton's smile was small and chilling—one of the most

chilling smiles Flint had ever seen. "It's hard to get my revenge from the Outlying Colonies."

Flint felt a shiver as he understood the implications of that. "You've killed others, haven't you?"

"Let's just say your gun doesn't frighten me. I've been in this situation before."

Flint hit the silent emergency controls on the cockpit console. Now no one could fly the *Emmeline* but him. "You planned this crisis with the Disty?"

Norton's smile grew wider. "I wish I'd been that smart. This entire thing has simply been a bonus. When I'm done, the Disty will destroy Sahara Dome. And that'll be a marvelous thing."

Then Norton lifted his right fist and opened it slowly. On his palm, a white disc rested.

"Do you know what this is?" he asked.

Flint shook his head.

"It's my guarantee that no one saves Sahara Dome. It's a concussion bomb."

Flint started. His system had searched Norton when he had come aboard and found nothing. Flint would have assumed that the police had searched him as well when they picked him up.

"Only at this range," Norton was saying, "you and I won't survive it."

Flint frowned. He could have his system scan again, but if this little device avoided detection the first time, he had a hunch it wouldn't register on the scans a second time either.

"This lovely yacht of yours won't survive it," Norton's smile faded. "Unless, of course, you hand me the gun."

"Why would I do that?" Flint asked.

"So that we can turn around, you and your six little friends can live, and this all ends without any bloodshed."

"Except for people on Mars." Flint said.

Norton nodded. "Except for them."

Flint's heart was beating hard.

Norton's thumb hovered over the disc. "Shoot me, and I

will press down on this little device here. So. Wouldn't you rather live?"

"Yes." Flint stepped away from the console and lowered his laser pistol ever so slightly. "I'd much rather live."

58

Iona Gennefort crouched on the curb, near the pile of bodies. She felt numb, overwhelmed, and completely responsible. So many dead, just because she had allowed the trains to pass through Wells. She had had no idea that would happen; if she had, she would have stopped the trains outside the Dome, just like the other cities had.

But unlike them, she had had no examples and no guidance. The Disty hadn't talked with her, and no one else seemed to know the intricacies of the Disty fear of death—if, indeed, fear was what it could be called.

Now she was in Wells's Disty section with her assistant, two police officers, and the medical examiner. The claustrophobic streets, with their narrow walkways and the low rooftops from the various buildings, seemed wider without the Disty.

But it was still unusually dark here, even though the Dome lighting was in midday. And the silence was unnerving. Gennefort had been here a dozen times before, and the noise—the constant conversation, the continued rustling of various Disty going from place to place, even the scratching they called music—had been the predominant feature. After the claustrophobic streets, of course.

The medical examiner, a small man who had enhancements that left his chocolate-brown head hairless, looked even more exhausted than she felt. He stood beside her, staring at the corpses, looking defeated.

"I don't know what they are," he said. "Or even how they died."

Gennefort leaned toward them. They were smaller than regular Disty, which made them the size of a four-year-old human child. They were thinner too, but Gennefort didn't think that was natural; it looked to her untrained eye like they simply hadn't been fed well.

"What killed them?" she asked.

They didn't look trampled like the other Disty she saw. Besides, these bodies were in an orderly pile, as if someone had gathered them here.

The medical examiner picked up a small hand and showed Gennefort the palm. The ridges in the center had turned a bright blue.

She shook her head. "What's that?"

"I field-tested it," he said. "It's just cayenne, but to the Disty, that's poison."

"Poison?" she asked. "This was deliberate?"

The medical examiner nodded.

"In the middle of all that panic, someone had time to poison these—what are they? Children?"

"I thought you didn't know how they died," said Shing Eccles, Gennefort's assistant. Eccles was a small man as well, but he was the brightest person Gennefort had ever known. If he had been with her in that control tower, she had a hunch she might have made a different decision.

"I know what they died of," the medical examiner said, "but I'm not sure how it was administered. Judging from the hands, I would guess they administered it themselves."

Gennefort felt a ripple of shock run through her. She leaned away from the hand that the medical examiner still held and looked at the body closest to her. The large eyes were open and had tiny blue lines running through the pupil. The entire face had a slight bluish tinge.

This death couldn't have been pleasant.

"Why?" she asked.

The medical examiner shook his head. "The Disty have never let us handle their bodies here. They let the Death Squads do it, so I've never even worked on a dead Disty. I've seen some, read about the intricacies of autopsying them, but I've never done it myself."

"You'd think there'd been enough death around here today to make something like this impossible," Gennefort said.

Eccles sighed. "I think these are hatchlings."

Gennefort looked at him. He was staring at the pile just like she had been. "The genderless Disty. I thought they were a myth made up to startle the humans."

"Apparently not," Eccles said. "But even I'm not sure."

"It would explain a lot of things," the medical examiner said. "It would . . ."

A red cloud fell across Gennefort's vision, and she stopped listening to the examiner. An emergency notification. She stood, wiped her hands on her pants even though she had touched nothing, and stepped into the middle of the street.

Her head brushed a nearby ledge, and she had to duck to make certain she didn't walk into a building's jutting corner.

She answered the notice. "What?"

The voice of another of her assistants filled her head. "The Disty have contacted us. They believe they have a way to decontaminate the Dome."

"You're kidding," she said.

"They'll let us know for certain in a few hours. Until then, we're to separate Disty bodies from human corpses, and mark on some kind of map where the deaths occurred. They say it's going to take a while, but they believe they can repair this whole thing."

"That's great news," she said.

"Except," her assistant added, "they want us to guarantee that no graves lurk beneath our soil."

Gennefort winced. In the hours since this mess began, she had learned how the crisis started. It still didn't make complete sense to her. She was beginning to realize how very little she had known about the Disty. It was quite a shock to her.

Before, she had always thought she understood them and did more than tolerate them, as so many other humans had.

"How can we make that guarantee?" she asked. "I'm sure Sahara Dome didn't know about that mass grave."

"They won't do anything until we make the guarantee," her assistant said.

Gennefort sighed. For a moment, she contemplated using imaging equipment to see what was beneath the surface of the Dome. But even if that were possible—and she wasn't sure it was, especially as deep as Sahara Dome's mass grave had been found—it would only work on open ground. So much of Wells was built up; there were only a few parks, and because of the Disty influence, very few open spaces outside of the human areas.

For all she knew, there could be graves hidden beneath the buildings all over Wells. The Dome had a frontier history, as so many Domes on Mars had.

But they needed the decontamination. They needed life to return to normal. The entire Dome would die without it. No one could do business with them as things stood at the moment.

No one could even send food.

"Guarantee it," she said.

"What?" her assistant sounded shocked.

"Do your best to keep the guarantee unofficial," Gennefort said, and signed off. Then she leaned against the Disty building, and felt the flimsy structure shift ever so slightly.

She hoped this decision wouldn't backfire on her as badly or as quickly as the last one had.

She hoped if bodies were ever discovered in the sand that provided Wells's base, she was no longer mayor of Wells City.

In fact, she hoped she was long dead.

She never wanted to live through anything like this again.

59

Flint kept a tight grip on his laser pistol as he slowly lowered it. He hoped Norton wasn't smart enough to ask Flint to drop it and kick it over. Flint wanted to catch Norton as he came to fetch the pistol himself.

Norton watched with a half-smile on his face. Then he glanced at the console, which was clearly his goal. Flint wondered if Norton would bother to return to the Moon, or if he would kill everyone and take the *Emmeline* out of the solar system.

"Now," Norton said. "We're going to—"

He stopped and tilted his head, obviously listening.

Flint listened too. Scuffling in the corridor. Voices came with it.

The other six had arrived.

Norton turned slightly. "Wait, everyone," he said. "I don't want you to get any closer. You—"

Flint saw his only opportunity.

"—don't quite understand what's happening here. Our pilot—"

He raised his pistol.

"—and I are having a stalemate. He—"

Fired.

Norton must have seen the shot from the corner of his eye. He twisted slightly and leaned away.

The shot caught him in the arm—the arm holding the

disc—and Norton's hand jerked upward. The disc flew from it. Norton kept twisting, then tripped, and fell into the hallway.

A woman screamed, and one of the men shouted something unintelligible.

The disc rose toward the ceiling. Flint hurried forward, thinking he might catch it, and didn't reach it in time. He winced as the disc clattered against the floor.

Norton sat up, his face gray, and scrambled for the disc, but Flint reached it first. He snatched it with his free hand, unbalancing himself.

Norton grabbed Flint's foot and pulled him over.

Flint landed on his back, the air rushing from his body. He clutched the disc in one hand, the laser pistol in the other, and tried to sit up. Norton still had a firm grasp on his foot. Flint gasped for air, seeing black dots across his vision.

The other six came into the room.

"Stop him!" Norton screamed. "He's kidnapping us."

But they didn't move. They stared at the whole tableau as if it sent them back to the helplessness of their childhood.

Flint finally sat up and aimed the laser pistol at Norton. "Let me go," Flint said.

Norton's grip grew tighter.

"Let me go or I will kill you this time," Flint said.

"And contaminate all of us?" Norton asked.

"If I have to," Flint said.

Norton let go. He used that hand to brace himself, his skin going even grayer.

"You don't know how to use that disc," he said. "It's dangerous."

Flint didn't answer him. Instead, he looked at Weiss, who stood in the front of the group.

"Would you people be kind enough to hold him down?" Flint asked.

"What did he do?" Weiss asked.

"I'll replay it for you," Flint said. "Just help me first."

Apparently, that was the right answer—the fact that they had come upon the attack and the fact that Flint's system had made a recording of it seemed to convince the group to take Flint's side, not Norton's.

They surrounded him. Two of the men held him down, careful not to touch the smoldering hole in his shoulder.

Flint stood. He carefully set the disc on the console, then reached under it and removed one of the pairs of handcuffs he kept in the cockpit. Then, holding the laser pistol in one hand and the handcuffs in other, he walked toward the group.

The seven of them watched him walk across the cockpit as if he were twenty times larger than he was. Their eyes were huge, their mouths thin. Even Marcos, the beautiful one, no longer looked sculpted. She looked frightened.

The men continued holding Norton, and he too watched as if he couldn't believe what he saw. The air smelled faintly of burned flesh, and Flint knew he would have to take care of Norton's wound.

"Turn him for me, will you?" Flint asked.

The men helped Norton up. Norton was hurt worse than Flint had thought. The pistol had shot all the way through his arm; the back of his shirt was scorched.

Flint looked up. A matching scorch mark marred the panels near the door.

Norton staggered slightly, and Flint tightened his grip on the laser pistol, although he didn't bring it all the way up. He wasn't sure if Norton was staggering from his injury or faking a loss of balance as a way to get to Flint's laser pistol.

"Hold him carefully," Flint said, not relinquishing the pistol.

He snapped one lock on Norton's right wrist, then without using his other hand, snapped the other lock on Norton's left wrist.

"All right," Flint said. "You can let him go."

Norton staggered again. His skin was even grayer than before.

"He needs treatment," Vajra said.

Flint nodded. "Let's get him to the brig and we'll do what we can for him there."

"You have a brig?" Weiss asked.

Flint shrugged. "This ship has all sorts of surprises."

But he wasn't going to share what they were. He didn't say anything. Instead, he went back to the console and picked up the disc.

He didn't see any trigger on the surface. In fact, the disc just looked like a piece of plastic. He held it closer to one of his scanners, and it didn't register the disc as a live device.

Flint suspected he had been bluffed. He wasn't going to let Norton know that, however, and he wasn't going to mention it to the others.

Flint slipped the disc into a built-in drawer in the console, a drawer that opened only to the touch of his warm fingerprint. Then he joined the others. He kept the laser pistol in his hand and walked behind them, telling them how to get to the brig.

No one spoke.

When they arrived at the brig, Flint grabbed the first aid kit outside it and handed it to Vajra. "Take care of him."

"How do you know I can?"

Flint shrugged. "You strike me as competent."

She went inside the small room with Norton and the two men. They laid him on the wall bed and ripped open his shirt. Edges of the fabric had burned into the wound.

"What if he dies?" Weiss asked Flint softly. "Doesn't that make us contaminated, according to all that Disty stuff?"

"He won't die." At least, not so that anyone knew. If Norton died before the rendezvous with the Disty, he would not be part of the passenger list. Flint would claim that Armstrong made the mistake in the count. He would also make sure the remaining six backed him up.

But he said nothing about any of that now. He watched Vajra follow the instructions playing on the kit's surface about how to handle a laser burn. She was doing well. If she had messed up, he would have stepped in. He'd treated more than a dozen of those wounds over the years in his work as a Space Traffic cop.

Finally, Vajra finished. Norton still hadn't opened his eyes, but his normal skin tone had returned and his breathing was even.

"So," she said, as she picked up the kit and stepped out of the tiny room, "are you going to tell us what happened?"

"Better yet," Flint said, "I'll show you. But first, let me make sure he's secure."

Flint closed the clear reinforced plastic door, then snapped the lock open and touched the surface in five separate places. He didn't care that the six passengers watched his movements. Like so many locks here, this was keyed to his fingerprint, but the fingerprint had to be part of a warm, living hand.

Then he turned around. The six looked like adult-sized children, with their large eyes and their solemn expressions. He had frightened them.

Norton had frightened them. Norton had frightened him.

Flint smiled at them, and this time he made sure his smile was warm—the smile he had used as a police officer, after someone went through a major trauma. A reassuring, you're-safe-now smile.

"He really didn't want to go back to Mars," Flint said. "And frankly, after all you people have been through, who could blame him?"

"But to shoot him," Vajra said. Her voice was soft. "You didn't have to do that."

"I didn't see any other choice," Flint said.

The six didn't move. He had frightened them too.

Which was probably good. They'd stay away from him for the rest of the trip to Mars.

60

Sharyn Scott-Olson was in the middle of her twentieth autopsy. The body, spread out on the table before her, belonged to a young human male. He was covered with bruises. His skull had been crushed, and so had his rib cage. Clearly, he was one of the many corpses she had seen that day that had been trampled to death.

What she had to figure out—besides his identity—was whether he had died from the crushed skull or the crushed chest. And if she couldn't figure it out quickly, she would set him aside and move to the next corpse, already waiting on a tabletop for her.

She didn't look behind her. She didn't want to see the amount of work that awaited her and her assistants, all of whom were working as hard as she was.

She kept mental score of the numbers she had already seen, but she couldn't tell anyone how many had been Disty and how many had been human.

By the end of this, she knew it would all be a blur.

One of her links pinged. She sighed and requested the urgency level, without taking her hands from the corpse's battered arm. The response was quick: *urgent*.

She directed the message to a nearby wall screen. If it was bad news or good news, she would have to tell them anyway, so she figured why not let them listen in?

The face of Gavin Trouvelot, the human liaison to the

Disty in Sahara Dome, appeared on the screen. Apparently, the image sent back to him allowed him to see the activity in the lab, because he visibly recoiled.

"Sharyn?" His voice was hoarse.

"Right here," she said. "I have more work than is humanly possible to ever finish, so make this quick."

"Good news," he said. "The Disty believe they have a way of decontaminating the Dome and everyone in it."

The noise around her stopped. She let go of the corpse's arm "How?"

"They found survivors of the massacre. They're coming in now from the Moon. It'll take a while, but they'll eventually get here. I thought you'd want to know. You'll all be fine. We're setting up priorities here, and we figure since you've suffered under this cloud the longest, your office should be among the first to meet with the Disty."

She blinked at his image. Obviously, no one was giving any of this much thought. She even had a guess as to how the reasoning went: The morgue dealt with the Death Squad off and on; they'd see if the ritual worked or not.

"I appreciate it," Scott-Olson said.

"Um—" Nigel started from beside her, but Scott-Olson waved her bloody, glove-covered right hand at him.

"However," she said, "we're really busy down here, and—"

"Still, I think this would take precedence," Trouvelot said.

She resisted the urge to shake her head at him. "It would be a waste of their time. We would just get recontaminated."

"How—? Oh." His gaze flickered downward. "When the autopsies are done, then?"

She suppressed a sigh. "It'll be a while. When we finish with the recent victims, we still have to deal with the corpses from the massacre."

"Oh." Trouvelot frowned.

She didn't ask about the skeleton. She hoped that the Disty had found someone to decontaminate Scott-Olson's lab team for that too, but she doubted it.

Maybe the best she could hope for was that the Disty would forget that one small detail.

"Is there anything else?" she asked.

"Um, how do we determine where you fit in?" Trouvelot asked.

"I'll have you work with Nigel," she said, and signed off. Nigel made a choking sound beside her. When she looked at him, he rolled his eyes.

"Don't I have enough to do?" he asked.

She let out a small, humorless laugh. "Don't worry. He won't contact us again for a while. We might even have to contact him when it comes time for our decontamination."

Nigel wheeled one of the finished corpses toward the back room. He no longer seemed squeamish about anything. When he reached the door, he stopped. "It is good news, though, isn't it? The decontamination?"

It was much too late. All of these people, as well as the Disty and the people in Wells and other parts of Mars, would still be alive if someone had taken care of this sooner.

Maybe Costard had done some good after all. The survivors were coming from the Moon. That Retrieval Artist had said he had some leads.

At least things weren't going to get worse.

"It's good," Scott-Olson said. "In fact, it's the best we can hope for."

61

Mars floated in Flint's view screen. The red-and-brown planet looked like its sandy surface had been mixed with blood.

He had all of the *Emmeline*'s defenses on high alert. Every angle of his ship monitored the exterior. He needed to know the moment something showed up on his sensors, and he needed that something evaluated. Too many Disty ships had exploded or been crippled because other ships crashed into them.

He wasn't going to die because Mars's Space Traffic Control system had gigantic holes.

Flint had taken other precautions. The six remaining survivors didn't know it, but they were locked into the passenger wing of the ship. They had no access to the maintenance areas or the cockpit—something he should have done when they first came on board.

Norton was still in the brig, where he would remain until the Disty came for him. He was seriously injured, but not in any immediate danger. With proper medical attention, he would be just fine.

Flint would tell the Disty that.

But he wouldn't tell them about the small disc that Norton had brought onto Flint's ship. Flint had made a study of that disc, and he was convinced that it wasn't a weapon at all. Norton had been improvising, and he had done it well. Still, Flint kept the disc in the small locked drawer on the console.

So far he had sent two messages to the surface, and had received no reply. He wasn't sure what he would do if the Disty refused to contact his ship. He had made certain that his survivors had had no outside access since he got within range of Mars's various systems, but he wasn't sure if things had changed.

His long-range sensors pinged. A square ship, completely black, was heading toward him from deep space. He put his weapons systems online and sent a message, asking the ship to identify itself.

The reply came quickly: "Disty vessel 665443: Death Squad. We have been appointed to rendezvous with your ship. Respond."

Flint let out the breath he had been holding. "We're waiting for you, Disty vessel. We were told you will dock with us?"

"We will. You will prepare for the docking."

Then the Disty signed out.

Flint watched as the ship got closer. Its design wasn't classically Disty, but it fit into the Death Squad configurations. He had studied a lot of Death Squad ships when he had worked Space Traffic Control so that he would recognize them when they came through.

The Disty ship reached his ship. Then the *Emmeline* shook as the Disty ship's grapplers attached. He heard faint bleets of nervousness coming from the game room. The poor survivors were probably more worried than they had ever been.

Perhaps they were even regretting their decision.

His outside cameras caught the entire maneuver. The grapplers were black and efficient, pulling his ship closer. Then the Disty ship sent its tunnel along the arms of the grapplers, creating an easy environment for the Disty to board the *Emmeline*.

Flint kept his main doors locked. He wouldn't open them until he was certain he needed to. He did, however, unlock the outside doors.

He stayed in the cockpit as he did this. He wasn't going to greet the Disty until he had seen them.

Ten Disty filed down the tunnel and into his airlock. They were so small they all fit into the tiny space. They were wearing black over their bodies. They wore a white cord around their necks. From the cord, a sheathed knife hung. Flint had only seen the knife blade once: It was also black, made of some kind of tempered glass, the strength reinforced through some sort of secret technique. The knife's dual edges were sharp enough to slice off a finger without much effort, and the flat part of the blade had little ridges that left slivers of glass inside the skin of anyone who touched it.

Those knives were used in many Death Squad rituals, including vengeance killings.

The Disty closed the exterior door. The tunnel remained attached to his ship. One Disty tried the interior door, then looked at the others. The look rippled through the crowd of Disty as if they could read an answer on the back wall.

"Your interior door is sealed," said one of the Disty.

"Standard precaution," Flint said. "I had to wait until the exterior door was sealed."

He opened the interior door, set the ship on autopilot, and grabbed his laser pistol, putting it in the holster he had saved from his police days. Then he left the cockpit. Before he walked down the corridor, he shut and locked the cockpit door. The lock was keyed to his left palm print.

Flint hurried down the corridor. He reached the main entrance as the last of the Disty stepped inside.

Individually, Disty were small and unthreatening. In a group, they usually seemed like overgrown human children. But this group had a level of menace to it; part of that was the clothing and the knives, but most of it was the level of confidence they exuded—the way they moved, almost as if they were a group mind instead of a group of individuals.

"Where are our passengers?" the lead Disty asked.

Flint could never tell the gender of these creatures, and he knew better than to ask for names. He did, however, ask for identification.

They presented him with a small pad. It had the Disty High Command's seal. When he tapped the seal, he saw dozens of official documents, all of them pertaining to this group of humans. He even saw two documents from DeRicci, swearing that the humans on this ship were survivors of the Sahara Dome massacre.

"Thank you," Flint said. "I will have to download a copy of this into my systems."

"Please do," the Disty said, and leaned back, its hands clasped at its waist. Its eyes glittered as it watched Flint.

He didn't take the pad to the nearest computer interface. Instead, he pushed a knuckle against the pad's surface, and downloaded into a chip he wore on his left hand.

The chip was not attached to any of his systems. It merely recorded the information. He then downloaded into one other chip—also an unattached chip—for backup, and handed the pad back to the Disty.

"I'll take you to the survivors," Flint said.

62

The news story had stalled. Ki Bowles sat in the broadcast booth and stared at the various wall screens. Disty ships still remained outside the Moon's perimeter. Moon-based ships, most from Armstrong, but some from the other port cities, lined the perimeter as if they were waiting for a fight.

But in the hours of the standoff, no fight ever came.

That alone stunned Bowles. She figured something else was going on. Someone had to know what was happening.

Someone was making deals.

The two freelancers in their rogue ship had gotten precious few Disty quotes. The Disty who initially contacted the rogue ship, thinking it was an official human vessel, signed off as soon as they realized it wasn't.

The footage was interesting. Some of those Disty ships were so crammed that half a dozen Disty were visible behind the pilot. And some of those Disty looked smaller than usual—children, probably. All of their eyes seemed unusually moist, and their faces a darker gray than normal.

So the freelancers were able to make the crisis personal, just like they had claimed. But their window to interview the Disty passed within five minutes.

It was a tribute the freelancers' talent that they were able to stretch those short contacts into much longer pieces.

Part of that was Bowles. She hunted for—and got—death tolls. They were unofficial and human-centered: two hundred human deaths total, most of them in Wells and Sahara Dome, most, it seemed, caused by trampling.

The Disty death tolls were tougher to get and kept changing all the time. She spoke to a human liaison with the Disty, someone who worked on Mars, and got an unofficial toll of three thousand, not counting the dead still in trains or those exploded in the ship collisions.

Bowles couldn't comprehend the number. She couldn't even think of ways to make it real for the news viewers, since there wasn't yet any available footage from Mars.

Her work was nearly done, and to make matters worse, it had begun to resemble the work of rival reporters from the other media companies. The story had become a universal one, which meant she would have to leave it soon and move on to other things.

She had one more angle, however, one she had more or less dropped as the crisis had gotten more immediate.

Noelle DeRicci.

Bowles would finish her profile of the woman who had left thousands of Disty to die in the space just beyond the Moon.

And the thing Bowles needed to finish that profile was DeRicci herself.

63

Flint used his links to silently disable the locks as he led the Disty into the passenger wing of his ship. It felt like old times—transferring prisoners from one jurisdiction to another—although he doubted the survivors in his game room would consider themselves prisoners.

When he reached the room, he found the door closed. It startled him; he had expected the door to remain open, as it had been throughout the trip.

He didn't let that surprise show, however. He didn't want the Disty to remove those knives from their sheaths.

Flint knocked once, more as a warning than anything, then pressed his hand on the automatic opener. The door slid back, revealing all six survivors standing in a line in the center of the room.

Weiss was in the center. When the door had opened all the way, he stepped forward, his meaty hand outstretched.

"You must be the Disty," he said, looking past Flint to the group behind him. "We're the Sahara Dome massacre survivors. I understand you need our help."

It was a masterful moment, a great attempt at taking power and control in a situation where these six people didn't have much control at all. Flint gave them a faint smile, and stepped aside.

But the Disty who had been the spokesperson all along caught Flint's arm. "I thought there were twelve."

"We found twelve," Flint said. "Five did not agree to come to Mars."

The Disty all whistled softly. The sound made the hairs on the back of Flint's neck rise.

"We're perfectly willing to help," Weiss said, as if the other conversation hadn't gone on at all. "You just have to tell us what to do."

"You said five." The Disty was still speaking to Flint. "There should be seven survivors, then. We only count six."

"The seventh is in my brig," Flint said. "He tried to take over the ship and blow it up."

The Disty's eyes grew even wider. "He is a criminal, then?"

"Yes," Flint said.

"So you are leaving us with six only. It is not enough."

Flint shrugged. "This is what we could do."

Weiss walked up to the group, forcing himself into the conversation. "We've agreed to remain on Mars as long as you need us. If it takes twice as long because there are only six of us, so be it."

The Disty slowly turned its head until it faced Weiss. "You know nothing of our customs."

Weiss's skin grew a little paler, but to his credit, he did not back away. Instead, he nodded. "We are willing to learn."

"It will be taxing," the Disty said.

"We were told that the rituals were not life-threatening for survivors. If that's the case, you have our full cooperation."

Flint looked past Weiss. The other survivors had their hands clasped in front so that they looked nonthreatening. Vajra was nodding as Weiss spoke. The others watched, looking nervous.

Flint had no doubt which two were behind this ploy.

"You have heard correctly," the Disty said. "The survivor ritual causes no harm to the participant. It does, however, take many hours to complete. And you will, given the number of times you must go through it, find yourselves quite exhausted before the months are through."

"Months?" Marcos asked, her beautiful face twisted with alarm.

"We have hundreds of thousands of Disty who must face you and receive the cleansing that can only come from survivors. Even if you were to do a purely human thing and shake hands, this would take days. We must do much more than that."

The Disty then looked pointedly at Weiss's hands. The Disty had noticed Weiss's attempt to be friendly, understood it, and ignored it.

"Months?" Weiss looked at Flint. "You said nothing about months."

"I didn't know," Flint said. "I told you I am not familiar with the ritual. However, my invitation still stands."

"Invitation?" The Disty asked.

"I told them that if they changed their minds, I would take them back to the Moon."

The Disty shifted all around him. Flint could feel their agitation as if it were a real, living thing.

Flint's skin crawled. He tried not to look at the knives.

"You do not have the authority," the lead Disty said.

"Yes, I do," Flint said. "They volunteered. They're here because they want to be, not because they're being forced. They have the right to change their minds."

All of the Disty faced the six survivors. Weiss looked over his shoulder at the others. Vajra shrugged. Marcos looked down, but the others did not move.

Finally, the lead Disty reached out with its long fingers and took Weiss's hand, shaking it awkwardly. "We appreciate your gesture. We are not used to kindness. We shall not take advantage of it, and we shall compensate you for your time."

"We'll be away from our families." The blue-haired woman, McEvoy, sounded frightened.

"We are aware of that," the Disty said. "Perhaps we can find a solution that will satisfy us all. If you will come with me, we can negotiate your terms. But we may not do so in front of your pilot, since he will not be part of the rituals."

"We won't leave this ship until we've made a decision." Weiss hadn't let go of the Disty's hand.

"Agreed. Perhaps we can speak in private here?" The Disty looked at Flint.

"Sure," he said. "But before I go, what about Norton? He's the seventh."

"He is a criminal. We have no use for him."

"You might," Flint said. "I think he's the one who placed the skeleton on top of the massacre site."

"The killer?" Another Disty asked that.

"Of the single human woman, yes," Flint said. "He had nothing to do with the massacre."

"Then that is different," the lead Disty said. "We have a use for him after all."

"I should bring him for the negotiation, then," Flint said.

"Whatever we decide, we'll hold him to it," Weiss said.

"We do not need to negotiate with criminals," the Disty said. "Our use for him will be different."

"How different?" Flint asked. "He's injured. I'm not sure he's up for something strenuous."

"We shall discuss this after we have finished here. Have him ready," the Disty said.

Weiss frowned at Flint ever so slightly. Flint shrugged. Then he backed out of the room and headed toward the main cabin. He used his internal links to monitor the conversation, although he did not listen closely.

He didn't want to know the rituals. He wanted to remain as uninvolved as possible.

But he did want to hear if anything went wrong.

64

"You have to be kidding," DeRicci said. "In no way am I sitting down with that bloodsucking reporter. She makes up lies."

The governor-general folded her hands together. She sat at DeRicci's desk as if it were her own. DeRicci was getting tired of having the woman around. Couldn't she co-opt someone else's office?

"I think you should consider it," the governor-general said. "The damage to your reputation has been severe. You could mitigate it, while the public thinks the crisis is still going on."

DeRicci glanced at the wall screens. All the public saw were the Disty ships outside the perimeter. Already, representatives for Armstrong's Disty community had contacted Mayor Soseki, worried about DeRicci. Soseki reassured them that DeRicci had nothing to do with the crisis, and that everything was under control.

Still, DeRicci didn't like how this was heading.

"So, I sit down with that woman, and she then asks under what authority I closed all the ports on the Moon. How do I answer?"

The governor-general frowned. "That could be an issue."

"No kidding." DeRicci refused to sit in one of the clear chairs scattered around the room. That was her desk, her chair, and this was her office. She didn't have to act like someone subordinate.

"I suppose," the governor-general said, "you tell Ms. Bowles that someone had to act to save lives, and you did so."

" 'At the expense of so many Disty lives?' " DeRicci mimicked Bowles. "I think this is a terrible idea."

"Yes, you already said that. But you'll have to get used to the media. Dealing with it is part of your job."

DeRicci paced toward the windows. The streets were filling up with Disty, many of whom had come to file complaints against her.

"You told me when you asked me to take this job that I could control how I talked to the media," DeRicci said. "Press releases, controlled press conferences, short meetings. You didn't say a thing about one-on-ones."

"I didn't expect a crisis so soon," the governor-general said. "I also didn't expect such bad publicity about you. Is it true that you tried to thwart the Disty when you were a police officer?"

DeRicci didn't turn. She just clenched her fists, made herself take several deep breaths, and then said, as calmly as she could, "Every police officer has a moment of disillusionment when dealing with alien laws. The cops have to do awful things—like giving up little boys, knowing that they're going to get their tongues cut out, and they're going to be denied healing treatment for the rest of their lives. Yeah, I had trouble with that. Find me someone who wouldn't."

The governor-general sighed. "So that story's true."

"It's an ugly fact of law enforcement. So what?" DeRicci did turn this time.

The governor-general was studying her hands. "Did you deny the Disty entry because you hate them?"

"You already asked me that, and I said no. I meant no. I denied them entry because we were about to get overrun. You heard the rituals, you saw what happened to Wells, you knew the risks. How can you ask me that again?"

"Because." The governor-general raised her head. "This issue will dog you for the rest of your political career."

"I made the best decision for the Moon," DeRicci said. "I *saved* the port cities. You know that."

"I know it," the governor-general said. "But unfortunately, with your history, it won't sound that way when the media gets through with it."

"My history?" DeRicci raised her voice. "I saved Armstrong from a killing virus. I've worked hard for this city and this place. I was a good cop, a better detective, and I make great decisions on the fly. You would have been afraid to close down the ports. I just did it."

She probably shouldn't have said that last bit. Her cheeks warmed, but she didn't take the words back.

The governor-general's gaze met hers. The governor-general's dark eyes seemed empty, almost as if she had coated them to hide any emotion.

"You're right, Noelle. I would have made the wrong choice. And we would have had a crisis. You stopped the crisis, and for that we're all grateful." She swept a hand toward the screens. "I'm already getting reports of ships turning back. Mars is accepting the contaminated Disty, so long as they land near Lowell. We're not going to have any more trouble here."

DeRicci was breathing shallowly. The governor-general didn't sound approving.

"But," the governor-general said, "you made that hasty decision—that correct decision—without political thought. You didn't ease the transition, nor did you make any kind of statement about it. You simply ordered it."

"I didn't have time for anything else," DeRicci said.

"There's always time," the governor-general said.

DeRicci shook her head.

The governor-general stood. She pushed DeRicci's chair under the desk, then tidied up the desk's surface. "And we took citizens from their homes without their permission."

"Not all of them. They had a choice. Five decided not to go. Besides, that was local police."

"Under someone's orders." The governor-general moved one of the plants to the edge the desk.

"You're going to blame all the problems with this on me, aren't you?" DeRicci asked.

"If you can think of a clean way to tell all of this to Ki

Bowles, maybe you'll come out of this just fine. People like you. And I think they like how decisive you are."

The heat in DeRicci's cheeks grew worse. "You want me to talk to Ki Bowles because you know how bad I am with the media. You want me to look like a damn fool, so that you can really blame all of this on me."

The governor-general gave her a sideways look. DeRicci guessed that the look was meant to be soothing, but it wasn't. "You can handle yourself just fine, Noelle."

"You bet I can, Celia," DeRicci said, mimicking the governor-general's patronizing tone. "Especially considering the fact that you've been in my office all afternoon, helping me make every single one of the decisions, and telling me that you would handle the media when the time was right."

The governor-general stepped around the desk and stopped in front of DeRicci. DeRicci had several inches on her, but for the first time, was not intimidated in her presence.

"You wouldn't dare," the governor-general said.

"I'm not getting fired for doing something right," DeRicci said. "And if I have to go down, I'll take everyone with me— you, the chicken councilors who wouldn't make a decision, and Armstrong's wimpy little mayor, as well as the heads of the police forces in all the Domed cities where the Sahara Dome survivors were. I may not be politic, but I do know how to speak my mind, and I can make anything sound bad if I have to."

The governor-general was silent. Then she stepped away from DeRicci and leaned on the desktop she'd straightened a moment before.

"It would be easier if you just resigned," she said calmly. "Then we could let the scandal float by, and this office would get the strength it needs. I think this situation proves that we need a Moon-wide security chief. I'm just not sure you're the person for the job."

"I'm exactly the person," DeRicci said. "You need some-one decisive and nonpolitical. Otherwise, we'd have been in the same situation as Mars, and all those deaths would have been your fault."

The governor-general closed her eyes. She obviously didn't want to hear this.

"And," DeRicci said, moving close enough to get the governor-general to open her eyes in alarm, "if you force me to resign to avoid a scandal, I'll be happy to tell everyone how indecisive you were, and how awful the council was, and how no one would help me."

"I don't like threats," the governor-general said.

"Neither do I," said DeRicci. "I also don't like martyring myself for no good cause. If I step down to avoid your scandal, my life will be ruined. I'd probably have to leave Armstrong. I might even have to leave the Moon. You're not doing that to me, Celia. You're working with me, whether you like it or not."

"But you're not political," the governor-general said.

"Then come to the interview with me," DeRicci said. "Answer most of the questions. Be the political one, and protect me from my worst instincts. Let me talk about my past, and let the people decide."

"Do you realize what kind of risk that is?" The governor-general's voice actually shook.

DeRicci stared at her. The governor-general seemed even smaller than she had a moment ago.

"Yeah," DeRicci said. "I know the risk. It's a risk to your political career, that's all. And considering the risks I faced today—the risk of being overwhelmed by panicked Disty, the risk of hundreds, maybe thousands of deaths—I think the risk we would take talking to Ki Bowles is pretty small."

The governor-general bent her head. Then she shook it.

"You say you're not political," the governor-general said softly, almost to herself, "and yet you've boxed me in."

"So," DeRicci said, "we're facing this together?"

The governor-general stood. "It seems I have no other choice."

65

Two hours later, the Disty and the Sahara Dome survivors came to an agreement. Flint was proud of the survivors. Because they knew the Disty needed them, the survivors took control of the situation entirely. They got the Disty to agree to payments, days off, and a duration for the ritual help.

Weiss and Vajra proved able negotiators. They even got the Disty to contact the High Command and lock the agreement in stone. Flint was impressed with the structure they placed on the entire affair—a structure no one else had thought to impose.

When the negotiations were finished, Weiss, Vajra, and the others went with nine of the Disty to the Disty vessel. Only the lead Disty remained. The others had gone through the airlock before the lead Disty asked Flint to take it to Norton.

When they arrived at the brig, they found Norton sitting up. His clumsily bandaged shoulder looked like it hurt him, but his color was still good.

"From one prison to another," he said when he saw the Disty.

"It is not that simple," the Disty said.

"I don't want to go to Mars. I've been back too many times. I hate it."

"You will not have to go to the surface," the Disty said. "I need one small thing from you."

Flint looked at it with surprise. He had thought the Disty was going to take Norton to the ship.

"What would that be?" Flint asked.

"Just a bit of blood to clean the site." The Disty reached into the pocket of its black cloak and removed a small vial. "If you can, tell us where you killed the woman so that we might reclaim that space as well."

Norton looked from the Disty to Flint. "What did you tell this thing?"

"I told him what you told me," Flint said. "That's why you're not going to the surface. The Disty don't want to be responsible for a criminal."

Norton frowned. "I told you that to scare you."

"Apparently," Flint said, "it scared them."

"Time is short," the Disty said. "Will you release the criminal so that I might take the blood?"

Norton scrunched backward on the cot, getting as close to the wall as he could. "I'm not volunteering for anything."

"You do not have to volunteer," the Disty said.

"I'm ill. Taking blood could hurt me."

"A consideration you did not have when you murdered your human friend," the Disty said.

"Or when you threatened us," Flint said.

"Yet you're not injured." Norton rubbed the bandage. "I'm going to complain to every authority I can find about this."

"Then complain." The Disty looked at Flint. "Will you let me into your brig?"

Flint unlocked the door. It swung open. He put a hand on his laser pistol, but to his surprise, Norton didn't try to bolt. Instead, he remained pushed against the wall, watching the Disty.

The Disty opened the vial, setting the cap in its pocket. Then it unsheathed its knife. The blade was as wicked as Flint remembered those ritual knives to be. The black glass absorbed the light—yet something deep within sparkled for just a moment.

Flint held his breath. He knew that the Disty couldn't commit a vengeance killing for a human-on-human crime, no matter what the outcome. Besides, it would take more than one Disty to do a proper vengeance killing, since most of the knife work happened before the victim died.

Still, Flint's grip on his laser pistol tightened.

"Thank you for remaining seated," the Disty said. "This makes my job so much easier."

Then it reached out with the knife and slashed forward, hitting Norton in the jugular vein. Blood spurted all over the brig, splashing the Disty.

"What the hell?" Flint sprang forward, shoving the Disty aside. It already had filled the vial.

Norton was grabbing his neck, his skin growing paler by the second. His fingers couldn't contain the blood.

Flint put his hands on the wound as well, but the blood continued to flow out.

"You said just a little blood!" Flint snapped.

The Disty held up the vial. "So it is."

"You had no right to kill him."

"Perhaps he will not die."

But they both knew that Norton wasn't going to survive this. Even Norton knew it, his eyes panic filled, his voice gone because he couldn't get enough oxygen into his lungs.

"What the hell am I supposed to do?" Flint asked.

"Try to save him," the Disty said. "I shall leave before he dies so as not to be contaminated."

"Wait!" Flint said.

"You can tell your government that he came to me willingly and participated in the ritual." The Disty held up the vial. "They agreed to that."

It nodded, then backed out of the brig, leaving a trail of blood as it hurried down the corridor.

Flint couldn't follow it. He kept his fingers on Norton's neck, grasping for the medical kit that had been replaced outside the brig.

He couldn't reach the kit. So he grabbed the bandage on Norton's shoulder. The bandage was designed to hold the pieces of the wound in place while nanohealers knitted the skin back together.

But he couldn't pull the bandage free. In fact, the bandage yelled at him, telling him he would destroy the work if he continued pulling. He ignored the voice, but the bandage didn't come off. It had incorporated itself into the healing skin.

Norton's own grip had slipped. His hand was loose beneath Flint's. Norton's eyes fluttered, and he made a slight gurgling sound.

The ship bounced. Flint recognized that motion. The automated tunnel had retracted. In a moment, the grapplers would let loose.

He cursed but kept his hand on Norton's neck. It was futile. Flint knew it, but couldn't stop himself, not until the blood stopped flowing completely.

It grew sticky against his fingers.

Flint looked up at Norton, his skin a pale grayish-white, and saw that his eyes were half open and glassy. Flint sprinted for the medical kit, placing a bandage on the neck, a bandage like the one stuck to Norton's arm.

The bandage informed Flint that the subject was dead, and therefore the bandage would be useless.

Flint flung it across the room.

He sank down onto the floor, looking at the dead man in his brig. The ship bounced again and then shook as the grapplers came free.

You can tell your government that he came to me willingly and participated in the ritual. They agreed to that.

Technically, the Disty was right. The government had agreed to that. But the death had occurred in Flint's ship, in his presence. He was not a government representative. He would be in trouble from the moment he returned to Armstrong.

He sat there for a long time as the blood pooled. Norton's body slipped down the wall slowly, leaving another blood trail.

Flint knew what he had to do. The Disty had given him the answer. Flint would claim—should anyone ask—that Norton had gone with the Disty. The Disty would back him up with the official language used previously.

Flint would have to change his records so that there were no complete recordings of the Disty taking the six out of the ship, and only a short moment of the lead Disty talking with Norton.

He stood slowly, furious at himself for being tricked. He had known better.

He would never do the government—even in the person of DeRicci—any more favors.

This one could have killed him.

But it wouldn't.

He would make sure of that.

66

Ki Bowles almost didn't believe her luck. Not only would she get an interview with Noelle DeRicci, she would also get to speak to the governor-general. Bowles hadn't expected anyone to answer her queries for an interview. The fact that DeRicci's assistant had gotten back to her quickly and had offered the governor-general was a coup.

Thaddeus Ling poked his head in the broadcast booth. He was grinning. "Great job. I expect you to make the most of this."

"I'm thinking of some puff questions and a light interview at first," Bowles said, "and then I'll get to the tougher stuff. That way I'll have some material for today's downloads, and more throughout the week."

"Whatever you need," he said. "I'm taking you off the overall story and giving you time to prepare. I want this perfect."

She nodded. The immediate story had pretty much ended. The Disty vessels that had ringed half the Moon were heading back to Mars. That would be a heck of a story—life among the contaminated Disty—but it wasn't her story.

Her story had to do with discrimination, bigotry, and a justification for keeping the Disty off the Moon.

The fact that the governor-general had allied herself with that was just a bonus.

Bowles was finally going to get the break of her career.

<u>67</u>

Flint put the *Emmeline* on autopilot, heading back to the Moon on one of the more unpopular routes. He also had the ship go very slowly.

Then he dragged Norton's body to the airlock. Flint made sure the environmental controls were on in the airlock before he took the body inside.

There he used one of the small surgical scalpels to remove Norton's ID chips, as well as any visible network chips. Flint placed those in a pile near the outer door. He leaned Norton against the door as well.

When he finished, he left the airlock and went back inside. He worked steadily, taking his time, making sure he took care of every little detail. Even with the help of his 'bots, it took Flint hours to clean the ship.

Finally, he went to the cockpit and checked the ship's location. He still had a long way to go before reaching the Moon. No other ships surrounded him, and nothing registered at all on his scans.

His stomach twisted. He did not believe in treating human beings—even human beings like Norton—in this way. But he had no choice.

Even if he managed to survive the inquiries, DeRicci wouldn't. No one would approve of a human's death in service of the Disty. If no one inquired about Norton, then it would simply be assumed that he had disappeared on Mars. A lot of people did that.

Flint turned on one of the internal cameras and looked at the body in his airlock. Norton didn't seem like a threat at all. He looked pathetic, a man who had had no chance since he was a small child, when his entire family had been murdered in front of him.

Flint had had to take Norton's word that he had murdered Jørgen, and maybe others. Flint doubted he would investigate that now.

He didn't want to find out if Norton had lied.

Flint double-checked his instruments again. The *Emmeline* was alone here. He was alone.

He pressed a part of his console screen and opened the exterior doors.

Norton's body got sucked outside, along with a flurry of chips. The chips immediately scattered. The body floated away as if it were on some kind of adventure all its own.

Flint closed the exterior doors. Then he hit the engines and sped up, hurrying away from the area.

He sat at the console, head down, for a long moment. Finally, he remembered to contact DeRicci. He did so, audio only.

"Flint here," he said. "I've given the survivors to the Disty, but you probably know that. I hope the whole thing works. Now that I'm out here, away from the Moon, I've decided to take advantage of the yacht like you've always told me to. I'm taking a short vacation. I'll be back in a month or so, and then we can talk. Good work on this."

And he signed off. He sent the message, encoded, along a slow channel, so it would arrive after he was too far away to receive an answer.

He didn't want DeRicci to see how shaken he truly was.

He took the ship off the preprogrammed route to the Moon and headed toward the outer reaches of the solar system. He hadn't been anywhere except the Moon, Mars, and Earth. Time to see a few other planets, or just be alone for a while on a very long journey, talking to no one, thinking of nothing. •

He felt contaminated, and he doubted anything would make that feeling go away.

68

DeRicci got the encoded message from Flint just before she sat down with Bowles and the governor-general for the interview. His voice sounded sturdy and strong—pleased that the transfer had gone well. Happy enough to take some much-needed time off. She wished she could.

She was trying not to be nervous. Bowles had come to her office. The assistants had moved the furniture, pushing the desk toward the back so that no one used it, and moving the couch out. Instead, three chairs sat in a triangle with a small table between them.

Bowles had already staked her place, in the chair that had a view of the wall screens, which DeRicci had shut off. De-Ricci let the governor-general choose her chair. DeRicci didn't want to sit until the last moment.

She felt calmer now that she had heard from Flint. She had had an odd feeling that something had gone wrong, although she hadn't heard it from the Disty High Command or anyone at the Alliance. In fact, everyone was thrilled that this crisis had been solved.

So thrilled, in fact, that her contact at the Alliance volunteered to make a statement supporting her to InterDome Media. Apparently, Bowles would talk to various officials about DeRicci's handling of this matter when this interview was over.

It was good that Flint was going to be away for a while.

This story would blow over and no one would hunt him down for an interview. DeRicci wasn't going to give his name to anyone, and she doubted anyone else knew of his involvement. Even the governor-general had no idea which pilot took the survivors to Mars.

DeRicci would keep it that way.

"Shall we begin?" Ki Bowles' voice was sickly smooth, fake in its niceness.

DeRicci swallowed the anger she had been feeling toward this woman all day, and sat down with a smile. "I'm ready."

"Have you started to record?" the governor-general asked.

"Just preliminary stuff," Bowles said. "The room, the entry, the way that the fledging security office looks."

"Good," the governor-general said. "Because I'm going to make a statement."

DeRicci tensed.

"You will use this statement in its entirety," the governor-general said, "or you will never be granted an interview with any member of my government again. Do you understand?"

"Governor, that's—"

"Those are my conditions." The governor-general spoke softly, yet there was great force in her words.

Bowles looked like she was about to be ill. "All right."

"Good, because the reporting you did today on Noelle De-Ricci amounts to the worst kind of journalism," the governor-general said. "You made up rationales for events you did not understand. You did not allow Chief DeRicci to defend herself before you aired your hate piece, and you combed through her sterling record to find some sort of case—any case—to support your claims. If you do the same thing with this interview, hack it to bits and make it say what you want it to say, the unedited version of this next hour will make it to your rivals' desks before your hack job finishes airing."

DeRicci felt her mouth open. No one had ever defended her like that.

"I don't appreciate being threatened, Governor," Bowles said. Her voice was calm, but her eyes flashed with something like hatred.

"I don't appreciate having an exemplary public servant being trashed for saving lives," the governor-general said.

DeRicci leaned back in her chair. She listened as the interview became a jousting session between Bowles and the governor-general, learned that manipulating the press had a whole new meaning when it was done by someone with experience and skill.

Bowles got in her questions, but DeRicci never had a chance to answer. The governor-general dominated the entire interview, allowing DeRicci only to describe the reasons she had made such quick decisions.

"Tell her what you told me about decisiveness," the governor-general said before DeRicci could answer. "Tell her about political decisions versus life-and-death decisions."

So DeRicci reiterated her case, and as she did, she felt increasingly lightheaded, as if everything she had understood about her world had shifted.

"The reason we chose Noelle DeRicci," the governor-general said, before DeRicci had a chance to finish, "is because she makes decisions like this, because she is not political, and because she thinks of lives first. I suggest the next time you come out with a hastily conceived story that could stir up the citizenry, you think of lives as well."

DeRicci tuned out the rest. She allowed herself a few moments of relaxation while the two women near her sparred. DeRicci had survived her first test as Security Chief, and she had survived it because she had defended herself.

Because she wasn't political; she was outspoken.

Because she was decisive.

And because she had a true friend in Miles Flint.

69

Sharyn Scott-Olson watched as her team carefully lifted the last body from the mass grave. One hundred and fifty people had died at this location one hundred years before. One hundred and fifty men, women, and children, piled on top of each other, their secret lost to time.

Until someone—an unknown someone—had tried to revive it with a single skeleton. The Disty claimed they knew who that someone was, and they would perform a ritual with that someone's help, clearing out the last of the contamination.

But first they had to clear the entire Dome, then this mass grave site, and finally the skeletal remains.

Scott-Olson had already been told to report to a Death Squad office as soon as the last of the autopsies were done. This last body meant that the victims of the massacre would be laid to rest. The victims of discovery of that massacre had already been cremated, most of them dead of crushed bones and shattered skulls.

Amazing how fragile humans were, even with the sophisticated medical techniques and life-expanding enhancements. No one ever thought to protect the body against outside violence. No one thought it necessary.

Even Scott-Olson, who had spent her last two weeks arm-deep in corpses who had died violently, wouldn't enhance her frame to take that kind of punishment. She would die how she would die, and she wasn't going to try to second-guess it.

The area around the mass grave was still empty. Most of Sahara Dome looked like a ghost town. The Disty wouldn't return until the Dome and its human occupants were decontaminated. And that process wouldn't end until these mummified corpses had their own funeral services, and Scott-Olson's team left the Dome for that weird decontamination ritual.

She was looking forward to it, in an odd way. She needed the closure as well.

She also needed time to mourn.

Not just for these unfortunate souls who had started the entire mess, but for the people she had known who had died, and for the poor Disty whom she still didn't entirely understand.

But most of all, she needed to find a way to grieve for Aisha Costard. Costard, who had died because she had come to help, had somehow managed to save them all.

Scott-Olson hadn't been able to reach the Retrieval Artist who had found the survivors. She hoped she would get a chance to thank him someday. He hadn't had to finish the case. When Aisha Costard died, he could have let the case lapse. But he had ethics, a thing she found was rarer than she expected.

Before she could go back to her own quiet life, she had to deal with her own choices. She had no idea if she could have done things differently, but she did know one thing:

From now on, she would not live in ignorance of her Disty neighbors, and she would not make assumptions about the knowledge of the people around her. She would explain the consequences of any request she made, no matter who she was talking to.

It was a small change, but an important one.

For the only way she could move forward was to learn from her mistakes. And she had to move forward. The surviving children of these poor victims had—and those children had enough courage to sacrifice weeks of their lives for people who may have descended from the people who murdered their families.

Scott-Olson didn't know if she was capable of that same generosity of spirit.

She hoped she was, deep down.

And she also hoped that, as long as she lived, her belief would never, ever be tested.

ABOUT THE AUTHOR

Kristine Kathryn Rusch is an award-winning writer in several genres. Winner of the 2001 Hugo Award for the novelette "Millennium Babies," she has also won the *Ellery Queen* Readers' Choice Award for best mystery short story. She is also a winner of the *Asimov's* Readers Choice Award, the *Locus* Award, the World Fantasy Award, and the John W. Campbell Award.

She has published more than fifty novels in almost a dozen languages, and she has hit bestseller lists in the *Wall Street Journal, USA Today,* and *Publishers Weekly.* Her science fiction and mystery short stories have been in many year's-best collections.

The *Retrieval Artist* novels are based on the Hugo-nominated novella "The Retrieval Artist," which was first published in *Analog.*